A CLAIRE WHITCOMB WESTERN COLLECTION: BOOKS 1-3
Retribution, Gunslinger Copyright © 2020
by D.V. Berkom
Legend Copyright © 2021 by D.V. Berkom

Published by

All rights reserved.
Printed in the United States of America
ISBN: 978-1-734-8599-2-8

***Join DV's readers' list to be the first to find out about new releases and exclusive, subscriber-only special offers. (*See the back of the book for details*)
Website: dvberkom.com

A CLAIRE WHITCOMB WESTERN BOOK 1
RETRIBUTION
DV BERKOM

A CLAIRE WHITCOMB WESTERN BOOK 1

RETRIBUTION

DV BERKOM

For my Grandfather

CHAPTER 1

Whitcomb Homestead, Leadville, Colorado – Spring 1880

Claire wiped the back of her hand across her forehead and tucked an errant strand of hair behind her ear. The bread dough was ready to go into the belly of the Beast—the cast iron stove she and her husband, Josiah had carted all those perilous miles to their new home in Colorado.

She was glad they'd brought it with them—glad for the warmth from the wood fire, especially in the winter, and for the comforting, steadfast way the Beast always turned out perfectly golden loaves of bread.

If she was truthful, she was glad to have that last, tenuous connection to their home and family back east. When Josiah had come home that day and announced his intention to move their family to the newly formed state of Colorado, Claire had balked. Their third child, Amy, was barely out of diapers, and the other two were happy with their schooling and friends. Claire herself was not opposed to change but was fiercely protective of her children and disliked disrupting their lives. The one argument she thought would win, that the area where he wanted to settle was dangerous and rife with heathen savages, didn't have the impact she thought it might. Her husband waved off her fears as overwrought gossip. Eventually, Josiah had worn her down with tales of striking it rich in the silver mines, and she relented.

The trip out West had been fraught with danger, although in comparison to other pioneering families she'd talked to, not nearly as tragic—they hadn't lost any lives, thankfully. Rattlesnakes, broken axles, heavy downpours—all normal events in a move west. Because of Claire's contacts where they lived in Philadelphia and her attention to detail, the family had been prepared for as many eventualities as she could think of, which meant they didn't go hungry or cold.

She'd just popped the loaves into the Beast when she heard Josiah yell a warning at the children. She wiped her hands on her apron and moved to the kitchen window to see what he was upset about. Probably some childish insurrection, which normally he'd redirect in a calm and rational matter.

She spotted Josiah first, standing stock-still with a look on his face that sent chills careening down her spine. Heart in her throat, Claire checked the front yard, searching feverishly for her children. Eight-year-old Nathan stood alone near the old pine, his eyes wide with fright. There was no trace of the two girls.

A bloodcurdling scream, the likes of which she'd never heard, erupted outside. Fear filled her and she raced for the Winchester rifle kept by the entrance.

She threw open the door and emerged onto the porch. Josiah turned to her, his mouth open to speak. From her right, the crack of a rifle split the air, the bullet ripping through his skull before he could utter a word.

Shock spiraled through her as her husband crumpled to the earth. Heart in her throat, she dove behind the metal horse trough they used for laundering and scrambled to the far end for a better view. Several yards away, an Indian wearing a blood red vest and leather breeches sat astride his horse, reloading his weapon. She brought up the rifle, sighted on the man, and squeezed the trigger.

Too nervous, she missed. She rammed the lever down, seating another cartridge into the chamber, and aimed again.

But he was already on the move, headed for the old pine.

Nathan.

"Nathan! Run!" She pivoted toward her son and aimed the rifle at a second Indian also bearing down upon her first-born.

Time slowed to a crawl. She took a deep breath, let it go, and fired. The bullet tore through the man's shoulder, but it didn't slow him down.

Already at a full gallop and holding his rifle high, the marauder bore down on Nathan. He swung his arm in an arc and smashed the stock against her child's head. Nathan tumbled to the ground and didn't move.

Claire shook with horror as she levered another cartridge into the chamber and fired, barely registering the acrid smell of gunpowder. She hit her son's attacker a second time. He fell from his mount, a pile of death on the ground. Tears coursed down her cheeks as she worked the lever again, hoping to hit the other man next. He came straight for her, howling unintelligibly, eyes snapping with rage. She steeled herself, and a calm descended over her. She raised the barrel, sighted him in, and squeezed the trigger.

At the last minute he reined his horse left, and the bullet went wide. She seated another cartridge and fired again, this time following his trajectory.

Somehow, she missed again.

Something whizzed over her head, and she craned her neck to see what it was. A flaming arrow had lodged in the roof. Tinder-dry from lack of rain, the fire would find willing fuel in the wooden shakes.

Claire glanced past her hiding place to see a third Indian let loose another fiery arrow. This one slammed into a different section of roof. She brought up the rifle and aimed again. At that moment, their eyes met. The coldness she found in their depths spilled ice through her veins.

She fired.

Another arrow.

By now, the roof was ablaze, flames crackling and licking hungrily at the bone-dry shakes. Keeping their distance from Claire, the two remaining attackers started for their fallen comrade. Rage overcame her fear and any sense she might have left. She climbed to her feet and strode down the steps, intending to destroy the men who had taken two of her family from her—shattering the fabric of her new life.

The first marauder turned as she raised her rifle and fired. The bullet hit the tree branch next to him. He said something to the other and fired back.

The round kicked up a fountain of dirt near her, but she kept walking. She ignored the ping of spent brass on gravel as she fired round after round after round. Gun smoke hung thick in the air.

The man shot at her once more, but he either intentionally missed or his gun misfired. He barked something at the second man, who had dismounted and was struggling with the dead attacker. The second man let the third fall back to the dirt, mounted his horse, and the two thundered off.

She stopped and took a breath.

Where were her daughters?

The thought tore through her grief like sunlight on an overcast day.

"Laura? Amy?" Her voice echoed through the trees, the wind taking their names to the valley below. "It's all right. You can come out now," she called.

Even though it wasn't all right.

There was no answer.

Dread settling in the pit of her stomach, she made her way to the shed, unsure what she'd find, or if she even wanted to find it.

Her girls weren't hiding there, nor were they behind it, concealed by the long, fresh grass of spring. She took another deep breath, a kind of relief flowing through her, and turned to go to Nathan. The girls were fine. They had to be. They knew enough to hide at the sound of gunfire.

They'd return soon.

Something next to the well caught her eye. She walked over to the hand pump. A moment of mild annoyance skated through her, as she wondered who had left out the mound of laundry.

It wasn't laundry.

Amy and Laura lay still and silent in death—a near impossibility for them both under normal circumstances. The two girls appeared to be sleeping but for the sticky, wet blood that pooled in the shadow of Laura's smashed collar bone, and the grotesque hoofprint marring Amy's face. Tears streamed down her cheeks as Claire sank to her knees and pulled first one, then the other to her, cradling their lifeless bodies. She rocked them, her grief escaping in massive, wracking sobs.

Sometime later—a moment? an hour?—she dried her tears and gently laid them back down, her clothes soaked in their blood. She carefully crossed each girl's hands over their hearts and closed their eyes.

Choking back a sob, she climbed to her feet.

What if the men come back?

Numb, she glanced at the burning house, now completely engulfed, the skeletal ruins outlined against orange-yellow flames and a heartbreaking blue sky.

Why hadn't they killed her when they had the chance?

A fresh set of tears streamed down her cheeks. Claire stumbled to Nathan, knowing he was gone, not wanting to believe it.

Dark blood matted the place where his sandy-brown hair always kicked up in a cowlick, and she had to stop herself from smoothing it down.

Tenderness welled within her.

"He was only eight years old," she said to the trees, but the crackling fire stole her words.

Her energy waning, she fought the impulse to go to Josiah. She'd seen him killed, his lifeblood ripped from him in an instant. She couldn't bear the thought of her beloved husband, so full of life and vigor—her champion, her knight in shining armor —dead. Couldn't bear the weight of what his death now meant.

In the end, she lost the battle. She staggered to where he lay and crumpled to the ground beside him, her face in the crook of his arm, nestled to his body one last time. He smelled of soap and sweat and the tang of blood. Breathing him in, she closed her eyes, believing for a moment the fiction that he was still alive.

The screech of a jay woke her. Claire opened her eyes, unsure for a moment where she was. She sat up and took it all in once more, bringing everything back. A sob welled deep within her and escaped.

The nightmare was real.

Don't let them win, Claire. It was Josiah's voice in her head, as surely as if he'd spoken the words aloud.

Anger nudged at her like an annoying insect, hopscotching to a crescendo of rage in a matter of seconds. She struggled to stand and sighted on the dead Indian, footsteps away.

Snatching the rifle from the ground she strode to where he lay. She stared at his face, her chest heaving with anguish. He wore the braids of the local Ute tribe, buckskin leggings, and a beaded vest. Why had they targeted them? Josiah experienced nothing but peaceable encounters with the local natives, and found them good and fair traders, if a little standoffish.

The rage inside her crested. Claire raised the butt of the rifle and brought it down, again and again.

And again.

And more.

Her anger spent, she lowered the gun and rested it against her thigh. Her violent episode had done more than release her rage. The man's hair had shifted such that it appeared she'd detached his scalp.

She knelt to take a closer look. She plucked at his blood-soaked hair, dislodging it, and sat back hard on the ground in surprise. In her hand was a wig, its texture similar to the tail of her beloved horse, Rose.

Underneath, the man's real hair lay matted to his skull, partially covered by a woman's bonnet.

Claire dropped the wig and crawled closer. Though bloody, the lower portion of his face was still visible. Dark stubble peppered his jaw. A memory surfaced of Josiah joking with a local Ute man who'd come to trade buffalo hides about the other man's inability to grow facial hair.

Utes don't grow beards.

Claire touched his chin. Definitely stubble. She glanced at her finger. A dark stain covered the tip. She withdrew a handkerchief from her pocket and wiped it across his neck. The white material came away brown. She held it to her nose, then jerked it away at the rancid odor of beef tallow mixed with blood.

This man is no Indian.

The memory emerged of locking gazes with the savage who came at her. His eyes were blue. Not brown, like most all the other Indians she'd seen.

Claire stood and picked up her gun, confused by the idea of a white man dressing as an Indian. Had the other two attackers been white, too? She closed her eyes trying to remember, but the details wouldn't come.

They must have been. Otherwise, why would two natives join with a white man dressed like them to destroy another man's homestead?

But who would do such a thing? Try as she might, Claire couldn't figure a reason to kill her husband and children and burn her home to the ground. They owned little, had yet to "strike it rich" on any of Josiah's claims.

She vowed not to rest until she found out.

With the rifle close, Claire retrieved a shovel from the shed and set about the grim job of burying her family.

HOURS LATER, dazed and exhausted, Claire set the shovel down and stared at the four freshly dug graves. The unyielding ground had demanded much, and she was spent. Used up.

Numb.

She'd had to roll Josiah into his final resting place, unable to pick him up or even drag his body to the shallow hole she'd managed to form from the hard-packed earth.

Nate, Amy, and Laura had been so much more difficult, and not because of their weight. There would be no more laughter from her cheerful, loving children. Nate would no longer tease his sisters with frogs from the creek. The sisters would never again gang up on their brother. Or play, or sing, or release their joyful energy with their rough-and-tumble fights. She'd never see another twinkle in Josiah's eyes when he told them to behave.

As the shadows lengthened into early evening, Claire Whitcomb said a prayer for her family, entrusting their souls into the everlasting care of the Creator. She ignored the battered body of the man she'd killed.

His two accomplices hadn't returned.

She didn't care.

The rifle at her side, Claire sank to the earth next to her children's graves. She rolled onto her back to stare at the brilliant stars, and silently prayed for God to take her, too.

CHAPTER 3

The next day, Claire awoke to birdsong and sun streaming through the old pine's branches. It was a beautiful morning, with a gentle breeze soughing through the pines and scrub oaks. Bits and pieces of her memory from the attack returned, unbidden. She choked back an anguished sob and bit down hard on her knuckles to keep from crying.

Stop it, Claire. Cry later.

Right now, she had work to do.

Stiff with cold from sleeping on the ground, she climbed to her feet and brushed the dirt from her clothes, realizing as she did that she was still covered in blood. She glanced at the burned-out husk of her home. She doubted anything survived the fire—certainly not clothing or material.

Rifle in hand, she made her way to the barn. Rose snorted a welcome as Claire waited for her eyes to adjust to the dim interior.

"Hey there, lovely," she cooed as she rubbed her horse's nose. Josiah's horse, Brick, whinnied in tandem. Rose snuffled her hand, expecting a lump of sugar or a carrot. Instead, Claire put a lead on them both and walked them outside to a grassy area next to the house so they could graze.

Claire walked back into the barn and took one of Josiah's work shirts from a hook on the wall. She exchanged her bloody shirt for his and tucked the shirttails into her dirty, blood-stained skirt. It would have to do.

Next, she cleaned her face at the horse trough and did her best to make herself presentable. Once Rose and Brick had eaten their fill, Claire put Brick back in his stall, saddled Rose, and headed for town.

It would have been an understatement to say that Leadville was hopping. Currently in the middle of a silver boom, the town was jam-packed with thousands of speculators and miners vying for space on the wide dirt streets. Men five-deep jostled for dominance, some of them newly rich, day-drunk, and shooting their pistols into the air. City lots that could be had for twenty-five dollars that morning might sell for upwards of ten thousand that night. Emotions and speculation ran sky-high, creating an exciting, combustible atmosphere with murder, robbery, and double-dealing the norm.

Thankful for her rifle, Claire pushed her way through the crowds to the marshal's office, garnering looks of annoyance and mild curiosity.

The dried blood on her skirt probably didn't help.

Self-conscious, she'd bunched her skirt with her hands, trying to hide the dark stains, but soon abandoned the effort. Leadville was as close to a lawless settlement as you could get. Most likely bloody clothing didn't matter, even that worn by a member of the gentler sex.

She finally reached the one-story, slat-wood building that housed the jail, but the sign on the door told her the marshal was out and wouldn't be back until later that day.

Her heart sank as she turned to look at the teeming street. She wanted to rail at all the life and bustle of so many people going about their business as though nothing was wrong. Didn't they know her family had been slaughtered? Murdered in cold blood by three ruthless, uncaring, and savage criminals who didn't have the guts to show their faces. Men who used the local tribe as scapegoats for committing heinous acts.

And what had they gained? They'd ruined anything that might be of value, including the family who lived there.

Claire fought back tears at the thought of never seeing her beloved husband again. Of never feeling his strong arms around her, nor his soft lips brushing against hers, or his words of love.

What should I do?

She could wait for the marshal to return, but that might be hours. She didn't know anyone in town except the owner of the general store, a banker, and one of the ladies at the milliner's shop, having been too busy making a home and rearing her children to be sociable. Josiah made most of the trips to town, often bringing one of the older children with him, and Claire had remained back at the homestead to care for Amy. She hadn't minded. She found most of the townspeople brash and rough and not much for niceties.

Find Henry.

Henry Blankenship was head of the First Silver Bank of Leadville and had taken a shine to Josiah and his family. An important and highly respected man in town, Henry would know what to do.

Claire fought her way through the streets to the bank and muscled the heavy wood and brass door open. She walked in, garnering stares from several men as they took in her disheveled appearance, but she paid them no mind. Inside was calm and somewhat ordered, in contrast to the crowded streets outside.

She scanned the high-ceilinged room beyond the teller cages, searching for the bank's vice president. When she didn't see Henry at his desk, she took her place in line to wait for the cashier.

"Next, please." Philip Jenkins, a thin, bespectacled man behind the brass bars, motioned her forward. Claire walked over and placed both hands on the counter to steady herself.

Jenkins eyed her askance and asked, "May I help you?"

Claire took a deep breath before replying. "I need to speak with Mr. Blankenship."

"I'm sorry, but Mr. Blankenship is indisposed at the moment. Is there something I can do for you?"

She shook her head, willing the tears not to fall. "No. I—I need to speak to him directly. Now."

"I can make you an appointment for next Wednesday, if you like." Philip Jenkins busied himself straightening the papers splayed out before him.

She stared at him uncomprehendingly. "Next Wednesday? No. I said I need to speak to him *now.*"

He gave her a disapproving glance and shook his head. "Mr. Blankenship is a very busy man." She was surprised he didn't add, *and he can't be bothered with an obviously hysterical woman.*

"Then I will wait." Claire nodded toward the empty chair next to Blankenship's desk.

"I really can't allow—" He took one look at her expression and sighed. "If you must." Jenkins waved over the next person in line. Claire took her leave and sat down next to Blankenship's desk.

Dozens of men milled about the lobby of the cavernous building—well-to-do investors, rough-looking miners, dandies in fine clothes—all acting as though they were on some kind of important business and couldn't be delayed. Their conceit left her cold, reminding her that life was raw, a matter of survival, and that nothing would ever be the same again. A veil had lifted, giving her a glimpse of reality—no longer sheltered in her role as wife and mother.

She waited for the better part of an hour before Henry Blankenship made an appearance. Before he could reach his desk, Jenkins pulled him aside and whispered in his ear. Both men's gazes flickered toward her before they resumed their shared conversation. Claire rose from her chair as Blankenship finally joined her.

"Mrs. Whitcomb. What a pleasant surprise." His gaze took in her bloody skirt, but politeness stopped him from remarking on her appearance. He wrapped his arm around her shoulders and steered her to a back room, murmuring, "My dear woman, what has happened to you?"

Relieved to have someone to lean on, Claire's shoulders inched down. She fought the tears welling in her eyes and allowed herself to be guided to safety.

Blankenship closed the door behind them and led her to a heavy wooden chair. He produced a handkerchief and handed it to her, which she used to dab at her eyes. The smell of wood and leather and a trace of cigar smoke gave her a sense of masculine protection. Her old life in Philadelphia was like that—civilized, peaceful.

Safe.

He drew up another chair and perched on the edge of it, concern etching his face. "What on earth happened? Where's Josiah?"

She lost the battle with her tears. She wiped angrily at them as they fell, and haltingly told him of the attack.

"The children?" he asked, a hard set to his mouth.

She shook her head as fresh tears tracked down her cheeks. "Gone. Everyone's gone." Hopelessness descended on her, as she fought through overwhelming panic.

"My God." His expression was one of disbelief. "They killed the children."

Claire nodded and continued to dab at her eyes, her misery settling like an anvil in her stomach.

Perspiration beaded on Blankenship's forehead. He produced

a second handkerchief and wiped it away. "And you're certain the attack wasn't the result of savages?"

"Absolutely certain. The man I killed wore a wig. Ride with me to our property and you'll see. I didn't...bury him."

He winced as though he felt her pain. "You're certain you want to return? Won't seeing the shell of your home be a terrible price to pay? The marshal and his men can take care of things for you."

After seeing my family slaughtered? She was certain there couldn't be anything worse. "I'm sure."

Blankenship took a deep breath and exhaled. "Then we must go immediately." He stood and offered his hand. "I will alert the marshal and let him know we require his services."

"The sign on the door said he would be gone until this afternoon."

"Ah. Well, then, I shall inform his deputies. They'll know how to get a message to him, and can stand in for him if he's unreachable."

Claire nodded and rose from the chair. "Thank you, Henry. I —I didn't know what to do."

"You made the right choice." Blankenship smiled sadly as he took her hand in both of his. "You've had a terrible shock to the system, Mrs. Whitcomb. I and the townspeople are here for you."

THE SUN banked low on the horizon when the small party of four arrived back at Claire's homestead: Claire, Henry Blankenship, and Eli Sutter and Joe Pendergast, two deputies from town. The house, now a charred ruin, still smoldered, proof of what had once been a home. The rock chimney towered above the wreckage, its shadows stretching from the damaged front porch to the old pine. The Beast and the metal laundry trough were the only other survivors, both blackened from the fire.

Blankenship dismounted and walked over to the four freshly dug graves. He removed his bowler hat and bowed his head. Eli and Joe removed theirs, as well. All fell silent in respect for the dead.

Blankenship was the first to speak. "I'm deeply sorry for your loss, Mrs. Whitcomb."

Claire nodded. The grief caught in her throat. "Thank you."

He turned toward the skeletal remains of the house. "Show me the cur you shot." His voice rose in righteous anger. "I want to see the kind of man who could do such a heinous thing to a God-fearing family."

Claire slid off her mount. "He's just over here." She walked to where she'd left the body but stopped, confused. She searched the ground, her panic growing.

"What's wrong?" Blankenship advanced toward her, a look of concern on his face.

"I left him here." She indicated the spot where the man with the wig had fallen. The body was gone. She dropped to her knees and pawed at the earth, searching for something, anything that would show the others that someone had been there. The earth had been scraped free of grass and blood, leaving only packed dirt.

"Grief has a way of confusing the mind," Blankenship said gently.

Claire shook her head. "No. No, I shot him," she said, pointing at the ground, "right there. He fell from his horse. I beat him with my rifle..."

Eli and Blankenship exchanged a worried look.

"You beat a dead man?" Eli asked, surprise creeping into his voice. Joe shifted nervously.

"I was... distraught." The word didn't begin to describe how she'd felt, but her upbringing mandated understatement.

"Of course you were." Blankenship helped her to her feet.

"You need some rest. You've been through a terrible, terrible tragedy."

"But I have nowhere to go." The crushing realization that she was homeless tunneled its way through her. All she had left in the world were the two horses, her rifle, the clothes on her back, a burned-out husk of a home, and a worthless claim. She'd have to sell their land.

The land they'd spent their savings on.

Blankenship put his arm around her shoulders reassuringly. "Now don't you worry about that, Mrs. Whitcomb. We'll sort it all out."

Claire nodded, unable to speak. Where had the dead man gone? She clenched her fists in her skirt pockets. A wad of material reminded her of the handkerchief she'd used on the man's neck. She pulled the material free and held it up.

"I used this to wipe his neck." She offered it to Blankenship. "The brown stain came from the man I killed."

Blankenship took the handkerchief from her and studied it before handing it to Eli.

Eli folded it up and put it in his pocket. "I'll keep this safe for when we find the men who did this." He leaned over and said something to Joe. Joe nodded and took off toward the barn.

"Will it help?" Claire asked.

"That all depends on what the stain represents," Eli said.

"I just told you. It was some kind of face coloring to lead me to believe he was an Indian."

Eli spat on the ground and wiped his chin. "Beg to differ, ma'am. Looked like it coulda been blood on that kerchief."

"What? No. I told you it was some kind of—"

Joe reappeared, holding Claire's bloody shirt. He handed the garment to his boss.

Eli's expression hardened. "Whatcha got there, Joe?"

"Found it bunched up in a corner of the barn. It was underneath the hay, like someone wanted to hide it."

Eli narrowed his eyes. "That's a lot of blood."

"I told you—" Claire took a step toward the two men. Joe straightened and drew his gun.

"That's far enough, ma'am."

"That blood is from my children." She choked back a sob.

"Why'd you hide it?" Eli asked.

"I couldn't stand the thought of wearing it…"

"It was because of the guilt of killing your family, wasn't it?" Eli gave her an accusing stare.

"You can't be serious." A spark of fear ignited inside Claire. She looked to Henry Blankenship for help. "Why would I do such a thing?"

Eli shrugged. "Mebbe you and the mister had a fight or something. Mebbe you didn't want him to put the place up for collateral."

"What?" Claire shook her head. She couldn't make sense of his words.

"Tell her, Henry."

She turned to the banker. "What is he talking about?"

Henry Blankenship frowned at Eli before he turned to Claire. "You know about the claim, Claire."

Disbelief bubbled up inside her. "You mean the property we own?"

Blankenship sighed. "Surely you were aware that your family was in dire straits. Your husband took out a second loan using the claim as collateral." He added in a quiet voice, "He was unable to make the payments."

"We what?" Cold shock slid to her gut. "No. No, he would have told me—" Dire straits? Josiah had never indicated they were in financial trouble. Indeed, just the opposite was true. He'd been upbeat and excited to work their claim. It was too much for her to take in. She closed her eyes, trying to come to terms with what Henry had said.

Eli gestured to his deputy. "Joe, I'm gonna need you to take Mrs. Whitcomb here into custody."

Joe took a step toward Claire, but Claire backed away, looking from Joe to Eli, and then to Blankenship.

"What are you doing? Henry?" she asked, her gaze skating to the banker's. "Stop him."

Henry Blankenship spread his hands. "Calm down, Claire. I'm certain this is just a big misunderstanding." He turned to Eli and Joe. "Gentlemen. The woman has lost her entire family. Do you really think she had anything to do with it?"

Joe stood motionless, waiting for Eli's instructions.

Eli shook his head. "Seems pretty straightforward to me, Mr. Blankenship. There's four freshly dug graves, blood-covered evidence that she hid inside the barn, a bloody kerchief, and a crazy story about so-called marauders dressed up like savages, but no body." He shot a glance at Claire. "And, she's the sole survivor of a so-called raid on the homestead. If her story about them outlaws is true, why'd they leave her be?"

Claire looked from Blankenship to Eli, then back to the banker. "You're not serious?"

Eli spat tobacco juice on the ground and leveled his gaze at her. "Seems to me we got us a female Jesse James."

"You think I killed my family?" Claire would have laughed if the notion hadn't been so bizarre. Joe moved in, coming toward her. She shot a glance at Rose, wondering if she could get to her rifle before he caught her.

Blankenship stepped between them, blocking Joe's access. "Now, gentlemen. Let's use some sense here." He looked at Claire, then at the two men. "Does this woman look like a killer to you?"

Joe frowned and nodded at her. "She already confessed to killing a man and then beatin' hell out of him. What if that's just a story to throw us off the scent?"

Blankenship made a show of looking around him. "Do you see a dead body anywhere?"

"That's not—" Joe began.

"What about the freshly dug graves?" Eli asked. "And the family's financial trouble? If her family's dead, the property would belong to her." He nodded at Claire. "You heard her yourself. She didn't know anything about the second loan. Why wouldn't her husband tell her?"

"Why would I bury them if I killed them in cold blood?"

Claire asked, certain now of the two men's intention to take her into custody. Preposterous as the charges were, frontier justice was rarely just. The chance that she'd hang from the gallows was slightly better than her chance of going free. She backed up toward Rose, slowly closing the distance.

Blankenship drew his revolver and aimed it at Joe. "Don't take another step, gentlemen."

Eli put his hand on his gun and gave him a warning look. "You're interferin' with the law, Blankenship."

"What if I take responsibility?"

"What do you mean?" Eli narrowed his eyes.

"I mean if you release her into my care, I'll guarantee that she'll appear in court when the time comes. Until then, she'll be my ward, so to speak." He glanced over his shoulder at Claire. "I've an empty bedroom for her to use."

"Won't people talk?" Joe asked.

Eli added, "What if she escapes?"

"I assure you, I will nail all the windows shut and lock her inside her room, negating any worries you may have of her escape."

Claire continued to edge toward Rose. She couldn't find her family's killers if she was locked up in Blankenship's house, and she'd be damned if she was going to allow these men to dictate what would happen to her.

Even with Blankenship's offer of help, she'd hang for sure.

When she judged the distance to be close enough she sprinted the last few feet to her horse, grabbed the saddle horn with one hand and her skirt with the other, and threw herself into the saddle. Blankenship shoved Joe to the ground as Eli drew his weapon. Claire spurred Rose and headed straight toward them. She turned sharply at the last moment, throwing Eli off balance so his shot went wild. Joe recovered too late and missed her by a wide margin.

Heart in her throat and tensing for the sting of a bullet, Claire bent forward, her head inches from Rose's mane, and urged the mare on.

She cleared the property at a full gallop, heading cross-country toward Leadville. She didn't know where else to go. She'd figure things out once she got to town and lost herself in the crowds. In the meantime, the sparse trees didn't give her much cover. The only thing on her side was a head start.

And a fast horse.

She glanced over her shoulder several times, fearing someone would follow her, but so far, no one came.

Perhaps they thought she'd be easy to find, or that a woman wouldn't get far on her own. Claire was determined to prove them wrong. They'd have a wanted poster with her face plastered all over town in short order. A reward would be a huge motivation. She'd have to keep to lesser-known areas.

The sun had set when she slowed Rose to a canter, cooling down both her horse and herself. It wouldn't do to make a show coming into town—too many people would remember her. Thankfully, nightfall was at hand. The streetlamps had all been lit, casting everything in a harsh glow. She'd be difficult to identify as long as she kept to the shadows.

She passed the main entrance to town and rode a little farther, hoping to come at it from a different angle with fewer witnesses. She chose a street that was little more than a rutted, nameless dirt road. She found herself in a residential section of town, evidenced by yellow lamplight glowing through parlor windows.

One of the homes she passed had laundry left hanging on the line. She slowed Rose to a halt and dismounted, leaving the chestnut mare to graze on a patch of grass nearby. No one walked or rode the street in either direction, so she sneaked into the backyard and quickly searched the dried laundry for something to wear. She eyed a woman's blouse and long skirt, estimated they would most likely fit her, and quickly pulled down the garments. She was back on her horse in moments and continued her course along the quiet street.

Half a block later, she turned down yet another no-name street with clapboard houses to each side. She stopped outside of a boarding house that was three stories high with a wide front porch. She dismounted and tied Rose to the hitching post. A sign next to the walkway read *Willoughby House—Rooms for Let by the Day or Week. Enquire within.*

Claire moved behind a large hydrangea bush and quickly changed into the newly acquired clothing. The high-necked, button-down white shirt fit well, although the blue twill skirt was overly large. This she corrected by securing it with her leather belt. She turned the bloody skirt inside out so the stains weren't obvious, and folded Josiah's shirt before stowing both pieces in one of Rose's saddlebags.

Satisfied with her wardrobe change, she took a deep breath and smoothed the new skirt, then patted her hair into place, most of which had fallen loose during her wild ride to town. She climbed the wooden steps to the front porch and knocked on the screen door. When there was no answer, she opened the door and called out. "Hello?"

The sound of indistinct voices, clattering dishes, and tinkling glassware reached her, and she let the door close. *They must be sitting down to dinner.*

She descended the steps and started for Rose, intending to find another place to stay, when a female voice behind her said, "Can I help you?"

Claire turned. A middle-aged woman wearing a green velvet dress smiled down at her. Renegade wisps of curly gray hair had escaped their confines and framed her head like a halo.

"I'm looking for accommodations." Claire returned the smile. "Would you happen to have a room?"

The woman nodded. "I do. It's three dollars, and includes what's left of supper and a good breakfast in the morning."

Claire's mouth watered at the prospect of food, but the price was steep. "That sounds perfect. Except I won't have any money until the bank opens in the morning."

The woman's smile vanished, and a wary look came over her face. "I'm afraid I don't take IOUs. Cash or silver only."

"Oh." Crestfallen, Claire turned back toward Rose. "I'm sorry to bother you. I'll be on my way."

The woman sighed. "Hold on."

Claire stopped and looked up hopefully.

She gestured at Claire to join her on the porch. "The least I can do is get a good meal into you. C'mon."

Claire's spirits rose for the first time since the attack, and she eagerly climbed the steps.

"There ain't much left. My boarders are mostly menfolk, and goodness, can they eat."

Claire followed her through the well-appointed parlor into the dining room. A younger woman scurried around the table clearing the dinner dishes. Most of the chairs at the long table were vacant except for a lone man who was still eating. He stood when the two women entered.

"Oh, sit down, Mart, and enjoy your dinner." He did, and she turned to Claire. "What was your name, dear?"

"Rose." No sense giving her real name. Rose would be easy to remember.

"Well, Miss Rose, don't pay Mart no mind. He's harmless." She gave him a broad grin, which he returned. "You can call me Esther, by the way."

Mart had a kind face, Claire decided. Dressed in traveling clothes with his sleeves rolled to his elbows, he had a shock of dark blond hair that fell across his high forehead, and intelligent eyes. She sat where Esther told her to and unfolded a linen napkin, which she put in her lap. Esther poured her a glass of claret, and told her she'd be right out with her dinner.

"Been travelin' long?" Mart asked, his fork halfway to his

mouth. He looked directly at Claire. His eyes reminded her of the peaceful glade near her home—deep and dark, yet soothing.

Correction. Near the burned-out husk of her home.

"Denver." Best not to let on that she was local—it would only raise questions.

Mart nodded and resumed eating. "I've been there a few times. Too many people, you ask me."

"So you came to Leadville?" She shook her head. "Seems like there are more people here per mile than in Denver."

"That might have been true a few months ago, but Denver's booming now." He studied her a moment. "How long's it been since you were there?"

Claire sipped her wine to cover her nervousness. "A while."

To her immense relief, Mart let it go and returned to his meal.

"Are you staying here?" she asked.

He shook his head. "The wife's visiting family in Michigan, and I like a home cooked meal now and then."

Esther returned carrying a plate piled high with roast beef, potatoes, and cooked peas and carrots. The younger woman followed and set down a smaller plate with a piece of delicious-looking cake.

"Thank you," Claire said, and smiled. The younger woman nodded and performed a little curtsey before hurrying back into the kitchen.

Esther walked around the table to clear Mart's plate. He grinned and leaned back in his chair. "Much obliged, Miss Esther. Your culinary skills are second to none."

Esther blushed and gave him a playful swat. "Go on with you." She walked back to the kitchen. "Enjoy your supper, Rose," she called over her shoulder.

Claire's mouth watered at the wonderful smell emanating from her plate. She attacked her food with gusto, making sure to eat as much as she could. She didn't know when her next meal would be, or where it would come from. As Mart had attested, the food was some of the best she'd ever eaten.

Mart studied her as she ate. "Are you traveling alone?"

Claire nodded, her mouth full of roast.

"I don't see any bags with you. May I help with your luggage?"

Claire slowed her eating long enough to answer. "Thank you for your kind offer, but I'm afraid I won't be staying the night."

"You have other accommodations, then?"

"Something like that."

He nodded, then stood and shrugged his coat on. The flash of a marshal's badge on the coat almost took her breath. Claire forced herself to remain calm.

"Then I'll take my leave." He drained his glass before he donned his hat and tapped the brim. "It was a pleasure meeting you, Rose. Perhaps we'll see each other again."

She wiped her mouth with her napkin, glad her hand didn't shake. "The pleasure was mine."

He stepped from the room and exited through the front door. Claire took a deep breath to steady her nerves. *Don't worry. He doesn't know who you are.* She busied herself by soaking up the last of the gravy on her plate with a biscuit and followed that with a big gulp of wine.

She doubted the marshal would hear about the goings-on at the homestead before morning, by which time she'd be miles away from Leadville. She just needed time to withdraw her money from the bank. By the way Henry Blankenship kept Eli and Joe from arresting her, she was certain he wouldn't stand in her way.

But where was she going to sleep? It would have to be somewhere no one would discover her before morning. Somewhere Rose would be able to graze her fill so she'd be ready for whatever lay ahead.

But where should she go? Philadelphia was a long train ride, and the marshal and his men would surely have someone watching the station. And what would she do with Rose? She couldn't leave the only friend she had in the world behind.

Perhaps Denver? If what the marshal said was true, the city to the northeast would be easy to get lost in. With the right provisions and good weather, she and Rose would be able to make it there in four or five days.

She brushed the thought away. *I'll figure it out in the morning.*

Finished with her meal, she brought the dishes into the kitchen and handed them to the younger woman.

"Thank you for your hospitality, Esther."

Esther turned and smiled. "Of course, Rose."

"I'll come back and pay you tomorrow."

Esther studied her for a moment. She wiped her hands on a dishtowel and set it on the sink. "I can't send you out into the night looking for someplace to stay. I've got an extra cot in the back room. I'm sure Laura here won't mind sharing her room for a night or two." She turned to the younger woman for confirmation. Laura nodded.

Claire's breath caught and tears welled in her eyes.

Alarmed, Esther put her hand on Claire's arm. "Whatever is the matter?"

Claire shook her head as she wiped at her tears. "I'm sorry. It's just that my eldest daughter was named Laura."

Esther and Laura exchanged a look. Esther took Claire by the elbow and led her to a chair next to the stove.

"You said *was.*" Esther's gentle voice was full of concern.

Claire couldn't stem her grief any longer. Fresh tears flowed down her cheeks. "She's—she and her sister—they're both—dead." She choked out a sob and hung her head in despair.

"Oh my goodness. You've been through it, haven't you?" She turned to Laura. "Get her a glass of water, would you?"

"Yes, ma'am." Laura disappeared into the dining room.

"You've already been so kind." Claire shook her head, misery clouding her thoughts. "I should go."

"Don't be silly. We'll have none of this talk of you going out into the middle of the night alone." She took both Claire's hands in hers and said, "Losing a child is a terrible thing. Losing two must be nigh on impossible."

Gathering herself, Claire closed her eyes and sighed. When she opened them, Esther was looking straight at her, as though she could see inside her soul. *Don't tell her anything else. You need to find out who killed your family, and you can't do that behind bars.*

"When did it happen?" Esther asked in a quiet voice.

"It seems like yesterday."

Esther nodded. Laura returned with a cup of ice-cold well water. Claire didn't think anything could taste so delicious. She finished it in short order and handed the cup back to the other woman.

"Thank you." She moved to stand. "I'd better see to my horse."

"Laura," Esther said, "would you mind? There's plenty of room in the barn."

"Of course." Laura set the glass on the counter and left the room.

"Please, keep an account of what I owe you. Once I go to the bank tomorrow, I can withdraw enough money to pay for everything."

"Don't you worry, dear. Everybody needs a helping hand at some point in their life. This is yours."

Claire gave her a weak smile. *If you only knew.*

Mart Duggan walked into the marshal's office and shut the door behind him. No reason to go home early with his wife gone. Eli and Joe had their heads together at his desk and both looked up as he entered. By the expressions on their faces, they appeared to have news.

"Hey, boys. What's going on?"

Eli leaned back and put his hands behind his head. The metal badge he wore on his vest flashed in the lamplight.

"Had some excitement while you was gone."

"Oh yeah? Like what, exactly?" With these two, Duggan never knew if the excitement was more or less because of them. He'd been tempted to let them both go for cause on several occasions, but he'd already fired all the deputies from the previous administration, and good, honest gunmen were hard to come by in these parts.

Not that they were all that good.

Or honest.

"The Whitcomb house burned to the ground and the whole family's dead, except for the missus."

Duggan took off his hat and pulled up a chair. "What happened?"

Joe took up the narrative. "Mrs. Whitcomb comes into town, cryin' and carryin' on about how some white men dressed as savages attacked her husband and children and kilt them all, except for her. Claims she shot one of them, and tells Blankenship to see for himself."

This was getting interesting. Duggan didn't know the Whitcombs personally. They'd kept to themselves, unlike many of the citizens in Leadville, who tended to let their lesser natures overcome their common sense. Even so, who could have planned such a thing?

"So, Blankenship finds us and asks us to go with him to check her story," Eli added, "and when we get there, there weren't no dead Indian."

"But there were four fresh graves," Joe added. "And the house was burned to the ground."

"Four graves?"

Joe nodded. "The husband and her three children."

Someone killed three children? An old, familiar anger ignited in Duggan's belly at the thought of three innocents lost to senseless violence. "Do we have an idea who might have done this and why?" He leaned forward, his elbows on his knees.

Eli nodded. "Mrs. Whitcomb."

Duggan scoffed. "No, really. Who do you think did it?"

"I told you. Mrs. Whitcomb. Joe here found a ladies' shirt soaked in blood hid in the barn under some hay. She was wearin' a man's work shirt. She insisted she'd killed one of the attackers, and gave me a kerchief with some dried blood on it to prove her point. That just didn't sound right to me. 'Specially since she was the lone survivor of the attack."

"Don't forget to tell him what she done, Eli," Joe urged.

Duggan looked at Eli. "What?"

Eli nodded. "She confessed to beating the man *after he was dead.*" He emphasized the words as though beating a dead man was the most scandalous thing he'd ever heard.

"I need to talk to Mrs. Whitcomb." Duggan rose from his chair. "Where are you keeping her?"

Eli avoided his eyes. "We ain't got her."

Duggan gave him a sharp glance. "Then where is she?"

"She took off on her horse, hell-for-leather toward town, but she was too quick and we lost her."

"You're certain she came to town?" *What the hell?* "And you're not looking for her?"

"Where's she gonna go?" Joe asked, looking smug. "A lady alone in these parts ain't gonna get far."

"So, you allowed a murder suspect to disappear into the night? Is that it?"

Eli stood and squared his shoulders. "We thought to wait until you come back to put together a posse."

"And when did all this transpire, pray tell?" he asked, not bothering to hide his sarcasm. Duggan's Irish temper may have been on a simmer, but his deputies knew from experience that he could explode without warning.

"A couple of hours ago."

A couple of hours? "All right then. Get to it. Now."

"Yessir." Both Eli and Joe scrambled for their hats and coats and hurried outside.

Damn. The suspect had a hell of a head start.

Duggan grabbed his hat off the desk and strode to the gun rack. As he reached for a box of ammunition he thought of the woman he'd met at Esther's boarding house.

A woman alone with no luggage, she was certainly not dressed for travel. Come to think of it, he didn't remember there being a woman's coat or hat on the coat rack in the front hallway. When he left the house, he'd checked over the woman's ride. The chestnut horse had been outfitted with a saddle and a rifle and only had what appeared to be one change of clothes in her saddlebags. If she'd come all the way from Denver, she'd at least have a coat and some provisions.

He made sure his weapons were loaded, and that he had enough extra ammunition, then walked out the door to join his men. Eli and Joe were on their way back from the saloon with several men in tow. The gaslights flickered, illuminating drunkards careening from saloon to saloon, searching for their next thrill.

When both men were within earshot, Duggan asked, "What does Mrs. Whitcomb look like?"

Eli pondered the question for a moment. "She's a fine-looking woman, but her eyes held a cunning I ain't never seen afore in the weaker sex."

"That's a fact." Joe nodded his assent.

Mart sighed. "What color was her hair? How tall was she? Any unusual marks?"

Eli and Joe looked at each other. Eli shrugged. "Longish hair, same color as a buck in summer, mebbe a little darker. Not fat nor skinny, neither. No marks that I could see."

Joe took up the narrative. "Fiery eyes. Inch or two taller than Eli here, if I was to guess."

Eli gave Joe a dirty look. "Her skirt had blood on it, that I do remember. And she rode off on a red mare."

Maybe the suspect didn't have such a good head start after all.

CHAPTER 6

Claire bolted upright on the cot where she'd been sleeping, unsure what had woken her. A moment later, a loud thud sounded near the front of the house. Laura shifted restlessly, but didn't wake.

Someone was at the front door and insistent on gaining access.

Claire wasn't about to wait around to find out who that might be.

The pitch dark room didn't make it easy for her, and Claire stubbed her toe on the dresser next to the cot. She stifled a yelp of pain as she groped for her skirt. Laura mumbled something, but remained asleep. Claire found her skirt and put it on before she grabbed her shoes and slipped out the door to the empty kitchen.

"All right, all right. I'm coming," Esther grumbled loud enough for Claire to hear, her voice echoing from the front hall.

Heart thudding in her ears, Claire tiptoed to the back door and eased it open. The door swung noiselessly and she said a silent thank you to whoever maintained the hinges. She eased outside and closed it gently behind her.

The hulking shadow of the barn loomed several yards before her across the gloomy backyard. The moon was almost full in a sky filled with glimmering stars, which did not bode well for her escape. She raced to the barn, certain that at any moment someone would burst through the backdoor and yell for her to stop.

But no one did.

She felt her way past several stalls until she heard a familiar whinny.

"That you, Rose?" she whispered. A loud snort gave her the answer. She ducked into the stall and walked toward the glint of her horse's eye. "Hi there, sweetheart." Claire breathed in her horse's familiar scent as she gave Rose's forehead a gentle rub. The saddle and tack had been left on the side of the stall. She draped the blanket across the mare's back and hoisted the saddle into place, then quickly secured the cinch.

"Time to go, girl," she whispered. Rose seemed to sense the urgency and followed Claire out of the stall.

"Where you going?"

Claire froze at the man's voice. Her heart sank as her mind raced for an excuse to be saddling her horse in the middle of the night. "I—I need to get to my mother's. She's ill." She lied without thinking, not knowing what else to say.

The man sighed and walked toward her. His silhouette resolved and became the man she'd met that evening at dinner.

"Rose, right? From Denver?" he said.

Claire cleared her throat. "Yes. That's right. And you're Mart."

He nodded. "You're not really going to your mother's, are you?"

Claire closed her eyes, her defeat crashing around her. She couldn't even manage to leave town before getting caught. She'd never make a fugitive.

"No."

Mart nodded again. "I heard about what happened to your home. And your family."

"I didn't do it." Her voice cracked. "They were my *family*. My life." She was going to hang for something she would never, ever dream of doing. Her eyes burned with unshed tears. Rose pushed her head against Claire, obviously concerned. Without thinking, Claire rubbed the horse's silky nose in an attempt to calm her. "Shh, now. It's all right," she soothed.

"I know."

At first, Claire didn't quite believe what she'd heard. "What did you say?"

"I said I know you didn't do it."

"Then why are you here?" A glimmer of hope ignited inside Claire. Someone believed her? *Please God, let it be so.*

"Not now. One of my deputies is going through Esther's place. He'll be headed this way in a few minutes, so I suggest we come to an agreement before he does."

"What kind of agreement?" She didn't know if she liked the sound of that. But what could she do? He held the cards.

"Come with me. You can stay at my place until I get to the bottom of this."

Claire narrowed her eyes. "And what do you want in return?" Did he expect her to sleep with him? Be his slave? What was she getting into?

"I assure you, I mean you no harm. You need to disappear while my deputies and their posse are searching for you. Buy yourself some time. They're hell-bent on pinning the murders of your husband and children on you and you alone."

"Why don't you think I did it?"

The back door of the house slammed open and voices could be heard.

"We should probably talk about that later," Mart said in a clipped tone. "Right now, we need to get you clear of my men."

She followed the marshal through the barn to the back alley, where a fine-looking Appaloosa had been tethered to a shrub. He mounted his horse, as did Claire, and the two raced off into the night.

42

The next morning, Claire awoke to brilliant sunshine and the sound of songbirds through a partially open window. Mart's home turned out to be a pleasant two-story clapboard house on the outskirts of town. He'd made certain she was squared away in a second bedroom and Rose was fed and watered before he headed back into town to rejoin his men and the posse searching for her. They hadn't exchanged many words before he left.

She still didn't know why he'd decided to believe her, nor why he'd taken her under his wing. She got dressed and made the bed, then went downstairs to the kitchen. A pot of what Josiah referred to as cowboy coffee simmered on the cast-iron stove, and she poured herself a cup before walking onto the front porch.

The thought of her deceased husband brought tears to her eyes, and she set the cup down on a wicker stand next to the willow branch loveseat to gather herself.

Don't think about them, Claire. You have to be strong right now. There'll be time to mourn them later.

Mart Duggan might be the perfect person to help her find out who was responsible for her family's massacre. He was the town's head marshal, although from what Claire had gleaned from Josiah's trips into town, marshals in Leadville didn't hold the position long before they were either shot or run out of town by the local roughs. Claire had a feeling that Mart Duggan was a different kind of lawman—one who didn't suffer fools gladly, a man who wasn't afraid to do what he felt was right.

She finished her coffee and went to the barn to see to Rose. The chestnut mare nickered in greeting, obviously glad to see her. Claire had finished brushing her down and mucking out the stall when she heard the sound of hoofbeats pounding up the drive toward the house. Her heart skipped a beat at the thought of one of Mart's deputies coming for her, but at the sight of Mart Duggan astride the horse she relaxed. He led Josiah's horse, Brick.

She went out to meet him. He dismounted and handed her the reins.

"Are you just getting back now?" she asked.

He nodded. "Posse's headed for Denver. I'm here to have a rest and then go back to town."

"If you're here, then who's guarding Leadville?" She wasn't an expert, but as lawless as Leadville was, she couldn't imagine leaving the place without some kind of justice for very long.

"Some of my men."

"Not Eli and Joe?"

Mart shook his head. "Nope. If I'm lucky, maybe they'll both get their asses shot up. Apologies for the rough language, ma'am." He lifted his chin.

"No apology necessary. Josiah—my husband—used plenty of salty language." Another block formed in her throat at the thought of him. *Not now, Claire.* She led the Appaloosa and Josiah's horse into the barn. Mart removed the saddle from his ride and hauled it into the tack room, while Claire used a curry comb on his horse.

"You're going to need to tell me what happened, exactly, Mrs. Whitcomb, so I can start to piece together who might have..." Mart let the sentence dangle, obviously sensitive to her pain.

Claire nodded and took a deep breath, then let it go. "Please, call me Claire." She proceeded to tell him exactly what she'd seen, what the man she'd killed looked like, and that the other two men had seemed to intentionally miss her when they fired at her.

"Is it true that you beat the man after he was dead?"

Claire glanced at the ground, avoiding his eyes. "Yes." She exhaled, hard, wondering how to explain. "I'm not proud of my actions, but the grief took hold of me and wouldn't let go. Not until I'd spent it all on the bastard who killed my son."

Mart nodded, as if confirming something to himself. "Anger can be a mighty powerful motivator."

Claire studied the man in front of her. There was something about him, a confidence, yes, but also a lethality she hadn't picked up on the evening before. "Last night, Esther said you were harmless. But I don't think that's right."

Without answering, he took the comb from her and continued to brush down his horse.

"I think you can cause a lot of harm, but only to those you think deserve it."

Mart stopped what he was doing and stared long and hard at her. Uncomfortable, she shifted on her feet but returned the stare. He was the first to break it off, and resumed grooming his horse.

"What makes you think that?" The casualness of his tone held a warning.

Claire leaned against the stall and crossed her arms. "Because you don't travel with the herd, and anyone who lives like that has their own brand of justice. I think that's why you've lasted as marshal for as long as you have."

A smile creased his lips for a moment before it disappeared.

"I've been known to skirt the law on occasion, if it means putting away an evildoer."

Claire's heart leapt. *Perfect.* "There was something I forgot to mention." Mart shot her a glance. "Eli said my husband was in dire straits, that he had taken out a loan against our property and had reneged."

Mart considered that, then asked, "What did Blankenship say?"

"He said everyone knew. He thought Josiah had told me, but he hadn't. I had no idea."

"Who has the deed to the property now?"

Claire shook her head. "I don't know. My plan was to go into the bank this morning after I woke up, but your raid on Esther's place stopped that idea in its tracks."

"Good thing, too."

"Why is that?"

"If you waltzed into the bank now, a fugitive—because that's what you are—you'd soon be looking through bars, waiting on a trial."

"But how am I going to find out what happened?"

Mart Duggan lifted his chin. "Leave that to me."

He finished grooming his horse, then fed and watered him and Brick.

"What's his name?" Claire asked.

"Lightning."

"That's an interesting name. He's fast?"

"Fast, sure, but I named him that when a bolt of lightning hit the ground next to him and he didn't buck me off. I knew right then he'd be a good horse for a lawman."

"I take it he doesn't react to gunfire."

"Not much."

She followed him into the house and poured another cup of coffee for herself and one for him.

"Would you like me to make you breakfast?" she asked.

Mart smiled. "Why, I think I would like that very much, Claire. Thank you. I'll go get us some eggs." He was gone for several minutes while she familiarized herself with the kitchen, and came back with a wire basket of fresh eggs and a good-sized piece of salt pork.

Claire mixed up some biscuits and sliced and fried the pork in a cast-iron skillet. Using the same skillet, she cracked several eggs into the hot pan. She served him first, then filled her plate.

"You still haven't told me why you believed me last night," she said between bites.

Mart took a swig of coffee. "You take good care of your horse."

Claire frowned. "I don't understand."

"To my way of thinkin', a person takes care of their horse, they can't be all bad."

"Ah. I see. And how did you know I took care of my horse?"

"I looked her over last night as I was leaving Esther's. But the main reason is how she responds to you. Horses know people." He slathered butter and preserves on a biscuit and took a bite.

"That horse is the best friend I've ever had." Her eyes got misty at the thought. What would she ever do without Rose?

Mart nodded. "That's a fact."

"So, what's your plan? What happens if Eli and Joe come back? I can't stay here forever."

"My wife won't be back for a while, and those two don't come out this way. I'll make sure they don't, anyway. So you're all right for now."

"What about Josiah's and my property? I need to know if Henry was telling the truth about Josiah reneging on the loan."

"I've got an idea for that." He finished his breakfast and pushed the plate away. "In the meantime, I suggest you practice your shootin' skills. Never know when you're going to need them."

Claire bristled at his assumption. "I know how to shoot. I shot that man off his horse."

Mart held up his hand. "I don't mean to insult you. Hell, I practice every day. But from what you told me about the roughs who attacked your place, sounds to me like they're some bad actors and you should brush up on your ability to defend yourself."

"Oh." Claire felt her cheeks flush. "I'm sorry. I didn't mean to bite your head off."

"That's all right. If I were in your shoes I'd be prickly too. In fact," he leaned forward on his elbows, "you seem to be taking this all in your stride. Most women would be hard put to stop crying long enough to cook a meal, let alone plan their revenge."

Again, heat flushed her cheeks. This time from anger. "Mr. Duggan—"

"Call me Mart."

"Mr. Duggan, if you don't believe that I mourn my family as much as any other woman, you're sadly mistaken." Her anger rose along with her voice. "I only see the necessity of ignoring this horrible tragedy in order to make things right—I will not rest until my husband's and children's murderers are brought to justice. I'll have plenty of time to mourn them when I've avenged their deaths."

Mart studied her for a moment, then nodded as if to himself. "If you survive."

Claire shot the last round from one of Mart's six-shooters, a Colt Single Action Army gun better known as a Peacemaker, and slid the gun into the borrowed holster she wore. After he'd rested, Mart had ridden into town, citing an acquaintance who might be able to help clear up a few things.

She walked over to the tin cans to check her accuracy. Four out of five had holes where the bullets had pierced through the metal. She'd missed the fifth.

Not bad, but not perfect. She was determined to be as good a shot as possible. Like Mart had warned, the men who killed her family were obviously hardened criminals if they'd killed children. If she threatened them and they fired back, they most likely wouldn't hesitate to kill her this time.

She still didn't have an explanation as to why they'd left her alive. Nor why they'd targeted her family in the first place.

The sun rode high in the cloudless sky, telling Claire it was close to noon. After she'd fed Rose and Brick and mucked out the stalls, she saddled Rose and took a ride along the creek that ran next to the Duggans' property. As she sat beneath a giant weeping willow the dam of tears broke. She cried for all the plans she and Josiah had made going up in smoke, for the death of her family and her dreams, for being left alone in an inhospitable place. She prayed for Mart and his wife, for the strength to see justice for her family, for reason and help and to resume a normal life.

But what was normal? None of what happened could be thought of as anywhere close to normal. She was setting upon a new road, one filled with vengeance and danger, and she wasn't sure how to stop, or even if she wanted to.

Had she fallen so far that she wanted to return a kill for a kill? She thought long and hard about it and decided that no, what she wanted was justice. But what did justice look like? If she was being honest with herself, it did involve killing—but rather than a bullet, death would come by a hangman's noose.

The peace that resulted from these thoughts gave her a welcome respite from the turmoil that raged within. Once she was clear on her intentions, she felt stronger, ready to take action and bring whoever was behind the attack to justice—no matter who it was, or what that justice entailed. Mart had warned her that things could get rough, that she'd be called upon to defend herself and maybe others, depending upon what the guilty parties decided to do.

"When you corner a badger," he'd said, "that badger will fight the only way it knows how, which might involve drawing blood to get away. You have to be ready to stop him before he stops you."

Well, she was ready. She'd already decided that if she died in her quest for justice, then that was Providence. It would be a relief, if she was honest. She wouldn't have to relive the nightmare of the attack, or be alone, or feel any number of emotions warring for dominance within her. Because right now, the future looked bleak, even if she succeeded in exacting some form of justice.

The sound of hoofbeats in the distance brought her out of her reverie, and she shaded her eyes to look. A rider and a horse and wagon were coming up the drive. The rider was Mart on Lightning, but the person on the buckboard was a woman.

Claire climbed back into the saddle and headed to the house.

Mart dismounted first and went over to help the woman down from the wagon. She struck Claire as a woman of means—her fine clothes and regal bearing were those of a woman people answered to.

"Claire—this is Mrs. Horace Tabor. Mrs. Tabor, this is Claire Whitcomb, the woman I told you about."

Mrs. Tabor smiled and held out her hand. "Please, call me Augusta."

Claire didn't know if she should curtsey in addition to shaking the woman's hand. Augusta Tabor was Leadville royalty. Married to Horace Tabor, the man who had almost single-handedly built Leadville from a miner's camp into the boomtown it was today, Augusta was a formidable businesswoman in her own right. She'd run several businesses including the general store and post office while her husband prospected and grub-staked miners. Two of the miners struck it rich with what was known as the Little Silver Mine, and with a thirty percent stake the Tabors became wealthy overnight.

"I'm pleased to meet you. Mrs. Tab—I mean, Augusta." Claire shook her hand and dipped in a modified curtsey.

"Mart told me of the horrific events you've had to endure." The sympathy on Augusta Tabor's face seemed genuine. "I can't imagine how awful you must be feeling right now."

"Thank you for your kind words." Claire was at a loss as to why Mart would tell the most well-known woman in Leadville of her problems. She assumed the fewer people who knew her location and predicament the better. Now that Augusta was privy to where Claire was staying, what would stop her from telling others?

A lot of others?

"Would you mind if we went inside?" Augusta asked, fanning herself. "The sun is something fierce today, and I could use a cool drink."

"Of course," Mart said, and offered his arm. Augusta accepted, and the three of them went inside.

Once everyone had a cool glass of water in hand and a seat in the parlor, Claire broached the subject. "I'm sorry to appear thick-headed, but why did you bring Mrs. Tabor here?"

"I figured if anyone could find out information about your finances," Mart said, "it would be Augusta."

"Indeed," Augusta said. "I've met far too many women who don't have any idea of the extent of their family's holdings. Which, to my way of thinking, isn't smart business."

Claire bristled. "It wasn't like my husband to withhold the state of our finances. He was always quite fair and open about such things." She didn't appreciate Augusta's insinuation that Claire didn't think the family finances important.

"I meant no insult, dear. May I ask, what exactly have you been told in regards to you and your husband's accounts?"

"Before the…attack, I was under the impression that our holdings were solid. My husband was eager to work our claim." Claire looked down at her clasped hands and relaxed them. "According to the men who wanted to arrest me for the murder of my family—" She paused as she choked back the emotion welling in her throat.

Augusta placed her hand on hers in silent support, urging her to continue.

Claire took a deep breath and went on. "According to those two men and Henry Blankenship, who was also present, my husband was in arrears on a second loan, and our claim was reverting or had reverted back to the bank. I—I was quite upset, as you might imagine."

Augusta patted her hand reassuringly. "What was said, exactly, to give you that impression?"

"Their exact words were that we were in dire straits."

Augusta nodded and gave her hand a gentle squeeze before she let go. "I would be happy to look into this for you if you'd like, Claire." She turned to Mart. "Give me some time to find out what I can."

"I'd be much obliged, Augusta." He glanced at Claire and gave her a slight nod. "If you wouldn't mind, I'd prefer you not let on where she's holed up. No sense tipping off anyone to her whereabouts."

"I'll be discreet." Augusta took a sip of water and stood. Claire and Mart followed suit. "It appears that you've got a champion in Mr. Duggan, Claire." She smiled at Mart. "You'll find no one better to come to your defense. My husband has always spoken highly of him, and I would have to concur with his assessment."

Mart looked at the floor, his cheeks coloring.

Augusta laughed. "And I now have one more piece of the Mart Duggan personality puzzle—he blushes when praised."

Mart and Claire followed Augusta out. Mart handed Augusta up into her wagon, then pulled Claire aside.

"What's wrong?" Alarmed at his obvious urgency, Claire's throat went dry.

"There's a wanted poster with your likeness going up around town. I noticed one on my way here."

"How could that be? I thought you said you weren't going to post one."

Mart shook his head slowly. "Ain't me, or any of my men. I'll check around town, see if I can get an idea of who might be taking it upon themselves." He gave her a look. "You probably shouldn't be seen anywhere near Leadville. Least for a while."

"Obviously."

He gave her a short nod and mounted his horse. "I'll accompany Mrs. Tabor into town, and then have some things I need to do. I should be home in time for supper."

Claire watched them until they disappeared over a slight rise.

Conflicting feelings warred within her, vying for dominance. It was real—she was now a fugitive. And she was trapped on Mart's property. She found it hard to breathe.

Calm down, Claire. Mart won't let anything happen to you. No one but he and Augusta know you're here. You're safe.

For now.

Part of her was glad of Augusta's support, relieved to have another person on her side. But the other part of her, the suspicious part that had made itself known after the attack on her home, wasn't so sure telling anyone else her location had been such a good idea.

CHAPTER 9

Claire sat on the front porch watching the sun drop low on the horizon. She helped herself to a glass of whiskey, hoping it would soothe her nerves. The longer she waited without taking action, the more agitated she became. Mart hadn't returned yet, and Mrs. Duggan's books on embroidery and other feminine pursuits had failed to keep her engaged.

She'd taken Brick for a ride along the river, stopping to enjoy the warm summer day, then returned and did whatever chores needed tending before going in to make supper. She'd waited as long as she could, but eventually succumbed to hunger and ate a bowl of the stew she'd made.

With a few hours of daylight left, after supper she'd set up some targets to practice with the six-shooter, then cleaned the piece and put it away. Now, having run out of things to do to keep her mind off her circumstances, she'd become tense and nervous and couldn't sit still.

What if Mart had a change of heart and decided she was guilty? What if Augusta slipped and told someone where she was? In Leadville, like any town, gossip spread fast. What if she never found out who had killed her family and burned down her house? What would happen to her then? Going back to Pennsylvania seemed the only course of action. But she'd come to enjoy the freedom the West represented. She had a feeling she'd chafe under the niceties of "civilized" society now.

She drained her glass and stood, preparing to go inside and retire for the night, when a crunching sound came from the side of the house. She froze in place, listening. There'd been no sound of hooves on the drive, and Mart wasn't one to be quiet. The crickets had gone silent, which wasn't unusual in itself, but the absence of their song gave rise to an eerie stillness. She waited, straining to hear. After several seconds, the crickets started up again. She shook off her unease, telling herself it was just a figment of her imagination.

She crossed the porch and reached for the screen door. A floorboard creaked behind her. She tensed and started to turn when a gloved hand clamped down on her mouth, and an iron-strong arm snaked around her waist.

Claire screamed through the leather trapping her mouth. The odor of unwashed humanity floated up to meet her as she struggled against the assailant's grip. The more she fought, the tighter their hold became, until she was scarcely able to breathe. The vision of Mart's Peacemaker flashed in her mind, but there was no way she could reach the revolver unless she broke free.

"Be quiet, woman," the man's voice hissed in her ear. "Stop fightin' me or I'll break your damn arm."

Claire forced herself to relax. The man chuckled.

"That's it. Nice and easy." Keeping his hand over her mouth, he dragged her off the porch toward the darkness beyond. A fresh dose of panic surged through her, and she started kicking and twisting, trying to squirm out of his grip.

"Goddammit, you're a hellcat." With his arm still around her waist, he shifted his grip on her mouth.

Claire took advantage of the break in contact, and with as

much strength as she could muster, twisted her body a half turn and sagged to the ground, pulling his upper body down with her. At the same time, she sank her teeth into his arm.

With a yelp of pain, he loosened his grip for an instant, but an instant was all she required. She slipped from his grasp and scrambled toward the house.

She made it up three steps before he grabbed her skirt and yanked her backward onto the ground. Claire screamed, as much in pain as in rage and fear, and kicked and hit at the man as he tried to subdue her.

A loud *crack* split the night. Her attacker cried out and staggered.

Heart pounding, Claire clawed the dirt to get away from him. The man gripped his side as he fell. Blood leaked through his fingers.

Rifle in hand, Mart emerged from the shadows and walked up to the injured man. He relieved her attacker of his gun and glanced at Claire. "You all right?"

Claire nodded. "I think so." Her heart was still beating so fast she thought it might split her open, but she doubted that was what he meant.

He turned his attention to the man in front of him. "Who the hell are you and what are you doing here?"

Panting from the pain, her attacker didn't say anything.

Mart prodded the wound with his rifle. The man yelped.

"Answer me."

"Go to hell, marshal," the gunman rasped.

"Looks like you're gonna get there before me." Mart studied him like a bug pinned to a bug board. "Why not make it easy on yourself and tell me who sent you?"

"The devil."

Mart's eyes glittered in the light from the lantern on the porch. "You'd best do as I say, or you will surely regret tonight."

When he didn't get a reaction, Mart shoved his rifle into the man's face.

"I will count to five real slow-like. If you don't tell me who sent you and why by the time I get to one, you'll be shoveling coal in the devil's furnace."

Again, the man didn't answer, but something in his eyes shifted. Claire wondered if he'd take the answers to his grave.

"Five."

Nothing.

"Four."

Still nothing.

"Three."

Sweat beaded on the man's forehead and he squeezed his eyes shut. His lower lip quivered.

"Two." Mart pushed the barrel even harder into his face. The man swallowed.

"One—"

"Don't shoot." The man threw his hand up, palm out. "I'll tell you. Don't shoot—"

"That's better." Triumph lit Mart's features for a second, before his face grew taut with anger. He prodded him with the gun. "I'm waiting."

The man tried to take a deep breath but couldn't. "Name's Cody Wilson."

"Okay, Cody. Who sent you?"

"I don't know."

Mart prodded him again, this time closer to the wound. He cried out.

"I'm telling the truth. I don't know the man's name. I only met him recently."

"Okay. Then where can I find this acquaintance of yours?"

Cody shook his head. "I don't know. He don't live in town. I seen him at the Golden Nugget."

"What does he want with Claire?"

"All's I know is he told me to take the woman who was stayin' at the marshal's place and he'd pay me five dollars."

"How did he know she was staying here?"

"I don't have no idea."

"What were you going to do with her? Hold her for ransom?"

Cody didn't answer. His breath came in shallow bursts. From the amount of blood on his shirt, Claire didn't think he'd survive much longer.

Mart shoved the barrel against his forehead. The barely suppressed rage on Mart's face would have been reason enough to elicit a confession from Claire, let alone someone who had something to hide.

"What were you going to do with her?" he repeated, his voice edgy and hard.

Cody's eyes crossed as he looked up at the gun barrel. Sweat gleamed on his forehead. He licked his lips. "I—I was s'posed to... I was—"

"You were supposed to kill her, weren't you? You're just a sniveling, yellow gun for hire."

"No," he rasped, his quavering voice evidence of his waning life force. "You got it all wrong—"

"Then tell me what's right. What were you supposed to do, if not kill her?"

The gunman didn't reply. His eyes glazed over. The shallow rise and fall of his chest slowed, then ceased. Mart scowled.

"Is he gone?" Claire looked from the gunman to Mart.

"Yep." He sighed. "Hard to get answers from a dead man."

Mart walked over to where she sat and perfunctorily looked her over, searching for damage.

"I'm fine," she said, but she wasn't. Tears coursed down her cheeks, a reaction to almost losing her life and watching the outlaw lose his. "Are there others?"

"There was only the one horse that I could see." Mart sat

down in the dirt next to her and wrapped his arm around her shoulders. Claire leaned into him and cried.

She was getting damned sick of crying.

She took a shaky breath and sat up. Mart offered his handkerchief, which she took to dry her face.

"I don't know what I would've done if you hadn't been here, Mart." The cold, hard reality that she would have been dead like her family catapulted through her, knocking her off balance.

Mart climbed to his feet and helped her up. "I don't know how the cur knew where to find you, but I got roped into stoppin' a fight in the Golden Nugget right about when I was fixing to leave town and come home. If I'd have done what I first intended, this would-be murderer wouldn't have gotten so close to you."

"Or he would have ended up trying to kill us both." Claire took a deep breath to calm her nerves. "I should leave town. Go back east to Philadelphia where I won't cause any trouble."

"And let your family's murderers go free? Is that what you want?"

Claire looked at the ground. "No. But I couldn't live with myself if someone else got hurt because of me."

Mart guided her up the porch steps and into the house. "Why don't you let me worry about that?"

He deposited her on the settee in the parlor and went to the sideboard to pour her a glass of water. He handed her the glass and sat on a chair across from her.

"The presence of ol' Cody out there tells me someone wants you dead, and it's my job to find out who that might be. But it's also my job to make sure you're safe."

"That's why I suggested leaving town."

"Maybe there's another way."

She frowned at him, wondering what on earth he was talking about. "What do you mean by 'another way'?"

"Well, you know when you have a nest of wasps somewhere you don't want?"

Claire nodded. "Josiah used to smoke them out."

He nodded. "We need to do that to whoever's behind this."

"How?"

Mart's smile lacked levity. "Leave it to me. First off, you need to learn the art of fightin' the enemy. And I've got just the person to help with that."

Claire woke early the next morning and went downstairs to make breakfast, but Mart had beaten her to it. Flapjacks and bacon and a couple of fresh eggs crowded a plate where she normally sat. She poured herself a cup of coffee from the pot on the stove and sat down.

"That is a lot of food." She eyed the stack of pancakes with trepidation. "I'm not sure I can eat it all."

"You're gonna need your strength today."

Claire eyed him skeptically. He looked tired. "What's going to happen today?"

Mart buried his nose in his cup of coffee. "You'll see."

Claire sipped the coffee and pushed the food around on the plate with her fork. Mart glanced at her above the edge of his newspaper.

"Did you sleep?" he asked.

She shook her head. "Had a hard time after last night." Every sound had frozen her blood. She kept Mart's loaded revolver on the nightstand and propped pillows behind her so she could sleep sitting up, but in reality she'd barely dozed, expecting someone to attack again. Even though Mart had assured her he would keep her safe.

Mart lowered the paper. "You need somewhere else to stay while I set up my plan."

"What plan, exactly?" He still hadn't told her what he intended to do to bring the killers to justice.

"All in good time. For now, you need to move off the premises. I have a friend down the road a piece who will take you in for the time being."

Claire stared at her food and nodded. "All right." She didn't want to be away from Mart—he made her feel safe, but he wouldn't always be home, and she'd be a wreck having to stay vigilant the entire time he was gone.

She tried to eat, but could only force down a few bites. Her nerves had stolen her appetite.

Mart cleared his throat and said, "I think you should see this." He unfolded the paper and turned it toward her.

On the front page was a drawing of a woman with the words *Wanted! Dead or alive* in large print underneath. A reward was listed below. Claire leaned in closer to get a better look at the likeness, and caught her breath.

The drawing looked like her.

She glanced at Mart. "Is that…"

He nodded. "It is. Like I told you yesterday, your picture is all over Leadville, and I've heard tell they started posting them in some nearby towns."

Claire leaned back in her chair.

"Are you all right? Your face is as white as a sheet."

Mart studied her.

"I'm a wanted woman."

"You were the same yesterday, Claire. Don't let it get to you. You'll be fine."

Claire swallowed and tried to take a breath, but her heart raced, making it difficult. The wanted poster made it all too real. Her anxiety spiraled out of control and she started to panic, fighting to breathe. Mart slid the paper back toward him and folded it so she couldn't see the image.

"It's going to be all right, Claire. Trust me. You'll make it through this." His quiet voice had a soothing effect, and eventually her breathing became even. Her heartbeat slowed, and the spots before her eyes disappeared.

"Thank you, Mart." Her gratitude for his kindness overwhelmed her. Where would she be without his steady hand? What would she do when this was all over, if she survived? His wife would never agree to her living here—what wife would? She'd have to harden off, like the seedlings she brought outdoors in the spring.

After they finished breakfast, Claire followed Mart outside to see to the horses. The outlaw, Cody, lay in Mart's buckboard wagon, waiting to be taken to the undertaker for burial. The outlaw's horse was tied to the wagon. The horses whinnied as they approached. Rose and Lightning appeared to have established a rapport, which made Claire happy. Although Brick was Josiah's horse, the gelding had been a new addition to the homestead and she hadn't developed a bond with him. In essence, Rose was the only family she had left. Claire constantly worried about her, making sure she was comfortable and had plenty of feed and water. But companionship wasn't something Claire could provide, other than riding her every day. Lightning had befriended Rose the way Mart had Claire.

Claire went to the tack room to get the brushes and bridles, while Mart fed the horses. On her way back, she overheard Mart talking to someone. She froze in her tracks, scarcely breathing.

"Claire, come here," Mart said. "There's someone I want you to meet."

The other man wore the long, dark braids of the local Ute tribe, as well as buckskin leggings and a beaded calfskin shirt with fringe on the sleeves. A pair of knee-high leather moccasins completed the outfit. Claire choked back a cry as images of the attack returned. She gripped the side of the stall until her knuckles went white.

Remember, Claire, white men attacked your family, not Indians.

She took a deep breath and let it go.

"Claire, I'd like you to meet my good friend Thomas."

Thomas caught and held her gaze, unnerving her with his boldness. She looked away.

"I'm pleased to make your acquaintance, Thomas."

Thomas glanced at Mart. "This is the woman?"

Mart nodded. "Claire, remember when I said you needed to learn how to fight the enemy?" Claire nodded. "Well, Thomas is here at my behest to help you in that endeavor."

Surprised, Claire glanced at Mart. "You mean he's going to teach me to fight?"

Thomas answered for him. "Mart has told me that you know how to shoot. I will show you the ways of my people, which will help you survive."

His elocution surprised her. If judged solely on the delivery of his words, he'd not have stood out in the drawing rooms back East.

"You speak very well..." *for an Indian,* Claire thought, but didn't voice it aloud.

"Not all Utes are uneducated savages, I assure you." She noted the slight sarcasm in his tone. "I attended school in England." He walked over to Lightning and smiled when the Appaloosa nickered at him. He pulled a carrot from his pocket and fed it to the horse.

"Why did you return to Colorado?" she asked. The new governor of Colorado had run on a platform of "The Utes Must Go!" and a majority of the tribes had been pushed onto reservations as a result. If he'd remained in England, Thomas would have been celebrated in London's high society as an "educated heathen"—which would have been more accommodating than the fate that awaited him in his own country.

Thomas made a face. "Too much rain."

Rose stretched her neck toward Thomas and snuffled his hand. He produced another carrot and fed it to her. He scratched her forelock and Rose snorted her approval.

"I dare say Rose likes you, Thomas." Claire relaxed a notch.

"She's a fine horse." He rubbed her neck, eliciting soft snuffles from the chestnut mare. He pulled another small carrot from his coat pocket and fed it to Brick. It disappeared in no time.

"Where are we to commence the training?" Claire asked. She might as well jump in with both feet. She was leery of staying with a complete stranger—an Indian, at that. Would she be expected to sleep in a wickiup? Or did his people erect tipis made of buffalo hide? She'd seen both while roaming the West. It couldn't be any worse than when she and her family traveled to Colorado, sleeping on bedrolls in all kinds of weather.

"You'll be staying at his place for the time being," Mart said.

Thomas looked her up and down with an appraising eye. Unnerved, Claire crossed her arms. "You will need to change your clothes," he said.

She glanced at her stolen skirt and high-necked blouse. "What's wrong with what I'm wearing?"

Thomas pantomimed grabbing hold of a section of her skirt. "Can you run in this? The skirt is too easy to grasp, and can give an attacker the advantage."

The memory of Cody grabbing her skirt and yanking her off the porch surfaced and she shivered.

"You'll also want to conceal that you're a woman at some point," Mart added. "I took the liberty of picking up some clothes yesterday from the general store."

Mart walked to the back of the barn with Claire close behind him. "How long will I be staying with Thomas?"

Mart shrugged. "As long as you need to."

He went over to a shelf on the back wall and picked up a package wrapped in brown paper and tied with string. He opened it to reveal a pair of dark blue dungarees and a cotton twill button-down shirt. He held the trousers up to her and squinted.

"Yep. These should do nicely." He handed the pants and the shirt to her, then disappeared behind a sawhorse doubling as a saddle mount. He returned with a pair of dusty-looking Wellingtons. "Afraid you'll have to find your own pair of boots, but these'll do for now." A bright red bandana, a wide-brimmed hat, and pair of leather gloves completed the look.

"How did you know what size?"

"You and my wife favor each other, so I used that as a guide. Whatever don't fit, we'll bring back."

"What about my husband's horse?"

"What about him?"

"I'd like you to have him, if it's not too much trouble. To thank you for your help."

"I don't need payment, Claire. I'm doing this because I believe you're innocent."

"I know. Please accept the horse as my everlasting gratitude." She looked at him, hoping that he'd at least grant her this one request.

He hesitated for a moment, but then nodded. "Well, thank you. I accept your generous offer." He touched the brim of his hat and left the tack room.

Claire changed out of her skirt and blouse and into the trousers and shirt. She'd worn Josiah's dungarees before when she mucked out the stalls, but no one outside her family had seen her in anything but skirts and dresses and women's shoes.

She stepped into the Wellingtons, which were a size too big, but serviceable, and returned to where the men were. Thomas nodded his approval, giving Claire an odd surge of happiness.

Mart took the wagon into town to bury the outlaw and do whatever work necessary to keep the peace and monitor the hunt for Claire. Claire and Thomas followed the creek on horseback until they came to a small cabin with a barn and a corral containing three other horses.

Thomas dismounted, removed the palomino's bridle and saddle, and turned the horse loose in the pen with the others. Claire slid off Rose and studied the homestead.

"This is your place?" she asked.

Thomas gave her a deadpan look. "Expecting a tipi?"

"No, I—" She felt her cheeks heat from embarrassment. Thomas chuckled.

"Some of us have learned to embrace the white man's ways, whether we like it or not."

"Of course. I'm just surprised." Relieved would have been a better word. Although, the cabin didn't look large enough to have more than one room.

The next several hours were spent learning to ride Rose and one of the other horses bareback, and how to quickly mount and dismount both, saddled and not. Once she'd shown proficiency in that, Thomas set up a target on a stump and instructed her to practice shooting while riding. After several attempts, she got the hang of timing her shots to the rhythm of the horse, and was thrilled when she hit the target dead center. Thomas didn't show much emotion, and she worked hard to elicit a response. Although she knew she was being ridiculous, a quirk of Thomas's lips, or a crease near the eyes showing her that he was indeed appreciative of her work, gave her immense satisfaction.

By sundown, Claire was so exhausted, she could barely walk. Thankful for the leather gloves, she pulled them off as she dropped into one of the rocking chairs in the front yard. Good. No blisters.

Yet.

Thomas disappeared into the cabin and reemerged with a canteen of water, a plate of hardtack, and an apple. "You have done well today, Claire. You show ability, but more importantly, you show a strong willingness to learn."

She took a sip of water and smiled, inordinately proud of the praise. "I enjoyed today very much."

They sat in companionable silence, eating and drinking. Dragonflies danced in the air as the sun set, and Claire's eyes grew heavy.

Thomas stood and gathered both plates. "I will take my leave. Sleep well."

Claire sat up straight in her chair. "Wait. Aren't you staying?"

"I will sleep with the horses this evening."

"I can't let you do that. I'm perfectly willing to sleep in the barn." She couldn't put him out of his own home.

"I don't mind. It's more comfortable than many of the places I've stayed."

"Will we continue the same tomorrow?"

He shook his head. Claire's spirits plunged. She'd enjoyed working hard, learning new and practical things she'd never thought to learn. She felt stronger, more capable. And, if she was honest, she enjoyed working to win his approval.

"But surely I'm not ready yet?"

Thomas smiled. "No, you're not ready, but you will be. Tomorrow you will learn strategy. The day after we will continue your physical training."

Claire's heart leapt and she returned his smile.

"That pleases you?" Thomas asked, his eyes sparkling in the twilight.

"It does, yes."

He turned to leave. "We shall see if you still feel that way in the morning."

The next morning, Claire couldn't get out of bed. She tried to raise herself up onto her elbows, but her arms wouldn't do what she wanted them to. She ached from head to toe, and wondered if this was what it felt like being run over by a team of horses.

She peeked underneath the bedclothes, expecting to see ugly welts and bruises, but saw only unblemished skin. How could her body have betrayed her this way? She couldn't even lift her arms above her head.

With a groan, she managed to heave herself to a sitting position and put her feet flat on the floor. Using the metal post on the bedframe, she maneuvered herself to a standing position and then hobbled over to the washstand next to the window. She glanced in the cracked mirror, unsure what to expect, and was relieved to see she didn't look like she felt.

Thomas's words filtered through her brain, and she finally understood what he'd meant. He'd worked her hard the day before and knew she wouldn't be in any shape to continue the physical lessons. The way she felt, she wondered if she'd be able to do what was required after a month.

Claire poured water in the basin and proceeded to wash her face and arms, then turned back to the chair where she draped her clothes the night before.

She'd been right about the size of the cabin—one room served as bedroom, sitting room, and kitchen. The bed was surprisingly comfortable, although the mattress needed to be re-stuffed, and the place was clean enough—another surprise, as Thomas was a single man. In Claire's experience, single men didn't care much for housework.

She eyed the trousers but decided the skirt would be easier to put on, then ran her hands through her hair and fastened it back with a couple of hairpins. Her fingers were barely able to button her shirt and she had to rub her knuckles halfway through to make them work right.

By the time she stepped out the door and onto the porch, she thought she might make it through the day. Her muscles were beginning to loosen and she was able to walk and move, although bending over presented a challenge.

Thomas waited for her on one of the rocking chairs next to a small fire, a cup of coffee in his hand. She stood in the doorway and breathed in the fresh morning air. Bright sun illuminated the lush grassland beyond the corral, with dots of yellow, red, and blue from the wildflowers scattered across the gently rolling land. The sound of the creek gurgling nearby and the singing of the birds in the cottonwood trees gave Claire a sense of serenity she hadn't had since the attack.

"This place is beautiful."

Thomas nodded. "The Great Spirit is pleased today." He gave her a sidelong glance as she lowered herself into the other rocking chair. "How are you feeling?"

Claire grimaced. "I've been better." She shook her head. "You were right. I've never been this sore."

"I have taken the liberty of feeding and watering Rose with the rest of the horses, so that we may begin our lessons in earnest. This morning we will look at the tactics my people use to attack and fight."

"We heard news of the Meeker Massacre," Claire said. In September of the previous year, Nathan Meeker, an Indian Agent posted at the White River Ute Indian Reservation, had an argument with a Ute chief and was killed along with ten other men working at the agency. At the same time, another band of Utes attacked the military camped at Mill Creek and killed several soldiers. Both attacks enraged a large contingent of white settlers, fomenting a rabid desire to remove all Utes from the territory and either kill them or force them onto a reservation.

"My people did not take part in the massacre, but their anger was warranted. Your governor lied and made spurious claims against the Utes, forcing us to abandon our ways and convert to Christianity."

"The chief took women and children as hostages," she protested. Claire and many of the settlers held their collective breath, hoping and praying until they heard the hostages were released, nearly a month later.

"That is so. Our great leader, Chief Ouray, negotiated for their release. But now, all Utes are considered criminals regardless of what we have done, or which band we belong to. My people are starving—the white settlers have fished and hunted and chased away the game, leaving none for the rest of us. And they force us to live on ever smaller pieces of land. All in the name of profit." He shrugged. "We might as well do what we're accused of—at least then we'll survive."

Claire had a hard time reconciling what she'd heard and read in the newspaper and what Thomas had just told her. She'd been led to believe Indians weren't trustworthy and had worried every time Josiah had dealings with them. Had she been wrong?

"I'm sorry, Thomas." Her words seemed a poor substitute for all that had transpired.

Thomas lifted his chin in acknowledgement. He set his cup down and leaned forward in his chair. Using a nearby stick he traced a design in the dirt. "Imagine this as an enemy encampment." He then drew two parallel lines radiating out from the designated camp, the distance between them narrowing toward the end. He glanced at Claire. "If you were planning to attack with few men, how would you do it?"

Claire studied the markings. "How many men are inside the camp?"

"Let's say there are a dozen."

"And what do these two lines represent?"

"A canyon."

"I'd figure out a way to lure the enemy into the canyon toward the narrow end, block their escape, and surprise them."

"A good solution," he said with a nod.

Claire felt a flush of pride for answering well.

"But an even better one would be to attack from above."

"Above? You mean station men on the walls of the canyon?"

He nodded. "Wouldn't this give the attackers a superior position?"

"I suppose so, yes. Especially if they had long-range rifles."

"Or bows and arrows."

"Right. Or bows and arrows." She glanced at him with interest. "Am I going to learn to use a bow and arrow?" That sounded interesting, except the idea caused her pain just thinking about it.

"Perhaps. Let's continue our strategy lesson for now."

Thomas scrubbed away the first drawing and drew others, each time positing a different scenario to Claire, asking her to devise the best plan of attack. Some she got right, some she didn't feel she had enough information but still offered her ideas.

After a couple of hours, Thomas set the stick aside and leaned back in his chair.

"You have a quick mind and pick up strategy well. A warrior

has to be prepared for any eventuality—to be able to see all sides of a situation before committing his men to battle."

"But what if I have no one to help me fight?"

"We shall cover sabotage and being outnumbered in our next lessons. But first, we must eat."

After the midday meal, which consisted of dried venison, a biscuit, a carrot from Thomas's garden, and another apple, they resumed her tutoring by taking a long walk next to the creek and discussing various situations. Claire found she had a knack for strategy and became excited to learn even more. She also found that by the time they returned from their walk, she felt much better physically.

"Set up several targets and practice with the revolver until sundown," Thomas told her. "Work on the speed of your draw." She did what he asked until she could barely lift her arm.

The next few days took on a familiarity that Claire clung to— a simple breakfast followed by training, either physical or mental. Thomas kept her busy, not giving her time to wallow in the grief that continued to stalk her. At the end of the day she'd be so tired, thinking was a chore. She was surprised to find she relished his instruction in hand-to-hand combat, which included escape from different holds, and moves intended to incapacitate a larger assailant. With the memory of the attack still fresh from the night before, Claire worked doubly hard to master Thomas's instructions.

At the end of the fourth day, Mart arrived.

Thomas and the marshal conferred for several minutes, and Claire found she had a hard time concentrating. She assumed Thomas was giving Mart an update on her progress, and she wanted to know what he was telling him. Unable to contain her curiosity, she stopped what she was doing and joined them.

The two men turned as she approached. Mart had a hard set to his jaw.

"What is it?" she asked. She wanted to say, *what is it now?* but that sounded like she was whining, so she held her tongue.

Mart and Thomas exchanged a glance before the marshal said, "Looks like there's a change of plan."

"Why?" She looked from one man to the other. Mart still hadn't told her anything about what he'd planned to do.

"Henry Blankenship wants to meet with you. He says he has information on your claim."

"How did he know I was still in town?"

"Horace Tabor told him."

"How—"

"Augusta mentioned your problem to Horace to see if there was anything he could do, and it appears he took it up with Blankenship."

"But won't it be dangerous for me to be seen in town?"

Mart nodded. "I told him about the attempt on your life. He's agreed to meet with you at a place of my choosing. Says he believes you're innocent and that he wants to help."

"But that's good news, isn't it?" At least she'd know what happened to the claim and their land. And having Henry vouch for her would go a long way toward keeping her out of jail and away from the hangman's noose.

"We'll see."

Claire studied Mart for a moment. "You still don't know how Cody knew where to find me."

Mart nodded. "I'm inclined to believe that Augusta may have unintentionally let your location slip to the wrong person. That's my fault. I brought her out to talk to you. There's a bounty on your head. Money makes strange enemies—enemies you might never suspect."

"You haven't told anyone where I am now, have you?"

"Of course not. Just the same, I'm going to suggest that you both remain vigilant until we catch whoever wants you dead."

"When am I to meet with Henry?" The sooner, the better, as far as Claire was concerned.

"Tonight, out at the old Hoover cabin."

"Will you come with me?"

"That was my plan."

CHAPTER 12

Claire and Mart reached the old Hoover cabin at dusk. Bats flitted above their heads, snatching insects. A lonely coyote howled in the distance, its call echoing through the night. Blankenship was due to arrive after his required attendance at a dinner party.

The abandoned cabin sat next to a small creek that ran through a narrow canyon. A crude outhouse perched to the north of the cabin. Both structures were badly in need of repair. After several unproductive years of panning for gold, Old Man Hoover had left for greener pastures. No one took his place, adding another abandoned claim to the dozens in the area.

Claire dismounted and walked around the site, wondering what it had been like to live alone for so many years, working day in and day out, hoping, waiting, expecting to strike it rich, and then realizing the dream was just that—a dream. She thought of Josiah, wonderful, naïve, optimistic Josiah, doing much the same. Well, tonight Henry Blankenship would put to rest the mystery surrounding her husband's folly.

At least then she'd be able to move on, whether there was any money left or not. Hopefully she'd find a way forward.

"I've been meaning to ask you." Claire shoved her hands in her pockets to keep them warm. "Were you able to find out anything about the man Cody mentioned?"

Mart shook his head. "Hard to find something without at least a description."

Claire shivered. The heavy work shirt and long coat Mart had given her helped some, but nighttime in the mountains could be cold. She was glad she wore the trousers. She reached up and removed her hairpins, allowing her hair to fall to her shoulders, hoping it would help keep her ears warm.

Mart gathered some twigs and branches and started a small fire next to a large log near the cabin. He motioned for Claire to sit.

"Thank you. Aren't you going to join me?"

"No, ma'am. I'd prefer to stand, if you don't mind." He walked to his horse and slid his rifle from its scabbard.

She eyed the two revolvers in his gun belt and nodded at the rifle in his hand. "Expecting trouble?"

"I like to be prepared."

That didn't bode well for the meeting. Was he worried about Henry? Did he think the banker might let their whereabouts be known? Or was it just a precaution, in case someone followed Henry to the meet?

Claire stared at the fire, willing herself to forget for the moment why she was there. "Thank you for introducing me to Thomas. I've learned so much from him."

Mart nodded. "A woman in your position needs to be able to take care of herself."

Claire sighed. "A woman in my position. What exactly does that mean?" She glanced at the marshal. "What am I to do? I've no husband, no family, most likely no money or property. I can't stay in Leadville forever."

"Once we clear your name, I could speak to Esther for you,

see if there's anything you could do for her at the boarding house."

"I don't mean to sound ungrateful, but if I'm going to take in washing and mending or cook for someone, I'd rather it not be strangers."

"Thomas says you have a talent for shooting and such." Mart studied her, his expression hard to read in the orange light of the fire. "Ever thought about hiring yourself out?"

Claire looked at him in disbelief. "As a gunman?" She shook her head, the idea absurd. "If you hadn't noticed, I'm a woman, and women don't do those kinds of things."

"Don't tell that to Alice Ivers."

"I assume you're referring to Poker Alice?"

"The very same. She makes a fine living gambling—and gets to wear the latest fashions, too."

"I'm not a gambler, and don't much care for frilly things."

"That's not what I'm saying. Alice has a talent for gambling, and she lives a good life. Or, if you prefer, there's Eleanor Dumont, or Calamity Jane. Both women make a living doing what they're good at, although I will admit, Jane has a fondness for the bottle that you don't. Besides being a good shot, you have a mind for strategy. And according to Thomas you're a quick learner. Those talents can be turned into a different kind of living—one where you're able to come and go as free as a man."

Claire had to admit, the idea was intriguing. But until she avenged Josiah and her children, she couldn't think about the future.

Somewhere, an owl hooted. Claire wrapped her arms around herself, strangely ill at ease. "When did you say Henry was going to meet—"

The crack of a gunshot split the still air. A round ricocheted off the log next to Claire.

"Get down," Mart yelled. Lightning and Rose whinnied and strained at their leads.

Claire dropped flat next to the log as Mart took cover near the cabin and returned fire. A volley of gunfire pierced the night, kicking up a fountain of dirt close to the log.

"They can see you. The fire."

Claire turned her head. The flames weren't more than two feet from her. Careful to keep low, she grabbed a handful of dirt and threw it on the flames. Another round splintered the log, this time closer than the last. Heart in her throat, she threw another handful and kept going until the fire sputtered out. A deep glow from the embers remained, but the area around her was much darker.

"Claire—" Mart whispered loud enough to hear. She coughed, letting him know she'd heard him. "I'm going to count to three," he continued in a low voice. "When I get to three, get up, stay low, and run toward me. I'll cover you."

Claire squeezed her eyes shut. She was going to die. If she got up and ran she'd be a moving target, like the deer Josiah loved to hunt. "I—I can't."

"Yes you can."

His voice held an urgency she hadn't heard before.

"No, Mart I—"

"One."

"Oh my God," she breathed. *I can't do this. I can't. I can't. I can't. I can't.*

"Two."

Another round ricocheted off the log. Too close.

Oh my God oh my God oh my God. You have to move, Claire. Do it. Now.

"Three!"

Heart hammering in her ears, Claire scrambled to her feet and ran headlong toward the cabin. Good to his word, the marshal fired rounds into the darkness, delaying the other gunman's attempt to shoot her.

She made it to the cabin. Gasping, Claire flattened her back against the wall. "What now?"

"Take this." Mart handed her one of his Peacemakers and extra ammunition. "When I say go, start shooting."

"Wait. What are you doing?"

"Going for the rifles."

"Oh, shit." She barely registered that she'd uttered the cuss word—one of Josiah's favorites. Mart waited until she'd taken a position near the corner of the cabin before he gave her a nod. Mart headed for the horses, and Claire popped out from behind the wall and fired five rounds in the gunman's general direction. The gunman returned fire, and she ducked back behind the building to reload.

Mart made it to the horses, but both of them were twitchy and danced back and forth, acting like they were ready to run. Lightning was accustomed to gunfire, but the echo through the canyon amplified the sound, most likely hurting the horse's sensitive ears.

Mart disappeared into the shadows behind Lightning. A moment later, both horses started moving toward the cabin.

He's using the horses for cover. Claire shoved her anxiety for Rose deep, bobbed around the corner of the cabin once more, and fired again at the unseen gunman. Mart reached the cabin and handed the reins to Claire.

"Take them behind the cabin."

She nodded and did as he asked. On her way back, she slid her rifle from its scabbard and took up a position next to Mart.

"I got no quarrel with you, Marshal." The man's voice echoed eerily in the canyon. "I want the woman."

Mart seated a round in the chamber of his Winchester. "Eli? That you?"

There was a pause, then, "I don't want to kill you, Mart. Just hand over the woman and you can go on home."

Claire glanced at Mart. The man trying to kill them was his deputy? "I thought he was on his way to Denver?"

"Guess he circled back." Mart turned toward the sound of Eli's voice. "You know that ain't going to happen, Eli. Why not give yourself up and we can all go home?"

"You know *that* ain't gonna happen. Lay down your guns. We got the place surrounded."

"Where's Blankenship?" Mart called.

"I don't know what you're getting' at. All I know is I need the woman."

Mart frowned at Claire. "If Eli isn't working for Blankenship, how in hell did he know where to find you?"

Claire shrugged. She closed her eyes, waiting for the gunman to say something.

"Marshal? I'm waitin'."

She opened her eyes and turned to Mart. She knew where Eli was. "He's near that clump of trees on the rise. You know the one we saw when we rode up?"

Mart looked at her. "You sure?"

She nodded. "I'm sure."

"All right, then. I'm going around back, see if I can sneak up on him. Can you distract him?" Claire nodded.

Mart disappeared behind the building, leaving her alone.

CHAPTER 13

Claire brought her rifle up, eased the barrel past the corner of the cabin, and started firing.

A few moments later there was another shot, this one farther away. Claire reloaded and fired again, unsure if or when to stop.

"Hold your fire, Claire," Mart called. His voice echoed from where the earlier shots had been fired.

Claire stopped. "Can I come out?"

There was a pause, then, "Yep—it's safe."

Claire lowered the rifle and took a tentative step away from the cabin, expecting gunfire. When none came, she headed toward the sound of Mart's voice, careful of her steps in the darkness.

As she approached the small grove of trees, she slowed her pace. There were two men standing over someone else on the ground. She drew closer and gasped.

"Thomas?"

The Ute warrior turned at her voice. "Claire."

She glanced at Mart. "How is he here?"

"I asked him to come."

She had more questions, but the man on the ground raised even more of them. Eli was still alive. A dark stain soaked his pant leg.

Eli narrowed his eyes at Claire. "I shoulda kilt you when I had the chance."

At that moment, she knew. It was his eyes. How did she not see it before? Memories of the attack returned with so much force her knees grew weak. "You were one of the bastards that attacked my place." Her cheeks began to heat. "You killed my husband and children." The rage inside her built like a fire consuming dry grass. She clenched her fists in an attempt to stop from clawing his eyes.

The man's expression turned icy. "And you kilt my brother in cold blood." He spit at her feet. Thomas slammed the butt of his rifle into his face. His head snapped back and he grunted. Blood gushed from his nose.

"Fuckid sabbage," he managed.

Thomas and Claire trained their weapons on Eli, and Mart dropped to his haunches in front of him.

"I don't really care what happens to you, to be honest. But I sure as hell want to know who sent you and why."

"Or whad? You gooda kill be?"

"Probably. Although if you work with me I might be persuaded to reconsider."

The man's laugh came out more like a gurgle. "Sure, Barshal. Whadebber you say."

Thomas stepped on his wounded leg and Eli screamed, the sound muffled by the amount of blood that surely must have been in his throat.

Mart watched Eli with the inscrutable expression he'd used on Cody, the first man sent to kill Claire. "It's gonna be a long, painful night if you don't cooperate." He nodded toward Thomas. "This here's a member of the Ute tribe. I reckon he knows more about causing pain to a man than most."

Keeping his hand on the bridge of his nose, Eli glanced at Thomas. Fear flickered in his eyes. "You wouldit leab be alode wid a sabbitch."

"What's it gonna be?" Mart continued. "A night of terror at the hands of a heathen? Or will you cooperate so it ends quick?" He made a show of looking around the area. "Ain't nobody gonna hear you scream, Eli. Not up here."

Eli closed his eyes for a moment, then opened them. "The bangger."

"You mean Blankenship."

Eli nodded.

Claire gasped. "Henry?" She looked at Mart, confused. "But he wanted to help me..."

Mart shook his head. "No, Claire. He didn't."

"That's why you asked Thomas to come tonight, isn't it?"

Mart nodded. "Blankenship was the only one who knew about this meeting. I wasn't one hundred percent sure it was him behind the attempts on your life. I am now."

Everything tumbled into place—the attack on the homestead and the attempt to blame it on the local tribe. Henry telling her not to worry, that the law would work it all out. Mentioning to the deputies that Josiah had taken a large mortgage out on the property and that they were in "dire straits." Henry aiding her escape, making her look even guiltier.

"What are we going to do?" Claire's heart sank. Blankenship was a powerful man. As head of one of the larger banks in Leadville, he was above reproach. Justice rarely came to the rich.

"I tell you what I'm going to do," Mart said as he pulled free a pair of handcuffs. "I'm going to take you into custody, Eli. We'll get a sworn statement from you and then arrest Blankenship."

At that moment a twig snapped, followed by the sound of a horse riding away.

Mart and Thomas exchanged looks.

"Blankenship," Mart said.

Claire was already halfway to the cabin.

"Wait. Claire—it's too dangerous—" Mart yelled.

"I don't care," she yelled back. She reached Rose, untied the reins, and was in the saddle and after Blankenship before anyone could stop her.

"Follow them," Mart said to Thomas. "Make sure she doesn't do anything stupid. I'll take care of Eli."

Thomas started for his horse. Taking advantage of the momentary distraction, Eli lunged at Mart, going for the Peacemaker. Mart pivoted, drew his pistol, and fired, killing him. He dropped where he was.

"Kind of takes care of your only witness," Thomas said drily.

"Which means we have to get to Blankenship before she does."

Leaving the dead outlaw where he lay, Mart and Thomas mounted their horses to follow Claire and the escaping banker through the darkness. In spite of their narrow lead, soon they lost them both. Thomas got down from his horse to search for clues. Mart did the same. The moon lit the terrain with a ghostly blue glow.

It didn't take long before Thomas found evidence of the banker's and Claire's paths, and they made their way along the tree line, following the obvious trail. The broken branches and hoofprints gave them plenty of indication as to which direction they were both riding.

Hours later, the trail led them to a small cabin in the middle of nowhere. Early on, the prints had diverged, indicating Claire had lost her way. Mart and Thomas continued tracking Blankenship, hopeful that Claire would take a while to locate his trail again.

A fine bay could be seen tethered to a crude hitching post, looking like he'd been rode hard. There was no sign of Claire. A faint light was visible from one of the two windows.

"I'll see who and what we're up against," Mart said, preparing to go.

Thomas stuck his hand out, stopping him. "A buffalo would have a better chance sneaking up on him."

Mart gave him an annoyed look, then nodded. "Fine. You tippy-toe up there, then."

A short time later, Thomas returned.

"It is as you thought," he said. "There is one man inside. He has black hair and wears a mustache and expensive clothing. He also has a bowler hat that doesn't look as though it has been used."

"That's our man. Weapons?"

"A revolver and a long gun."

"Any sign of Claire?"

Thomas shook his head.

"Best take him into custody as soon as we can." He gazed at the sky. They had maybe an hour before daylight. "No telling when or if she'll show up." He gave his friend a sideways glance. "You teach her how to track?"

Thomas avoided his eyes. "I might have mentioned something."

"Shit." Mart sighed. "Well, then I suggest you cover the far side of the cabin. I'll take the front. Stay out of sight. We don't know if he saw you up at Hoover's place."

❧

CLAIRE WHITCOMB STARED at the expanse of switchgrass billowing gently down the slope below her. The earthy scent of pine and dirt rose to greet her as a slight wind rustled through the trees. A fiery red sunrise colored the horizon—it would soon be daylight.

Smoke drifted from the chimney of the one-room cabin. Rose shifted anxiously, swishing her tail, her breath exploding in short puffs from flared nostrils.

Images of greedy flames licking the sides of the one-story farmhouse she'd built with her husband filled her mind. She swatted them away, much like Rose had done with the flies circling them.

Not now.

Claire took a deep breath, steeling herself. She was so close. All she had to do was ride down the embankment, dismount, slide her rifle from its scabbard, and open fire on the cabin's occupant.

Simple.

Everything had led her to this one, true moment.

She released her hair from its confines and shook it free, allowing it to flow down her back. Thomas had insisted that appearances mattered. Especially when attacking.

She'd worn her long tresses tucked under the leather hat Mart had given her. Along with the button-down shirt, dark dungarees and boots, and a fine red bandana, from a distance she could pass for a man.

How much she'd changed.

No longer Mrs. Claire Whitcomb, devoted wife of Josiah Whitcomb, and mother of Nathan, Amy, and Laura, she was now just Claire—drifter. Wanderer.

Avenging angel.

At the thought of her children, tears welled in her eyes, and she angrily wiped them away.

Not now.

Rose pawed the earth, sensing her rider's unease. Claire shook off the melancholy that threatened to overcome her and squeezed her thighs, signaling to the mare it was time to go.

Rose picked her way down the embankment, her head bobbing with the movement. Filled with trepidation, Claire kept a firm but gentle hold on the reins to keep her horse from stumbling.

What if Blankenship wasn't alone? Or her gun jammed?

Or he got off the first shot?

Not now, Claire.

She took another deep breath and let it go, releasing the fear.

By the time she reached the cabin, any remaining anxiety had hardened into determination. She'd killed a man once before. True, that man had murdered her boy, Nathan, but the man in the cabin had instigated far worse—he'd destroyed any semblance of a normal life for Claire and used his elevated standing to get away with it.

She was tempted to go in guns blazing but heard both Mart's and Thomas's voices in her head, talking her out of that particular approach. There were too many variables to consider, and stealth was required.

Claire had watched the cabin for a time, hoping to catch Blankenship on his way to relieve himself, but it was not to be. Either he remained inside from an abundance of caution, or he just didn't feel the need to go out.

There was no corral or barn nearby. Again, she swept her gaze over the area around the cabin, searching for evidence of a horse. Had he sent it packing in an attempt to throw off his pursuers?

She draped Rose's reins across a shrub, allowing her to graze.

Mart wanted to take the banker into custody and hold him for trial, but if that happened she'd never get justice. She needed to confront Blankenship, needed him to pay for the destruction of her family—her life. With his influence and money, he wouldn't spend a day in jail much less swing at the end of a hangman's noose.

She offered a silent prayer of thanks for the marshal—without his help, she'd have taken the coward's way out and gone back to Philadelphia to lick her wounds amongst a family for which she felt nothing but a tepid connection.

But Blankenship's misdeeds ended now.

Her real family was here, in the West. Thomas, and Mart, and Esther, and Augusta Tabor. All four had proven supportive and helpful, had seemed to understand the pain of losing her family as a deep, abiding agony housed inside of her, one which would never dissipate.

She slid her rifle free. With the sound of the waking birds drowning her footsteps, Claire crept across the empty yard and up to the small front porch. Her heart thudded in her ears, the excitement and danger of what she was about to do enlivening her senses. Each twig snap, each birdcall, each swoop of a bat lent a heightened, surreal aspect to her mission.

Claire was ready to die, if this was the end. But she'd be damned if she didn't take Henry Blankenship with her.

She picked up a couple of rocks and slipped them into her pocket. Careful to step on the outside of the wood plank stairs leading up to the cabin, Claire eased her way to the front door.

She took a position opposite the handle, removed one of the stones, and tossed it away from her. The rock clattered across the porch, coming to rest at the far end.

Silence.

She took the second rock and did the same.

Nothing happened.

Fine. She'd need to be more direct.

"Henry Blankenship," she called. "Show yourself."

She waited a few moments before trying again. "Come out here, now."

Still nothing.

Had he already gone? Her spirits plunged. He would be much more difficult to kill if he'd gotten away.

Or was he lying in wait to cut her down as she entered the cabin?

So be it. She'd get off at least one shot before he tried.

She'd better make that shot count.

Claire grasped the handle and pushed the door open. It swung wide easily and she took a step back, braced for gunfire.

There was none.

She entered the cabin, rifle first.

It was empty.

A chair lay on its side in the middle of the one-room shack. Broken dishes littered the floor. A banked fire crackled in the stove. Blankenship's bowler sat on the table, looking as though its owner had just stepped out for some air.

There'd obviously been a scuffle.

Thomas and Mart had gotten there ahead of her. They took Blankenship into custody, just like Mart said he would.

A flash of anger started slow and deep in her belly, then raced up her spine, igniting a conflagration in her heart and her soul. She left the cabin and headed for Rose.

She'd find them.

She had to.

Claire caught up with them two hours later. Mart and Thomas had stopped near a stream to rest their horses. Mart filled his canteen with water, while Thomas tended to the horses. Henry Blankenship sat at the base of a young cottonwood, wrists handcuffed behind him around the tree.

She slid from Rose and tied off the reins so she wouldn't bolt at the sound of gunfire. Then she pulled her rifle free and walked into the clearing.

Thomas was the first to notice, and he whistled at Mart. The marshal turned. At the sight of Claire, he slowly rose to his feet. Blankenship's eyes grew wide. His face blanched white.

She aimed her rifle at the banker. "I'm here for justice, Mart. Don't try to stop me."

Thomas and Mart exchanged looks. Mart reached for his gun. "I'm taking him in, Claire. He'll stand for trial. I promise he'll get what's coming to him."

"You tell her, Marshal." Blankenship gave Claire a look that told her he didn't believe he'd be in jail any time soon.

Claire hesitated. Could she go through with it? The man couldn't shoot back. If she killed him, it would be as cold and heartless a thing as she'd ever done. "At least let me ask him some questions."

Thomas stepped between Mart and Claire. Mart frowned in warning.

"Let her at least have this," Thomas said.

Mart moved his hand from his holster. "Fine."

Claire turned to the man on the ground. She lowered the barrel of her rifle slightly and said, "You had my family killed—you had *three children* murdered. Why?" She needed to hear his reasons. Had to know what drove someone like him to do a deed so evil.

"Now, Claire. You've got it all wrong. I don't know who you've been listening to, but—"

"Stop it, Blankenship. Horace and Augusta Tabor had your clerk, Philip Jenkins, audit my husband's bank account and found the loan you'd given him. But you called in your marker before he had a chance to make good on his claim, transferring the land and mineral rights to you." She studied him for a reaction, but his face had turned to stone. Claire had the eerie sensation of being outside her body, watching the scene.

"Josiah wasn't a businessman," he scoffed. Blankenship tried to shift his body, found he couldn't. "He'd have frittered away your holdings. You needed someone with experience to manage your claim." He sighed. "I thought we could do it together, but obviously that was not to be."

"So you had my family *killed*? You monster." She had no words. He'd tried to transfer his guilt to her with his confession. She raised the rifle back into position.

Blankenship glanced at Mart and Thomas, both of whom were listening intently to their conversation. He turned back to Claire. "I'm truly sorry about the children, Claire. But you have no evidence."

"The deputy marshal would beg to differ." Claire lifted her chin.

A look of superiority came over Blankenship's features. "I'm afraid, my dear, that Eli's dead."

She glanced at Mart. "Is this true?"

Thomas answered. "He tried to take Mart's gun."

She stared at Blankenship. No witnesses. No jail time. He wouldn't stand trial.

"Claire—" The warning in Mart's voice was clear. "Don't do it. Let justice work."

And the realization hit her. *The rich never pay.*

She pulled the trigger.

Leadville, Colorado - Two months later

Claire finished securing her saddlebags and turned to say her goodbyes to Mart and Thomas, who had both come to see her off. They stood in the shade of the old pine next to the burned-out shell of her home. Horace and Augusta Tabor had offered her a fair price for the property, and she'd agreed. The thought of rebuilding a life in the same place that elicited so many horrible memories held no attraction for her, and, truth be told, she'd been relieved to sell.

Thomas stepped forward and handed her something wrapped in a colorful Indian blanket. She unfolded it to see an honest-to-goodness tomahawk alongside a bow and a quiver of arrows.

"Oh, Thomas. I—I don't know what to say. They're beautiful." The tomahawk had a carved handle, and the quiver and bow each had beaded decorations in the Ute way.

"The tomahawk has been through several wars, and the bow

and arrows I had made for you. But I've seen you use these weapons. You need more practice." Claire had spent the last two months training with Thomas at his cabin. She still hadn't quite mastered throwing the tomahawk with any accuracy, although she was much better with the bow.

"The next time we meet," he continued, "I expect you to be able to hit a moving target from Rose's back."

"Thank you, Thomas, for everything." Overcome with emotion, she threw her arms around the Ute, but then caught herself and quickly stepped away. He gave her a nod and the slightest of smiles before going to see to his horse.

She turned to Mart. "Words cannot express how grateful I am that you believed in me, and for all your help. I don't know what I would have done without you." Claire choked back tears. He'd also covered for her when questions arose regarding Blankenship's death. She owed him her life.

The ex-lawman gazed at her with genuine affection. "You would have found a different life. One that wouldn't have suited you as well." From his pocket he withdrew an envelope, which he handed to her.

"What's this?" she asked. Inside was a folded piece of paper. She took it out to read. When she was finished, she glanced at him. "A letter of introduction?"

He nodded. "For whenever you decide you want to hire yourself out. It'll come in handy, I'll wager."

She put the letter away. "The Tabors paid well for this place. If I'm careful, I won't need to work, at least for a while."

Mart looked at the ground, attempting to hide his smile. "Whatever you say, Claire."

"Fine. You think whatever you want, Mart Duggan." She turned to Rose and secured the gifts. Mart had grown tired of being a lawman. He'd handed in his notice and was poised to write another chapter in his life. Claire wondered if the realities of how justice prevailed in the West—or didn't—had anything to do with his decision.

"I almost forgot," Mart said, and walked over to his horse. He pulled something out of one of the saddlebags and handed it to Claire. It was a hand-tooled gun belt with a pistol tucked into one of the holsters.

She looked at him in surprise. "A Peacemaker?"

Mart nodded as he mounted Lightning. "You earned it. Give my regards to Luke and Wyatt." Mart Duggan touched the brim of his hat and gave her a quick smile before he and Thomas rode away.

Claire watched them until they disappeared, then turned to her family's four graves. With tears in her eyes, she said goodbye, placing a kiss on each of the mounds. She stood silently for several minutes, remembering them as they were, not as they died.

When she was finished, she made her way back to Rose and climbed in the saddle.

She didn't know where she would end up, but that didn't matter. She'd find a new life, somewhere. The mining town of Tombstone in the Arizona Territories sounded like a good place to start. Leadville held too many bad memories.

She could only hope that she'd be able to outride them.

ACKNOWLEDGMENTS

There are so many people to thank for making Retribution possible: first and foremost, a huge debt of gratitude to my partner in crime and first reader, Mark, who has a wicked sense of humor and is a saint for putting up with the vicissitudes of living with a writer; to editors Laurie Boris and Ruth Ross for their amazing attention to detail and expert comma-wrangling; to author and early reader Charles Ray for his experience in the Western genre, and for his much-appreciated encouragement to keep writing this story; to Mike Foster for his horse expertise; to longtime early readers and writing partners Michelle, Ali, and Jenni—I especially appreciate that they don't pull their punches when it comes to getting the story right; to good friend Jim Van Houghten for his expertise with Old West firearms and time-period authentication; to Bob Metz for his invaluable information regarding Leadville and its surroundings; and last but not least, to my advance reader team—there's no question that you guys make me a better writer. Thank you.

Writing is never a solitary endeavor.

A CLAIRE WHITCOMB WESTERN BOOK 2
GUNSLINGER
DV BERKOM

A CLAIRE WHITCOMB WESTERN BOOK 2

GUNSLINGER

DV BERKOM

For my father

CHAPTER 1

Leadville, Colorado – Fall 1880

Claire Whitcomb rubbed the nose of her chestnut mare, Rose, before she handed the reins to the train steward.

"Sweet Rose," she murmured. "You'll be all right." The horse nickered and lifted her head, then nudged her. Claire stood back as the steward led Rose up the ramp—she'd made certain that the railroad company was using a specially made stock car before she'd purchased her ticket. This one had eight stalls and provisions for feed and water, as well as a bed of straw for the animal's comfort.

Once she was sure Rose had been taken care of, she made her way through the throng of people to her car—everyone was abuzz about the Denver & Rio Grande's new narrow-gauge railway, recently completed to Leadville. She'd been tempted to follow the stagecoach to Pueblo, but decided to take the train when she heard about the new stock car. The alarming number of animal deaths on railway journeys had always dissuaded her—

she'd never risk Rose's life, especially now that her family was gone.

Her eyes misted over as thoughts of her husband and three children crowded her mind. Clutching her reticule, she tugged at her waistcoat, uncomfortable in the confinement of her traveling clothes. She'd gotten used to wearing men's clothing during her training with the Leadville marshal and Thomas, a local Ute warrior, but polite society would frown upon her traveling as such in the railcar.

She carried a single-action army revolver strapped to her thigh, accessed through a specially made slit in her skirt hidden by folds of fabric—an invention she'd insisted the seamstress include when Claire had the outfit made. In her carpetbag she carried a gun belt, boxes of ammunition, and her trusty Winchester rifle, along with a decorated tomahawk, a bow, and a set of arrows. If trousers would upset the stuffed shirts in the rail carriage, how much more upset would they be seeing she carried Thomas's gifts?

She continued toward the front of the train to find her seat, passing a private car with rich green paneling instead of bright yellow like the others. Red velvet curtains peeked above wooden shutters covering the thick glass windows.

Probably built for some rich miner to take his family—or his mistress—traveling.

She found her car and boarded. The space smelled of oil-rubbed wood and new leather. The bench seats looked brand new and the wood floor didn't yet have the scuff marks acquired from passengers wearing boots with spurs. Claire stowed her bag in the overhead rack and settled in with a sigh of relief. She hadn't realized how tense she'd been.

"Good day to you, miss." The young man sitting across from her smiled. His too-short coat sleeves revealed worn cuffs and freshly scrubbed fingernails. The coat's corduroy material strained across his boney shoulders, evidence of either a hand-me-down or a too-hot wash. But he and his clothes were clean. He wore his sandy-blond hair slicked back.

Claire warmed to him immediately. "And the same to you. My name's Claire."

"Ian." Ian stuck out his hand for a shake. Claire obliged and then leaned back in her seat.

"Your accent. You must be Irish."

He worried the brim of his hat and nodded. "Is it that obvious, then?"

She smiled. "A little. Would you happen to know Mart Duggan?" The marshal was as Irish as they came, and mentioned keeping an eye on his people.

He grinned, nodded. "Oh, yes. Everyone knows Marshal Duggan."

"Pity he's no longer the marshal." Her friend and protector had grown weary of being a lawman and turned in his badge earlier that summer. He now owned a livery stable. If it hadn't been for Mart, Claire would most likely either be in jail or sentenced to hang for murder.

Ian's expression grew somber. "And Leadville's the poorer for it."

"He was certainly an effective lawman."

Ian nodded. "He'll be back. Mark my words. Ye can't keep a good Irishman out of the politics of a place."

She wondered if that were true for Mart. His wife had been the main reason behind his retirement. With a penchant for disregarding the law, he'd been the most effective lawman Leadville had ever seen, but he'd also amassed many enemies. Claire figured Mart's wife preferred him alive.

"Where are ye headed, if I may be so bold?" Ian asked.

"Tombstone, eventually."

"That's a fair piece. I'm going as far as Pueblo. My girl is waiting for me there." His face split into a wide grin, telling Claire all she needed to know about his feelings for "his girl."

"Are you coming back to Leadville?"

"Aye. I've been given two days off but must return come Monday."

"And what is it that you do?"

"I'm workin' a claim with me older brother."

"Mining's hard work. I wish you luck."

"Thank ye. Did ye see the private car?" Ian asked, nodding toward the back of the train.

"I did. Do you know whose it is?"

Ian leaned forward conspiratorially. "I heard it belongs to Isabella King herself."

Claire drew a blank. "I'm sorry, I don't know the name."

He gave her a surprised look. "Only the most talented actress this side of the Mississippi. And," he lowered his voice even more, "rumor has it she's Jay Gould's fancy woman."

That was a name Claire did know. Well known for his ruthless business practices, Jay Gould was one of the richest men in America, if not the world.

"Jay Gould, the railroad magnate?"

Ian nodded. "I saw her at the Opera House night before last." His eyes got a faraway look in them and he sighed.

"She must have been good."

"Miss King outshines the stars."

A middle-aged couple boarded and took their seats across the aisle from Claire and Ian. Claire greeted them both with a smile. The husband touched the brim of his hat in acknowledgement, but the scowl on his wife's face was unmistakable.

Ian leaned over and whispered, "She appears to have gotten up on the wrong side of the bed this mornin'."

Claire smiled at his attempt to make her feel better. "She must have." Truth be told, she was used to being snubbed by the fine, "upstanding" women of Leadville ever since Claire's likeness had appeared on a wanted poster earlier that spring. Mart had cleared her of the charges, but the stigma remained.

Once marked a killer, always a killer. Decent women didn't get tangled up with criminals.

She couldn't argue the point. She *had* killed two men.

The first whistle blew long and loud, and several last-minute passengers boarded, filling the car. The conductor came through to check everyone's tickets as the train began to move, its warning bell clanging. Steam escaped with a *whoosh* and the locomotive *chug-chug-chugged* up to speed. Claire settled back in her seat and contented herself watching the mountainous terrain slide by. It was late September and the aspens had begun to turn color. The first snow was likely weeks away.

As the scenery flowed past, her melancholia got the better of her. This could be the last time she saw Leadville.

It was best to move on—forget the past.

"Do ye know how fast this train can go?" Ian asked, obviously impressed.

"I imagine it would depend on the terrain."

"Aye. But in a straightaway I've heard tell she can move along at quite a clip."

"I hope they aren't out to break any records," Claire said. Train travel could be dangerous, especially if the routes were shared. Stories abounded of collisions between locomotives, and deaths weren't unheard of. Most cities set their own time, which often resulted in timetable confusion. Some stations got around the problem by using the telegraph to set their clocks, but the practice was far from standard.

The warm fall sun streamed through the window, and Claire allowed the gentle rocking of the train to lull her to sleep.

"Claire. Wake up."

Claire opened her eyes. Ian was looking at her in earnest, the excitement on his face unmistakable.

"We're traveling through the Royal Gorge. You must rouse yourself and take a look."

Disoriented, Claire shook off the vestiges of sleep and

glanced out the window. The Arkansas River surged by, its white water rushing along the majestic rock walls of the canyon.

"How long have I been asleep?"

"Quite a while. I hated to wake ye, but I didn't think anyone would want to miss this. We're about to cross the hanging bridge." Ian's excitement was palpable. "It's a marvel. The engineers attached a one hundred and seventy-five-foot girder to a sheer rock wall that hangs over the river. This is the narrowest part of the canyon at thirty feet."

Claire glanced at the track. The river churned against the low-slung bridge, looking for all the world like a raging spirit, fighting to dislodge the steel girder. Two steel A-frames supported the bridge. The sheer granite cliffs soaring up each side of the canyon sent a spear of claustrophobia through her.

"Fascinating." She leaned back in her seat. Ian may have been excited by the idea of man's ability to tame nature, and indeed, it was a marvel, but Claire's own thoughts strayed to the beauty of that nature, and how man inexplicably changed its rhythm just because he could.

"You don't seem particularly impressed." Ian gave her a look that said he was disappointed in his new friend.

Claire smiled and said, "I must still be tired."

He seemed to take her excuse in stride and returned his gaze to the window. Claire retrieved a book from her bag and settled in. Soon, the canyon opened its rock walls to the sky, easing the sense of being hemmed in. The river had slowed as well, meandering through a wider section between the cliffs. Then, without warning, the train ground to a halt, its brakes screeching in protest. Claire braced her feet against the floor to keep her seat.

"Why are we stopping?" she asked. She glanced out the window to see only sparse grass on each side of the tracks, joined to the river and the rocky cliffs.

Ian shrugged. "I'm not sure." He consulted a map of their journey. "We aren't due in Cañon City yet."

Tired of sitting, Claire stood and stretched. The other passengers were murmuring to themselves, equally confused by the delay. She lowered the window near her seat and breathed in the fresh mountain air.

A moment later, gunfire thundered through the canyon.

A chorus of screams rose up from the women in the car. Claire climbed onto her seat to lean farther out the window to see what was going on. At first nothing appeared amiss, but moments later a man dressed in dark clothing with a bandana covering the lower half of his face jumped to the ground from between two train cars up the line. He had a gun.

Heart pounding, Claire pushed back from the window before he saw her. She grabbed Ian's arm. "The train's being robbed."

"Oh my goodness," exclaimed the woman who'd snubbed Claire earlier. Her eyes widened as she placed her hand on her ample chest. With a grim expression her husband moved aside his jacket to reveal a revolver, which he pulled from his gun belt.

Claire opened her bag to grab her rifle and extra ammunition. The man across the aisle looked at her in surprise.

"I assure you," she said to him, ignoring his wife. "I'm well versed in its use."

"Aye. I am, as well." Ian had produced an older-model revolver—the kind Union soldiers used in the war.

The other man nodded. "Anyone else?" he asked the rest of the passengers.

"I've got a gun," offered a tall, thin gentleman two rows to the back. He held up a six-shooter.

"And me, as well." Another man, wearing the clothes of a miner, tugged down his bag from the luggage rack and pulled out a shotgun.

Claire studied the others. Many were women, although there were a couple of children and a handful of men—none of whom looked like they wanted to fight.

The first man nodded at the others. "Let's get to it, then."

"I believe it would be prudent if the smaller children hid underneath the seats," Claire suggested. "Everyone else should get down below the windows."

The man across from her nodded. "I agree." He gestured at a woman sitting with two younger children. "Madam, I suggest you hide your children immediately." She did as he instructed.

Claire eased next to the open window to see where the gunman had gone. His gun raised and moving low, he was making his way toward their car at a fast clip.

"He's coming." She climbed off the seat. "At least one of us should remain in the car to protect the others. Ian, myself, and this gentleman—" She glanced at the husband.

"George," was his reply.

"Ian, myself, and George will go to the back of the train, split up and—"

George held up his hand. "I'm afraid I can't let you put yourself in danger, Miss—"

"It's Claire. And I must object—"

"You'll stay here." His expression hardened. He turned to Ian and the other men. "Come with me."

Claire choked back a retort and took a deep breath. Arguing with him would just waste precious time. *Let him go.* Ian gave her an apologetic look as he followed George to the back of the train, exactly what she'd suggested.

She glanced at the miner with the shotgun. "Cover the front of the car. I'll do what I can from here."

The miner nodded and moved to the front door.

Claire turned to address the passengers. "Please, everyone, get down and stay down."

The women and remaining children immediately did as she asked, even the rude woman. The men were a little slow to respond, not used to taking orders from a woman.

Frustrated, Claire hissed, "If you're not going to fight, I suggest you get *down*. Now."

Reluctantly, the men did as she said. Claire eased back to the window to check on the gunman's progress, but he was nowhere in sight.

Where had he gone? She gestured to the miner, but he shook his head. No one was attempting to board from his viewpoint. George and his band of armed passengers were visible sneaking alongside the car on the side opposite her, headed for the front of the train. She turned to look toward the rear of the train. No sign of anyone there, either.

Had he passed by unnoticed? If so, where was he? He could have ducked underneath the carriage if he saw Ian and the other men headed his way. But why hadn't he boarded? She glanced at the passengers' belongings in the overhead rack. There were most likely plenty of valuables.

Then it hit her.

The private car.

Of course. The private car had set tongues wagging among the passengers. The outlaws would certainly be interested in the car's contents. In addition to the baggage car, there was also a pay car carrying wages for railroad employees, but that was further forward, near the front of the train. She assumed the thieves' main target would be the money in the safe, but the presence of the private quarters would certainly be tempting.

Claire made her way to the miner covering the front. "I'm going to check the private car behind us. Can you manage?"

"Yes, ma'am." He nodded at his shotgun. "Ol' Bessie here ain't never done me wrong in a fight."

"Good." She turned to leave.

"You be careful, miss. I reckon them's not your everyday roughs. What with stoppin' a train and all."

"I reckon." She stopped and rapped on the wall to get everyone's attention. "I'm going to check on another car. The man at the front of this car is to be respected and his orders to be followed." She looked directly at one of the men who had stayed behind. "Once I leave, I suggest you bar the back door to anyone with harmful intent."

The man nodded and stood, then gestured to his companion to join him.

Claire slipped past the rest of the passengers who were still hunkered low in their seats, to the back of the car where she eased the door open. She peeked around the corner but didn't see anyone, so she climbed down to the gravel bed.

She peered underneath the carriage and looked to the front of the train and to the back to make sure no one was hiding there. Then she quietly made her way to the private car.

As she drew closer, she flattened herself to the side of the railcar so she could listen. Besides her heart thrumming in her ears, she heard nothing. She was about to move to the rear door when a thud sounded inside. Claire froze.

Another thud. A muffled cry, and the crack of gunfire.

Claire moved swiftly to the rear entrance and climbed the steps, staying out of sight of the occupants. The rear window shutters were closed, so she was unable to look inside.

Someone cried out a second time. Claire held her breath and grasped the door handle.

She exhaled, got her rifle ready, and eased the door open.

CHAPTER 3

A chaotic scene greeted Claire when she entered the train car. Fine upholstered chairs lay overturned on the floor. A smashed lamp lay nearby, the smell of kerosene permeating the air. Shards of glass littered the rich carpet. A trunk had spilled open, clothes scattered everywhere. The drawers of a large secretary littered the floor, their contents strewn across the car.

A man lay face up on the floor next to a red velvet settee, a bloodstain on his shirt. His eyes were closed and he wasn't moving. The outlaw she'd seen sneaking along the tracks stood near the rich mahogany door at the far end of the car, the bandana no longer hiding his face. He held a revolver in his right hand.

"Open the damned door—*now*," he shouted, slamming his fist against the dark wood.

Claire raised her rifle. "Drop your gun, raise your hands, and turn around, slowly." Her voice was much calmer than she felt.

He straightened but didn't comply. She sighted on his back.

"I said, drop your gun."

He squared his shoulders but hesitated, as though deciding what to do. Revolver still in hand, he spun in place.

She fired and immediately levered another round into the chamber.

A second bullet turned out to be unnecessary.

The outlaw gripped his chest as a red stain spread beneath his hand. He stared at Claire in disbelief, then looked down at the bloody wound. His legs gave out and he staggered back against the door, lurching to one knee. With a wheeze, he dropped his gun and collapsed face down on the carpet.

Claire ran to him and kicked the revolver away from his hand. She shoved him onto his back and held her hand beneath his nostrils. There was no breath.

"What's happening? Earl?" Alarm laced the woman's voice coming from behind the door.

"The bandit is dead. It's safe to come out now." Claire glanced at the man near the entrance. He hadn't moved. She picked up the outlaw's gun, walked over to the other man, and checked him for life. He was dead, too.

The lock to the door at the other end of the compartment snicked back. A woman with hair the color of burnished copper appeared in the open doorway, her bright green eyes startling against a bloodless face. Pink spots colored her high cheekbones. She glanced at Claire, then at the dead outlaw. Another woman, this one with brown hair and a plain face, stood a good distance behind her with a fearful expression.

"Thank God." The redhead's gaze skated to the other man, then Claire. She took in a breath and began to shake. "Is he—is Earl—"

Claire nodded. She rose and walked back to the women, avoiding the mess on the floor. She wrapped her arm around the redhead's shoulders to steady her and led her to a chair that hadn't been turned over. The woman gripped Claire's forearm as though hoping to pull from her strength. The other woman followed at a discreet distance.

"Are you all right?" Claire asked. The shock of seeing her

family killed came back with a force she didn't expect. She remembered all too well the numbness that followed. "You've been through quite an ordeal."

The redhead closed her eyes and shuddered. "He was going to kill me."

"Very possibly, yes. He was looking for valuables. And I'm certain he's not alone." Claire turned to the woman. "What's your name?"

"Isabella King."

So Ian was right. "You're the actress?" Claire figured asking her inane questions would help to calm her. It worked.

Isabella nodded. "Yes."

"And Earl was your—"

She drew a deep breath and exhaled. "My personal bodyguard."

"I see." But she wasn't sure she did. Did actresses require bodyguards? Shrugging off the question, Claire handed her the outlaw's gun. "You know how to use one of these?"

Isabella nodded. "I'm not a crack shot, by any means." She glanced at Earl and shuddered again. "Hence the need for a bodyguard."

"I'm going to join the others. They may need my help. I suggest that you and she," Claire nodded at the younger woman, "retire to your sleeping quarters and throw the bolt on the door. If anyone tries to get inside, shoot them."

She turned to go and Isabella grasped her arm. "Please. Don't leave."

Claire gave her an understanding look. "You'll be fine. You're more capable than you imagine. I promise."

Isabella reluctantly released her grip. "Will you return? I mean afterward?"

"If you want me to, yes."

"Please."

Isabella and the younger woman returned to the bedroom

and shut and locked the door. Claire exited the private car and headed for the front of the train to join the others.

She got to her railcar and motioned for the miner to open the door. His gaze cut left and right as he stepped outside.

"Anyone come by here?" she asked.

The miner shook his head. "Nobody I seen."

"I'm going to lend a hand up front. I think the main target is the pay car."

"You may well be right. Hold up a minute." The miner disappeared into the car, then reappeared a moment later and climbed down the steps to the gravel bed below. Claire gave him a questioning look and he said, "Tole one of them city boys to take over. Let's go."

The sound of gunshots peppered the air, echoing against the walls of the canyon. Claire and the miner crept toward the sound, careful to stay low and check underneath for signs of anyone headed in their direction. They got as far as the third car before she saw the first dead body.

They both stopped, hidden from view of the opposite side by the train's wheels. The man was dressed in fine traveling clothes, most likely not an outlaw. Eyes wide open, a gunshot wound marred his forehead. The low hiss of steam from the train made it difficult to hear if anyone was nearby.

After checking the undercarriage and finding the way clear, they eased past the corpse and continued on, unsure what to expect.

Claire slowed as they neared the front of the first-class car. A second man, the tall, thin one who'd volunteered, lay in a shallow ditch next to the train. Blood seeped from a wound in his belly.

She swallowed the bile rising in her throat as they stepped past him, hoping against hope that Ian was all right. She glanced at the windows, searching for signs of passengers, but didn't see anyone. There was no sound from inside.

Either they were hunkered down for safety, or the outlaws were inside.

The pay car was ahead of the first-class carriage, which was where she figured the bandits would concentrate their attack. She and the miner crept to the front of the car. Claire peered over the coupler to the other side and caught sight of a pair of canvas-clad legs with leather boots and Mexican spurs. She couldn't see anything else with the pay car blocking her view.

Claire leaned close to the miner and said, "There's at least one bandit on the other side. I suggest we split up." She nodded above his head. "Give me time to climb to the roof. They won't expect gunfire from above."

The miner gave her a nod and headed for the front of the pay car. Claire clutched her skirt and rifle with one hand and grabbed hold of the metal ladder running up the side of the train. Snatches of conversation floated toward her and she froze, worried she'd be seen or heard by the outlaws. Escaping steam from the compressor hid some of her movements, but not all.

Cursing her clothes under her breath, she raised her skirts and tucked a corner into her bloomers as best she could. This would be the last time she wore women's clothes when traveling. To hell with the gossip mongers.

She reached the top of the car and lay flat on her belly. With her rifle in one hand, she slid to the middle. Hearing voices, she stopped, still hidden from below.

"What do *you* think I should do with them?" a man asked. His question was met with derisive laughter.

"Shoot 'em and be done with it."

A chorus of agreement rose up in answer.

"Now, wait a minute. You want me to gun down these fine gentlemen in cold blood? Is that what you think of me?"

"Well, yeah. Ain't you a stone-cold killer?"

More laughter.

"*Quiet.*" The command rendered his men mute, the *ch-ch-ch* of the idling engine punctuating his words.

Claire slowly raised her head to get a better view.

Three men wearing bandanas stood in a semicircle, holding Ian and George at gunpoint. The other men from Claire's railcar weren't visible. A fourth man in a brown Stetson and obviously the leader of the group stood in the center of the circle, his arms at his sides and legs apart in a gunfighter's stance. He wore stained buckskin leggings and a gun belt with a pair of Colt six-shooters. His bandana circled his neck rather than cover his face, revealing a hawkish nose over thin lips, a scarred chin, and a day's growth of whiskers.

He took a step toward George, a cruel smile playing on the corners of his mouth. "What do you think? Should I let you go?" He turned to his men and gestured at George. "Didn't he just try to kill us?"

The other gunmen nodded, their excited expressions telegraphing the anticipation of what their leader would do next.

Claire raised herself to her elbows—enough to get a view of the miner, who was almost in position. She eased back down and waited.

"Know what?" the outlaw wearing the Stetson asked. "These hombres ain't skeered enough for my taste. I think mebbe I need to make an example out of one—"

At that moment, the miner opened fire. The sound ricocheted off the cliffs, making it seem as though they were surrounded. Using the distraction, Claire sprang up and aimed. One of the bandits lay on the ground with a shotgun blast to his head. The outlaw's leader and the second and third gunmen turned and fired at the miner, but he'd already taken cover behind the front of the car.

Claire fired and the rifle bucked in her hands, the round hitting the third gunman in the shoulder. He staggered backward, but kept his feet. The biting, sulphur odor of black powder permeated the air. She levered another round into the rifle. The second gunman and the leader spun and fired at Claire, and she dropped and rolled to her side. That same moment, a window slid down in the first-class car, and a man wearing a bandana and holding a pistol leaned out. He looked up as Claire propped herself on her elbows and fired, hitting him square in the face. He dropped his pistol and slumped over the window ledge. A woman inside screamed.

The two gunmen on the ground continued firing at Claire, and she dropped flat as the bullets whistled past her. Another shotgun blast from the miner arrested their attention.

She popped up again and drew a bead on the second gunman, but Ian jumped onto the man's back and sunk his fingers into his eyes while George attempted to wrestle the outlaw's gun away. The gunman screamed and clawed at Ian's hands. Claire adjusted her aim, afraid to take the shot, worried she'd hit Ian or George.

The miner darted into view and opened fire on the lead outlaw, who had taken cover below grade in the shallow ditch. The miner fell back behind the train to reload as the third gunman returned fire. Taking advantage of the lull, the lead outlaw emerged with both pistols blazing, firing first at George, then at Claire. George cried out and staggered, falling back against the train. Claire returned fire. The leader pivoted, but one of her rounds still found him. He grimaced as the bullet hit his forearm, and his hand fell useless at his side. He stumbled back to the shallow ditch.

Claire's heart thundered in her chest. Time slowed and her hands shook as she reloaded. Gun smoke filled the air.

A shotgun blast from the miner hit the second gunman in the thigh and he went down to one knee, screaming in pain, Ian still on his back. Claire fired on the third gunman and hit him in the chest. He sprawled backward, dead.

The second gunman somehow managed to throw Ian off his back and draw his gun. He spun and pulled the trigger, hitting

Ian. Claire fired again, felling the second gunman. She seated the next round and aimed at the leader. Their eyes locked. Something flared in their depths. Surprise? Disbelief? He brought up his pistol.

She fired again.

Hit him dead center.

The outlaw fell.

As the gun smoke cleared, Claire scrambled down the ladder and ran to Ian. Blood soaked his torso.

Lifting his shirt to find a bullet hole in his stomach, Claire tore off her fitted waistcoat, balled it up, and pressed it against the wound. Sweat beaded his upper lip and dripped down the sides of his ash-colored face. His breath came in shallow, explosive puffs.

She cradled his head, attempting to make him more comfortable. "You're going to be all right, Ian," she said, trying to ignore the amount of blood he'd lost.

Breathless, the miner raced to her side. "The engineer and conductor are both dead."

"What about security guarding the pay car?"

"Ain't seen 'em, but I expect they're dead, too." He glanced at Ian, the concern in his eyes betraying his thoughts. "What can I do?"

"Run and see if there's a doctor on board."

He frowned at her. "Do you think that's a good—"

"I said, *run and see if there's a doctor on board the train.* Now."

The miner nodded. "Yes, ma'am." He ran off down the line of

train cars. She didn't have time for his assumption that Ian was as good as dead. A few passengers hesitantly disembarked from first class and milled about, uncertain what to do.

Claire returned her attention to Ian, putting as much pressure on the wound as she could, trying to stop the surging blood.

Ian gave her a shaky smile. "Showed them, didn't we, Claire?"

Claire couldn't help but smile back. Tears pricked at her eyes. *Don't you die, Ian.* "We sure did. You fought like a cornered wildcat."

"Ye did all right yerself." Ian grimaced. Red bubbles formed at the corner of his mouth. "Can't say as I ever saw a woman shoot like that."

"That would be thanks to Mart Duggan."

"Must've been a good teacher."

Claire glanced impatiently in the direction the miner had gone. *Please, please, please let there be a doctor.* She closed her eyes and said a quick prayer.

"Claire?"

She opened her eyes, stared into his. "Yes?"

"Would ye tell...tell her that I loved her...more than anything?"

"Your girl?"

He gave her a weak nod.

Claire's chest constricted, keeping the air from her lungs. "I think you should tell her yourself."

A wet cough rattled his chest, and he attempted to shake his head. "I won't be seeing her again. Not on this earthly realm." He grabbed her arm, his grip surprisingly strong. "Promise ye'll tell her that she was the last thing I thought of."

Tears brimmed in her eyes and she nodded. "Of course, Ian. But you never told me her name."

Ian closed his eyes, wincing from the pain. "Juliette," he said softly. Then his face went slack. His head rolled to the side as his life drained away.

Claire couldn't hold back any longer. Tears cascaded down her cheeks. She hugged him harder, wishing she could bring him back to life, knowing the thought was foolish.

The miner returned with two men. One was slender, with wire-rimmed spectacles, giving him a bookish appearance. The other had some years on him, with snow-white hair and a grizzled face. He wore a pinched expression as he limped toward them, grimacing with each step.

"This here is an animal doctor." The miner nodded at the older man. "I thought that since I couldn't find a regular one maybe he'd do…"

Miserable, Claire shook her head. "He's gone."

The miner said something to the two men in a low voice. Then he turned to Claire. "You did all you could, ma'am."

The older man nodded at Ian. "That boy was gut shot. Weren't nothin' you could do fer him." He nodded at the dead outlaw lying in the dirt next to the brown Stetson. "That there was Jack 'Sheriff Killer' Abrams. I seen his likeness on a wanted poster over in Pueblo." He shook his head. "Charley here tells us you was the one shot him."

She looked at the miner. "Your name is Charley?"

He nodded. "Yes, ma'am."

"Well? Was you?" the older man persisted.

Claire sighed. It seemed the specter of hanging followed her no matter where she went. "It was self-defense."

The younger man stared at her in disbelief. "You think we're accusing you?" He gave a halfhearted chuckle. "Ma'am, we're *grateful* to you and Charley here. Why, if it weren't for you two we'd most likely be dead, or worse."

"To tell you the truth," Charley added, "it was her idea that we sneak up on the outlaws. She even suggested it to those men right there." He nodded at Ian and George. "But hell if the one in fancy clothes thought he knew best."

Claire listened but didn't hear them. In her mind, she was

back at her homestead, watching her house burn, discovering the dead bodies of her husband and three children. How helpless she'd felt, how angry.

How numb.

The pain was so raw, she wasn't sure she could handle it. Panic rising in her chest, Claire gently laid Ian down and climbed to her feet. Charley tried to help her, but she brushed his hand away. "Leave me be. Please."

She stumbled toward the front of the train, away from people, from death. The sound of the river roared in her ears. Tears blinded her as she tried to find a private place to sit, far from everyone.

Trying to put space between her and what the good people of Leadville had referred to as the "Whitcomb Massacre."

She came to rest on a large granite boulder next to the tracks and doubled over as grief overcame her. Deep, wracking sobs tore up from deep inside. The kind she couldn't stop if she'd wanted to.

A while later—she wasn't sure how long—Charley approached, uncertainty on his weathered face. In his hand was her rifle. She glanced at him and dried her eyes.

Time to think about something other than yourself, Claire.

She stood and took the gun from him. "Thank you, Charley." Without another word, she strode off toward the train, leaving Charley with a puzzled look on his face.

"Where you goin'?"

"To see to my horse."

CLAIRE SAT in the shade on a flat rock worrying a smooth stone with her thumb as Rose grazed through the sparse grass near the tracks. Someone had sent a message to the railroad office in Cañon City about the attempted train robbery and the murders of the engineer and conductor. A clerk from the Denver & Rio Grande Railroad would send out replacements as soon as they could. A few of the male passengers had taken it upon themselves to load the bodies, including the outlaws, onto the pay car, so that the women and children wouldn't have to see them. They found the payroll guard inside, dead. The safe had its lock shot off, but the money was still inside.

A murmur went through the small group that had gathered near the first-class car as the crowd parted to let Isabella King through. She spotted Claire and headed her way. Her maid wasn't with her.

"I thought you were coming back." The actress stopped and stood before her, arms crossed.

"I'm sorry. So much happened, I forgot."

Isabella uncrossed her arms and nodded at the space next to Claire. "Mind if I join you?"

"Of course." She moved over to make room.

Isabella touched Claire's blood-soaked sleeve. Ian's blood had dried, hardening the material. "Were you hurt?"

Claire shook her head. "No." She closed her eyes, her failure to save Ian weighing heavily on her conscience. If only she'd been able to reload faster, be a better shot.

"Then what's wrong?" Isabella gestured at the passengers. "The would-be thieves are dead. Everyone is safe. There's talk you killed a notorious outlaw and two of his men." She shook her head. "That is quite a feat. Especially for a woman."

Claire choked back the emotion that rose inside her. "I could have saved him." She threw the rock in her hand with an anger that surprised her. It bounced a couple of times, coming to rest just short of the train.

"Who?"

"If I'd have been quicker with the rifle I could have killed that bastard before he did Ian."

Isabella put her arm around Claire. "You saved so many. Doesn't that count for something?"

Claire nodded. "It does." She sighed. "I'm sorry about your bodyguard."

The woman shrugged. "I didn't like him much."

"If you don't mind my asking, what do you need a guard for? I mean no offense, it's just that it seems unusual. Especially if you didn't like having him around."

"My paramour insisted." She leaned back on her palms. "He believes that traveling with a security guard in a private car is safer than traveling with my troupe." She rolled her eyes. "Personally, I feel safer in a crowd. Besides, if someone wished me ill, it would be quite easy to achieve when I'm onstage. Especially in rough towns where guns are carried as is the fashion."

"Logistically, I can see that could be problematic."

Isabella nodded at Claire. "If you don't mind my asking, where is your ultimate destination?"

"Tombstone."

Isabella smiled, seemingly delighted with her answer. "Then it's Providence. I myself am on my way to Tombstone to meet the Nellie Boyd Dramatic Company. We're going to join forces for their first performance there." She sat up and brushed off her hands. "Seeing as how we're both headed to the same destination, and my bodyguard is no longer, what would you say to working in his capacity?"

"You aren't serious."

Isabella nodded, obviously warming to the idea. "Deadly serious. My guard was a big bully, always telling me what to do, drinking too much, gambling. And," she wrinkled her nose, "he stank. Besides, no one has to know, if you're worried about that. I can pay you in cash."

Claire shook her head. "I'm not qualified."

"Don't be silly." She gestured toward the pay car, where the dead were stored. "The evidence of your qualification is on that train."

"Who is responsible for paying your security's wages, cash or not?"

"My sweetheart, Mr. Gould."

"Then he's the one who should hire your bodyguard."

Isabella tilted her head to the side, an enigmatic smile on her face. "I assure you, the position pays very, very well."

Claire studied her for a moment, trying to think of a reason to say no. "Tell you what. I'll consider it—" The other woman's face split into a wide grin. "I *said*, I'd consider it, on one condition."

"And what would that condition be?"

"That you tell him who I am, and that he agrees."

"And who are you? You haven't told me your name."

"It's Claire. Claire Whitcomb." She decided then and there she would keep Josiah's last name and be proud of it, whether people connected her to the "Whitcomb Massacre" or not.

Isabella stuck out her hand. "Then, Miss Whitcomb, I do believe we have a deal. I'll send Mr. Gould a telegram as soon as we pull into town."

Claire shook her hand, sealing the agreement.

She hoped she wasn't making a big mistake.

CHAPTER 5

William Cooke set his half-filled glass of brandy on the marble table next to his wingback chair and studied his companion. The scent of fine cigar smoke and old leather wafted through the rarified air of the exclusive club. Worry lines etched deeply into his companion's broad, high forehead, and although his full beard covered much of his face, his complexion lacked the healthy glow he'd had when the wealthy entrepreneur returned from his sojourn west. William understood how worry could change a man for the worse. He himself fought it with every breath and grown weary of the effort.

"What is it, Jay? Good news or ill?" Cooke's gaze settled on the paper his friend perused. The familiar form told him that Jay Gould had received yet another telegram. But this one seemed to affect the railroad magnate much more profoundly than missives from his many holdings.

Gould sighed and shook his head. "Nothing to worry about, William. A domestic matter. Shall we have another drink?"

The two men finished their after-dinner brandies as Gould attended to one of the many supplicants begging for the scraps of a powerful man at the height of his influence. With his friend's attention diverted, William Cooke covertly slid the telegram toward him to see what had so worried his friend.

MY DEAREST,

Train robbery foiled. I am well. Earl no longer available for service. Have hired replacement security (who goes by the name of C. Whitcomb) for completion of journey to Tombstone. Require more funds. Hope you are well.

Fondly,

Izzy

THE ACTRESS IS on her way to Tombstone. William Cooke hid his excitement at his stroke of good fortune. To Cooke's utter frustration, Gould had kept the woman's whereabouts close to his vest, only letting on that she was somewhere out west, performing at smaller venues. He'd also assured Cooke that she posed no risk to Cooke's freedom, as Gould had paid handsomely for her silence.

But William Cooke didn't trust the actress. She'd proven to be loose-lipped about her affair with the married Gould, and he didn't believe casting her away from the Eastern Seaboard would keep her from talking.

Especially not about his own transgression.

Cooke wasn't normally a man to allow his passions to get the better of him, but that night in March at the Fifth Avenue Hotel proved his undoing. True, he'd imbibed much too heavily during a private business meeting and normally would have allowed the man's insult to fade into the evening's festivities. But it was not to be. Cooke ended the life of the man who had mistakenly thought him a weak-willed elitist.

To her ill-fortune, the actress, who was apparently traveling under another stage name, had witnessed his lapse in judgement and run to her protector with the news. Gould confronted Cooke later that evening, after Cooke had the body of the man he'd killed disposed of before anyone discovered him. Initially, Cooke had bought silence from the hotel steward, but then paranoia got the better of him, and he changed his mind. Two days later, the poor wretch met with a mortal accident.

William Cooke slid the telegram back to its original spot as Gould concluded his discussion.

"I believe I shall call it a night, old friend." Gould finished off the last of his brandy and rose from his chair. "I will see you in the morning." With that, he stowed the telegram in his breast pocket and left.

William Cooke nursed the rest of his drink as he ran scenarios through his mind on how best to use this new information. Although he imagined several different possibilities, he kept coming back to the simplest of them all. It would most likely end his friendship with the railroad tycoon, but only if Gould discovered his plan. And he fully intended that Jay Gould would never find out.

He wrestled with his conscience a few moments longer but lost. He'd decided.

The actress and her new bodyguard would not be long for this world.

Claire relaxed against the rich brocade of the salon chair, marveling at the luxury of the private railcar. Dark mahogany and rich tapestries mingled with overstuffed furniture and ornate crystal chandeliers. Once she and Isabella and Isabella's maid had returned everything to its proper position, and Earl had been laid to rest in the pay car, the maid prepared them a pot of tea and served them sweet biscuits. Uncomfortable being waited on by the younger woman, Claire thanked her warmly for the tea and helped herself to a ladyfinger.

"Agnes, you may leave us," Isabella said to the maid.

"Yes, ma'am. I'll just tidy up the bedroom and whatnot." Agnes went into the other room and shut the door, leaving them alone in the swaying parlor.

"We should be arriving in Pueblo shortly. I expect a telegram from Mr. Gould to be imminent." Isabella took a dainty sip of her Darjeeling tea and settled back in her chair. She'd sent the telegram from the Western Union office in Cañon City, prior to the train's departure.

"And if he's decided not to hire me?"

Isabella smiled. "I doubt that will be a problem. He'd prefer I had protection."

"I've been meaning to ask you," Claire said, setting her cup on the table between them. "Why does Mr. Gould want you to have security? Are you that popular?"

"Unfortunately, it isn't because of my popularity, although that is quite well documented." Isabella sighed and shook her head. With an eye on the door leading to her bed chambers, she leaned closer and added in a low voice, "I witnessed an offense while in New York City. Because of this inopportune and unfortunate knowledge, Mr. Gould believes me to be in grave danger."

"What did you see, exactly?" When Isabella didn't reply, Claire raised her eyebrows. "If I am to work as your guard, surely I must be apprised of all possible encroachments on your safety."

"I see your meaning." Isabella nodded and set her own cup down. With another glance at the closed door to the bedroom, she said, "It was in March of this year. The weather was cold, with a sharp and biting wind." She shivered dramatically, obviously relishing her role in the story. "I was returning from the ladies' lounge when I came upon two men arguing in the empty stairwell of the hotel—the Fifth Avenue, if you're curious."

"Go on," Claire said, enjoying the performance.

"Being the genteel woman you see before you, I immediately attempted to vacate the premises, preferring not to become embroiled in their argument, which had turned quite heated, I must say."

"What happened then?"

"The first gentleman, Mr. Cooke, a friend of Mr. Gould's and someone of whom I'm not particularly fond, elevated his voice to the point that someone else would no doubt have heard, and the other man matched him. I feared they would come to blows, then and there. Little did I know, fisticuffs were the least of my worries."

"And then?"

Isabella fanned herself with her hand and fluttered her eyelashes, adding another element of drama to the tale. "There I was, standing in the darkness of the hallway, frozen with indecision, when Mr. Cooke produced a pistol and, without so much as a by-your-leave, shot the other man in the throat." Her complexion paled at the memory. "The poor man crumpled to the floor, obviously dead." She stared into space for a moment before recovering and giving Claire a brief smile.

"How dreadful." Claire herself had been in shock the first time she'd seen death.

"Yes. Very."

"Did Cooke know you were there?"

She shook her head. "Not me, exactly. Although he knew someone was. I ran as fast as I could straight to Mr. Gould. I could think of no safer place. But when Cooke reappeared, he could tell by my disposition that it was I who had witnessed his atrocity."

"That explains things. You believed that Mr. Cooke would do you harm?"

Isabella nodded vigorously. "I'm sure of it."

"Then how came you out west?"

"Mr. Gould talked Mr. Cooke into allowing me to leave the city–indeed, the entire Eastern Seaboard—alive, citing not only the great distance between me and any predisposition to present facts to the authorities, but also a goodly sum of money to ensure my silence."

"Hence the bodyguard."

Isabella nodded. "Hence the bodyguard."

"And have you noticed anything untoward—less desirable types, perhaps, or attempts on your life—in the past months since you've been out west?"

"No. Nothing. I'd begun to think I'd put the worst of it behind me. But then the train robbery happened."

"You can't think that was a ruse to silence you?"

Isabella leaned forward, an earnest look on her face. "I must be truthful. When the train stopped and that outlaw burst into the car brandishing a gun, I was absolutely certain he would end my life."

"Whom did Mr. Cooke kill?" If Isabella was this concerned about Cooke coming after her so far from civilization, surely the victim was someone of import.

"A wealthy businessman like himself."

"Couldn't Cooke have declared he'd killed the man in self-defense? That same story has been used extensively here in the West to keep men from going to prison, true or not." And women, Claire thought.

"Perhaps. That's what I asked Mr. Gould. But Mr. Cooke's actions following the murder solidified his guilt. A hotel employee mysteriously died in an accident not two days later."

"Are you certain this employee was involved?"

"There is no reason to believe otherwise. The body of Mr. Cooke's victim had been disposed of and the stairwell scrubbed clean. Someone did it, and I'll wager it wasn't Mr. Cooke."

"Couldn't anyone have done the same? Or do you have other reason to believe it to be this employee?" Surely Cooke wouldn't have shared his actions with Isabella, the only witness who could testify against him in court.

"Mr. Cooke confided in Mr. Gould. In turn, Mr. Gould told my security man, Earl, who in a fit of drunkenness blurted out the whole sordid story to me on our journey West."

"How much do you trust Mr. Gould? Would he ever let on where you were?"

"I trust him with my life."

"What about newspapers? Don't they report on your comings and goings?"

"Mr. Gould has made certain that the venues where I'm scheduled to appear use only my nom de guerre of Isabella King —which is different than the stage name I used back east."

Claire took another bite of her ladyfinger. "That's good. So the only person who knows your itinerary is Mr. Gould, is that right?"

"Yes. And as I said, I trust him with my life."

Claire was certain that Isabella believed what she said, and perhaps Claire herself was a step behind popular culture, but in her mind a married man who kept a mistress couldn't necessarily be trusted. Rich men could always replace a mistress.

Claire had a feeling that she'd bitten off a lot more than a ladyfinger.

CHAPTER 7

The meeting with Ian's love interest, Juliette, went about as well as could be expected. Once the conductor allowed passengers to disembark at Pueblo Station, Claire searched for the young woman on the platform. Juliette stood surrounded by a concerned group, many of whom were understandably quite protective and viewed Claire with some mistrust. When Claire mentioned she knew Ian and had spoken to him before he died, Juliette agreed to step away so that Claire might give her a message.

"I'm so sorry for your loss," Claire began. The unshed tears in the young woman's eyes wrenched Claire's heart.

"Did you know him well?" Juliette sniffled and used a dainty lace hanky to wipe her reddened nose.

Claire shook her head. "I met him on the train. I was with him when he died."

Juliette closed her eyes as tears slid down her cheeks. "Was he in pain?"

Not wanting to cause her further distress, she said, "Your name was the last word on his lips. He loved you so very much, Juliette."

The young woman's sobs brought curious stares, but she didn't seem to care. One of the women who'd been with her on the platform joined them, a worried expression on her face.

Frowning, she glanced at Claire. "What are ye telling the lass that makes her cry so?" She put a protective arm around Juliette's shoulders and drew her away.

Juliette pulled from her grasp and turned back to Claire. "Did he say anything else?"

"He said you were more precious to him than the sun."

Another rush of tears coursed down her cheeks as the disapproving older woman swept her away from the cause of her anguish. Claire sighed, remembering how she felt when she'd seen Josiah and her children slaughtered.

Juliette's reaction, though heart-rending, told Claire she would come through the shock all right. She was young and Ian was her first love, but she had family and friends who obviously cared for her. A tragic end to a love affair to be sure, but life in the West tended to deliver such challenges, hardening off each recipient until they were either destroyed or as strong as honed steel.

Claire was making ready to board for the next leg of their journey when Isabella ran up to her, breathless, leading a small group of lively young men and women.

"Claire. I'd like you to meet my closest confidants." She turned to the woman next to her—a plump brunette with rosy cheeks. "This is Maxi. Maxine to be exact, but no one calls her that. Maxi, this is Claire, the lady gunslinger I told you about."

Maxi giggled and gave a little bow. "Pleased to meet you, Claire." She looked Claire up and down and leaned in to whisper, "Are you armed?"

Claire smiled and whispered back, "Never fear. There is a pistol secreted in the folds of my skirt."

Maxi looked properly scandalized and giggled again. One of

the men of the small group jostled her aside and swept his arm in an arc, following that with a dramatic bow.

"Blake Underwood at your service, madam." He straightened and let his gaze travel slowly up Claire's body in an unabashed attempt to either embarrass or perhaps seduce her.

Isabella gave him a playful push. "Pay no attention to Blake, Claire. Although a passable actor, he's all hat, no cattle."

Claire gave her a surprised look. "I thought you said you hailed from New York? That's as Texas a saying as I've ever heard."

Isabella smiled. "I've met my share of drovers."

"Remember the one in Denver?" Maxi fanned herself. "He was fine as cream gravy."

Isabella introduced the other two as Jojo and Orrin. They chattered on about Claire being a famous gunslinger and how she would be a good addition to the troupe.

Claire took Isabella aside and asked, "Are they joining us on the trip south?"

"Of course. Is there a problem?"

"There could well be, yes."

Isabella widened her eyes. "Whatever do you mean? I assure you, they're topnotch performers."

"Be that as it may, the addition of four passengers to your private car begs a change in logistical planning." At that moment, Claire was questioning her decision to accept the job guarding the actress. This was her first position handling security for anyone, much less a small group of show people.

"Don't be silly, Claire. They'll be fine. If it makes you feel any better, they'll only ride in the private car during daylight hours."

"And where will they sleep?"

"I've used some of my allowance to purchase first-class seats for them."

"Fine." Claire sighed, still unconvinced. "But you've compromised my role by informing your friends that I'm a 'gunslinger.'

How can you be certain none of them will drink too much and tell whoever is within earshot who or what I am? Part of my effectiveness is that most would underestimate my abilities."

"I hired you to be *my* security, not anyone else's. Pay them no mind, Claire. I promise they won't say anything. They're just excited to know a lady who makes her living with a gun, that's all. You should be glad that the rest of Nellie's troupe is meeting us in Tombstone."

Claire really didn't have much say in the matter. She'd agreed to terms and was now guarding Isabella, mistress to one of the most powerful men in the nation. She'd have to adapt.

After a quick word with the conductor, the six of them boarded Isabella's private car. Isabella regaled them with a somewhat fictionalized rendition of Claire coming upon the outlaw who had killed Earl, her security guard. After much cajoling, Claire then recounted the shootout with Jack "Sheriff Killer" Abrams, with Isabella playing Claire and Blake acting as the outlaw. Even Claire had to laugh at the actor's antics. Blake made for a perfect villain and played his part to the hilt.

After the impromptu show, Maxi produced a bottle of brandy and one of absinthe. Isabella rummaged through one of the drawers of the secretary and returned with six slotted spoons and a ceramic container of sugar cubes. She set these on the table between them as Blake and the others jostled for position on the banquette seats.

Everyone took a seat and Maxi opened the absinthe. She glanced at the group.

"What are you waiting for?" Isabella asked.

"The glasses?" Maxi suggested.

"Oh. Of course." Isabella pointed to a tray of six peculiarly shaped glasses near Jojo. "Would you be a dear and fetch them, Jojo?" A waif of a girl with big, dark eyes and hair the color of wheat, Jojo did as instructed and set the tray on the table in front of Maxi.

Maxi poured a measure of the bright green liquor to a line on each of the glasses. Then she set a slotted spoon across their tops, along with a sugar cube.

Blake grinned and rubbed his hands together in gleeful anticipation. "The Green Fairy shall visit us all tonight."

"May I ask what she's doing?" Claire asked Orrin, a young man with a striking resemblance to a pink-cheeked cherub.

"She's preparing the absinthe the way the French do it."

Claire glanced at the clock on the secretary. "It's a bit early, isn't it?"

Her question was met with guffaws, as though she'd made a particularly witty jest. *They'll be completely soaked by the time we pull into the next station if they finish the bottle*, she thought.

Maxi carefully poured cold water over the sugar cube, allowing the mixture to drain into the absinthe below. In the process, the bright green liquid turned opaque.

"She learned the process at an establishment in New Orleans," Jojo confided.

Isabella nodded solemnly. "The Absinthe Bar."

Claire had heard stories of the hallucinatory experiences of absinthe drinkers—that imbibers could suffer from convulsions and experience auditory and physical hallucinations. But she'd also heard the spirit occasioned drinkers to sloth and indolence. What better way to watch over and protect the lot of them than if they were in a comatose state?

So long as no one turned belligerent.

An hour later, three of them were happily ensconced on the settee, deep in conversation describing the quality of their inebriation. The other two, Blake and Isabella, had broken into the bottle of brandy and were babbling and laughing incoherently. Claire had deemed it prudent to abstain, as she was the one with a gun, as well as a mandate to protect her employer's mistress.

Soon, Isabella and Blake grew quiet. Taking advantage of the calm, Claire went into the bedroom, intending to use the water closet. Startled, Agnes straightened with an exclamation and slipped her hand into her skirt pocket. A jewelry box lay open on the bureau.

"Miss Whitcomb. Goodness. You startled me."

"May I see what's in your pocket?" Claire asked.

Agnes's cheeks colored. "What?"

"You slipped something into your pocket. May I see what it is?"

"See what it is?" Eyes wide, she took a step back.

The young woman's guilt couldn't be more apparent. Claire held out her hand. "Agnes, please. If you've taken something of Miss King's, you must confess. If you don't, the consequences will be far worse than if you had."

"I would never—"

"The contents of your pockets, Agnes."

Agnes's gaze skated from the door to Claire back to the door. Her expression went slack and her shoulders slumped as the realization hit her that there was no way out. Slowly, she reached into her pocket and brought out a ruby brooch, which she placed on the bureau.

"Is that everything?" Claire asked.

With a sheepish look, she dug in her pocket and brought out a sapphire ring. She placed it on top of the bureau, alongside the brooch.

Claire picked them up and said, "Have a seat, Agnes. I doubt your employer is in any condition to determine your fate, but at least she'll have the opportunity to see what you've done."

"Oh, please, miss, couldn't you see to letting it go this once? I've never done anything like it before, and that's the God's honest truth." She glanced at the floor, a contrite expression on her face. "I don't know what got into me. I—I promise I won't do anything like it ever again."

"I'm sorry, but I can't do that, Agnes. What would happen if she found out that I let you go with a warning? Especially something like stealing?"

Eyes bright with unshed tears, Agnes put her fist to her lips. "Please. I'll do whatever you want me to. She'll leave me off at the next station. I've no money and nowhere to go." The tears escaped down her cheeks.

Unmoved, Claire gave her a hanky. "I'm sorry, Agnes. But Miss King needs to know that someone in her employ is a thief."

The word 'thief' brought fresh tears, but Claire ignored her and walked out to the parlor, closing the door behind her. She went to Isabella and Blake and leaned down to whisper in Isabella's ear.

"I caught Agnes with these." Claire showed the two items to Isabella. "She'd put them in her pocket."

Isabella stared at the jewelry in her hand and looked up at Claire. "You mean she stole my jewelry?"

Claire nodded. Isabella snorted and turned to Blake. "Can you imagine? The maid is a thief." With that, she dissolved into laughter, with Blake joining her.

Mystified by her reaction, Claire said, "I'll secure your jewels so she is unable to rifle through them at will. Would you like to speak with her?"

That brought even more laughter from them both.

"What's funny? An employee has been caught stealing from you. Don't you care?"

Isabella wiped her eyes, her laughter spent. "Claire, my darling. All of the jewelry in the bedroom is what we call costume jewelry. It's not real. We use it during our shows. The sapphire you rescued is cut glass, as is the ruby. My valuable pieces are well hidden. Even I don't remember where I put them." With that, she dissolved again into laughter. Blake joined in.

"Be that as it may, she still attempted to steal your things. That in itself would be enough to make one wary of keeping her on as staff." Baffled by Isabella's reaction, Claire didn't know what to make of her disinterest in at least confronting Agnes. Had she consumed enough spirits to take leave of her senses? Or, was it something different? Perhaps when one was the mistress of the richest man in America, one didn't worry about such trivialities as honesty.

Claire gave up and returned to the bedroom where Agnes waited on the settee next to the bed, wringing a lace kerchief in her hands. She glanced behind Claire, then met her gaze, obviously relieved her employer wasn't in tow.

Claire put the costume jewelry back into the box and closed the lid. She turned to Agnes. "I've let Miss King know of your disloyalty, but she chooses not to mete out punishment at this time. I have no idea if she'll change her intentions by the time we arrive at the station. Either way, I suggest you don't attempt the same again. At least, not while I am in her employ."

Agnes stood and curtsied. "No, ma'am. I certainly won't do it again. Thank you."

With a sigh, Claire went into the ornate lavatory and shut the door. The chandelier's crystal pendants clinked overhead with the swaying of the train. The finest towels and facecloths had been draped over the towel rod, and intricate silver scrollwork cradled the ceramic wash basin. She glanced in the mirror and shook her head.

The rich were certainly different. Claire found herself looking forward to reaching Tombstone.

CHAPTER 8

The train tracks eventually ran out at a small town named Mowry City in the New Mexico Territory, which meant they would have to take the stage to San Marcial, then cross into Arizona Territory on the way to Benson. The journey had Claire longing for Isabella's private railcar.

The trip was not only uncomfortable but mentally taxing, too. Everyone was on edge, passenger and driver alike, bracing for attack by renegade Apache or ruthless road agents. According to the man riding shotgun, the Apache were known to favor horses more than valuables and rarely killed passengers unless given a reason to do so. Road agents were less predictable, well-armed, and often desperate. Many had no qualms about murder.

Claire was even more on edge than the driver, if that were possible. She couldn't bear the thought of losing her horse, Rose. To help combat her anxiety, she used the time on horseback to work out a faster way to reload and fire her rifle in one continuous action. The guilt of not being fast enough or good enough to save Ian still ate at her.

Claire kept a wide berth between Rose and the stage to

reduce choking on the dust and dirt kicked up by the team of horses and the Concord stagecoach. Riding all day was tiring, but also liberating. She'd taken to wearing the clothes given to her by Mart Duggan, which consisted of a pair of dungarees, a long-sleeve button-down shirt, a good pair of leather boots, and a wide-brim hat. The hand-tooled leather belt and six-shooter, also from Duggan, added to the look. So far, Claire couldn't think of any downside to the outfit. That she resembled a man from a distance, with her hair tucked up under the hat and her oilskin coat on, was an added bonus.

By the end of the first day, Claire and Rose were more than ready to turn in. Most evenings on the train, Maxi brought out libations, sharing with Isabella and the others. Although it was offered, Claire always refused. Liquor dulled her senses. All that day, an idea for the rifle had nagged at her, so she borrowed pencil and paper from the owner of that evening's lodgings to sketch it out.

Once she was satisfied, she put the drawings away. Now she needed to find a gunsmith who understood what she wanted.

The stage pulled into Benson late in the evening of the third day. The Benson Hotel, the only available choice for lodgings, turned out to be quite comfortable though hastily built, as were the rest of the buildings in town.

Claire made sure Rose was well fed and had good accommodations in the nearby corral before retiring for the night in a room that connected to Isabella's.

"Are you certain you wouldn't like a drink, Claire? This will be our last evening on the road." Isabella stood in the hallway outside her door. Blake and Maxi were already in her room with a bottle of whiskey Maxi had purchased from a gentleman she'd found loitering outside the hotel. Orrin and Jojo had gone to their respective rooms, opting not to partake in the evening's festivities. As usual, Agnes hovered nearby.

Claire shook her head. "Thank you, but I'd better not. I'll see you in the morning."

"Thank goodness we're almost to our destination. I don't know how much more I can take." She gave a nod toward her room, indicating Blake and Maxi and the bottle of whiskey.

I feel exactly the same way.

Claire was surprised Isabella hadn't let Agnes go. Against Claire's advice, the actress had decided to keep the maid on, not wanting to abandon a young woman alone in the middle of the Arizona Territory. When Claire argued she could easily pay for her ticket back to New York, Isabella had told her she felt responsible and would keep her on, regardless.

Agnes had been grateful for her employer's largesse, as evidenced by her doting on Isabella and her friends. She gave Claire a wide berth, clearly uncomfortable in her presence, which was fine with Claire.

Early the next morning, after seeing to Rose, Claire instructed the hotel clerk to transfer the group's bags to the stage company's holding room off the lobby in anticipation of the coach's arrival. She couldn't help herself—her excitement at finally reaching her destination after such a long journey brought a lightness to her step. The slight annoyance at Isabella's vehement aversion to mornings disappeared with each breath. Claire had to wake the hungover redhead several times before she waved Claire away with a croaking voice, promising to rise.

After a hearty breakfast at the hotel, which included coffee that would have cleaned the rust off an old ship, Claire took a short walk down the dusty street. Built in response to the arrival of the South Pacific Railroad earlier that summer, the town of Benson was still finding its feet. Even so, several buildings had already been erected as evidenced by a dozen or more saloons, a post office, the corral, and the Benson Hotel.

The town boasted no boardwalk, so she traversed the dusty

street to the end to view the deep red sunrise. For the first time since leaving Leadville, happiness filled her. She was on her way to a new life, one in which she had no past except a burgeoning reputation as an oddity: a female gunslinger who could take care of herself.

Breathtaking color filled the sky—it seemed as though she stood in the middle of a masterful painting. Dramatic clouds formed over the Dragoon Mountains to the south, indicating weather was on the way. The stillness of the air and faint smell of distant rain promised a rousing storm. The odd plants and dramatic sky lent everything a foreign quality.

Mountains here weren't nearly as tall as the Rockies. Even so, stories abounded of miners and settlers losing their way and their lives in the rocky crags. Also in contrast to Colorado, there weren't as many trees, although the stark, windswept landscape presented a beauty of its own. A carpet of short, green grass stretched to the dusty brown of the mountains, reminding her of the endless prairies during her trek West with her husband.

"Quite a sunrise, wouldn't you say?"

Claire's heart leapt as she spun in place, her hand reaching for her pistol. Not two feet away stood a gentleman dressed in traveling clothes and a bowler hat. His eyes widened, obviously surprised Claire was of the female persuasion.

"Oh," she said, easing her hand away from the gun. "How silent you were. I didn't hear your approach."

The gentleman recovered. Smiling, he touched the brim of his hat. His manner of dress and elocution gave the impression of someone from back East. "Sorry, ma'am. I have a habit of sneaking up on people without meaning to."

Claire relaxed a fraction at his demeanor. She smiled back. "You're forgiven." She moved to walk by him.

"Name's Worthington," he said, failing to move out of her way. "Ed Worthington."

"I'm Claire."

"Pleasure to meet you, Claire. Are you waiting for the stage to Tombstone, by chance?"

"Yes, I am. Why do you ask?"

He shrugged and glanced over her shoulder at the fading sunrise. "No reason. I'm headed there myself. I like to know with whom I'm traveling."

"Well, Mr. Worthington, it's been lovely to meet you, but I must return to the hotel to take care of some things before the stage arrives." She turned to leave but stopped. "Perhaps we'll have time to chat on the journey."

Worthington smiled and touched his brim once more. "I'd like that." He moved aside and allowed her to pass.

The man's actions gave her pause. To seek out passengers to determine who one was traveling with wasn't itself unusual, although under normal circumstances the information would be sought during the trip—conversation to pass the time. But there was something about him she couldn't quite put her finger on— an uneasy feeling she couldn't shake. She was most likely being paranoid, now that she was in the position to guard Isabella.

By the time Claire made it back to the Benson Hotel, Isabella and her entourage had managed to make their way to the restaurant for breakfast. They all looked horribly hungover except Blake, who appeared fit as a fiddle. The others obviously found the eggs and biscuits unpalatable, as they were mostly drinking coffee and ignoring their food.

"Good morning," Claire said in a chipper voice, stifling a smile at Isabella's and Maxi's groans.

Isabella covered her eyes and slowly shook her head. "Must you be so... cheerful?"

"And loud?" added Maxi.

Claire pulled an empty chair over from a nearby table and sat beside Isabella. "From what the hotel clerk tells me, we should arrive in Tombstone no later than eleven."

Isabella barely nodded. "I'm afraid I won't be good company.

My head feels like a full melon fit to explode, and my mouth is drier than the desert." She waved vaguely at the door. "Thankfully, opening night isn't until tomorrow. In the meantime, I shall pray for a swift demise."

Maxi fluttered her lashes and nodded in agreement. She reached in her pocket and brought out a silver flask, unscrewed the top, and poured a measure into her coffee cup. Claire raised her eyebrows and Maxi shrugged. "The only cure I've known to work." She offered it to Isabella, who shook her head. Maxi moved to put the spirits away.

"On second thought." Isabella grabbed the flask and added a dollop to her own cup. She then handed it back to Maxi.

Claire sighed. She had a hard time getting used to show folk. The frivolity with which they approached life struck her as irresponsible. She'd always been serious, even as a child, and had gravitated toward adults rather than those her own age. Josiah had celebrated that quality in her, and it stood their family in good stead while traveling west. Thankfully, Claire's contract as Isabella's security lasted only until they arrived in Tombstone, after which she'd be free to go her own way.

Isabella glanced at Claire with watery, bloodshot eyes. The misery she projected was in direct contrast to her smartly tailored outfit and coiffed hair. "Will you ride in the coach with us to Tombstone?"

Claire shook her head. "I'll do the same as I've done." She didn't like the idea of being stuck inside, listening to Isabella and her friends go on about silly things she couldn't have cared less about. Rose was more a companion to her liking.

Quiet.

She also wanted to be unfettered in case of an attack by renegade Apache or brigands who might wish to rob the passengers.

"I'll let you be, then," Claire said to Isabella. "Meet me outside when you've finished eating."

With that, Claire headed to the corral to saddle Rose. She then led the mare back to the hotel.

Surrounded by passengers and freight, the newly arrived, gaily painted stagecoach cut a cheerful figure in the early morning sunlight. Isabella and her entourage emerged from the breakfast room and milled about nearby, checking for the correct number of bags. Claire walked up to the two men loading the coach.

A young man, perhaps in his late twenties, handed a piece of freight to a slightly older man standing on the boot, who shoved it into place and reached for another.

"Excuse me, may I speak with the driver?" she asked the younger man.

He handed the next piece to the other gentleman before answering. "That'd be me," he said, turning to see who'd spoken. His eyes widened, evidently surprised by her attire, but he recovered quickly. "Eli P. Philpot at your service. But everyone calls me Bud." He extended his hand, which Claire shook. "That there is Bob Turner," he added with a nod at the other man. "He'll be riding shotgun today." Turner touched the brim of his hat, then resumed stacking freight.

"Claire Whitcomb," Claire said. "I plan to ride my horse with you to Tombstone." She glanced at Isabella and her friends, who were waiting to board. "I am employed as security for the redhead standing next to the stage."

Philpot nodded at the Peacemaker Claire wore. "You know how to shoot, I take it."

"I do. I've got a Winchester rifle, as well." She declined to tell him about the tomahawk and the bow and arrows. She doubted she'd need them, anyway.

"Good. Always glad for an extra gun." As if to emphasize his words he pulled his coat aside, revealing a pistol snugged into a shoulder holster. He gave her a meaningful look, then grabbed another piece of luggage and handed it up to Bob, who, having run out of room stacked it on the roof. "We should be headed out shortly. Might want to saddle up."

"Already did. What time do we arrive in Tombstone?"

"Round about eleven, long as things go smooth." He glanced at the sky. "Looks like we could have ourselves a bit of weather. But it shouldn't slow us up too bad."

Claire thanked him and joined Isabella and the others near the door to the stage. Six sleek bays stamped impatiently in their traces. "How are you holding up?"

Isabella shrugged. "As well as can be expected. What did the driver say?"

"He confirmed what the hotel clerk said. We should arrive in Tombstone by eleven."

A look of relief swept Isabella's face. "Oh, good. I doubt I'd survive much longer in another boneshaker."

Claire studied the stage. By Western standards, the bench seats of the coach were luxurious, with padding on both the seats and backs. But, as was typical, the floor didn't leave much room for passengers to put their feet. Space for a "treasure box" was located in the boot, although Claire doubted there'd be any bullion or silver being hauled from Benson to Tombstone. That kind of freight normally made the trip the other way—silver from the mines of Tombstone to the train in Benson to be shipped to Tucson and beyond.

When Bud Philpot called for everyone to board, Claire went to retrieve Rose. As Claire and her horse cantered up to the stage, she spotted the man she'd met that morning, Ed Worthington.

She'd relished his surprise at her manner of dress. Men had so much more freedom to be and do whatever they wanted, and took that freedom for granted. Women normally carried the yoke of civility and conformity, but once Claire had a taste of that freedom, she swore she'd never go back. If she thought about it, she realized she'd acquired even more independence than a man, for she was able to change back into feminine clothes when it suited her purpose.

Bob Turner climbed up to his seat, joining Bud Philpot on the box. Five more men sat on the roof next to the overflow luggage, referred to by passengers who paid for interior seats as hangers-on. Two of them were what most referred to as "celestials," immigrants from the Celestial Empire of China who came to America to work the railroad as evidenced by their manner of dress and long ponytails.

Philpot raised his whip. With a resounding *crack* and a rousing "He-yah," the team sprang to life and the stage rolled away from the hotel, headed for Tombstone.

Claire spent the first hour or so following the stage at a distance. For a time the terrain kept her attention—she marveled at the odd plants and animals, the birds flitting in and out of different types of cactus, tiny lizards skittering across Rose's path, the occasional coyote. Soon enough, she grew restless with her ignorance of the names of things and urged Rose closer to the front of the stage so she could engage Philpot in conversation.

They'd entered a stretch of the journey that required walking the horses, which suited Claire's purpose.

"Mr. Philpot," Claire called, coming up alongside the stage.

Bud Philpot nodded at her. "Call me Bud, ma'am. What can I do for you?"

"I was curious about the names of the flora we've had occasion to pass. I've not had the occasion to learn."

Philpot smiled and pointed at a low-growing cactus with white spines. "That there is called a cholla cactus. You want to steer clear of that one. Them spines can prick clear through horseflesh and boot leather easy as you please, and they're hard as Hades to pull out. Got little hooks on the end."

Claire took note and silently vowed to keep her distance.

"See that one there?" He continued. "The one with the long spikes?" He spit out a wad of tobacco and wiped his mouth with his sleeve. "The Mexicans call that one ocotillo. Gets real purty orange flowers in the springtime."

"They're so unusual."

"Think that's unusual, you should take a ride up Tucson way. They got these big tree-like things called saguaros. They grow arms out to the side, like this." He bent his arm at the elbow with his hand up. "Takes a mighty long time for them arms to grow. Old timers say the first one can take near to seventy-five years."

"How interesting. What are they used for?"

"The Indians was the first to use 'em for buildin' things—their insides are kinda wood-like—and if you're ever lost in the desert you can cut into 'em and get water. Most cacti are like that, though. The saguaro's flowers are something else, too. Big white things that look like a ladies' Easter hat."

"When do they bloom? That would surely be something to see."

"Generally early summer, though I've seen 'em as late as July, depending on the monsoons."

"I'll keep that in mind."

Claire and Philpot rode for a while in companionable silence. Soon, they passed a rock outcropping with crudely drawn symbols on its surface. She pointed at the drawings and asked if they were created by the Apache. Philpot nodded.

"It's their way of markin' time and tellin' stories."

"I heard there's been trouble with Indians in these parts." Claire glanced at Philpot for confirmation. He nodded. "In Colorado, where I'm from," she continued, "most belonged to the Ute tribe. The majority of them have been moved onto reservations, though."

She thought of Thomas. He'd been resigned to the fact that he must adopt the white ways if he was to survive and thrive, but he'd chafed like a raw-bit horse at having to do things that contradicted his upbringing. What little she'd learned from him about the Ute people had sparked an interest in their beliefs—they had a deity they called the Great Spirit and referred to the land as Mother Earth. She found she actually preferred the Ute's characterization. It seemed more in tune with the way things worked.

Philpot scratched his neck and squinted into the distance. "We done the same with the Apache. But we still got a few renegades who like to stir up trouble. Things were right peaceful after they signed the treaty with Cochise in seventy-two. Tom Jeffords was up at the agency back then. That didn't last long. Folks didn't like Jeffords. Called him 'Indian lover' and such. So the federal government got rid of ol' Tom and moved 'em all off their sacred lands to the San Carlos reservation. Cochise was dead by then, from natural causes."

"Then what happened?" Claire asked.

"Apache Wars started up again."

"But if Cochise was dead—?"

Philpot nodded. "Another warrior by the name of Geronimo took his place. The government sent him off to the reservation, too, so things've been kinda quiet lately. It's his followers that are causin' trouble." Philpot shook his head and spit another stream of tobacco over the side of the box. "That's what happens when them do-nothin's in Washington get involved."

"You sound like you sympathize with the Apache."

Philpot shrugged. "I surely get why they're angry. The federal government got a tendency to meddle where they ain't wanted, and that's a fact."

Claire rode alongside the stage half-listening to Philpot describe the terrain and thought about what he'd said. Folks in Leadville felt the same—federal interference was met with suspicion, if not outright anger. The West was supposed to be a place with fewer laws and regulations than back in the "civilized" East. Indeed, it was one of the main reasons Claire remained.

She hoped it wouldn't change any time soon.

ED WORTHINGTON surreptitiously studied the faces of his fellow passengers and wondered about the woman he'd met that morning. He'd heard stories of females out west donning men's clothes but had yet to meet one. It was too bad. A fine-looking woman like that would have had her pick of suitors if she dressed like a woman ought to.

The attractive young redhead sitting across from him was clearly the leader of four of the other passengers in the carriage. She'd tried flirting with him, but he'd only tipped his hat to her, not wanting to invite familiarity.

His job required cold professionalism. The pay Cooke offered was enough to retire on, and he meant to have it. He reckoned she'd be an easy mark—he only had to find the right place to carry out his orders. He was certain she was the woman in question. The locket-sized photograph given to him for targeting purposes might have been small, but this employer's description of her smile and red hair were unmistakable.

"Make it look like an accident," Cooke had told him.

Worthington knew all about that kind of killing. He'd made his mark back East doing exactly that before Cooke had him "take care of" the employee at the hotel last March. Indeed, he'd developed a reputation for his ability to stage a murder so it looked like the victim had encountered nothing more nefarious than bad luck and clumsiness.

To be honest, Ed Worthington enjoyed his work. Even though he made his living by violent means, the jobs enabled him to rub shoulders with the upper crust, netting him some mighty fine dalliances with a number of the rich men's bored wives. He figured their attraction came from the sense of danger he exuded. Not that he was unattractive, but the peril of a taboo liaison played exceptionally well in the swanky hotels and back rooms of mansions.

Powerful men eventually realized they needed people like Ed Worthington, especially when they wanted a leg up on the competition. Worthington had grown up around shifty, ruthless types, but the upper crust had them all beat. Killing women wasn't normally his bailiwick, but the amount offered was such that he'd made an exception. Truth be told, he rather looked forward to devising her death. Women were frail, yes, but they could be as calculating as men. Besides, she and her friends annoyed the hell out of him with their frivolous ways. He'd be doing society a favor.

Now he had to figure out who C. Whitcomb might be. Cooke had informed him that the redhead had lost her original bodyguard and hired a new one. Probably one of the three white men riding up top. He'd tried to find out names before the passengers embarked but had only ended up with two others, in addition to the woman from that morning. No matter. In case his first attempt didn't pan out, he'd readied a backup plan.

He was still ruminating on how and where he'd do the deed when the woman dressed like a man galloped to the front and struck up a conversation with the whip. Worthington strained to hear what was being said. After a few moments he gave up trying. With the sound of the horse's hooves and the incessant grind of the wheels clacking over dry ground, it proved impossible.

Unfortunately, the incessant giggling of his fellow travelers came through loud and clear. Cooke had mentioned something about the redhead being an actress but hadn't said anything about her traveling with friends—only her maid. That presented a slight problem. How to separate her from the herd, so to speak. He'd have to think on that. The two men in their party didn't pose a threat. Neither carried weapons that he could see, and the shorter one appeared to be a dandy. The other women didn't merit much more than a passing glance except the one sitting next to him whose name was Maxi. Her voluptuous curves were more to his liking, and she appeared interested.

Once he'd done his job, he'd look into taking her out behind the woodshed and having his way with her. Of course, then he'd most likely have to kill her, too. No sense leaving a witness.

Tired of the laughter and innuendo of the other passengers, the dust, and the stifling heat, Worthington brought out his copy of the *Arizona Daily Star* and fell to reading the headlines.

He had no doubt what he planned would become one of the major stories in that very same publication. Although the redhead's death would be deemed an unfortunate accident, he'd still disappear into the backcountry.

Like so many others who traveled west.

Several miles later, the stage pulled into Drew's Station. Isabella joined the rest of the passengers outside to stretch their legs, while Claire led Rose to the horse trough. After ensuring her mare had enough to drink and some shade, Claire went inside the thick-walled adobe station to inquire about feed.

The station turned out to be the Drew family home. The interior was dark and cool—a welcome change from the relentless heat outside. Claire took off her hat and shook her hair free.

An older woman standing near a pot-bellied stove looked at her twice, then beckoned her to sit at a small table. "You must be hotter than blazes wearing that get up," she said. "Still, I suppose it makes a certain kind of sense."

"I was wondering if I could get some grain for my horse."

"Which one are you riding?"

"The chestnut mare."

"My husband will see to her," Mrs. Drew assured her. "I'm Mrs. Drew, by the way. And you are?"

"Claire Whitcomb. It's good to meet you." The two women shook hands.

"While you're waiting, how about a slice of apple pie?" When

Claire didn't reply right away, Mrs. Drew added with a conspiratorial grin, "Fresh baked today. It's still warm from the oven."

Claire had to admit, the pie smelled delicious. What could one piece hurt? "I would be happy to have a piece of your pie, Mrs. Drew." Claire had a seat at the small table, positioning herself so she had a view out the tiny window where Isabella sat with the rest of her entourage in the shade of a sprawling *palo verde*. Mrs. Drew brought her a tin cup filled with water.

"Thank you," Claire said and drained the cup. She hadn't realized how thirsty she was. The older woman gave her more. "Is the weather always this hot?" Claire asked.

Mrs. Drew nodded. "It'll cool off some when it rains." She eyed Claire's Peacemaker with interest. "On your way to Tombstone?"

Claire nodded. "Yes, ma'am. From Leadville, Colorado." She kept her eye on Isabella, even though she didn't think she'd have to worry, not at such a small way station. Tombstone would be another matter.

"That's a far piece. If you don't mind my asking, why are you headed there? Not much of a place for a...lady."

"I'm not exactly sure yet." She patted her pocket. "I've got a letter of introduction from the Leadville marshal to Mr. Wyatt Earp."

An expression of distaste flickered across her face.

"You know him?" Claire asked.

Mrs. Drew gave a curt nod. "I do. But I don't have much good to say about the likes of him or his friends."

"I'd be grateful to hear what you know, since I haven't had the pleasure." Claire tensed, wondering what could possibly anger the woman. At that moment, two of the passengers who'd been riding on the upper seats on the stage walked in, breaking into her thoughts on the matter.

"I've said too much." Mrs. Drew waved away Claire's request and greeted the new customers with a smile.

Perhaps the Earp brothers weren't the kind of men Mart Duggan had made them out to be. True, many lawmen had checkered pasts, but that often lent effectiveness to their work. Sometimes it took a criminal to catch one.

Claire finished her pie, wanting to probe further, but decided it wouldn't be prudent. Not everyone had liked Mart, either, but she'd gotten along with him. She set her plate next to the wash basin, paid Mrs. Drew for the pie, and went outside.

Blake, Maxi, Orrin, Agnes, and Jojo were still in the shade where she left them, but Isabella was nowhere to be seen. Claire made her way to the little group.

"Where's Isabella?" she asked.

Fanning herself with her hand, Maxi nodded toward the back of the house. "Using the privy."

Claire thanked her and headed to the outhouse. Sweat trickled down her neck and shoulder blades, and she paused long enough to tuck her hair back up under her hat. The tightly woven felt was hotter than Hades, but it beat strands of hair plastered to the back of her neck. A gust kicked up as dark clouds scudded across the sky. Even though the breeze was warm, it helped cool her.

Bud Philpot waited near the metal-roofed outhouse and gave her a nod as she approached. "Did you try a piece of Mrs. Drew's pie?" he asked.

"I did. Delicious."

The door to the privy opened, and one of the men who'd been riding on top of the stage walked out. When he realized Claire was a woman, he took off his hat and gave her an awkward little bow as he walked by.

"Is this the only outhouse?" she asked Philpot. When he nodded, she added, "You haven't seen Isabella, have you?"

"Wasn't she enjoying the shade with her friends out front?"

"No longer."

"Probably taking the air, then."

"Probably." Claire studied the area for signs of the actress. Several yards away, a deep wash cut through the desert, evidence of a temporary source of water when it rained. Aside from prickly bushes and low-growing trees, there was no one and nothing in sight.

Philpot remained rooted to the spot. Realizing he hadn't availed himself of the privy out of politeness, she gestured to the wood structure. "I'm sorry. I don't mean to keep you."

With a quick bob of his head and a slightly embarrassed smile, Philpot disappeared inside. Claire headed toward the wash, wondering if Isabella had chosen to walk nearby. A drop of rain splatted her face.

As she neared the wash, she caught sight of something moving out of the corner of her eye. She edged closer. "Isabella?" she called. "Are you down here?" A wren swooped past her and landed in a mesquite tree, flicking its tail and chirping in annoyance.

Something scrabbled on the rocks below, and she cocked her head to listen. "Isabella?" she called again, moving toward the sound.

There was a muffled cry, but it was cut short. Alarmed, Claire pulled out her gun and half-slid, half-jumped down the bank to the rocky creek bed below.

Color flashed to her left, and she tracked it with the barrel of the revolver, working her way through the brush clinging to the bank.

Isabella lay on her back next to a flat rock. There wasn't anyone else nearby. Holstering her pistol, Claire rushed to the actress's side. The sound of footsteps running away across the gravel wash echoed toward them.

Torn between checking on Isabella and following a possible perpetrator, Claire chose Isabella.

"Are you all right?" Claire patted the actress's cheeks to rouse her. She checked her for injury but found only a small amount of blood from a scratch on her forehead where a bruise was beginning to form.

Isabella's eyes fluttered open and she groaned. She brought her hand to the back of her head and winced.

"What happened?" Claire asked.

"I—I don't know exactly. I must have slipped." She sat upright and grabbed Claire to steady herself. "I was walking along the creek bank."

Claire felt the back of her head and came away with blood on her fingers. Upon closer inspection, she discovered a gash along Isabella's hairline.

"Can you stand?" she asked.

Isabella nodded and Claire helped her up. The actress swayed, and Claire braced her so she wouldn't fall.

After making certain Isabella could stand on her own, Claire scoured the area for the cause of the gash. Besides the large flat rock, there were only smaller rocks and branches nearby—none of which had the heft or edge to leave a gash.

She turned to Isabella. "Did you hear anything before you fell? Footsteps? Something coming through the brush?"

"No, I don't think—" Isabella stopped midsentence. "Wait. There was movement behind me on the bank." She stared at Claire. "Something hit me on the back of my head."

Claire walked over to the place where Isabella had fallen and climbed the bank. The dirt had been disturbed, with a larger pair of footprints in evidence. She spread her fingers to get a rough measure of the length and width of the larger print, which was substantial. The deep indentation of a squared heel could be seen in the dirt. Claire returned to where she'd left Isabella. A quick glance at the woman's slender foot told her the other set of prints clearly didn't belong to the actress.

Concerned, Claire looked at Isabella. "I think someone just tried to kill you."

Claire helped Isabella back to the station and told Maxi and her other friends to keep an eye on her.

"She had a bad fall and hurt her head. I'm going to see if Mrs. Drew has something to dress the wound." She and Isabella had agreed to keep their suspicions about the attack quiet for now. Isabella would be in much less danger if she acted as though she'd hurt herself rather than alerting the offending party of their suspicions.

Mrs. Drew appeared with a bar of lye soap and a pan of water and set to cleaning the ugly gash on the back of Isabella's head. She then tore a section of white muslin into strips and bandaged the wound. Once she finished, she gave the acting troupe a fresh-baked pie to a chorus of thanks, then went back inside.

Claire kept her distance as Agnes and Maxi helped Isabella back to the stage for the last leg of the trip. She studied everyone as they took their places. When Philpot looked ready to resume the journey, she motioned him over.

"What can I do for you, Miss Claire?" he asked.

Her voice low, Claire replied, "I have reason to believe someone tried to kill Isabella."

Philpot frowned, alarm creasing his weather-beaten face. "Do you have any idea who might want to cause the young lady harm?"

"I've eliminated her friends and the man we saw leaving the privy earlier. They weren't anywhere near her when it happened. How well do you know the men riding on top of the stage?"

Philpot squinted as he thought. "One's a miner from Tombstone. The others I'm not familiar with, except the celestials. They wouldn't dare hurt a fly. Bob spent his time seeing to the horses, so you can count him out. Besides, I know him—he'd as soon be killed by renegades than harm a woman."

"That narrows the field a bit."

"How do you come by the assumption she was accosted?"

"The manner of injury at the back of her head."

Philpot nodded and cut a glance toward the stage.

"And," she continued, "there were footprints other than her own at the scene." She glanced at the sky, gauging the time. "How many more stops before we arrive in Tombstone?"

"Since we saw to the horses here, we won't be stopping in Contention, which is up the road a piece. So unless there's some kind of interference, Tombstone'll be our next stop." He glanced at the worsening weather. "There's one more wash we got to cross. Let's hope the rain holds up till we do."

"Fewer stops will narrow the attacker's opportunities. I'll need to remain vigilant, especially when we get to Tombstone."

"That you will. Tombstone ain't what I'd call the most law-abiding town, although it does have its fair share of lawmen."

Claire shrugged. "I'm accustomed to the lawlessness of mining towns." She climbed onto Rose and took up the reins. "I'll keep an eye on things and be glad to know you and Mr. Turner will do the same."

Claire rode behind the stage, far enough back to watch the horizon and be alert for trouble. A few miles out from Drew's Station, they came to the other wash. This one had a steep bank at the far end, requiring the stage to slow. Thankfully, the rain hadn't amounted to more than a light patter. Claire stayed back, watching the coach's progress.

"Hold!"

The commanding voice echoed through the air. Claire pulled her gun free and urged Rose behind a big clump of sagebrush in an effort at concealment.

"Whoa." Philpot brought the stage to a halt. The set of his and Bob Turner's shoulders told Claire this wasn't a routine stop. She guided Rose past a mesquite tree and quietly approached the stage from the left, keeping both her and the mare hidden. Through the branches, she could make out three men aiming their guns at Philpot and Turner. None of the three wore masks, which struck Claire as a bad sign.

They didn't care if anyone saw their faces.

"Throw down your weapons," the lead man called.

Philpot shook his head. "You know I can't do that. We don't want any trouble. We ain't transportin' a treasure box. Lower your weapons and let us pass."

The gunman next to the lead man fired at Turner. The bullet splintered the box near his leg.

"I said, throw down your weapons."

Turner tossed his rifle to the ground and raised his hands.

"You, too." The leader gestured at Philpot with his revolver. "Or don't you want to live?"

Philpot swore softly as he threw his rifle to the ground, his revolver still in the holster concealed by his coat.

"That's better. Now, what's inside the box?"

"All's we got is passengers. Like I told you, there ain't no gold nor silver."

The leader frowned in annoyance. "Well, then let's see them passengers."

"I'm coming out," came a man's voice from the coach. "Don't shoot." The door to the stage swung open and Ed Worthington stepped out. One of the gunmen aimed his rifle at him and motioned for him to come closer.

Worthington raised his hands and walked slowly toward them. The gunman tracked him like a rattlesnake with a mouse.

"Who else ya got inside there?" the lead gunman asked. "Come out, come out, wherever you are," he sang. His grin didn't match the coldness in his eyes.

"You'd best do as he says," Worthington called over his shoulder. "I believe he means to kill any of us who don't comply."

The stage rocked as the rest of the passengers climbed out to join him. The five men up top stayed where they were, hands in the air. The squall decided at that moment to let loose in a heavy downpour. Muddy water coursed down the sides of the coach, mixing with the dirt below. The horses shifted in their traces.

While two of the bandits held everyone at gunpoint, the leader went from person to person, collecting valuables. When he reached Isabella, he stopped. His gaze flicked to Worthington's, but only for an instant. Worthington's expression betrayed nothing. The road agent hadn't asked him to throw down his gun, even though the handle was visible beneath his jacket. No one else seemed to notice.

Claire's heart skipped. Did they know each other?

Claire dismounted and carefully slid her rifle from its scabbard, then crept through the brush to get closer to the stage. She picked up a small rock and tossed it at Philpot, hitting him in the arm. His face toward the gunmen, he dipped his chin, indicating he knew she was there.

Through the pouring rain, two of the gunmen's legs were visible beneath the thorough braces. Claire stole down the muddy wash, positioning herself near the underside of the coach. Thankfully, the rain masked her efforts. She took a deep breath to quiet her pounding heart, raised the rifle, and fired.

The first shot hit one of the gunman's kneecaps. Her target screamed and dropped his gun as she levered another round into the chamber and fired again. Pandemonium erupted as the next round hit the second gunman in the upper thigh. Passengers screamed in terror and ran in every direction. Philpot leapt to the ground and sprinted for cover. The five men on the roof thought it best to do the same. One misjudged the distance and hit the ground hard. His leg buckled and he screamed, his face contorting in pain as he scrambled to get away. Two of the other men went back for him and dragged him to safety.

Turner slapped the reins hard across the horses' backs and yelled, "Hey-ah!" The bays lurched forward as one, dragging the empty stage up the muddy bank and out of the line of fire.

Glad for the chaos, Claire ran to where some of the passengers had taken cover behind a copse of low-growing trees on the far side of the wash, but out of sight of the bandits. Jojo was the first to see her approach. Relief flooded her face.

Blake glanced at her, then back toward the gunmen. His ashen face and jerky movements told her he was terrified. "What are we going to do?" Eyes wide, he turned to Claire.

"Stay low and follow me," Claire commanded.

Jojo did as she was told. Maxi and Orrin both turned to see what was happening. Claire motioned for them to follow her.

Frozen to the spot, Blake shook his head. "We need to stay here. They'll kill us."

"It's not safe," Claire hissed. "You're too close."

"But—"

Claire leveled her gaze at the panicked actor. "Trust me."

Blake's shoulders drooped in resignation and he nodded.

Keeping low, Claire led them over a slight rise to a clump of brittlebush several yards away. "Stay here. I'll come for you when it's safe." The four of them nodded. She leaned over to Jojo and whispered, "Keep an eye on Blake, would you? He seems kinda skittish."

Jojo nodded. "I will."

Claire made her way along the creek bank to where Isabella

and Worthington had taken cover behind a dense thicket. A bright flash of lightning ignited the sky, bringing with it rolling thunder and sheets of rain, mixing with the sound of gunfire. Worthington had his back to her, watching the action.

Why isn't he shooting?

The bandit's leader had taken cover behind a gnarled tree trunk clinging to the wash's bank. The two wounded gunmen dragged themselves partway up the bank and returned fire from behind a large rock. Philpot and two of the men who'd been riding on top of the coach dug in and fired at the three gunmen. The celestials wore no guns, and stayed low as they tended to the injured man.

Claire was about to grasp Isabella's arm when Worthington turned away from the gunfight. He reached under his coat, his attention on Isabella.

Claire stepped in front of the actress and raised her rifle.

Worthington froze, his eyes narrowing. "What do you think you're doing?"

"Give me your pistol." She gestured at his coat. If he wasn't going to fight, then, by God, she was going to confiscate his gun and use it herself.

"We need to fight them off," Worthington snarled. "Not fight between ourselves." Gunfire punctuated his words. The heavy rain plastered their clothes to their bodies. Claire didn't move. Breathing heavily, Worthington kept his gaze riveted on Claire's. "Well?"

"I don't see you doing any fighting," she snarled back.

He glared at her. "That's because I wanted to make sure the young woman was safe."

Though she still didn't trust him, Claire lowered her rifle. Now wasn't the time to argue. "Join the others," she said to Isabella. "Over the rise." She nodded to where the rest of her group was hiding.

Isabella dashed over to join them. Claire turned back to

Worthington, who had pulled out his revolver. He was facing her, not the outlaws.

A moment passed between them. Would he shoot? Ignoring his obviously aggressive stance, Claire said in a commanding tone, "Draw their fire." After a moment's hesitation, Worthington nodded, then spun and fired at the outlaws.

Keeping low, Claire came at the lead outlaw from the side. His attention directed at Philpot and Worthington, he didn't notice her. The remaining two outlaws were more concerned with the other men shooting at them. She took cover, then rose and fired at the closer of the two outlaws. The first round carved a hole in the back of his head. He dropped his rifle and fell forward. The second gunman glanced at his compatriot, then spun and fired at Claire. She dropped back.

A low rumble shook the ground. Claire glanced at the sky. Angry gray clouds roiled against each other as they scudded past, but the rumble had a different tone than thunder. She wiped the rain off her face and tracked the sound to the far end of the wash.

Philpot had moved back, putting more distance between himself and the lead outlaw, as did the other men from the roof. The lead gunman used the lull to reload.

The rumbling grew. A moment later, a wall of muddy water burst over the bank and emptied into the wash, ripping trees and brush from their roots as it churned past, taking first the dead outlaw, then the second one with it, cutting short the surviving gunman's scream for help.

The lead outlaw looked up from his gun, but it was too late. He clutched at the tree, fighting to stay above the surface, but the water, a seething, roiling beast, tore at his grip and wrenched him free. He barreled past, rolling and bucking, first one hand, then the other grasping at air, his eyes wide with panic as the torrent claimed him.

Claire tore her gaze from the fury of the water in search of

Isabella and the others. One by one they appeared, gawking at the now thundering river where only moments before there'd been sand and rocks. Claire made her way back to them, relieved to see that Turner had brought the stage around.

"Have you seen Bud?" Claire asked Turner.

He shook his head as he climbed down to see to the passengers. "Last I saw, he was tradin' shots with the bandit."

"I'll go take a look." Claire set off to where she'd last seen him. She tamped down her worry as she fought rain-slick branches and skirted sharp cholla cactus. Thankfully, the rain had begun to let up, making it easier to see.

A few minutes later she found him. Relief swept through her. He gave her a nod, and they both walked back to the stage.

A crowd of townspeople met the stage when they rolled into Tombstone, eager to lure passengers to one establishment or the other. Allen Street was a muddy mess from the rainstorm, but that didn't deter the business owners. Rats and other furry critters didn't care, either. Several skittered underfoot—Claire kept a firm hand on the reins, but thankfully Rose didn't react. She pulled out a handkerchief and held it to her nose, attempting to tamp down the smell of garbage. Braying donkeys and the dull thud of the stamp mills joined in a sonorous chorus with the shriek of mine whistles.

An interesting introduction to Tombstone City.

Once populated by renegade Apache and with mountains on three sides, the area previously known as Goose Flats had lured Ed Schieffelin, a prospector with a penchant for bucking authority, to try his luck. After prospecting for several months, he discovered a motherlode of silver where others had failed. Early on, when Schieffelin had first come to the valley, soldiers at Fort Huachuca had warned him about the Apache element and told him the only thing he'd discover in the desert was his own tombstone. Within a year of his find, the town he named in honor of the warning was booming, and now included a mining camp, tented drinking establishments, dozens of elegantly furnished saloons and gambling houses, fine restaurants, and opulent hotels.

Before the passengers could escape to their accommodations, the town marshal, Fred White, interviewed each passenger, jotting down everyone's recollection about the attempted robbery. Since the robbers had most likely drowned in the raging arroyo, White sent several men to the area to see if they could recover the bodies.

Claire looked through the crowd for Ed Worthington, but he'd disappeared soon after giving his statement.

"At which livery should I board Rose?" Claire asked Bud Philpot once she finished speaking with the marshal. The mare had been a champion on the long journey and Claire was determined to let her have a well-deserved rest.

Philpot shaded his eyes and nodded toward a building down the street. "The OK Corral does a good business, and it's the closest. They'll do you right."

Claire made sure Isabella was safely checked into the Grand Hotel and warned her not to open the door to anyone but Claire before she led the chestnut mare to the corral.

On her way back, Claire decided to stretch her legs and see more of the town, so she took a roundabout way back to the Grand via Third and Fremont streets. As she passed, a woman sweeping the sidewalk outside of a boarding house stopped her.

"Mornin'." The woman greeted her with a smile. "You're new in town." She wiped the sweat from her face and leaned the broom against the building.

"I am." Claire held out her hand. "Claire Whitcomb."

"Mollie Fly. I run the boarding house with my husband, Camillus Fly. Everyone calls him Buck, though." She nodded at the sign above her with *Fly's Boarding House* written in bold black letters. Mollie, though shorter than Claire by a good six inches, had the dignified bearing of a much more imposing woman. "Our primary business is photography. Buck's out making photographs right now."

"I'd like to see them sometime."

"Our gallery is in back. I'd be happy to show them to you." She studied Claire's clothes with a practiced eye, her gaze lingering on the Peacemaker. "You're a gunslinger, then?"

Claire smiled and shook her head. "Not hardly. I am currently employed as security for a client. Although that's not normally how I earn a living."

"Like the Pinkertons, you mean?"

"Something like that, except I don't work for a company."

Mollie raised her eyebrows. "Well, if that ain't something. I should like to take your picture, if you'd be amenable. It's not every day we get a lady gunslinger in town."

Claire touched the wisps of hair that had escaped her hat. She probably looked like one of the town's rats had made a nest on her head. "I'll need a proper bath first. It's been a long journey."

"Of course. Perhaps tomorrow?"

"I'll let you know."

"How long do you expect to be in Tombstone?" Mollie asked.

"That depends."

"On what, exactly?"

"On whether Tombstone and I get along or not."

Mollie Fly nodded her approval. "When Mr. Fly and I arrived, we knew in our soul this was where we were supposed to be." She gazed into the distance, lost in her memories. "The photographic subjects here are extraordinary. Do come back. It will allow me to show off the gallery. Mr. Fly's photographs are utterly transforming."

"I'd love to see them." Claire thanked her and got directions to the telegraph office where she wired Jay Gould to tell him about the attack on Isabella and the attempted stage robbery. She then told him that the culprit who had attacked her hadn't yet been apprehended and that she'd stay on until the danger had passed. She added that once the culprit was caught, she would appreciate being released from her contract. She handed the missive to the telegraph operator and asked him to deliver any reply to the Grand Hotel.

Claire walked the remaining distance to the Grand, recognizable by the impressive arches over the entrance. The building was a testament to what money could buy, with walls covered in fine gilded paper, showing off the sleek walnut furniture and elegant carpets. Extravagant chandeliers graced high ceilings, and an ornate, mirrored gentleman's bar took up the entire east end of the building. She marveled at the contrast of the luxurious hotel and the dusty, loud, odiferous mining town outside its doors. She could have been back East at one of the finer establishments.

As she walked up to the front desk the clerk didn't bat an eye at her clothing. Claire collected her key and climbed the grand staircase to the second floor, pausing at the Bridal Suite. She rapped lightly.

"It's Claire."

"Come in."

Claire opened the door and stepped inside. The front room looked as though Isabella's steamer trunk had exploded—it could be the only rational explanation. Clothes in every color and texture imaginable spilled from her luggage onto a majority of surfaces, giving the room a festive air. A copper tub filled with used bathwater stood in the center of the room, next to an elegant settee. Tall windows stretched across the far wall, with views of the bustling street below.

"Is that you, Claire?" Isabella called from the other room. "I'm in here."

Claire followed her voice to the opulent bedroom. Clad in an emerald green day dress, Isabella lay sprawled on the bed atop a mound of clothes. Her wet hair and flushed skin told Claire she'd already bathed.

"Have you tried your bed?" Isabella gushed. "The spring mattress is *divine*." She stretched like a cat and smiled. Apparently her hangover had dissolved with the bath water.

"I haven't been to my room yet. All I can think of is having a proper soak."

Isabella grinned and sat up. "I had Agnes order one for you. It's probably already in your room."

"Really?" An inordinate amount of joy surged through Claire.

Isabella nodded. "Really. Have your bath. I'm going to rest a while before I go down to the dining room. Will you meet me there in an hour?"

All Claire really wanted to do was take a nap, but she was still on Mr. Gould's payroll. She nodded her assent and was about to leave when she realized she hadn't told Isabella about the telegram. "I sent a message to Mr. Gould detailing your attack and the attempted robbery."

Isabella widened her eyes. "Whatever for?"

"Because…your life is in danger?"

Isabella waved her off. "Oh, silly. No one's after me. Not way out here."

"Not long ago you were sure someone had pushed you down an embankment, intending to kill you. The gash on the back of your head would seem to confirm that theory."

"Now that I've had time to reflect, I think I was just clumsy." She touched the back of her head.

"Are you forgetting that I heard someone running away?" Claire asked.

"It must have been the wind."

"How's your injury?"

"It's nothing. See?" She turned her head to show Claire. The gash did indeed look less severe with the blood washed away, and her hair covered what remained, but that didn't change the fact that she'd received the cut.

"What about the attempted stage robbery?"

Isabella's laughter echoed through the room. "You can't think that was constructed to cover my demise? Quite elaborate, don't you think? Why not shoot me?"

"I still think—"

Someone walked into the front room and Claire moved to the doorway to see who it was. Agnes busied herself picking up towels and trying to corral Isabella's clothes. Their gazes met. An unguarded moment of anger swept across the maid's face, quickly replaced by a less malevolent expression. "Ma'am," she said and curtsied.

"Agnes." Claire turned back to Isabella. "I would feel better if you minded your surroundings while here in Tombstone. Take note of anything untoward, especially if you are approached."

Isabella drew her lips together in a pout. "But isn't that why I have you? You're supposed to protect me from rogues and ne'er-do-wells. Or are you trying to tell me that you've had enough of being a bodyguard?"

"Inasmuch as I believe that your life may still be in danger, I will continue to act as your security. But once the threat has passed, I've asked to be released from my contract."

"Oh, fiddle. I was hoping you'd agree to come back with me to San Francisco next month." Her eyes lit up. "Think of the fun we'd have."

Claire smiled and shook her head. "I dare say you'd have a good time wherever you went."

"You're probably right. But I still need a guiding hand to protect me from scoundrels. Although," she gave Claire a mischievous smile, "I would quite like to entertain one of the rogues I noticed upon checking in to the hotel."

"Who would that be?" Claire didn't notice any overly attractive men in the lobby. The clerk struck her as fairly bookish and not Isabella's type. The bar was sparsely attended, except for a trio of gentlemen drinking whiskey. She assumed a crowd would gather later.

"The man behind the bar. Did you see him? I asked the clerk at the front desk and he said his name was Johnny Behan. He's only been in town a short while." She studied her fingernails, avoiding Claire's gaze. "Apparently he used to be a territorial legislator and wants to run for sheriff in the special election."

Claire had seen the bartender but didn't note anything special about the man other than that he had the face of a cherub and appeared to be on friendly terms with the men drinking at the bar. She guessed that might be what attracted Isabella, although he wasn't Claire's type at all. She preferred someone tall and quiet, with strong features and strong hands, like her Josiah had been.

"I'll find you once I've had my bath," Claire assured her.

Claire went to her room, which was next door. As promised, a copper tub filled with piping hot water had been placed in the center of her smaller but still well-appointed room. Two clean towels were draped across the side of the tub, and a glass jar filled with lavender salts graced a small table nearby. Her trunk had been emptied and set aside in the bedroom, and her clothes hung in the armoire, eliminating the tedium of unpacking. She couldn't deny being in the employ of the wealthy had its benefits.

Perhaps working the job a little longer might be in everyone's best interests.

An hour later, Claire met Isabella and her entourage in the dining room. Everyone looked in good spirits having bathed and rested. Claire had sent out her "road clothes" for cleaning and opted to don one of the serge dresses she'd had made in Leadville before she left. The undergarments were a bit confining, although she didn't mind. She quite enjoyed the appreciative looks from the men she passed, reinforcing her belief that being able to switch between modes of dress was a distinct advantage. Also, she was able to wear her Peacemaker strapped to her thigh with no one the wiser.

Another distinct advantage.

"I'm so glad you could join us," Isabella enthused, popping a grape into her mouth from a bowl on the table. A plate of French bread with little pats of butter shaped like shells joined glasses of red wine on the linen-draped table. Elaborate chandeliers lent an elegant air to the restaurant, as did the polished silver and gleaming walnut accents. Claire took the seat next to Isabella and helped herself to some fruit. Maxi poured her a glass of whatever they were drinking and slid the crystal goblet across the table to her.

Claire lifted her glass in a toast and said, "To our safe arrival in Tombstone." They all drank and Claire added, "I almost didn't recognize the lot of you—everyone looks so different from the last time we were together."

Blake guffawed as the rest chuckled appreciatively. "Might I say the same of you?" He leaned closer and whispered, "You look quite fetching, Miss Claire. The dress becomes you."

Isabella watched the two of them with interest. "Is there something you two aren't telling me?" Maxi and the others turned their attention on Claire and Blake.

Claire laughed. "I think your imagination has run away with you, Isabella."

Blake's smile faltered, but only for an instant. He laughed loudly and raised his glass. "To Claire. The finest woman gunslinger this side of the Mississippi."

Everyone joined in the toast. Judging by the amount of wine in their glasses, they were well ahead of her.

After eating, Orrin, Blake, and Jojo left to check on the venue where they were to perform the next evening, leaving Claire and Isabella alone. Claire sipped her wine as she watched the other diners, intrigued by the disparity—many were likely the upper crust of Tombstone society, as evidenced by their fine clothes and elegant manners. But there was also the odd table with what looked to be freshly scrubbed miners and laborers, reminding her of Leadville.

"What are you looking at?" Isabella asked.

Claire shrugged and smiled. "People. Don't you find them fascinating?"

"I do. But it's my job to study them so that I can recreate a character when I'm on stage." She leaned in and nodded across the room at a table of three men. "What's their story?"

Claire studied them for a moment. "They're friends, obviously, and have known each other for some time." She cocked her head to one side, considering the group. "The one on the left is the leader."

"Why do you say that?"

"Because of the way the other two defer to him. I do think they consider each other equals, though." The man on the right looked up and their gazes met. A thrill skittered along Claire's back at the intensity of his china-blue eyes. His mouth quirked up in a smile, enhancing a slight unevenness in the line of his mustache. Claire felt her cheeks flush and she lowered her gaze.

Isabella looked at Claire, then back at the gentleman at the table. Her smile widened, revealing deep dimples. "Why, Claire Whitcomb. I dare say that dangerous-looking man over there is smitten with you."

Claire rolled her eyes. "Oh, stop. I doubt—"

At that moment, the gentleman in question patted the corners of his mouth with his napkin before he rose from his chair and made his way to their table. He was tall and walked with a relaxed swagger peculiar to confident men. He was also rather thin, although his clothes hid it well. He wore his sandy blond hair brushed back in the style of the day. The full mustache aged him. The closer he came, the younger he looked. She pegged him as late twenties—the same as Josiah.

"Ladies." He greeted them with a courtly bow, barely acknowledging Isabella before turning to Claire. He held out his hand, and Claire, without thinking, lifted hers. He grasped her fingers and leaned in to kiss her knuckles. A lazy smile stretched his lips as he straightened and released her.

"DOUBT THOU THE *stars are fire;*
 doubt the sun doth move;
 doubt truth to be a liar;
 but never doubt I love."

· · ·

"Shakespeare," Claire said with a smile. Blood warmed her cheeks.

The man nodded. "Allow me to introduce myself," he said with a drawl. "John Henry Holliday. But my friends call me Doc." He looked pointedly at Claire. "And you are?"

"Claire Whitcomb," Claire replied. Relieved to direct his attention elsewhere, she added, "This is Isabella King. She's appearing in tomorrow night's performance of *The Pirates of Penzance.*"

Doc Holliday swept his hand in an exaggerated arc as he bowed to Isabella. "I shall be sure to attend." He turned to Claire. "As long as you'll be there."

Surprised and oddly pleased with his audacity, Claire nodded. "I will, yes." She'd heard of Doc Holliday, knew of his ability with a gun, but she'd never imagined meeting the man.

Much less garnering his attentions.

"Claire is my security guard," Isabella said.

A light flickered in Holliday's eyes. "Security guard, you say?" He pulled out a chair and asked, "May I?"

"Of course," Claire replied.

Doc Holliday sat down and draped his arm over the back of his chair. "I heard the gentleman who was at your table earlier toast you as the 'finest gunslinger west of the Mississippi.' Is the accuracy of that august moniker true?"

Self-conscious, Claire laughed. "Not exactly."

"Then what *is* true, Miss Claire Whitcomb?" His hooded gaze slid along the lines of her dress, paused at her neckline, and then continued to her face. The man was quite bold. Claire resisted the urge to fan herself.

Remember, Claire, you're consorting with theater people. He probably thinks you have the same morals.

Isabella saved her from having to answer. "Who are your friends?" She nodded at the two men he'd left at his table. "And would they care to join us?"

Holliday glanced over his shoulder. "I should think they would, yes." He waved at them. The man who'd been sitting in the middle rose immediately and walked over, while the one Claire pegged as their leader took his time before doing the same.

"Wyatt Earp and Luke Short, may I introduce the lovely Miss Claire Whitcomb and her equally lovely friend, Miss Isabella King?"

"Ma'am," both men said and touched the brims of their hats.

Claire was struck by the serendipity of meeting the men to which Mart Duggan had written his letter of introduction on her first day in Tombstone. Wyatt Earp, the man she'd pegged as the leader, was slightly taller than Doc and had an intense look about him, as though impatient to get on with life and devil take the hindmost if anyone tried to stop him. Luke Short lived up to his name—although a head shorter than the others, his confident bearing held up well in comparison to his two friends. Claire guessed he'd be good in a gunfight, as opponents would surely underestimate him.

"It's a pleasure," Claire said. "Our meeting must be fate, as I have a letter of introduction from a mutual friend—Mart Duggan."

Luke's face split into a wide grin. "How the hell is the old bastard? Pardon my French, ladies."

"He hung up his badge, I'm sorry to say," Claire replied. "I think his wife and the dangers of lawing might have had something to do with his decision to purchase the livery, but as a friend of mine said once, Leadville's the poorer for it." A brief sadness sifted through Claire at the thought of young Ian. She mentally shook free of the depressing thought and smiled. He wasn't in any pain, and his first love, Juliette, would eventually move on.

Wyatt speared Claire with a look. "You were on this morning's stage from Benson?"

Claire nodded. "Both Isabella and I were."

"Do you know the woman who shot the bandits?" he asked.

Isabella grinned and pointed to Claire. "She's sitting right here."

Doc's look of interest brought a flush to Claire's cheeks.

Wyatt cocked his head to the side. "You're the one Bud Philpot spoke of?"

Claire nodded. Wyatt's intense stare gave her pause. Was he angry? Did he think she'd overstepped her bounds? A flicker of anger raced through her at the thought. She had as much right to defend the passengers as any man did. Maybe that was why Mrs. Drew didn't have much good to say about the lawman.

Wyatt held out his hand. Surprised, Claire shook it. His handshake was firm and confident. "Well, I'm damn glad to meet you, Claire. We need more women like you in Tombstone."

Doc Holliday studied her for a moment. "I think we should celebrate this momentous occasion. Shall we order a magnum of champagne?"

"I'm game, if you fellows are," Isabella said, smiling like a Cheshire cat.

Wyatt shook his head. "I'm afraid I have to refuse. I've got work to do."

"And what do you do, Mr. Earp?" Isabella fluttered her eyelashes at him, but he appeared unmoved and not a little amused.

"Deputy Sheriff," Luke Short answered for him. "He's running for county sheriff in the November elections."

"As is Johnny Behan." Wyatt didn't sound particularly excited about the prospect of running against Behan.

"Well, Mr. Wyatt, good luck to you." Isabella fluttered her lashes at him once more for good measure, apparently fishing for a response. When he didn't react, she transferred her charms to Luke Short, who was more than happy to return the attention. Wyatt said his goodbyes and left.

Doc leaned in closer to Claire and asked, "Does your friend always flirt so shamelessly?"

"I don't really know," she said truthfully. "This is the first we've socialized since our trip began."

"How came you to be a security guard? Another Mart Duggan introduction?"

Claire shook her head. "I met Isabella on the train from Leadville. An outlaw broke into her private car and threatened her life." She paused, wondering how much to tell him. "I shot him."

"How admirable. And how unusual to meet a woman who has killed someone. I'm sorry, two someones. I believe I'd like to take you shooting sometime."

She studied him for a moment. "I would like that. Thank you for the invitation." It wasn't every day that a man with Doc Holliday's reputation offered to shoot with her.

The barman, Johnny Behan, walked in with a magnum of champagne in a silver bucket, which he brought over and set on their table. A waiter delivered fresh glasses with a flourish and disappeared behind a swinging door.

"Mr. Behan, how are you?" Doc asked.

"Just fine, Doc." Behan perused the small group, his gaze lingering on Isabella. He acknowledged the others with a tip of his head. "Ladies. Luke."

"May I introduce the infamous Johnny Behan," Doc said. "Johnny, I'd like you to meet Isabella King and Claire Whitcomb, newly arrived this morning on the Benson stage."

"It's a pleasure to meet you both That must have been some trip." His gaze drifted back to Isabella. "I'm glad you are all safe."

"I hear you're running for sheriff, Mr. Behan." Isabella batted her eyelashes at him; the effect was immediate. Interest lit Behan's face just as sure as summer followed spring.

"Why yes, I am." He nodded at Doc and Luke. "I'd ask for your votes, gentlemen, but we all know who's gettin' yours." His gaze flickered back to Isabella. "May I ask your purpose for visiting Tombstone?"

Isabella's smile would have made the sun jealous. "Yes, you may. I'll be appearing tomorrow evening in *The Pirates of Penzance*."

Johnny grinned, his interest even more pronounced. "An actress. Well, welcome to Tombstone."

Impatient, Doc grabbed the magnum from the bucket, worked the top free with an explosive *pop!* and filled the glasses.

"A little early for you, isn't it, Doc?" Behan crossed his arms, a wary expression on his face.

"Don't you worry, Johnny. I'll behave myself," Doc said with a smile. "Put the bottle on my tab, good man."

Behan scowled. "Your tab is full to bursting, Doc."

Doc waved him away. "I'll settle up later this evening." Behan snorted his disbelief but took his leave.

Luke chuckled. "You sure know how to needle him, Doc."

Doc smiled. "One of my most cherished reasons for living, Luke."

After a few minutes of polite conversation, Luke and Isabella fell into an easy discussion about his adventures while out West.

Clearly uninterested in listening to his friend wax nostalgic about life on the trail, Doc moved his chair closer to Claire's. "Tell me, madam. How did a lovely woman like you become a gunslinger for hire?"

Claire sighed, wondering why she felt compelled to open up to someone she'd just met. There was something about him, something comfortable, like she'd known him a long time. The attraction wasn't really physical—she preferred men with a bit more meat on their bones—but he exuded something she couldn't put her finger on. Something that made her feel safe and valued.

"I came west with my husband, Josiah, a couple of years ago, and we settled in Leadville."

"Whose idea was it to move to Colorado?"

"His. I would not have chosen to move. Our children were quite young, you see." A wave of nostalgia came over her, and she tamped down the sadness that always rode its coattails.

"What happened to them?" His tone was gentle, similar to how a person spoke to a horse to calm them, which told her he'd guessed the answer would be painful.

"They were murdered."

"I'm so very sorry." He covered her hand with his own. His skin was cool and dry.

She nodded, unable to speak. Regaining her composure, she continued. "The man responsible was a prominent banker from Leadville who wanted our claim." She left out that he'd wanted her, too. The revelation struck her as sordid, so she always skipped over that part in the telling.

"What happened to the cur?"

She lifted her gaze to meet his. "I shot him, too."

Doc nodded. "A fitting end for such treachery. I'm curious, did your actions help or hinder your peace of mind?"

Claire stared at nothing, remembering the aftermath. "The consequence of his death was most unfulfilling."

"Vengeance usually is." Doc threw back the rest of his champagne and refilled the glass. Claire had barely touched hers. "Your erudition appears to be of Eastern origin. Where did you live prior to Leadville?"

"I could say the same for you. I started life in Pennsylvania."

"Philadelphia?"

Claire nodded. "It seems so far off now."

"Indeed. I know the state well. I attended the Pennsylvania College of Dental Surgery."

"Impressive. Do you still practice?"

Doc shifted in his chair. "Unfortunately, I left my dental equipment in Prescott, believing faro and poker to be my salvation." His sardonic laughter turned into a body-wrenching cough, which he covered with a handkerchief from his pocket. Isabella glanced at him in alarm, but then turned back to Luke, apparently not wanting to draw attention to the outburst. The moment passed, and Doc folded the handkerchief and put it back in his pocket. "Funny how patients don't enjoy being coughed upon by their dentist."

"A chronic illness?"

He nodded and sipped his drink. "Isn't everything?"

His behavior suggested he preferred not to dwell on his malady, so Claire changed the subject. "Your manner of speaking tells me you weren't raised in Pennsylvania."

"You are correct, madam. My origins are the great state of Georgia."

"I thought I detected a southern sensibility." Claire smiled. "What brought you west?"

"The dryness of the air. And the amicable women."

"There is certainly an abundance of the former." She took a sip of champagne and rolled it around her tongue. It was crisp and dry with the essence of apples and figs. "Forgive my asking, but are the rumors about your reputation true?" Stories of his prowess with a gun preceded him, as did his gambling habit and hair trigger temper.

"That would depend on which rumors." There was a twinkle in his eye as he spoke. "I should ask you the same."

Surprised, Claire said, "Have I been the subject of rumor so soon? I've barely arrived."

Doc Holliday smiled. "News travels fast, dear Claire. It should be no surprise that tongues are wagging about a woman gunfighter. That's rare enough."

"I suspect you're right." She hadn't realized she'd have to deal with the fallout from her actions. She wasn't sure if she liked the idea of having a reputation, but there was nothing to be done about it now. Perhaps she could use it to her benefit.

"Have you been in Tombstone long?" she asked.

"Define long."

"What brought you here?"

He took another sip and placed the glass on the table. "Friendship. And gambling. Now it's my turn. Whatever possessed you to travel all this way?" He looked around the room at the clientele before returning his attention to her. "There are much finer towns."

"I'd decided to leave Leadville, and Mart mentioned how nice the weather could be in the Arizona Territory this time of year."

"That might be the only nice thing you experience here."

Their gazes met. Claire smiled and said, "I doubt that." He returned the smile with his own. She sipped more of the champagne, wondering if she dared ask him what he thought about her sketches. *Fortune favors the bold, Claire.*

She swallowed her nervousness and asked, "Would you be so kind as to look at something I'm working on to improve the speed of reloading my rifle?"

Doc straightened in his chair, his interest obvious. "I'd be delighted, madam." He nodded at her to proceed.

Claire brought out her reticule and fished for the latest draft she'd done of the mechanism to assist with loading and firing her rifle. She put it on the table and smoothed the paper flat.

"What have we here?" Doc asked. Claire slid it across the table to him. "Did you draw this?"

She nodded. "I wanted something that would both seat a new cartridge and at the same time fire the gun, eliminating the need to pull the trigger every time."

Doc studied it for a moment. "What happens if you want to delay the shot? Is there a way to release the mechanism?"

Claire pointed to a small piece near the lever. "You can push this part aside to disengage the trigger, returning it to its original configuration."

"It's ingenious."

Luke and Isabella paused in their conversation and turned their attention to the drawing.

"Do you really think so?" Claire asked.

"Yes, I do." Doc slid it back to her. "What made you think of it?"

As Isabella and Luke looked on, Claire told the story of Ian and the attempted train robbery by Jack "Sheriff Killer" Abrams and the other outlaws. When she finished, a grin slowly formed on Doc's face.

"So, it was you who killed Abrams?"

Claire nodded. "And two of his gang."

He leaned back in his chair and let out a low whistle. "Well, I for one am pleased as punch to meet a fellow gun devotee." He held out his hand. "Let me see that rendering again."

Claire slid it back over the table toward him, and he glanced at it once more. He downed the rest of his drink and stood.

"Come with me, Claire Whitcomb."

Doc assured Claire that Isabella would be in good hands with Luke, especially with so much champagne left, so after she had a word with them, Doc took her to the gunsmith on Fourth Street.

He showed Claire's invention to the proprietor, George Spangenberg, who told them to give him a few days and he'd see what he could do.

As they started for the hotel, Claire patted his arm. "Thank you, Doc, for not shooting down my idea, so to speak."

Doc smiled at her play on words. "It was my pleasure, Miss Claire. I may make use of your invention myself—not that I'm partial to rifles, mind you. My preference is a pistol. But I'm not against an idea that could help in a fight."

"Earlier, you mentioned a practice shoot. Would you be interested in doing that now? I'm not sure whether I'll have much time in the future, depending on Isabella's requirements, and I would hate to miss the opportunity."

"Why, I'd be honored, Miss Claire. I'll need to go back to my room to retrieve my weapon of choice. It's over on Fremont Street. Would you care to accompany me?"

"Of course."

They stopped outside of the same boarding house where Claire had met Mollie Fly earlier that morning. Claire walked inside and had a seat in the parlor while Doc went to his room. Mollie brought her a glass of water while she waited.

"Have you known Doc long?" she asked.

"I met him today, as a matter of fact. Why?"

Mollie shrugged. "He's got—an unsavory reputation. I'm not sure you want to be associated with a man of his caliber."

Claire smiled. "He's been nothing but a gentleman." She was going to add that she didn't care much about her reputation but decided against it.

Mollie patted Claire's knee. "Well, dear, you be careful. He tends to be quite volatile when he drinks." She leaned closer and whispered, "He likes to shoot things."

"I will. Thank you, Mollie."

Doc reappeared, a leather satchel in hand. "Mollie. What atrocious untruths are you telling my new friend?" Smiling, he turned to Claire. "Don't believe a word she says, Claire. She makes a mean strawberry crumble, but she's a sharp tongue."

Mollie waved him away. "Oh, stop it. You behave, Mr. Holliday. Claire isn't the type of woman you're accustomed to keeping company with," she added with a reproving look.

Doc smiled at Claire with a mischievous glint in his eyes. "Oh, don't I know it, Miss Mollie. Don't I know it."

They rented a buggy from the livery and rode north of town to set up targets at varying distances. Self-conscious at first, after a few practice shots Claire relaxed into the friendly competition. She held her own, although Doc was much faster on the draw. He hit every target, while she made nine out of ten.

"What would you do if someone had a hold of another person you didn't want to shoot and was threatening their life?" The memory of not being able to get a clear shot of the gunman who held Ian haunted her.

Doc considered her question. "Well, that would depend on how they were holding them. If he's got them around the neck like this—" He demonstrated by standing behind Claire and wrapping his arm around her throat. "Then you've usually got a good shot at the bastard's head."

Acutely aware of his presence behind her, Claire tamped down the carnal thoughts running through her mind and concentrated on what he was saying. "You mean you'd take the shot? What if you hit the victim?"

Doc released her with a chuckle. "If you can't hit a target the size of someone's head, then I would recommend another line of work."

"I see your point."

"You, on the other hand, most certainly are proficient enough to do so. I must profess my admiration, Miss Claire. Not since Calamity Jane Cannery have I been witness to such expert shooting by a member of the fairer sex."

"You know her?" Claire had heard tales of the woman sharp-shooter, how she'd been a drover and a scout, and lived life her own way and on her own terms.

"Met her in Deadwood, before Hickok was shot. That woman did love a drink."

"Her choice of lifestyle wouldn't be an easy one. I daresay drink would be one way to cope."

"Indeed."

They continued shooting for a while longer, with Doc giving Claire some more pointers. By the end of their session, she felt much improved.

"Thank you, Doc. I've learned so much. I don't know how to repay you."

Doc smiled as he put away his pearl-handled Colt Lightning. "There's no need, Miss Claire. Our little sojourn has been a grand diversion. Perhaps we'll have another chance later on, if you decide to make your home in Tombstone."

"Perhaps," Claire replied. She'd been in town for less than a day but already felt as though fate had a hand in things. She'd sleep on it and see what came of it in the morning.

∽

Claire and Doc returned to the hotel to find Isabella and Johnny deep in conversation in the lobby, with Luke Short nowhere to be found.

"I should stay here with Isabella. She is my responsibility, at least for the time being," Claire said to Doc.

Doc touched the brim of his hat and gave her a half-bow. "Then I shall take my leave. I hope to see you in the near future, Miss Claire. I will hold you to the second practice session we spoke of."

"I look forward to it, Mr. Holliday." Claire turned, intending to join Isabella and Johnny, when a well-dressed woman with striking eyes walked through the entrance. She narrowed those eyes as she spotted the couple. With a resolute look, the woman straightened her shoulders and made her way toward them.

"Darling! Where've you been?" she sang, belying her obvious anger at the hapless bartender. Johnny's face drained of color and he immediately stood, distancing himself from Isabella.

Isabella wore a bemused expression as she watched the other woman's approach. "Who is this?"

Johnny plastered a bright smile across his face. "Josie, my love. I've been here all afternoon. I was helping to orient one of the town's new arrivals."

It was Isabella's turn to narrow her eyes at Johnny. She directed her attention at Josie and gave the woman her most dazzling smile as she offered her hand. "I'm afraid we haven't met. I'm Isabella King."

Ignoring the gesture, Josie wondered aloud, "Isabella King— where have I heard that name before?" She tapped her finger against her chin. "Oh, yes. You're a member of Nellie Boyd's troupe appearing in the play tomorrow evening, aren't you? A showgirl." Derision laced her words.

Isabella kept her smile in place as she replied. "I am, yes. I'm appearing as one of the lead characters. I do hope you'll come?"

"Wouldn't miss it for the world."

Johnny appeared to relax a bit, adding helpfully, "Josie is an actress herself."

Josie's posture practically screamed possession, both of the space around her and the man within it. "A thespian, darling." She gave Isabella a calculating look. "A bit different than a showgirl."

"Oh? What's your stage name?"

"I go by Josephine Marcus," she answered, raising her chin.

Isabella took a sip of her drink and smiled. "I'm afraid I'm not familiar with your work. Which troupes have you toured with?"

"I was most recently a member of Pauline Markham's Theater Company, in a production of *H.M.S. Pinafore*."

"How extraordinary. And now?"

"I'm between performances."

"I see." Isabella's disbelief was obvious, but manners dictated politeness. The high color on Josephine's cheeks portended a fight brewing.

Deciding it would be a good time to intervene, Claire interrupted the standoff. "Are you ready to go, Isabella?"

Isabella gave Claire a blank look. "Go?"

"For your dress fitting?"

Understanding lit Isabella's eyes and she nodded. "Of course." She drained her drink and slid her hand over Johnny's, giving it a pat under Josephine's hawk-like gaze. "It's been lovely getting to know you, Johnny. I do hope to continue our conversation in the near future."

"Uh, I—I look forward to it." He glanced nervously at Josephine.

Claire grasped Isabella's elbow and led her from the room. "What are you doing?" she whispered. "You do remember Mr. Gould? The man who pays your bills?"

"Whatever do you mean, Claire?"

Claire pulled her outside the hotel onto the sidewalk that lined bustling Allen Street. She couldn't help but giggle at Isabella's innocent expression. Isabella joined in, and they both leaned against the wall, helpless with laughter.

"Did you see her face?" Isabella asked, eliciting another round of giggles.

"I actually thought the two of you would come to blows," Claire replied, trying to catch her breath. "Over a bartender." She shook her head.

Isabella clapped her hand over her mouth in an attempt to stifle her merriment. Passersby gave them odd looks. "Poor Johnny—I'm sure he wished the earth would open and swallow him whole."

Claire was the first to gain control. "I sincerely hope that you don't intend to pursue the man. I'm afraid of the lengths Josephine would go to defend her claim."

Isabella gave her an enigmatic look. "I may, and I may not. I find it great fun to trifle with men's affections. A bad habit to be sure, but entertaining nonetheless."

"You're a scandal, Isabella King."

"When one is an actress, one must be larger than life, don't you think?"

"Please do it when I'm not around, though. I'd hate to have to pull my gun."

That brought another squeal of laughter from them both.

"What say we do as you suggested in the lobby and visit a dressmaker? I feel the need for a new frock." Isabella studied Claire's outfit. "And you could do with something a bit more daring."

"What's wrong with this?" Claire quite liked her dress. True, it wasn't the most up-to-date style, but it worked well for what she needed.

"It's…serviceable." She grabbed Claire's elbow and pulled her down the street. "Come on, Claire. I dare you."

Claire grinned. "I've never been one to shy away from a dare."

ED WORTHINGTON WATCHED as Isabella and the Claire woman made their way along Fremont Street, laughing like a pair of schoolgirls. Claire, the woman who had threatened him with a gun during the botched stage holdup had changed into clothes more suitable for a woman. He had to admit he'd been right—the brunette cleaned up very well.

Too bad she had to be collateral damage. He assumed that she suspected him for Isabella's mishap at the station, although she had no proof. He'd have to take care of her before she raised her suspicions with the local lawmen.

Ed straightened his vest and entered the Grand Hotel lobby, looking for the actress's maid, Agnes. Not seeing her, he politely inquired as to the availability of the so-called Bridal Suite for the evening but was told it had been occupied and would be for the foreseeable future.

"For future reference, what kind of view does the room have?" he asked the obsequious clerk.

"The suite occupies nearly half the front on the upper floor and has windows along its main wall with views of Allen Street," replied the clerk proudly.

"And how does one access it?"

The clerk pointed to the grand staircase leading to the upper level. "Up those stairs and turn right. You can't miss it. May I interest you in one of our other well-appointed rooms?"

"Thank you, but not at this time." Ed walked to the other end of the lobby, waiting for the clerk's attention to turn elsewhere before climbing the stairs to the upper floor.

The gleaming black walnut doors boasted a brass plaque that read *Bridal Suite*. He jiggled the handle to check if it was locked and the door opened, revealing a surprised Agnes holding an armful of clothes. Apparently she recognized him, and she gave him a quick smile.

"May I help you?" she asked, exiting the room and closing the door behind her.

"I'm here to inquire as to how your mistress is settling in. Is she available?"

"She's settling in fine, sir. But she's out at the moment." She indicated the clothes she carried. "I'm taking some of her dresses to be freshened up."

"Of course." Ed Worthington stepped aside to let her pass but stopped her as she did. "If I may, how much does Miss King pay you for your services?"

"She pays well enough. Why do you ask?"

Ed gave her a look he hoped she took to mean he was embarrassed. "I'm quite taken with her, you see, and I should like to arrange a meeting with the young lady. Away from prying eyes, if you get my meaning."

Agnes nodded, a conspiratorial look on her face. Clearly she'd been approached with similar requests in the past. "It'll cost you. Getting her away from her security guard isn't easy."

"I shall be resolute in my attempts to evade him."

Agnes gave him a scornful look. "Her guard ain't a 'he.' It's a she. Her name's Claire. You seen her on the trip from Benson. She was dressed like a man and rode a horse the whole way."

Worthington frowned in confusion. Claire was C. Whitcomb? How did his employer, Cooke, not know that? *I should have shot her when I had the chance.*

"Really? My goodness, that's a novel idea, isn't it? A woman gunslinger."

"She can go to hell, for all I care," Agnes grumbled.

Aha, thought Worthington. *A rebellious employee. Perfect.* "I may have an idea that would work to both of our advantage. Interested?" He showed her a wad of bills in his pocket.

Her eyes lit up and she nodded. "I'm all ears."

CHAPTER 15

The next evening, Claire checked herself in the mirror, making sure the off-the-shoulder, royal blue satin evening dress trimmed in black sequins looked all right. Isabella had insisted on buying the matching elbow-length gloves and blue slippers to complete the outfit.

Claire pinched her cheeks to bring up the color and smiled at her reflection. How fun it was to wear fine clothes one moment, then don men's rugged, practical clothing the next, depending on the activity. Truly, she had the best of both worlds.

She slid her hand through the folds of the dress's hidden access and curled her fingers around the grip of the revolver strapped to her thigh. The opening had been easy enough to create, and the seamstress had remarked how she'd like to have one herself.

Isabella's attacker was still at large. Even though the actress had declared the injury she'd received at Drew's Station an accident, Claire still believed her life was in danger.

Truth be told, her main suspect was Ed Worthington, and she wanted to be prepared.

She was taking a slight risk, though. Tombstone had an ordinance against carrying concealed weapons. Like most of the weapon bans in the Arizona Territory, this one didn't have teeth unless a person was on the wrong side of the ruling faction in town. At most, a fine would be imposed, and her gun might be confiscated for the evening. If she was caught, she'd argue that assassins didn't play by the rules.

She picked up her reticule and made her way from the hotel to Ritchie Hall on Fifth Street, where Isabella and the rest of the troupe were performing that evening.

The cramped hall was at capacity. Filled with raucous miners, prospectors, and several prominent citizens, the crowd was a good blend of all classes of Tombstone society. The gaslights cast a golden glow over the animated patrons, all eager to see and be seen during the festive evening. At the side of the stage, Maxi peeked out from behind the velvet curtain for a glimpse of the room. Spotting Claire, she waved her over. Claire waved back and began her journey through the throng.

"Well, if it isn't Miss Claire." Doc Holliday smiled as he stepped in her path. "I hoped we'd run into each other."

He'd clearly been drinking—aside from his flushed cheeks, he appeared to be having difficulty focusing.

Claire smiled back at him. "It's good to see you, too, Mr. Holliday. It seems you're enjoying the evening."

"Oh, I always enjoy my evenings. I should like to spot you a drink later on, after your charge's august performance, of course."

"I should enjoy that. Shall we meet somewhere afterward? I'm certain my 'charge' and her friends would be interested in joining me." If past behavior was any indication, Isabella and the rest of the troupe would be looking for a place to blow off steam after the performance.

"I'll be dealing faro at the Alhambra Saloon. Please do come by and grace us with your lovely presence." Doc bowed over her hand, tickling her knuckles with his mustache. He released her with a wicked smile. Claire returned the same before making her way to the stage.

She'd almost gained the steps when Ed Worthington brushed against her. Tensing, Claire gave him a most insincere smile. "Mr. Worthington."

"Pardon me, Miss Whitcomb." He nodded at her before disappearing into the crowd.

She turned to see where he'd gone but lost him to the shadows. She wondered how he'd known her last name was Whitcomb. When they first met in Benson, she'd only given him her Christian name. Claire shook off the foreboding his presence had elicited and went backstage.

The troupe was gathered around Isabella and Nellie Boyd, listening to what turned out to be a rallying cry meant to put everyone in high spirits before going on stage. They ended their pep talk, and Isabella turned back to her mirror to put the finishing touches on her makeup.

Maxi gave Claire a nudge with her elbow and grinned. "Ever think about joining an acting troupe, Claire?"

"I'm afraid I'd be about as good an actress as I am a dog sledder."

"Izzy said that you wouldn't be coming with us to San Francisco when we leave." She made a moue with her mouth. "None of us want to see you go. We've all felt so safe with you around." She glanced at Blake, who was practicing with a sword on the other side of the set. He was dressed for the role of Major-General. "Blake was shattered when she told us."

"I'm sure that Isabella will be able to find someone better suited as a bodyguard. Besides, a month isn't long enough to really get to know a place, and I aim to know Tombstone."

Maxi shrugged. "Well, please know we'll miss you when we leave."

"And I'll miss the lot of you. Life will be much duller, believe me."

Claire wished her good luck on the performance and walked over to where Isabella was seated, brushing her hair. "It's so busy back here. I had no idea of the amount of activity that went on before a show."

Isabella set her brush on the table and adjusted her pirate costume. "The expectation, you mean." She closed her eyes and took a deep breath. "I live for this. Whenever I'm not onstage, I feel a bit like a wilted flower." She gave Claire's dress an appreciative look. "Your new gown becomes you."

Claire smiled at the compliment. "And may I say you look the perfect pirate."

Isabella bowed. "Thank you, milady. Have you been to your seat yet? I made sure to save you one of the best in the house."

"Not yet, no. But I am looking forward to the show."

Claire left them to their preparations and found her seat. Isabella hadn't exaggerated—the box had a full view of the stage and orchestra. She took her place and settled in for the performance.

The audience laughed at the rapid-fire dialogue and witty Gilbert and Sullivan numbers, as well as the quick changes the members of the small troupe had to make to cover the roles. The other half of the group had arrived the week before and had set tongues wagging with their outrageous antics—all done to drum up anticipation for the nightly performances. Their objective had appeared to work.

Claire went backstage during intermission and watched from the sidelines as the actors and actresses went through their paces, changing backdrops and costumes. She marveled at how well managed the production seemed. A "well-oiled machine" as Josiah would have said.

On her way back to her seat, one of the ushers pressed a glass of wine into her hand. She accepted out of politeness, not intending to drink until they were safely ensconced in the

Alhambra Saloon with Doc nearby. She planned to keep her wits about her until then.

She got to her seat as the curtain parted, revealing the new set. Claire moved her chair forward to see the stage more clearly, and nearly knocked over the wineglass. Movement below caught her attention, and she realized Ed Worthington was staring up at her from his seat on the main floor. His attention made her skin crawl, and she eased the pistol from inside her skirt.

The rest of the performance went well. The appreciative audience whistled and stomped their feet, demanding several curtain calls. Claire took that moment to leave her seat and return backstage. She slid the pistol back into its holster and walked out of the box into the narrow hallway. As she started down the stairs, she sensed a presence behind her. She turned, but no one was there.

The lobby was empty except for the head usher cleaning up with his assistant, and a few audience members leaving before the rush for the exit. Claire couldn't shake the feeling that she was being watched and slipped her hand around the butt of the pistol. As she walked through the double doors leading to the raucous main floor, there was movement to her left. Startled, she stepped back as a shadowy figure rushed toward her. Without warning, the figure changed course, dissolving into the crowd.

Puzzled, Claire glanced behind her to see Doc. All evidence of drunkenness gone, he caught her by the arm.

"Did you see who it was?" she asked, her heart pounding.

Doc shook his head. "No, but I believe he meant you harm."

"You're certain it was a he?"

"Do you know many six-foot-tall women with exceptionally broad shoulders?" He drew Claire back into the light of the lobby and checked her over. "You're certain you are unharmed?"

"I'm sure. Who do you think—" At that moment there was a shriek from the other side of the room, near the stairs to the box seats. A well-dressed woman staggered from the stairwell, her face drained of color.

"He's—my husband—he's—" Her eyelids fluttered and she fainted, collapsing to the floor. The usher and his assistant rushed to help her.

Claire started for the stairwell, with Doc close behind. They raced up the steps and checked each box. When they came to Claire's seat, they found an older gentleman lying on the floor, his arm outstretched with Claire's empty wineglass by his hand. Vomit dribbled from his lips, puddling near his head.

Claire dropped to her knees and listened to the man's chest. She could detect no heartbeat. She held her finger beneath his nose but knew it was a futile gesture. She glanced at Doc. "He's dead."

Doc picked up the empty wineglass and sniffed it. "Smells like wine. But his expectoration professes otherwise."

"Poison?" Shocked, Claire stared at the dead man. "That wine was meant for me."

Doc put the glass back where he'd found it. "And most likely would have killed the usher or his assistant had this gentleman passed the opportunity by."

"But what poison kills so quickly? Arsenic would have taken hours, if not days. As would hemlock."

Doc looked at her with interest. "How much you know of poison, Miss Claire. Remind me never to get on your bad side."

She waved his comment away. "I studied Socrates in school, and I've used arsenic to poison rats. What else?"

"Cyanide? Mercury? All are easily procurable in a mining town."

"Clearly the person you deflected downstairs meant me harm."

"Indeed."

Dread seized her as she realized the implications. "I need to warn Isabella." Claire was on her feet and halfway down the stairs before Doc caught up to her.

"Be wary, Claire. The rogue is still at large."

Claire and Doc raced backstage. Several actors remained, helping to clear the area, but Isabella wasn't there. Agnes walked by with an armload of costumes on her way to the door. Claire stopped her.

"Where's Isabella?"

Startled, Agnes widened her eyes. "She left after the last curtain call. Said she was going to meet someone over at the Cosmopolitan."

Claire and Doc exchanged a glance. "Did she leave with anyone?" Doc asked.

"I don't think so, no."

"Is there a back door?" Claire asked.

Agnes pointed to a piece of set painted to resemble a ship. "Over there, behind the boat."

Outside, Claire turned to Doc, her heart racing. "I asked her to meet me at the Alhambra, not the Cosmopolitan."

"Then either that woman is lying—"

Claire finished his thought for him. "Or the would-be attacker somehow redirected her." She clenched her fists. "He's going to try to kill her."

"Do you have any suspects?"

Claire nodded. "Ed Worthington. One of the passengers from the stagecoach we traveled with. He seems to always be close by when bad things happen."

"Then might I suggest we find her before he does?"

Claire pulled her pistol free, and they started for the saloon.

Isabella wasn't at the Cosmopolitan, and no one Claire and Doc spoke to had seen her. Foreboding filled Claire as they checked Hafford's and the Oriental Saloon but came up empty.

"She can't have just disappeared." Agitated, Claire paced in front of the Alhambra. The party was in full swing—laughter coupled with piano music and glassware tinkling intended to lure passersby inside. At that moment, a man bashed through the swinging doors. Unable to conquer his velocity, he dove headlong into the street.

"And don't come back!" The man responsible for his flight scowled at Doc. "Hope you ain't comin' in to start anythin', Doc. I got no patience for trouble tonight."

Doc tipped his hat and smiled. "Wouldn't think of it, Sam."

Sam scowled again and stalked back inside, the doors swinging behind him. Claire raised her eyebrows. "Somebody's having a bad night."

"Indeed." Doc searched both sides of the street. "Perhaps we should split up—double our ability to scour the area. You take the south side—there are fewer establishments. I'll cover the north side. I need to poke my head inside the Alhambra to let them know I'll be there presently. I'll meet you on Sixth Street."

The Red Light District—a place not meant for well-bred ladies. Well, hell, Claire thought. It wasn't like she was trying to save her reputation. She nodded. "All right."

"Good luck." Doc went into the Alhambra.

Claire crossed the street and headed east. Isabella wasn't in the bowling alley or any of the saloons that had sprung up wherever space allowed. Most were busy, although the finer establishments like the Oriental and the Alhambra had better clientele, as well as more refined prostitutes. A lot of the establishments were nothing fancy, a basic place to have a drink, catering to a majority of the miners.

Claire was out of luck by the time she reached Sixth Street. She glanced behind her, searching for Doc, but he was nowhere to be found.

She turned right and headed southeast along Sixth, avoiding the Red Light District. She'd wait for Doc to show up so he could work his way through those establishments. This section of town was dark and deserted—a backstreet in Tombstone.

Halfway between Allen and Tough Nut, she came upon a darkened alleyway. Something shifted in the shadows, capturing her attention.

Partway in, she heard scuffling and froze. What was she getting into? Ever more cautious and alert, she continued on, the pistol cocked and ready. She took deep breaths to still her thudding heart as she crept farther into the darkness. Most of the lots lining the alley were vacant, and the storefronts she did pass were dark—none here catered to Tombstone's considerable nightlife.

Several yards in, she stopped. The blue light of the moon illuminated two shadowy figures, seemingly entwined in an intimate embrace. What if she'd stumbled on a miner and that evening's entertainment? They were close enough to the Red Light District that it wasn't a stretch, and Claire didn't want to interrupt a late-night tryst. Surprising a miner wasn't a good idea under most circumstances—she could get shot for her trouble.

She was about to retrace her steps when one of the figures cried out. Claire squinted into the darkness, trying to see what was going on.

"No! Let me go—"

Isabella. Heart in her throat, Claire crept closer.

"Quiet," a man's voice warned. Taking a bead on the taller of the two figures, Claire couldn't get a clean shot. The shadows were too dense. She didn't want to miss him and hit Isabella.

Frustrated, Claire moved closer. As she did, her foot hit a rock and it skittered across the gravel. The man looked up and the moon lit his face.

Ed Worthington.

"Let her go, Ed." Claire's voice was strong and clear, which surprised her. She thought her galloping heart would beat out of her chest.

Worthington wrapped his arm around Isabella's neck as he pressed his pistol against her temple, holding her in front of him like a shield. "Would that be the great C. Whitcomb?" Scorn oozed from his lips. "My, my. Lucky me. Two for the price of one."

Claire moved, but he shook his head and pulled Isabella tighter.

"Not one more step." He sneered. "Didn't anyone tell you ladies can't be gunslingers? Too emotional." Worthington nodded at Claire. "Drop your gun, or I'll kill her."

"You might want to rethink that idea." Doc stepped from the shadows, his nickel-plated Colt gleaming in the moonlight.

Claire took aim at Worthington, her heart beating wildly in her ears.

She only had one shot.

It had to count.

Claire pulled in a deep breath.

Still using Isabella as a shield, Worthington spun and fired at Doc. Claire squeezed the trigger, hitting the assassin in the side of the head. Isabella screamed as Worthington dropped his pistol and sank to the ground like a marionette with its strings cut.

Free of his grasp, Isabella raced to Claire, a sob escaping her lips.

"Are you hurt?" Claire asked, checking to see if she had any injuries.

Isabella shook her head. "I'm fine. He said he didn't kill me right off because he wanted us both." She took a shaky breath. "To think I shared a coach with that man." She shuddered.

"Can you wait here?" Claire asked. "I've got to check on Doc—"

"No need, Miss Claire." Doc emerged from the shadows and walked toward them, the shadow of a smile on his face. "That was some fine shootin'."

"Thanks to you." Relieved that Doc was all right, Claire turned back to Isabella. "You're safe for now—until whoever hired Worthington hears about his death."

"It's Jay's friend, William Cooke. Worthington said as much." There was bitterness in Isabella's tone. "Cooke's the one who killed that man in New York."

"Do tell." Holliday cocked his head to the side. "This sounds juicy."

"Is it possible that Mr. Gould told him where you were?" Claire asked.

Isabella shook her head emphatically. "No. He knew what William had done. But he's one of his oldest friends. Jay got me out of the way so that he wouldn't have to choose between us."

Doc slid his gun into his holster. "I daresay he already made that choice."

"He's got a point," Claire said.

The actress's hurt expression told Claire Isabella hadn't thought the railroad magnate's actions through.

Then, as though appropriating a part in a play, Isabella set her jaw and squared her shoulders, transforming her from victim to heroine. "You know what? You're both right. I'm tired of living like this, looking over my shoulder, wondering when he's coming for me. I'm through being afraid. I'm going back to New York and I'm going to offer myself as a witness."

Doc gave her a sidelong look. "You really think that's a good idea?"

"Probably not. But I can't run scared all my life." Isabella hugged herself. She looked lost, suddenly. The confident party girl had all but disappeared.

"What do you think Mr. Gould's reaction will be?" Claire had a feeling that Isabella's days as mistress to one of the richest men in America were numbered.

Isabella shrugged. "I can't let that stop me from doing what I ought." She nodded at Worthington's corpse. "What do we do about him?"

Claire looked at Doc, who smiled.

"I know just the gentleman to take care of that."

One Week Later

Claire stood at her hotel room window and studied the fancy private coach on the street below. Six sleek bays danced in their traces, looking for all the world as though they might take off at the slightest provocation. The whip and the shotgun messenger were busy unloading luggage, while several men bristling with weapons surrounded the coach. Considering the passenger, local law enforcement had decided to make an exception to the ordinance prohibiting concealed weapons—although from what Claire could see, most of theirs were plenty visible.

Isabella had been surprised when Jay Gould rolled into town like royalty in the state-of-the-art stagecoach. She'd been nervous but excited, thinking that perhaps he'd missed her and was anxious about her well-being. The morning after the shooting, Claire had wired him about Ed Worthington's attempts to murder Isabella and his subsequent death. He'd wired back his thanks but didn't express concern for his mistress in the curt telegram. He'd also canceled Claire's contract, releasing her from her obligation to the actress. Isabella had pleaded with Claire to stay until she found a suitable replacement, paying her salary from her own pocket.

Worthington's body had been dealt with by an undertaker who was friends with Wyatt Earp. An unmarked wooden cross served as his headstone in the busy cemetery. Since the assassin had kept largely to himself and wasn't well known in Tombstone, his disappearance went unnoticed by the townspeople.

Outside her room, a door banged shut and footsteps rumbled down the carpeted stairs. A moment later, the same door opened and closed with much less force and was soon followed by a tap on Claire's own hotel room door.

"Coming." Claire walked to the door and cracked it open to reveal a distraught Isabella. Claire opened it wider and stepped aside to let her in. "You look like death."

Isabella strode into the room, wringing her hands. "I'm finished," she said, her voice an octave higher than usual. She turned to Claire. "Jay left me." Tears brimmed in her eyes.

Claire wrapped her arms around the distressed young woman. "Come, now. You'll get through this. You're stronger than you know."

Isabella buried her face in Claire's shoulder and shook her head. "He said he can't have the scandal that my testifying against Cooke would evoke." A heartrending wail escaped her, followed by several choking sobs.

"But if you don't testify, how will you ever be safe from Cooke's attempts on your life?"

"Jay assures me that he's spoken with him and that Cooke will leave me in peace. Jay hired someone to make certain he doesn't come after me again."

"And you believe him?"

Isabella nodded. "I take him at his word."

"Well, then, consider it a gift."

Isabella lifted her head and frowned at Claire. "A gift?"

"Now you're free to pursue whatever life you can imagine."

With another sob, Isabella returned her head to its original position on Claire's shoulder. "But I don't want to be free," she wailed. "I want to be his mistress."

Claire rolled her eyes, glad of her own freedom from the tyranny of men like Jay Gould. "Didn't you say you had money put aside?" At the actress's nod, Claire forged on. "Then what's the downside? Now you can openly pursue Behan without fear of it getting back to Gould."

Isabella's sobs quieted, and she raised her head once more. Searching Claire's eyes, she said, "But what about that woman?"

'That woman' was Josephine Marcus, the angry beauty who had objected to Johnny Behan's flirtations with Isabella that day at the hotel. Apparently, Behan had promised marriage, and Josie wasn't about to allow another woman, another *actress*, to stop her from achieving the respectability she obviously craved.

"You're more than capable of winning his affections, I'm certain of it. But you may want to cast your net wider. There are plenty of rich, single men in Tombstone, as well as San Francisco, who would be more than happy to engage your attentions."

Isabella's tears slowed to a trickle and she grew silent, apparently thinking about what Claire had said. Then she nodded and stepped back, a resolute expression on her face.

"You're right," she said, squaring her shoulders. "Jay Gould isn't the only fish in the sea." Then, as though she'd just noticed, she exclaimed, "You're wearing your traveling clothes. Are you leaving?"

Claire looked down at her outfit of dungarees, long-sleeve button-down shirt, and Western boots, complete with Cuban heels and spurs. "I've got an interview later today for a job with Kinnear and Company."

"The stage line? What position?"

"Shotgun messenger," Claire said, still amazed at the opportunity. After the shooting, Doc Holliday had talked her up to the station agent and recommended Claire for the position, suggesting she take over as shotgun messenger when Morgan Earp, Wyatt's younger brother, was engaged on another route. Claire was excited, but nervous at the prospect of proving herself to the owner, J. D. Kinnear.

"That's wonderful," Isabella exclaimed. "You'll be perfect for the job. How I envy you and your ability to live life however you please."

"What's stopping you from doing the same?"

She gave Claire a resigned look and said, "I care too much what people think."

Claire laughed. "Which is why you chose to become a married man's mistress and an actress?"

Isabella giggled. "When you put it that way, it doesn't seem like I do. Still, I have no desire to be uncomfortable, which your job will undoubtedly be. Thankfully, the troupe and I will only have to endure the stage to Benson. After that, we'll take a train to the coast and then have our choice of train or steamship to San Francisco." She smiled and hugged Claire. "Oh, how I'll miss you." She broke free. "I consider us great friends, and I hope that we'll stay that way."

"I feel the same." Even though Claire didn't partake in the endless parties and flirtations of Isabella and her friends, she was still going to miss them. They'd added a lively dimension to her life, to say the least.

"Take care, friend." Isabella started for the door.

"One suggestion?"

The actress turned. "Yes?"

"Fire Agnes." Although Claire didn't have proof, she was certain the maid had a hand in Worthington's scheme. "The woman is bad news."

Isabella smiled. "I've already foisted her off on Mr. Gould."

She studied her fingernails. "I told him that since I was no longer receiving a stipend, I was unable to keep her on. I convinced him that it would look unseemly if he left the poor girl, his mistress's maid, alone in a rough mining camp. Especially if someone were to offer a salacious narrative to the press regarding such." Isabella gave Claire a mischievous grin.

Claire laughed and shook her head. "Isabella, you are a scandal. I think you'll do just fine. I expect to be regularly informed of your escapades."

"Of course. We're best friends, aren't we? Best friends keep in touch." Isabella kissed Claire on both cheeks and left.

Claire put on her hat and gun belt and grabbed her oilskin coat, then walked out the door on her way to meet Doc.

He was waiting outside the Occidental Saloon and smiled when he saw her. As she drew closer, she was struck by the sparkle in his clear blue eyes. Consumption was a fickle and demanding mistress, with the illness ravaging the lungs of even the heartiest of patients. Often, Doc didn't have enough energy to climb out of bed until late afternoon, especially if he'd been drinking hard the night before. Obviously, today was a good day.

"Good morning, Doc," Claire said in a cheerful voice.

"Good morning to you, my dear." He stepped back, revealing her rifle leaning against the wall.

Claire's heart skipped a beat as she recognized her invention attached to the lever. She widened her eyes at Doc. "How does it shoot?"

"That's the burning question, isn't it?" he asked with a drawl, handing her the gun. "We'll try it out after your meeting with Mr. Kinnear."

Claire and Doc rode to the horse racing track where Claire was to prove herself for the job. Due to recommendations by Doc, Wyatt Earp, and Bud Philpot, J. D. Kinnear had agreed to give Claire a chance—although he was leery of hiring a woman for such a dangerous position.

An empty stage with a team of four bays was standing ready on the track. Bud Philpot was there, standing with a group of three other men, one of whom turned out to be Wyatt. Doc and Claire walked over to the group.

"Gentlemen, may I introduce Claire Whitcomb, the woman about whom you've heard glowing reviews from many of those in attendance. Claire, may I present Mr. J. D. Kinnear." Doc nodded at an older gentleman with a worn but friendly face. "The man next to Mr. Kinnear is Mr. Marshall Williams, the station agent for Wells Fargo."

Claire's nervousness skyrocketed at the prospect of trying out in front of the owner of the stage line *and* a Wells Fargo representative. *All I need now is to be introduced to the president of the United States.*

"You already know Bud and Wyatt."

"Gentlemen." She swallowed her anxiety and shook hands all around.

Kinnear turned to Claire. "I'm sure you understand my reticence in placing a member of the fairer sex in a position of such danger, but you come highly recommended." He nodded at Wyatt and Bud. "I assure you, Mrs. Whitcomb, I will judge you solely on your ability to defend my stage."

"Thank you, Mr. Kinnear. I appreciate your fairness." *The West truly was the new frontier,* Claire marveled. A woman applying for such a position back east would have been laughed out of the stage office.

"I've asked Bud to be your driver." Kinnear pointed to several objects placed at various intervals around the track. "I want to see how well you shoot while under pressure on a moving stage." He glanced at the Peacemaker in her holster. "How proficient are you with a rifle?"

"I prefer a rifle over a pistol, although I'm proficient with both."

Kinnear smiled broadly. "I admire your confidence, Claire.

Feel free to use any and all weapons you are comfortable with." He rubbed his hands together. "Shall we commence?"

Claire and Bud walked over to the empty stage. Doc followed, giving her some last-minute pointers. Before she climbed up onto the box, Doc handed her the Winchester.

She shook her head. "I can't use this. I don't know if it works yet."

Doc gave her a sheepish smile. "I must confess, and please don't be angry with me, but I already put it through its paces." He shrugged. "The temptation was too great."

Claire couldn't help but smile at him. "And? How did it perform?"

"It's a marvel, Claire. You should be proud." He took a step back and added, "Now, do *us* proud."

Claire climbed up to her seat beside Bud and placed her rifle across her lap. Then she adjusted her holster so that she had easy access. She took a deep breath and let it go.

Bud grabbed the reins and looked at her. "Ready?"

She nodded. "Ready."

Bud Philpot slapped the reins and yelled, "He-yaw." The horses raced forward, unencumbered by a heavy load. Claire kept her seat by riding the sway of the coach, alternately bracing her feet against the floorboards and shifting her weight.

The first target was at the straightaway and proved to be an easy mark. Using the rifle, she drilled the wood stand at its center, knocking it backward. The stage gathered speed and rounded the first corner. The second and third targets were placed next to each other on the turn, and she engaged the rifle's new mechanism. She fired once and levered the next cartridge into the chamber while shifting her aim to the second target. As she pulled the lever home, the mechanism depressed the trigger and the rifle fired instantly, hitting the next target square in the middle and proving her theory correct.

Claire's heart sang as she prepared for the next target—a

crudely built whirligig that Marshall Williams had set to spinning. She rose to a crouch and braced herself as the Wells Fargo agent removed himself from the line of fire.

You can do this, Claire. Concentrate.

She squeezed off a shot and there was a loud *ping!* as the round hit and sent the thing spinning even faster. But Claire wasn't through. Keeping her eye on the target as they passed, she levered another round into the rifle and fired another immediate shot.

The stage had already cleared the target, so the bullet hit from the opposite side and set it spinning the other way. Elated, Claire turned back to set her sights on the next objective, which was a man-sized dummy on a child's wagon. As she homed in on the target she was surprised to see it move. A quick glance at the handle showed a rope tied off with Williams pulling from several yards away. She sighted on the moving target as she seated the next round, and shot the dummy through the head.

At that moment, the wheel hit something and the stage rocked to the side, throwing both Bud and Claire up off the box. Bud landed in his seat, the ribbons still in his hands, but Claire lost her footing and felt herself fall.

Gripping the Winchester, she grabbed for the stage with her other hand as she dangled off the side, and barely latched on to the railing that surrounded the rooftop.

"Whoa," Bud called, but the horses kept running.

Holding on with one hand, Claire strained to pull a knee up on the open window ledge. She tossed her rifle on the seat inside the stage and pulled her pistol free. The stage had just driven past the next and last target—a whiskey barrel with a stack of crabapples on top.

Claire took a bead on the top apple and fired the pistol. The target exploded, with pieces of fruit flying every which way.

Bud finally managed to slow the horses and the stage rolled to a stop. Claire slid the pistol back into her holster, grabbed her rifle, and climbed down. Blood pounded in her ears from the excitement of almost falling off a moving stage, and her knees went weak. She braced herself against the stage as she worked to still her hammering heart.

Bud came running around the side of the stage, worry obvious on his face. When he saw that she was all right, he stopped and closed his eyes in relief. "I thought you were a goner," he blurted.

Still shaky, Claire laughed. "I hit the apples, right?"

Bud shook his head, clearly amazed. "You plumb demolished 'em, Claire."

Wyatt got to the stage first, out of breath from running. He leaned over and put his hands on his knees. "Damnation, Claire. You gave us a fright. We couldn't see what happened after you fell off the box from all the damn dust."

Doc came after him, walking as fast as he could manage.

Alarmed at his heavy wheezing and deathly white face, Claire raced to meet him. "Doc, I'm all right." Coughing uncontrollably, he nodded and waved her away, fumbling for his handkerchief.

J.D. Kinnear was the last to join them, huffing and puffing from the effort. He held out his hand and said, "That was some fine shooting, Mrs. Whitcomb. I'd be proud to have you on the payroll. Welcome to Kinnear and Company."

ACKNOWLEDGMENTS

Writing a book is often a team effort: research rabbit holes often lead to helpful experts, not to mention the valuable feedback from early readers, editors, and long-suffering partners/spouses. *Gunslinger* is no exception. Huge thanks to my partner, Mark, whose culinary and listening/brainstorming skills are second to none; to editors Ruth Ross and Laurie Boris, whose attention to detail make these books so much better than the original draft; to early readers and writing partners Ali, Jenni, and Michelle—the trust we've built up over so many years and manuscripts is a gift for which I'm eternally grateful; to early reader Charles Ray; to Ryan Ehrfurth, Arizona State Library Archives & Public Records for pointing me in the right direction and for links to information I didn't know I needed; to George F. Shaw, AT&SFRyCo Collection Archivist, Arizona State Railroad Museum Foundation, for the fantastic spreadsheet and meticulously researched information on where and how my characters would travel in the 1880s; to Jim Van Houghten for his insight into weapons and gear of the times; to K.C. Curtis for her insights on the terrain near Tombstone; and of course to the ARTeam-you guys seriously rock.

Doc Holliday was indeed in Tombstone in the fall of 1880, having recently arrived at the urging of his good friend, Wyatt Earp. The description of the town (and of Doc and Wyatt and some of the other characters) is based on extensive research, much of it available online (although there are several conflicting reports regarding such—I used the most respected sources I could find). Isabella King, though fictional, is an amalgamation of various actresses who performed in the Old West. Her paramour, Jay Gould, was one of the infamous railroad "Robber Barons" of the 19th century. Johnny Behan and Josephine Marcus were also historical figures involved in one way or another in Tombstone lore. Claire's modification of the Winchester rifle is fictional, but certainly possible. Several gunfighters in that time modified their weapons (as gun owners do today), often improving their range and/or efficacy. Even so, I was unable to locate the exact mechanism I described in the book, so fabricated what I needed. I've been assured it would work as advertised.

Writing is never a solitary endeavor.

A CLAIRE WHITCOMB WESTERN BOOK 3
LEGEND
DV BERKOM

LEGEND

DV BERKOM

For all the legends in my life.

CHAPTER 1

March 1881- Tombstone, Arizona Territory

Claire Whitcomb glanced out the window of her room at Fly's Boarding House as she prepared to leave. Day and night, seven days a week, Tombstone teemed with wagons and miners and townspeople. Business and commerce waited for no one, as evidenced by the ever-present thud of the stamp mills. Even the vacant lot next to the boarding house was abuzz with wagons pulling into and out of the nearby O.K. Corral.

At the urging of Mollie Fly and Doc Holliday, Claire moved her belongings from the Grand Hotel to the less expensive Fly's Boarding House on Fremont Street. Claire decided she didn't need the deluxe accommodations, now that her contract as bodyguard to the actress Isabella King had expired. Fly's suited her and kept her in close contact with her good friend and mentor, Doc.

Claire checked the amount of ammunition she had before donning her gun belt and viewing herself in the full-length mirror. Her long brown hair, high cheekbones, and deep green eyes contrasted with the masculine attire. In addition to her oilcloth duster, she wore a favorite pair of dungarees with the leather gun belt, a long-sleeved shirt, and leather boots to ward against the chilly March morning. She and Doc had plans to ride into the desert to see if they could scare up some quail for dinner.

Winter in the desert hadn't been the picnic her friend Mart Duggan assured her it would be. Even so, the cold wind whistling through the dirt streets and light dusting of snow Tombstone had experienced in recent days wasn't as bad as winters in the mountains of Colorado.

Still, she would have liked a bit warmer temperatures while serving as shotgun messenger for the J. D. Kinnear and Company stage. Thankfully, she didn't have to go on that evening's trip to Benson. She let the newly-elected Pima County sheriff, Bob Paul, take her shift while his case for election fraud made its way through the courts.

With one last look, Claire grabbed her wide-brimmed hat, slid her six-shooter into her holster, and opened the door.

A fist came at her from out of nowhere and Claire ducked. Unable to connect, the woman outside her door muttered a curse and tried again. Claire dodged the second blow and slammed her fist into her assailant's jaw. The woman staggered back, momentarily stunned. Claire rushed her, knocking them both to the floor with a resounding *thud*. The attacker flailed, attempting to strike Claire, but Claire managed to grab her wrists and hold her still.

"What in blazes are you trying to do, kill me?" Claire gasped, working to keep her aggressor immobile.

"Get off," the other woman cried as she tried to squirm out from under her. The brunette's accent was one Claire hadn't heard before—like a cross between German and some other exotic locale.

"I will if you stop trying to hit me."

The woman narrowed her eyes and tried to wrest her hands free. Claire tightened her grip, determined to hold her still. When she realized Claire had the upper hand she sighed and went limp. Wary, Claire eased up on the pressure. Like a fish wriggling off the hook the woman resumed her attack. Claire corralled her wrists again.

"Get. Off. Me." Tears of frustration coursed down her attacker's cheeks as she struggled to break free.

"Hush," Claire said, in a vain attempt to quiet her. "I have no idea why you're so all fired mad at me. I don't even know you, for Pete's sake. Recite the charges and I'll set you straight."

That pissed off the would-be assailant even more and she renewed her struggle. "I can't do it anymore," she wailed. "Not only do I have to contend with Wyatt stealing his affections, but now you!"

"What? Who?" Bewildered, Claire stared at her. The only Wyatt she knew in Tombstone was Wyatt Earp—but he was a married man, and she was talking about...

The woman squeezed her eyes shut and started to sob.

Claire determined her foe wouldn't be much of a threat crying so hard, so she eased off and climbed to her feet, pulling her pistol free just in case. The woman struggled to a sitting position.

"What are you going on about?" Claire asked. Tears coursed down the woman's cheeks. "Oh, for heaven's sake." Claire reached in her pocket for a handkerchief and handed it to her.

The woman accepted and blew her nose. Loudly. When she offered the kerchief back, Claire shook her head.

"Keep it." Claire helped her to her feet and quickly put distance between them in case she tried to hit her again. "Seems only fitting that I know the name of my attacker."

The woman sniffed and held her head high. "Mrs. John H. Holliday."

Claire widened her eyes in shock. "Holliday? Doc's wife?" The woman nodded. Claire's spirits plunged at her confirmation. "He never told me he was married."

Mrs. Holliday scoffed. "He wouldn't." She dabbed at her eyes.

"Why accost me? Surprising someone at their door isn't very sporting."

The sound of someone hurrying down the hallway toward them heralded the appearance of a red-faced Mollie Fly, huffing from the effort. "What in tarnation's going on?" She paused to catch her breath before adding, "Sounded like a herd of buffalo dancing the tango."

Claire waved at the other woman. "This gal just tried to buffalo me so I can certainly see your point."

Mollie Fly looked from one to the other, giving Doc's wife a disapproving scowl. "So you've met the so-called 'Mrs. Holliday,' have you?" She crossed her arms and narrowed her eyes. "Can't say I ever thought of Doc as the marrying kind."

"Mr. Holliday and I have been together for many years." Mrs. Holliday sucked in a ragged breath. All the fight appeared to have left her. "I'm quite aware of his proclivities."

"I've known him since last fall," Claire said, "and he's never so much as mentioned you."

The wounded look on her face gave Claire pause. She glanced at Mollie, who shrugged.

"I run a boarding house in the town of Globe," Mrs. Holliday explained. "I have traveled to Tombstone several times." She nodded at the door to Doc's room. "I stay with him when I am here." She gave Claire an appraising look. "You don't seem his type."

"His—wait a minute. We're not—" Claire scrambled to refute the implication. But in a sense, Doc's wife was right—they were —or at least they had been. Once. During the Christmas holidays, they'd both been quite drunk and Claire had thrown caution to the wind. For whatever reason the relationship became awkward, and they both agreed to remain friends instead of lovers. Claire's cheeks grew warm with shame. *You didn't know he had a wife, Claire.* A flicker of anger shoved away her embarrassment. Good thing Doc wasn't there—especially since she was wearing a gun.

Mrs. Holliday studied her. "It's obvious he never told you of me. I am inclined to let bygones be bygones." She squared her shoulders, all trace of tears gone. "Now, if you would be so kind as to tell me where he is?"

"Have you tried the Alhambra?" Claire wasn't about to let Doc's wife get to him first. She preferred to talk to him before he could formulate some kind of story to cover his lies. "I'm Claire Whitcomb." She held out her hand.

Mrs. Holliday clasped hers with a firm grip. "Kate Holliday, neé Elder."

"You're Big Nose Kate?" Claire exclaimed. Mollie chuckled. Wyatt had mentioned a Kate Elder by the derogatory nickname on a couple of occasions, citing Kate's meddlesome ways. But he'd never so much as hinted that Doc was married to her. Neither had Doc.

Kate grimaced. "I see you have spent time in the unpleasant company of Wyatt Earp."

"Hold on a minute there," Mollie warned. "I'll thank you to keep whatever problem you have with the Earps to yourself. Their family's been nothing but helpful to my husband and me."

"Wyatt Earp is the devil." Kate spat and glared at Mollie.

Claire shook her head in bewilderment. "I can't imagine why you'd have it in for Wyatt, but I've got errands to run." She put on her hat and nodded to both women as she passed, glad she didn't have to stay and explain herself further to Doc's wife. "We're fine here, right?" She looked pointedly at Kate.

"Yes. We're fine." Doc's wife nodded.

"Good." Claire continued down the steps, determined to find Doc and give him hell.

Claire picked up the dead quail and stuffed it into the bag with the others. She and Doc had shot enough of the birds for a good-sized dinner that evening. She hadn't brought up Kate's appearance yet, waiting for the right time to broach the subject. Doc had an unpredictable temper and could fly into a rage at the smallest provocation. True, he had reason to be angry —suffering from consumption, especially at his age, would cause anyone to be ornery—but that didn't make confronting him any easier. Claire took solace in the small mercy that he didn't appear to be drunk and was low on ammunition. Besides, her anger had cooled and she was in a more charitable mood.

Doc waited on his rented horse as she climbed back into her saddle. Her horse, Rose, didn't appear to mind the arid terrain and had proved a champion when it came to packing through the desert. Even through the extremes in temperatures she'd been a calm and steadfast companion. Claire gave the chestnut mare a loving pat on the neck. They'd been through a lot together.

"Miss Claire, I do believe something's weighing on your mind," Doc remarked as they rode back to town.

Claire nodded. "There is. And I'm of a mind to tell you, but I am wary of getting into a row."

"Say your piece, madam. I'm happy as a lark out here with you in the vast, dry spaces. I don't wish to argue—with you or anyone."

"All right." Claire reined in Rose, and Doc did the same with his horse. "I met Big Nose Kate this morning."

Doc didn't seem surprised. "She's in town?"

Claire could have sworn his eye twitched, although it could have been a trick of the light. "She ambushed me this morning at Fly's." She decided not to mention Kate's attempts to strike her— it would just stir up trouble.

Doc sighed and closed his eyes. "I'm sorry not to have told you about her."

"You certainly should be. If I'd have known you were married I never would have..." Claire choked back a flash of anger. "What transpired between us would have never happened."

"She said we were married?" He scowled as he answered his own question. "Of course she did." He looked at Claire, holding her gaze. "I profess to you most earnestly we are not now, nor have we ever been, formally joined in matrimony."

"But she said—"

"I know what she *said* but I can promise you that we have never officially married, in the eyes of God or society at large."

"Then why tell me she had?"

"My dear, what's to stop her? Her establishing ownership is the move of a desperate woman."

"Desperate?"

Doc nodded. "She's been trying to lure me from Tombstone since I arrived. For obvious reasons I have resisted her efforts."

"If she's so desperate, why not live here with you?"

He gazed into the distance. "She hates Wyatt and refuses to live anywhere near him. Believes he's a bad influence." Doc's laughter transformed into a coughing fit, wracking his failing body.

"You have feelings for her."

Doc pulled his handkerchief free as he regained his composure. "She's a familiar kind of devil. We're not what I'd call two peas in a pod. I'd liken us to two scorpions in a coffee can—we will most likely end up stinging each other to death." He wiped his mouth, then folded and put the handkerchief away. "Please believe me, Claire. I never meant to hurt you."

He appeared contrite. Claire studied him for a moment before she said, "I accept your apology. Now, what do you say we go back to town and deliver the birds to your friend, Nellie, before this blasted cold weather freezes them solid?"

They continued toward town in silence, each with their own thoughts. Claire's anger had cooled again. It was difficult to stay mad at Doc, and not only because of his frail health. He was a curious mixture of erudition and scoundrel; a man to whom guns and gambling were like air or water, yet he was possessed of a devastating southern charm and good manners. Yes, he had a bad temper—she'd seen it more than once, although never directed at her—but his sarcasm and anger hid a deeper, unfortunate reality; that of a man sentenced to a lingering, painful death through no fault of his own.

They returned to Tombstone and Doc took the birds to Nellie Cashman's restaurant, while Claire returned to her room. Doc's door was partially open so she tiptoed past, not wanting to alert Big Nose Kate to her presence.

Once inside her room she shucked off her boots, clothes, and gun belt, and rinsed the grit of the desert from her face and body at the wash basin in the corner. Finished, she sat on the bed and leaned against the headboard.

She truly liked Doc, possibly even loved him in a friendly kind of way, and didn't want to see him embroiled in an unhappy relationship. But he was his own man and capable of dealing with his own life. Kate Elder wasn't Claire's problem, she was Doc's. Whatever happened, Claire vowed to stay out of things. Keeping Doc out of trouble would be a full-time job—and futile, if she was any judge. Riding shotgun on the stages a few times a week kept Claire busy enough.

Claire sighed and closed her eyes, intending to take a short nap before dinner. The warmth of the room and the pounding of the stamp mills lulled her to sleep.

She jolted awake at the sound of a woman screaming across the hall.

"You are ruining your life, John." Kate's heavily accented voice reverberated through the walls of the boarding house. "This place is not good for you. You must come back with me to Globe."

"Be still, woman," Doc roared. The sound of glass breaking punctuated his words.

Pulling on her robe, Claire walked to the door and cracked it open. Mollie Fly stood motionless in the hallway listening to the row. Another loud crash emanated from behind Doc's closed door and Mollie rolled her eyes and shook her head. Claire slipped out of her room and joined her. The fight continued its stormy intensity, both Doc and Kate hurling epithets at each other like bullets from a pistol. Claire winced at the sound of something large hitting the floor.

"Are they always like this?" she asked Mollie.

Mollie pursed her lips in disapproval. "Some people thrive on contentiousness. I daresay Kate Elder is such a person."

"She and Doc are a combustible combination."

"They certainly are." Mollie gave Claire a sideways glance. "How are you holding up?"

"What do you mean?"

"I know how close you and he are."

The shame of someone knowing her private business

warmed Claire's cheeks. "We're…not that close," was all she could manage.

"If you say so."

To her relief, Mollie changed the subject.

"I swear, every time those two are together something gets broken." Mollie paused as another loud crash reverberated from inside the room. "At least he always settles up. Although getting hold of replacements is a bear."

Claire grew tired of listening to Doc and Kate scream at each other so she returned to her room where she changed into a blue serge dress. Her stomach growled, and she was looking forward to having dinner at Russ House, the restaurant of Doc's friend, Nellie. She'd assumed that she and Doc would sup together, but that appeared not to be the case this evening.

She concealed a small Smith & Wesson .38 double-action revolver in her specially made skirt pocket, picked up her reticule, and checked herself once more in the mirror before opening the door. The empty hallway told Claire that Mollie Fly had grown weary of the dramatics coming from Doc's room as well. Claire stepped into the hall as the door to Doc's room flew open and Kate Elder ran out. Tears streamed down her cheeks, and a smear of blood stained her lower lip.

"Kate—are you all right?" Claire made a move toward the distressed woman.

With a deep sob she shook her head as she ran past. The front door to the boarding house opened and slammed closed, signifying Kate's departure.

Claire glanced in the partially open door to Doc's room, unsure how to respond. Doc stood next to the bed rubbing his knuckles, a storm of emotions pulsing across his face. He looked up and their eyes met. The china blue of his irises had darkened to the shade of the Atlantic in winter. With a weary expression he closed the door.

CHAPTER 3

That same evening Claire went to Russ House for the quail she and Doc shot earlier in the day. Doc had raved about Nellie's culinary skills and Claire was looking forward to the meal. She'd just been seated at a table next to a window when Doc entered through the front door and searched the crowd. He smiled when he saw her and made his way to the table. As did most of the professional gamblers in Tombstone, he wore his six-shooter openly in case of an altercation, many of which arose without warning.

"May I?" he asked, indicating the chair across from her.

"Of course."

Doc sat down and waved at one of the waiters for a drink. By the look of him he'd already had a few. He smiled at Claire and said, "I hoped you'd be here."

"Judging by the fervor of your testament to Nellie's culinary abilities I dare not miss the chance."

The waiter brought over a bottle of Old Overholt rye whiskey, a bottle of red wine, and three glasses—a shot glass and two wineglasses.

Apparently, Doc had decided to celebrate.

"Where's Kate?" Claire asked. She'd been shocked to discover Doc would hit a woman even though he and Kate had been hurling insults at each other. For Claire, hitting a woman, any woman, revealed a man's lesser nature and offered disturbing insight into his character. She'd been acquainted with violent men in the past, many of whom kept secret their baser instincts.

She'd just never expected Doc to be one of them.

Doc drained his whiskey and poured himself another. "I haven't had the pleasure of seeing her since this afternoon at Fly's."

Claire studied him. "Is this a normal occurrence between you?"

"Fighting? Yes." He threw back his drink and set the glass on the table. He didn't move to pour another.

"I was referring to the outcome of the fight."

Doc poured another drink while Claire sipped her wine. "I have only ever hit a woman twice in my lifetime. You witnessed the second and last occurrence." This time he sipped at the rye. "I don't plan to do so ever again."

Claire didn't press him on who the first victim might have been. "I should hope you don't."

With an earnest expression Doc leaned across the table and took her hand in his. "I promise I will never raise a hand to you, lovely Claire."

"I would likely shoot you if you did."

Doc grinned as he released her hand and relaxed back in his chair. "And thus you reveal what it is that I love about you." He raised his glass. "To Claire Whitcomb—the finest, most accurate lady with a gun I've ever had the pleasure to meet—and would never, ever cross."

Claire smiled, glad to have broken the tension that had pervaded their time together. The waiter appeared with their first course, and the rest of the meal soon followed. The quail was indeed some of the best she'd ever eaten.

They'd just finished their dessert when one of the other diners, a rough-looking man with reddish brown hair, banged his hand on the table and, in a loud voice, complained about his meal.

Nellie Cashman had been making the rounds ensuring her customer's satisfaction and froze at his words. Before she could make her way to the table to find out what was wrong, Doc stood up, drew his gun, and aimed at the man who'd complained.

"Would you care to repeat that?" he drawled, his voice low and deadly calm.

A hush fell over the restaurant as if the diners had taken a collective breath. Nellie's wary expression spoke of experience with Doc's moods as she looked anxiously from Doc to the diner who'd complained. The diner's face reddened and he looked down at his meal, grumbling something Claire couldn't make out.

Doc walked over to his table and stood across from him, an icy smile frozen on his lips. The man's dinner companions scooted their chairs away from their friend in an attempt to distance themselves. "I said, would you care to repeat that?"

The man muttered something. Doc leaned closer. "Could you say that a bit louder? I don't think your companions heard you."

The man raised his head, a contrite look on his face. "It's the best I ever ate."

Doc smiled as he uncocked his revolver and slid it back in his holster. "I thought that's what you said." He returned to the table and poured himself another drink. A collective sigh of relief filtered through the restaurant as everyone resumed their meals, acting as though nothing had happened.

"Remind me to never complain about my food." Claire shook her head in amazement. Doc's sense of loyalty to his friends, though mostly commendable, revealed a devil-may-care attitude that was likely a direct result of his impending demise. On more than one occasion he'd remarked on his indifference to danger, citing his utter lack of fear once he'd learned his prognosis.

"Every day is a gift, Claire," he'd often said. "Let that knowledge guide you through life and you can't go far wrong."

After dinner Doc left for a poker game in nearby Charleston, while Claire went to the Occidental Saloon where she enjoyed the company of gunslingers Luke Short, Wyatt Earp, and newfound friend, Bat Masterson. Later in the evening they gathered around a faro table to watch Wyatt deal and hopefully win money. Wyatt's older brother, Virgil, strode into the saloon, looking tense. A chill skittered through the room.

"The Benson stage's been robbed," he told Wyatt, his expression fierce.

"What happened?" Wyatt asked, handing the cards to another dealer as he slid his chair back.

"Arthur Cowen just rode in from Contention City with the news. Bob Paul drove the stage to Benson with the Wells Fargo treasure box. Reports are that three men attempted to hold up the stage outside of Drew's Station." Virgil's gaze flickered to Claire and then returned to Wyatt. In a low voice he added, "Philpot's dead."

Shock pooled in Claire's gut. "Bud's dead?" she repeated, disbelief sliding through her. Tears pricked at her eyes. She'd often worked shotgun when Bud Philpot drove—he was well known by everyone in town and well liked, too. He was the first resident of Tombstone she'd met when she arrived, and he'd been kind and immensely helpful. "I just spoke to him yesterday. I was supposed to ride with him tomorrow." The stage company's owner, J. D. Kinnear, didn't often schedule her on night runs, citing the danger. Now she wondered if it would have made a difference if she'd been there.

"Behan and I are rounding up a posse," Virgil declared.

"I'm in," Luke said.

"Me, too," offered Masterson.

"You know I am." Wyatt reached for his coat. "Where's Morgan?"

"Getting the horses."

"I'd like to go." Claire stood with the rest of the men. It would be a long, cold ride, but she was more than ready to saddle up. She wanted to be there when the posse arrested the curs. "Bud was a good friend."

Virgil took her aside. "I know how you feel about Bud, Claire, but I need you to stay here to let Doc know what's going on."

"Come on, Virgil. The news will be through town before you can say 'bandit.' He'll find out soon enough."

"Be that as it may I'd feel a whole lot better if you stayed here in Tombstone. Depending on how much of a head start the outlaws have we may not be back for days. A posse is no place for a woman, even one with your abilities."

"But—"

Virgil gave her a stern look. "I'm sorry, Claire. But I can't deputize you like I can the others."

"I don't care about the pay, Virgil. I just want to see justice for Bud."

Virgil sighed and shook his head. "Behan'll fight it and that's going to waste time."

As county sheriff, Johnny Behan would lead the posse. Since the attempted crime involved a stage carrying the US mail, as a federal marshal Virgil would be required to go too.

Virgil put his hand on her shoulder. "We all want justice for Bud, Claire. Stay here. He'd want you to be safe, not risk your life looking for his killers."

Claire swallowed her anger. Once again her frustration at being viewed as nothing more than a defenseless woman in the eyes of the law threatened to boil over. It wasn't fair, especially when she could shoot as well or better than any of the men joining the posse that night.

She took a deep breath to calm herself and nodded. "I understand, Virgil. Good luck. Find the bastards and bring them to justice."

The posse, led by Johnny Behan and Virgil, galloped out of town headed for Drew's Station. Claire tamped down the yearning to join them and ordered another drink. The only subject on everyone's mind that evening was the botched Benson stage robbery and the murder of Bud Philpot and a passenger, Peter Roerig.

Sometime after midnight Claire left the Occidental to go back to Fly's when she noticed Doc riding down Allen Street. She walked out to greet him, and he reined in his horse.

"Miss Claire." He tipped his hat in greeting. "What brings you out at this ungodly hour?"

His horse snorted, creating a puff of white mist in the cool air, and pawed the ground, its flanks gleaming with sweat. Claire rubbed its nose and said, "Looks like you put your horse through its paces. Did you have any luck tonight?"

Doc shook his head. "Alas, I was too late—the game had ended by the time I arrived." He shrugged. "At least it was cold enough to freeze the balls off a brass monkey—made for a most enjoyable ride." He nodded toward the Occidental. "Is the erstwhile Wyatt at large?"

Claire shook her head. "He and Virgil joined Johnny Behan's posse. Someone tried to rob the Benson stage tonight." She teared up at the freshness of Bud's murder. "Bud Philpot was killed."

The shock on Doc Holliday's face told Claire he hadn't heard.

"There's news that a passenger named Peter Roerig died, too," she added.

"My God. A double murder *and* an attempted robbery? Do they know the infidels who did this?"

She shook her head. "There's been no word. They lit out of here a few hours ago, headed for Drew's Station where it happened."

"Ah. Then I won't join in the hunt unless they send word." A coughing fit wracked his body, and he pulled his coat tighter. "I am worn down from the ride and the cold, as is my steed."

"Shall I accompany you back to Fly's?" Claire asked.

"I think I will head over to the Alhambra for a while. Try to recoup my losses from missing the poker game." He touched the brim of his hat. "Ma'am."

"Have a good night, Doc. Don't overtax yourself." Claire stepped away, and he started for the Alhambra. She watched his receding figure for a long moment, the urge to envelop him in safety and nurse him to health overwhelming. She reminded herself that he was a grown man who would live as he deemed his right. Doc Holliday was not her concern.

Especially now that Kate was in town.

Six days later, Kate Elder went back to Globe without Doc, and Johnny Behan and Wells Fargo agent Marshall Williams returned to Tombstone with one of the fugitives—a man named Luther King.

After King had been secured at the jail Claire sought out Williams and took him aside.

"Luther didn't do it alone," she said. "Bob Paul swore there were at least three outlaws."

"You're right about that," Williams answered.

"Did he say anything about who might have helped?"

Williams's lips quirked up in a grim smile. "When Wyatt got hold of him—well, let's just say Mr. King implicated his cowboy friends right quick."

"And?" Claire prompted. The cowboys were a loosely affiliated gang of cattle rustlers and ranchers known for questionable behavior. Mostly, the good citizens of Tombstone turned a blind eye to their antics since they brought plenty of business to town.

"He says he only held the reins while the other three did the shootin'." He snorted. "Likely story."

"Who were the others?"

"Billy Leonard, Jim Crane, and Harry Head."

"How'd you know where to find him?"

"They were hard to track, I'll tell you that. At first they headed into the Dragoons, riding single file over rocky terrain so's they wouldn't leave tracks. But then they made the mistake of circling back this way. We found King milkin' a cow at Redfield's ranch with his goldarned gun belt on. Had his rifle nearby too."

Claire shook her head. Who milked their cows armed? "What about the rest of them? Any leads on where they're going?"

"King says they're makin' for the boot heel out in New Mexico Territory."

"That's not good." The territory was known for its lawlessness and cowboy-friendly hideouts.

"The Earps are good trackers. They'll find them."

The yearning to be part of the posse came back with a force that Claire quickly tamped down. "I surely hope so."

~

MARCH 29, 1881

"HE'S GONE." Williams peeled off his hat and slumped into the seat across from Claire.

"Who?" Claire had just finished her plate of eggs and ham and was sipping a cup of strong coffee, having tried and failed to rouse Doc to join her at the hotel for breakfast. He'd had another late night and told her what she could do with her breakfast.

Williams sighed and gave her a serious look. "Luther King."

Claire almost dropped her cup. "He escaped from jail?"

He nodded. "Damned if Woods didn't forget to lock the cell

last night when he stepped out to do some business." Woods was Johnny Behan's new undersheriff and the man he'd left in charge of guarding the prisoner while Behan rejoined the Earps and the rest of the posse.

"Sounds like it was planned," Claire said. "You check to see if Woods been spending lots of money lately?"

Williams snorted. "Somebody had a horse waitin' for Luther out the back door." He gave a disgusted sigh. "I'll bet he's headed to warn his outlaw friends right now."

"The posse has a good head start. They'll find them first."

Williams got an uncomfortable look on his face. He shifted in his chair and said in a low voice, "Rumors been making the rounds that Doc had a hand in settin' him free."

Claire scoffed. "Why on earth would Doc want to help Luther King escape?"

"People think he had a hand in the Benson stage robbery and that King was gonna testify against him because Doc and Billy Leonard had dealins' when they was both in New Mexico."

"You know as well as I do Doc would sooner shoot a person who had something incriminating on him than let him go."

Williams leaned back in his chair. "You know it and I know it, but some folks around here don't take to Doc like you and me. They're putting all them rumors together and comin' up with what they think is the truth."

Claire dismissed the rumor as just that: a rumor. But the night of the robbery kept niggling at the back of her mind. The way Doc's horse looked like it had been ridden so hard. His story about arriving in Charleston after the poker game broke up, giving him a flimsy alibi around the time of the attempted robbery. And now the newest piece of the puzzle: Doc being known to work with Leonard.

Had he been involved? It seemed far-fetched, especially since none of the money in the strong box had been touched.

But it was hard to argue—twenty-six thousand dollars was a

lot of money. Had Doc joined forces with the outlaws, attempted a holdup, and failed? Bob Paul, the driver, would have recognized Doc if he'd been there, even if he'd been wearing a mask. Doc had a way about him that was hard to disguise. But she still wondered.

And hated herself for doing it.

Days later the posse straggled back to Tombstone looking tired and defeated. Since they hadn't located the other three outlaws believed to be loosely associated with the cowboys, another rumor started making the rounds. Not only had Doc Holliday been part of the attempted robbery and murders the night of March fifteenth, but the Earps were part of it, too—all to steal the money in the strongbox.

Claire had a good idea who started that rumor. Wyatt planned to run against Johnny Behan for county sheriff in the next election, with all the tax money that implied hanging in the balance. The hefty amount a sheriff could collect in a year's time was a major incentive, and Johnny Behan wasn't about to let anyone else, especially Wyatt Earp, win the coveted job. Especially since the town held Behan responsible for Luther King's escape. Not long afterward, to Behan's chagrin, two of the three remaining Benson stage robbers turned up dead, invalidating his attempt to capture the outlaws involved and regain his reputation as an effective lawman.

Even though the idea that Wyatt would be part of a plan to help the cowboys/outlaws when he was banking on getting rid of them was ludicrous, anti-cowboy sentiment ran deep in Tombstone and the rumor took hold.

~

THE HEAT SIZZLED that spring and summer, igniting the worst fire in Tombstone's short history when a barrel of whiskey exploded from the too-close proximity of a lit cigar. Tinder-dry from the excessive heat and lack of rain, over sixty businesses in four square blocks were destroyed in a matter of hours. Towns-people worked to douse the flames as best they could, but there was only so much to be done. Claire gave a hand to flatten build-ings and throw water on the rest, but the smoldering remains were a blaring testament to the lack of a proper fire engine. Iron-ically, the mayor of Tombstone was at that moment back east, in part on a quest to secure one.

Within hours of the fire lot jumpers showed up, attempting to take possession of the destroyed property. The uproar from the townspeople was immediate. Virgil Earp, having been designated acting chief of police after the original chief skipped town, and in addition to his federal status as marshal, convinced the jumpers to leave with the business end of his gun. A week later the ring of hammers and carpentry joined the pounding of the stamp mills as the townsfolk set to rebuilding Tombstone.

In appreciation, the city council made Virgil's position permanent.

By Independence Day several of the buildings destroyed in the fire had been partially rebuilt and plans for a subdued cele-bration had been set in motion. News of an attempt to assassi-nate President Garfield was one reason for the somberness of the occasion. Another being the money set aside for fireworks had gone toward purchasing the fire wagon.

Claire woke early, anticipating a day of celebration to coun-teract the grim resolve so prevalent in town. After looking out the window she decided to bring an umbrella. Dark clouds had gathered, threatening rain. She put on the blue serge dress and pinned on a dark blue hat with a short veil. Then she slipped her pistol into her secret pocket and with a quick look in the mirror opened the door and stepped into the hallway.

"Hello, Claire." Kate Elder stood next to Doc's door, fist raised as if to knock.

Claire flinched, her hand instinctively going for the gun in her skirt. "Kate." She nodded at the other woman.

"Have you seen Doc?" Kate asked.

"I didn't hear him come home last night, although he may have slipped in while I was asleep." The boarding house was such that most everything in one room could be heard in the others, making privacy almost nonexistent.

Kate gave her a tentative smile and took a step toward her. "I believe that we got off on the wrong foot the last time I was here. I would like to remedy that." She offered her hand.

Claire studied her for a moment, remembering that her old mentor, Thomas, had taught her to remain wary of adversaries but at the same time act charitable to throw them off. "That sounds good to me." Claire shook her hand and then stepped back to put distance between them.

Kate smiled and nodded. "Good. Doc always speaks well of you. I'm grateful for your…" She frowned as she struggled to find the word. "Your sympathy? Is that right?"

"Close enough. I'm very fond of Doc. It's no burden." Claire started for the stairs and stopped. She turned back and said, "Perhaps we'll see each other this evening during the festivities?"

The woman's relieved expression told Claire that Kate was most likely genuine in her attempt at reconciliation.

"That would be nice."

Claire continued down the stairs and into town, a weight lifted from her shoulders that she hadn't even known was there.

~

LATER IN THE day Claire made her way to the grandstand for a reading of the Declaration of Independence. Red, white, and blue bunting had been draped everywhere, giving the town a festive air. The citizens themselves were having a high time, drowning out much of what amounted to stump speeches by the local politicos with their animated laughter and hijinks. The Tombstone Brass Band was on hand, lending a truly patriotic theme to events.

She caught a glimpse of Doc but didn't see Kate, so she walked over to speak to him. He wore his gun belt, having requested and received a permit to carry a weapon in town. The new ordinance recently passed by the Citizens' Safety Committee was apparently intended to control only certain visitors to the town of Tombstone. Oddly enough not Doc, whose reputation would normally require oversight.

"You've seen Kate?" she asked.

Doc nodded. The nervous tic she'd noticed before was back. "Indeed I have. She's not feeling well this evening."

"I'm sorry to hear that. She attempted to make amends with me earlier today at the boarding house."

"You don't say. And, pray tell, what was your reaction?"

"I accepted. Peace in the valley, you know."

Doc snorted and shook his head.

"Would you mind some company?" Claire grinned at the gunslinger and batted her eyelashes in an attempt to make him laugh. It didn't work. "Is something wrong?" she asked.

"The scalawag cowboys are in town. Wyatt and his brothers are patrolling the streets as are some of Virgil's men, but we've been put on notice in advance of any possible hooliganism." He nodded toward a small group across the street that included Wyatt and Morgan. "If you'll excuse me for a moment, I'd like to see if there's any news."

Doc left Claire to talk with Wyatt and the others. The rain had begun in earnest so she allowed the merry tinkle of piano music to draw her into the Alhambra.

Inside, Johnny Behan and several of his deputies were crowded around a table. One of them moved aside, revealing Kate Elder sitting in their midst. Curious as to what they were talking about Claire edged closer but only caught snippets of their conversation.

"Will you swear to that?" Behan asked Kate. By the looks of things she'd been drinking heavily. Her bodice was askew and her normally impeccable hair had escaped its confines.

Kate nodded and replied, "Damn right I will."

Behan's expression resembled the cat that ate the canary as he poured her another shot, which she threw back with alacrity.

Was Kate looking to make Doc jealous? Sidling up to Behan or any of his friends would likely get the job done. The more Claire watched, the less that appeared to be the case—Behan didn't comport himself like a man who was interested in Kate. More like he was urging her on as he plied her with drinks.

Claire studied Kate. A bruise had formed next to her left eye, evidence of a possible altercation with Doc. So much for Doc promising to never hit a woman again.

Kate laughed raucously at something one of the deputies said. The other men nudged each other and smiled. Behan had a most determined expression on his face and didn't join in their laughter.

Something was off—and Claire had a feeling that whatever it was didn't bode well for Doc.

CHAPTER 6

July 6, 1881 – Tombstone, Arizona Territory

Claire saw them first.

Doc was dealing faro at the Alhambra when Johnny Behan and three of his deputies strode into the saloon and made a beeline to Doc's table. Claire gave him a nudge and nodded toward the group.

Doc watched them approach with interest. "Why, I believe they're coming for yours truly. What do you think?"

"I think you might just want to leave while you still can," Claire said drily. She'd told him about Kate meeting with Behan and his men on the Fourth of July but he'd laughed off her concerns.

"She's got a temper but she'd never do anything to harm me," he'd said, adding, "except perhaps hit me over the head with a paperweight." He'd winced as he touched the back of his head.

Behan was the first to reach them. "John Henry Holliday—you're under arrest for the murder of Bud Philpot and Peter

Roerig and the attempted stage robbery near Contention on the night of March the fifteenth."

Claire's heart stuttered and she glanced at Doc. His face, already pale in the best of circumstances, had drained of color. He passed the cards to another dealer and stood.

"I beg your pardon, gentlemen, but I must profess my innocence."

Behan smiled coldly. "That's not what your lady friend says." He waved a piece of paper in his face. "I have in my hand a signed affidavit stating that you confessed your misdeeds to Miss Kate Elder."

Doc sighed in resignation. "Claire, darlin'," he said in a weary voice, "would you be so kind as to collect my gun from the bartender?"

"Of course, Doc." Claire waited until Behan and his deputies marched Doc out of the saloon before she retrieved his gun belt and went in search of Kate.

Claire found her drinking at the Hatch Saloon on Allen Street. Two men were playing billiards while a small group stood at the bar drinking. The men tipped their hats to Claire before going back to their conversation.

"Come, Claire," Kate slurred from her table of one, a half-empty bottle of whiskey and an empty shot glass in front of her. "Siddown."

Claire pulled out the chair next to her and slammed Doc's gun belt on the table. Kate attempted to focus but wasn't able to, so she closed one eye and looked at Claire. "What?"

"Recognize that?" Claire asked, nodding at the leather gun belt. She'd given Doc's gun to Wyatt after she informed him of his friend's arrest.

Kate took another look at the belt and shrugged. "Looks like Doc's."

Claire leaned in close and grabbed Kate's wrist. "He's been arrested," she hissed, her anger at a boil. "Because of you."

"Ow. That hurts." Kate tried to pull her hand away but Claire held firm.

"I don't care if it's broken. Do you realize what you've done?"

"Vat do you mean? Let go." Her accent had grown thicker with drink.

"Your 'sworn affidavit' put your so-called husband in jail for *murder.*" Claire let out a disgusted sigh. "He could hang, Kate." She released the woman's wrist and crossed her arms.

"He told me himself he vas there that night," Kate said, wrinkling her nose as she tried to focus on Claire. Evidently, there were two of her. "How do you like our beloved Doc now, hmm?"

"Listen," Claire said, softening her voice. "I know he hit you and I'm sorry."

Kate touched the bruise near her eye as her gaze drifted to the floor.

"But that's not a good enough reason to let him hang. That's a good reason to leave him."

Kate leaned her head back and laughed. "And there it is. The real reason you're here." She threw her arms wide, almost unseating herself. Claire reached out to steady her. "You vant me to leave so you can haf him for yourself."

"No, Kate. I'm here to ask you to recant your testimony. Doc isn't an angel by any means, but he doesn't deserve to die at the end of a rope."

Kate waved her hand at Claire. "He von't hang. He's a lucky bastard."

"But what if he does? How will you feel then? When you've sobered up?"

A stormy expression crossed her features, and she slammed her fist on the table. "I vill not be lectured to by a woman who can't even hold onto her man." Drunken fury raged in her eyes. "He sent you, didn't he?" She rose on unsteady legs and raised her hand. There was a flash of metal as she lunged for Claire.

Claire easily sidestepped Kate's knife but Kate continued to rage, slashing indiscriminately at the air. One of the men at the bar rushed her from behind while Claire grabbed her wrist and squeezed. The knife fell to the floor. Tears streamed down Kate's cheeks as she realized the futility of her struggle.

"Kate Elder, you're under arrest," the man holding her said. Claire glanced at his overcoat. He wore a badge designating him as one of Virgil Earp's newly installed policemen.

"I don't think she meant to kill me. She's quite drunk."

"If it's all the same to you, miss, I saw what I saw. She needs to sleep it off. Jail would be the best place for her."

Claire nodded, conceding his point. "You're probably right." She'd talk to Kate in the morning once she sobered up.

Word of Kate's drunkenness and subsequent arrest spread, and her testimony was deemed tainted. After consideration of the evidence, Doc was released.

Kate finally left for her boarding house in Globe, and Doc continued as he always had—drinking and gambling in Tombstone and the surrounding areas, and sometimes traveling to Tucson for a change of pace.

Throughout the chaotic summer and early fall Claire practiced shooting and gambling, and became quite good at counting cards, which gave her an edge in most of the games. She won more often than not, which further burnished her reputation as a force to be reckoned with.

Most eligible men didn't dare approach Claire because of her reputation as a gunslinger and because of her friendship with Doc and the Earps, which suited her just fine. She didn't have time to waste on a man who lacked the courage to court her because of her abilities or her associations. The ones who did try weren't worth the price of salt and were usually liquored up, which didn't leave a good first impression. Generally she didn't mind being alone, but every once in a while she caught herself wondering if she'd ever find someone with whom to share her life.

Late one evening, Claire had just finished a successful game of faro at the Oriental Saloon when she decided to call it a night. She nodded at Wyatt, who'd been dealing, collected her winnings, and stood to leave.

"Ain't no way you won that pot fair," Ike Clanton, one of the players, growled. Ike's slurred speech and unfocused eyes told Claire and everyone around him that he was yet again on one of his benders, but that didn't make him any less dangerous. In fact, spirits made him more unpredictable if that were possible. Connected to the cowboys, he was known for being a hothead.

Claire brought her hand to the gun in the hidden pocket in her skirt and leveled her gaze at him. "You'd best sleep it off, Ike. You're not seeing what you think."

Ike's face turned red at the admonishment. His curly blond hair and cherubic face gave him a chip on his shoulder the size of a buffalo, especially in the macho world of Tombstone. Always trying to prove himself, Ike would drink for long stretches, building up the courage—some called it stupidity—to take on whoever looked at him crosswise. His father had reined him in, but with Old Man Clanton's recent death Ike was unfettered and free to act however he liked.

Ike's eyes narrowed, and he spit a stream of tobacco on the floor, missing the spittoon by a mile. "You think yer so damn smart. Well, you ain't. Yer jest an uppity bitch who cain't figure out whether she's a girl or a boy." His laughter ricocheted through the room.

Claire and Wyatt exchanged looks, and Wyatt gave her an almost imperceptible shake of his head. She nodded and turned to leave, secure in the fact that he'd take care of Ike.

Without warning Ike lunged across the table for Claire, upending chips and cards and drinks. Wyatt grabbed him from behind and slammed him facedown on the table as Claire leapt out of reach. She stopped short of drawing her pistol, not wanting to alert anyone to the concealed weapon.

Just another night in Tombstone.

"Damn you, Earp." Pinned to the table, Ike Clanton's muffled curse had less of an impact than it otherwise might. "You cain't even keep yer trap shut 'bout things that shouldn't be said."

"What the hell are you goin' on about, Ike?" Wyatt's look of annoyance was about as emotive as he usually got.

"I know you tol' Doc 'bout our agreement."

Wyatt rolled his eyes. "We ain't got no agreement, Clanton. Now shut your mouth before I have you arrested for drunk and disorderly."

"You tol' Doc 'bout our plan to ambush them fugitives—I know you did. You and yer brothers're gonna get me killed."

"Damn it, Ike. I don't know what else I can say to stop your confounded, paranoid imagination. I did not tell Doc about any so-called ambush."

"I don't believe you."

Wyatt turned and shouted at his younger brother, Morgan. "Get over to Tucson and tell Doc to come back to town. Tell him I need him here to refute Ike's everlasting stupidity and get him off my back."

"Will do, Wyatt," Morgan replied.

Claire figured it was time to go. Ike wouldn't bother her anymore that evening. "Thank you, Wyatt," she said, and took her leave.

As she made her way back to her room at Fly's, she glanced at the stars and thought of Doc, wishing he'd been there tonight. He'd grown distant; she assumed it was because he'd been seeing Kate more often on his trips out of town. The only thing that kept Claire from leaving town was Doc. She wasn't fond of the unpredictable Arizona weather—the blazing hot summers and freezing winters, the floods and relentless wind—and she'd grown tired of the dirt and dust and danger of living in a desert mining town. True, she'd grown in her shooting abilities because of Doc's tutelage, and she'd gotten better with the tomahawk and the bow, but she couldn't shake her restlessness. If she needed to, she could probably make a living as a gambler, especially since most men tended to underestimate her. There were lots of places to gamble.

Maybe it was time to move on.

October 1881 – Tombstone, Arizona Territory

Not long after the altercation between Wyatt and Ike at the Oriental, Morgan located Doc. He and Kate returned to Tombstone and took a room at Fly's. Claire welcomed them back, happy to see the two of them getting along for once. She studied Kate for signs that Doc had hit her. From what she could observe, he hadn't.

Kate's boarding house in Globe had burned to the ground and she'd been cast adrift, unmoored in a town that hadn't captured Doc's interest. Claire asked her what her plans might be going forward.

"I will stay with Doc for now."

"I thought you hated Tombstone." And Wyatt Earp, Claire thought, but didn't say.

Kate gave her a resigned look. "This is where Doc is happy. I must be where Doc is happy."

Doc had forgiven Kate for bearing witness against him in the Benson robbery, and Claire realized that no matter what happened, the two of them would always be connected. Even though Claire had no romantic interest in Doc, she grew wistful at the thought of someone loving her enough to forgive any transgression. No one was perfect, and Claire was acutely aware of her own faults.

The afternoon of October twenty-sixth, Claire retired to her room at Fly's to work on some ideas to improve her skirt's pistol pocket. The mood in town was tense—Ike Clanton had been drinking heavily all night and was running his mouth off about the Earp brothers, threatening to kill them on sight. Although Ike was a blustering fool by most accounts, Claire had ensured that Doc and Kate knew about the rumors before retiring to her room. Kate mentioned seeing Ike Clanton near the boarding house that morning, still drunk and wearing a bandage on his head.

"Claire—" Kate yelled as she banged on Claire's door. "Come quick."

Claire ran to the door and opened it wide. Clearly upset, Kate beckoned for Claire to follow her. Her fear-filled eyes appeared coal black in her pale face.

"What's wrong?"

"It's Doc." Kate grabbed Claire's hand and dragged her to their room. Once inside, she pointed out the window. "There."

The window looked onto the vacant lot next door where several men squared off with each other. Virgil, Wyatt, and Morgan Earp stood on Fremont Street near the lot entrance, while Ike Clanton, his brother Billy, and well-known ranchers and cattle rustlers Tom and Frank McLaury stood farther in. Tom held the reins of his horse and wore a guarded expression. Doc stood in the middle of Fremont wearing a knee-length duster and a deadly serious expression.

Claire pointed at Virgil, who'd just stepped into the lot. "Virgil's got Doc's cane." The lawman held the silver-headed walking stick in his right hand.

"What's he going to do with that?" Kate asked, annoyed. "Hit someone over the head?"

Claire clenched her fists. "I should be there to back them up." She turned to leave, but Kate gripped her arm.

"No, you should not, Claire Whitcomb." Kate's fierce expression made Claire rethink her decision. "Unless you want to die."

Kate had a point. This wasn't Claire's fight. She took a deep breath, fighting the urge to join the men in the lot, and turned back to the window. Maybe Virgil would deescalate the situation. With all the bad blood between them the chance seemed remote.

Kate cracked the window open in an attempt to hear what was being said. A cold wind slithered into the room, and Claire hugged herself against the chill. A crowd had formed on Fremont Street, comprised of an eager audience—it wasn't every day that there was an honest-to-goodness shootout.

Let this be over soon, Claire thought.

To Claire's left, Wyatt took up a position at the southwest corner of Fly's. Morgan stood on the street near the entrance to the lot. Doc remained in the center of Fremont Street, most likely to keep an eye out for anyone coming toward them. Virgil stayed where he was.

There was movement to Claire's left as Tom McClaury appeared to go for the rifle in his saddle scabbard. Doc swept his coat aside to reveal a double-barreled shotgun. Tom froze.

"Throw up your hands, boys. I intend to disarm you." Virgil's voice rang out in the cold October air.

"We will—" Frank McLaury began, but Virgil's words set everyone in motion. Frank went for his pistol at the same time as Wyatt.

Wyatt beat Frank to the draw and fired, hitting him in the stomach. Frank doubled over but kept his feet.

Virgil waved the cane and yelled, "Hold!" but his words had no effect. Billy Clanton, standing next to the wood frame house across the lot from Fly's, fired at Wyatt, but his shot went wide. Ike threw himself at Wyatt and grabbed him around the middle, unintentionally shielding him from Billy's next shot.

"Don't shoot, Wyatt. I ain't armed," Ike pleaded. Wyatt tried and failed to throw off the tenacious cowboy. Billy worked to get a clean shot at Wyatt, but Ike was in the way. Seeing an opening, Morgan shot the younger Clanton, who collapsed against the house but kept shooting.

Black smoke thickened the air as the gunfight intensified. It was hard to keep track of who shot whom.

"Virgil's down." Claire gasped as the veteran lawman fell to one knee.

Virgil struggled to his feet and fired at Frank as Frank staggered toward Fremont, but the outlaw's horse got in the way and Virgil missed.

Ike and Wyatt were still locked in a struggle when Wyatt's pistol went off. Kate stifled a scream, startling Claire. Outside, Morgan yelled, "I'm hit," and went down. He attempted to stand but tripped and fell.

Wyatt finally managed to shake Ike free and bellowed, "The fighting's commenced. Get fightin', or go away."

Ike chose the latter. He took off running and disappeared from view.

"I'm going after Ike." Claire turned from the window, a mixture of anger and fear for Doc and the Earps firing through her.

"No—you must stay here. You will be shot—" Kate pleaded.

Claire's anger reached a boiling point, and she turned on Kate. "This is Ike's fault and he's getting away. I'm going to find him and either kill him or bring him to justice."

More shots rang out, and the two women turned toward the window, momentarily forgetting Ike Clanton. Tom McLaury's horse bolted, leaving Tom wide open. Doc fired the shotgun, hitting Tom under the arm. Tom staggered from the lot, his right side a bloody mess. Doc threw down the shotgun and pulled his pistol free, searching for his next target. He honed in on Billy.

His hand bloodied by a bullet wound, Billy switched his gun from his right to his left, but his wounds were too grave and his aim was off. Seeing that Billy was no longer a threat, Doc turned his attention to Frank.

Frank McLaury fired at Morgan but Frank's horse spooked and took off, leaving Frank exposed and bleeding in the middle of the street. Morgan managed to pull himself up to take aim at Frank, but Doc was already coming for him.

With difficulty Frank straightened. He drew on Doc and yelled, "I've got you now."

Doc smiled at his audacity. "Blaze away. You're a daisy if you have."

Frank fired.

Doc staggered. "I'm shot through," he bellowed. Both he and Morgan fired at Frank. Frank collapsed to the ground. Doc towered over the fallen cowboy and said, "The son of a bitch has shot me, and I mean to kill him."

But Frank was already dead.

A steam whistle from a nearby mine shrieked, breaking the onlookers' stunned silence. Armed men swarmed the street but balked at the sight of the dead. Obviously they were too late to help.

Claire raced from the room with Kate close on her heels, and met Doc as he crashed through the door and headed for his room. Kate followed.

Mollie Fly stopped Claire and handed her a bar of soap and a kettle of hot water. "He might need these," she said as she pulled strips of clean muslin from her apron pocket. Claire took everything to Doc's room. Doc was in the process of unbuttoning his trousers. With a grimace he pulled the fabric away from his hip. Blood marked the wound.

Claire handed Kate a damp cloth, which she used to clean him. Kate leaned back, relief obvious on her face. "It's just a graze." Claire let out a sigh, unaware she'd been holding her breath.

Doc grabbed a wad of muslin, secured it to the wound to stanch the blood, then pulled his pants back on. "I've got to go to

Wyatt. The cowboys will be looking for revenge." He nodded at Claire. "I would appreciate your company."

"I'll get my rifle." Claire hurried to her room to grab the modified Winchester and joined Doc outside.

Wyatt stood guard over Virgil and Morgan and chatted quietly with bystanders while they waited for a wagon to take his wounded brothers home to be looked after. Out of the eight involved, Wyatt was the only one who hadn't been shot—except for a bullet hole punched through the bottom of his coat. When Claire pointed it out Wyatt inspected the damage and raised an eyebrow. "Well, I'll be. Billy got a shot off after all."

"You want to take his gun?" someone behind Claire asked.

Claire turned to see Camillus "Buck" Fly—Mollie's husband—and Bob Hatch, the owner of Hatch's Saloon, standing near Billy Clanton. Weak and bleeding from multiple gunshot wounds, Billy worked feverishly to reload his gun.

"Aw, hell. I'll do it." Fly bent down and wrested Billy's gun from his hand.

"I need more bullets," Billy cried as he attempted to retake his gun. He fell back, writhing in pain. Several men walked over and picked him up to take him to a nearby house. Billy's screams echoed through the vacant lot as they carried him away.

Not long after, the wagon arrived to cart Virgil and Morgan off to be seen by one of the town's doctors. Sheriff Johnny Behan, missing throughout the gunfight, walked out from behind Fly's Photography Studio and joined Wyatt, Doc, and Claire.

"Wyatt Earp and John H. Holliday, you're under arrest for the murders of Frank and Tom McLaury and Billy Clanton."

Wyatt rounded on the sheriff, his anger on full display. "I'll tell you plain, Johnny, I will not be arrested."

Clearly taken aback at Wyatt's outburst, Johnny sputtered a response. "You and Doc need to answer for what you done."

A Tombstone businessman who was standing nearby interrupted. "There's no hurry arresting this man," he claimed, nodding at Wyatt. "He's done right in killing them, and I'm certain the town will agree."

"You bet we did right," Wyatt admonished Behan. "We had to do it. And you threw us, Johnny. You told us they were disarmed."

Outnumbered, Johnny gave in. "See to your brothers, but stay in town."

"Someone needs to find Ike," Claire suggested. "Last I saw he was running toward Allen Street."

Johnny eyed Claire's rifle and shook his head. "It's a good thing you weren't involved. I'd hate to put a lady behind bars. Or worse, bury you."

"Go after Ike," Claire replied. "It's the least you can do, Johnny."

Johnny glared at Wyatt and Doc and said, "I'll find Ike, but it won't be good for either of you."

After Behan left, one of the bartenders from the Alhambra ran up to Wyatt, breathless. "The Safety Committee's talkin' about lynchin' Ike Clanton."

Doc and Wyatt exchanged glances. "I'd say Sheriff Behan will have his hands full tonight."

With Behan out of the way, Claire, Doc, and Wyatt started for Virgil's house. On the way, Claire asked Wyatt, "Will there be a trial?"

Wyatt narrowed his eyes and stared into the distance. "If there is I have no doubt the town will back us."

"I'm not so sure, Wyatt," Doc said. He had a slight limp but didn't appear to be in too much pain. He'd recovered his cane, which he used now. "This town has a way of turning on you. Look at the election last year—we all expected you to win."

Wyatt frowned. "Citizens don't like Behan much, especially

since he's partial to cowboys. Virgil's the law and he appointed Morgan and me as his deputies. We were in the right, all the way through. We gave those cowboys plenty of opportunities to either give up their guns or leave town."

"But is that enough?" Doc asked. "Three of the cowboys died today. At the very least their compatriots will be looking for revenge, disrupting Tombstone's serenity. The town's collective memory may run short if that happens. The shootout will be top of mind."

Wyatt looked at Claire. "You saw it. What do you think?"

"It all happened so fast, I can't say for sure exactly," Claire said. "I do know that Ike Clanton's had it in for you and your brothers for a while now. The whole town knows that. But I also know there's been bad blood between you and the cowboys for longer than that. A standoff has been a long time coming."

"Did you see who shot first?" Doc asked.

"I didn't have a clear view because of McLaury's horse but Tom looked like he was going for his rifle and thought better of it when Doc pulled out the shotgun."

"Indeed." Doc nodded at her recollection.

"Would you swear to it in court if it came to that?" Wyatt asked.

"I don't know how effective my testimony would be in a trial —everybody knows I'm partial to you boys."

Doc's mustache quirked up as he gave her the briefest of smiles. A second later the grim expression he'd worn since the shootout returned. "I think we're in for it, Wyatt."

"We'll be fine, Doc. Don't worry about things that ain't gonna happen."

Surprisingly, the next morning both newspapers backed the lawmen, although rumor had it that close to half the town sided with the cowboys.

That afternoon, the dead cowboys' funeral procession commenced. Mourners numbered in the hundreds and included a stagecoach and twenty-two carriages. Close to two thousand townspeople lined the streets of Tombstone in respectful silence. Claire wondered how many were on the side of the dead.

Whatever the number, it didn't look like a town that was going to back Doc and Wyatt.

CHAPTER 9

C laire was right.

"What will happen now?" Claire asked Doc. She'd just finished breakfast at the Grand Hotel. She and Doc sat at a table talking.

"It doesn't look good, Miss Claire." He made circles on the table with his cup and stared into the distance. He'd taken to adding a splash or two of rye whiskey to his morning coffee. "The governor denied Virgil's request for federal troops to fend off what he sees as an impending cowboy assault."

"They don't think that will happen? I'd expect the cowboys would want vengeance. Especially if the courts don't rule in their favor."

Doc shifted in his chair. "I don't think we need to worry about an all-out assault on the town. I believe Virgil made the request to rehabilitate his reputation. The cowboys may be rash but they're not stupid. They will exact their revenge in a more surreptitious manner."

At that moment, Johnny Behan and two of his deputies entered the restaurant and strode to their table.

"John H. Holliday," Behan declared, "you're under arrest for the murders of Billy Clanton, and Tom and Frank McLaury."

Doc sighed and placed his linen napkin on the table. "This is getting tiresome." He stood and bent to kiss Claire's hand and murmured, "I'm sorry to leave you so soon, my dear." He turned to Behan. "And you, sir, have the tedious habit of repeating yourself. You might want to check with your doctor—you may well be succumbing to feeble-mindedness."

Behan scowled at Doc. "That's enough, Holliday. Time to go."

The inquest lasted several weeks, and it appeared that the cowboys were favored to win. That is, until Tom and Frank McLaury's older brother, Will, requested that Ike Clanton take the stand. After a few easy questions, the Earp brothers' attorney, Tom Fitch, showed Ike a telegram from Wells Fargo to Marshall Williams stating that the company would pay a reward for the apprehension of the Benson stage robbers, dead or alive.

"Did you or did you not strike a deal with Wyatt Earp to lure the stage robbers to a predetermined place," Fitch asked, "so that Mr. Earp could take the fugitives into custody and collect the reward—all of which he would then pay to you?"

Ike's face turned red, and he stammered his answer. "I—uh, Wyatt came to me to help him kill the men that robbed the stage. He said there was a lot of money to be had—twelve hundred dollars for each bandit captured—and that I could have it all." He turned to Justice of the Peace Wells Spicer, and added, "Wyatt even offered twenty-four hundred dollars of his own money if I agreed to betray my friends.

"Naturally, I wanted to know why Wyatt wanted them three dead so bad. He told me him and Morgan gave Doc and Billy Leonard money from the treasure box even before the stage left town. They was afraid the others would squeal on 'em if they was caught."

Fitch listened to his story, then prompted, "Why didn't you tell anyone else about this sinister scheme?"

Ike's gaze darted to Wyatt as he answered. "Wyatt made me promise on my honor as a gentleman not to repeat the conversation if I did not like the proposition."

Wyatt scoffed. Attendees buzzed with conjecture.

Fitch ended his questioning. Will McLaury asked to question Ike further, to which Spicer agreed. Fitch whispered something to Wyatt and then settled back in his chair. Doc scribbled on a scrap of paper and slid it to his attorney. What other lies would Ike dream up?

Apparently thinking Will's request to keep him on the stand implied his support of the direction Ike's testimony was taking, Ike continued his blatant perjury.

"A few days after the holdup, Doc Holliday came around askin' to talk with me. I told him no sir, don't take me into your confidence, but he went ahead and confessed to takin' part in the ambush and that he himself shot Bud Philpot through the heart."

A collective gasp erupted from the room at this supposed confession. The excitement was palpable as the spectators whispered among themselves.

Ike sat straighter in his chair, clearly buoyed by his time in the limelight.

"That ain't all. The day after that, Virgil Earp told me he was in league with his brothers and that he'd thrown off the posse chasing 'em so's they could escape into New Mexico Territory."

"Why did you wait until this hearing to mention these crimes?" Will asked Ike.

Ike leaned forward in his chair. "I never would've said a word 'cept for being called up on this stand." He swept his gaze over the room. "I was afraid after the outlaws was found dead that the Earps and Doc Holliday would surely kill me for what I knew." He leaned back triumphantly. "That's why they started the gunfight."

A collective murmur filled the room. Claire studied Wells Spicer, looking for some kind of tell for which way he was leaning. Surely he didn't believe Ike Clanton. Ike's "confession" was so over the top as to be comical. It was well known that none of the money in the Wells Fargo treasure box had been taken in the attempted robbery and had been delivered to Tucson that same night. Plus, Ike's description of Virgil being in league with the robbers didn't ring true and everyone knew it. His insistence that Doc would kill him didn't hold water either. Doc could have easily killed him during the gunfight and didn't, weakening Ike's testimony considerably.

More witnesses were called, and the prosecution rested. When it came time for the defense, Fitch asked if Wyatt could read a statement. Overruling the prosecution's objections, Spicer allowed it and Wyatt gave his version of events.

On the afternoon of November thirtieth, Wells Spicer called everyone back to render his verdict. Claire filed into the room with the rest of the spectators and took a seat. The crowd was abuzz with speculation and rumor. From what Claire could glean, half were anti-cowboy, half wanted Wyatt and Doc to stand trial for murder. Claire did her best to ignore what was being said and waited for Spicer to begin.

"Virgil Earp's decision to enlist his brothers and Doc Holliday in disarming the cowboys," Spicer began, "was an injudicious and censurable act."

That didn't sound promising. Claire glanced at Doc. His jaw pulsed but he remained stone-faced. Wyatt stared straight ahead.

Spicer continued. "But I can attach no criminality to his unwise act. The cowboys were violating the town's ordinances, and Virgil, Wyatt, Morgan, and Doc were doing what it was their right and duty to do. I cannot resist the conclusion that the defendants were fully justified in committing these homicides—that it was a necessary act, done in the discharge of an official duty.

"There being no sufficient cause to believe the within named

Wyatt S. Earp and John H. Holliday guilty of the offense mentioned, I order them to be released."

Claire let out a breath and laughed with relief. Grinning, Wyatt and Doc stood up and slapped each other and their counselors on the back. Several folks in the room shot to their feet to clap and whistle. Wells Spicer banged his gavel trying to restore order, but it was not to be.

Afterward, Wyatt, Doc, and Claire met up with Virgil and Morgan at the Cosmopolitan, where the two Earp brothers had been convalescing. Drinks flowed freely—even Wyatt had a glass of whiskey to celebrate. Virgil's and Morgan's wives, Allie and Louisa, joined them at the hotel and the group prepared to go to dinner.

"Isn't Mattie coming?" Claire asked Doc. Mattie Earp often stayed home citing a headache. Even so Claire figured Wyatt's wife would want to celebrate the important occasion. At that moment an attractive woman walked through the door and greeted Wyatt with an intimate smile. Claire raised her eyebrows at Doc. "Josie and Wyatt?"

Doc nodded and said, "Unfortunately, yes," before throwing back his drink.

Josie was Josephine Marcus, the former actress from San Francisco who had most recently lived with Johnny Behan. Claire had met her the year before when Claire had first come to town and wasn't at all impressed. Josie was beautiful and knew it, using her feminine wiles to manipulate men to get what she wanted.

Except Johnny had promised Josie marriage and kept putting her off time and again. Eventually Josie had caught him with another woman (or two) and had made it known that their impending nuptials were off.

"Do you think she's trying to get back at Behan?" Claire wouldn't put it past her—she'd earned a reputation as a proud woman who expected to be treated like royalty.

Doc shrugged. "That may have been her original intention but I fear they're both smitten now."

"How on earth did they keep their relationship from the rumor mill?" It always amazed Claire at how quickly gossip traveled through Tombstone. Keeping anything a secret from the town busybodies was a full-time job.

"I assume it was mostly Wyatt's doing."

The group moved to the dining room, and Doc offered Claire his arm. "Miss Whitcomb, will you do me the great honor of accompanying me to dinner?"

Claire smiled and slipped her hand in the crook of his elbow. "I'd be delighted, Mr. Holliday."

Kate Elder wouldn't be joining the celebration. When it appeared the preliminary hearing wasn't going well for Doc and Wyatt, Kate had skipped town after securing a gift of fifty dollars from Doc's nemesis, John Ringo. Apparently Kate and the cowboy had a history. Doc didn't appreciate Ringo financing his woman's travel—indeed, he'd been beyond enraged when he found out. Doc vowed to escape from his cell to hunt the cattle rustler down. Luckily, Claire managed to calm him before he did anything rash.

Dinner was festive and everyone had a lovely time, but when Claire sat back in her chair and studied the group, a sense of uneasiness settled over her.

The cowboys weren't going to let the Earps' victory stand—they'd get their revenge. She just didn't know how or when.

Late in December, as Virgil Earp made his way to the Cosmopolitan from the Oriental Saloon, an unseen gunman shot him in the back. He survived, but lost the use of his left arm. Certain the shooting was the work of the cowboys, Wyatt asked for and was granted US marshal status and began to put together a posse.

Then Morgan was killed, ambushed as he played billiards at Hatch's Saloon with Wyatt looking on. Two bullets smashed through the backdoor window—one of the rounds missed Wyatt's head by inches, while the other ripped through Morgan's spine. Morgan died less than an hour later.

Wyatt was beyond angry, beyond grief. One brother maimed for life, another dead. That Sunday on Wyatt's' thirty-fourth birthday he sent his brother's body home via railcar to their parents in California. The next day he and Doc and another member of the posse escorted Virgil and Allie to Tucson. While there, another cowboy named Frank Stilwell attempted to ambush Virgil and kill him, but Wyatt shot and killed him first. The group returned home, and Wyatt immediately called together another posse. Tucson authorities deemed Stilwell's death a murder and issued a warrant for Wyatt's arrest.

When Claire heard that Wyatt was planning a "vendetta ride" to hunt down those responsible for Morgan's murder, she searched him out and found him at the Oriental Saloon.

"I want to join the posse."

Wyatt finished entering a posse member's name in his ledger and looked Claire in the eyes. "I appreciate your offer, Claire. But I won't have a woman's safety on my conscience. This isn't like protecting a stage."

Claire's anger spiked and she glared at Wyatt. "I'd appreciate it if you didn't put me in a box with other women. You know I can shoot as well as anyone joining up." When he didn't respond she added, "You need me. I can track and shoot and ride and I've got better eyesight than half the men in this saloon. Besides, you know how much I care for you boys. Isn't that worth something?"

There was a set to his jaw as he shook his head. "I'm sorry, Claire. I can't allow it."

Claire pulled in a deep breath, fighting the retort that sprang to her lips. Arguing with Wyatt wouldn't solve anything. He was the leader of the posse. His word was final.

"When Virgil didn't let me join the posse to hunt down Bud's killers, I figured it was because he didn't know me well enough. I thought you'd be more open-minded since you know what I can do. Obviously I was wrong."

Someone entered the saloon through the swinging doors, and she caught a glimpse of Doc standing outside on the boardwalk. With a frustrated sigh, she brushed past Wyatt and went out to meet him.

When he saw the look on her face he pulled her aside.

"You have to talk to Wyatt," Claire protested, pinning his gaze. "I *have* to—no, I *need* to be part of this posse."

"I can't help you, Claire." Doc sighed. "Wyatt's mind is made up."

She pulled back, searching his eyes. "You talked to him for me?"

He nodded. "Of course I did. Don't you think I want you along? You're a better shot than half these men and likely better at strategic thinking than all of us put together."

"Oh." His admission took the wind out of her sails. At least Doc had the good sense to want her along. "I could follow at a distance, keep out of sight until you find them."

"I'm sure you could. But when Wyatt finds out you disregarded his edict I guarantee he'd never trust you again. Wyatt sees the world in black and white. Your defiance would be a bridge too far. Is that what you want?"

"I see how it is," Claire said. "No matter how capable I am, men like Wyatt won't ever allow me to live to my potential." She shook her head, her anger building at the stupidity of it. "You need me, Doc." She waved her hand at the posse. "They need me."

Doc nodded. "You're right. We do. But nothing you or I say is going to change Wyatt's mind." He lifted her chin. "You'll find your place, Claire Whitcomb. Besides, I could never forgive myself if you were killed."

Doc gave her a chaste kiss on the cheek and climbed onto his horse. Claire watched the posse ride out of town, wishing with every fiber of her being that she could join them.

THE NEXT DAY, Claire met Mollie Fly at the Cosmopolitan for lunch. Mollie was Claire's only source for gossip since Claire didn't put much stock in most rumors. Mollie could be counted on for the straight story.

"Apparently Johnny Behan tried to arrest Wyatt last night."

"Again?" Claire shook her head. "When is he going to figure

out he won't win with the Earps?"

Mollie smiled, the devil in her eye. "Johnny's mad at Wyatt for stealing his girl."

Claire rolled her eyes. "Josie? Behan never had her in the first place. The end was obvious when she caught that lowlife cheating on her."

Mollie studied her with interest. "I thought you didn't like the woman?"

"What I don't like are men who can't be trusted. No woman deserves that kind of scoundrel in her life."

"Hear, hear," Mollie agreed. "I was wondering." She looked up and caught Claire's gaze. "Would you be interested in a job?"

Claire leaned forward. "What do you have in mind?"

"Buck has a friend who needs help moving a prisoner from Fort Huachuca to Tucson where they'll take the train to Yuma Territorial Prison."

Still stinging from Wyatt's rebuke the night before Claire said, "Does your husband's friend know I'm a woman?"

"He does. And to be truthful he wouldn't normally choose someone of the female persuasion. But with all the good marksmen joining Wyatt's posse and your sterling reputation, he was most amenable to the proposition."

Claire sat back, considering. "Does he want someone to guard the prisoner on the train?" She'd certainly had experience in that regard.

"No, just to Tucson. There are extenuating circumstances." She waved Claire's next question away. "I'll let him tell you the rest. I took the liberty of setting up a meeting at the boarding house this afternoon."

Claire smiled at her friend. "And if I decide not to?"

"That's your choice. But if I could put in a good word, Buck's friend is an upstanding gentleman who never reneges on his promises and holds women in the highest regard."

"We'll see."

The meeting with Buck's friend, Mr. Van Houten, took place that afternoon at the boarding house. Quite a bit older than Claire, Van Houten was professional in his request, and his reasons for hiring her matched with Mollie's explanation. Both went a long way toward alleviating Claire's unease.

"May I ask why you are coordinating the transport of prisoners since you're not a federal marshal or a lawman?" Claire asked.

"A fair question," Van Houten said with a nod. "I've been tasked with such by my good friend, Governor Tritle. I have heard nothing but sterling recommendations of your abilities as a gunfighter and security guard." His gaze held hers. "I've heard differing accounts of your character, many of which were positive."

"May I ask what you've heard that is not?" Not that she cared much anymore, but she was curious what people said.

Van Houten's cheeks reddened and he shifted uneasily in his chair. "Only in regard to your association with a certain John H. Holliday. And, well, to be quite frank because of your support of the Earps."

Claire nodded. "I make no excuse for my friendliness with all of whom you speak. Those men have been nothing but helpful and supportive since I arrived in Tombstone." Although Wyatt's stance against her joining the posse rankled, she wouldn't hold it against him. Some men were just bullheaded.

Van Houten nodded, seemingly satisfied with her answer. "That was all I needed to know, Mrs. Whitcomb."

"Please, call me Claire. Who am I to transport?"

"A man known as Sam Peters."

"Sam Peters, the man who killed that family near the fort?"

"The very same."

Sam Peters had been captured and charged with multiple murders when a family of seven was discovered dead at a remote ranch near Fort Huachuca. Peters and his gang of rustlers and thieves had been sighted nearby at the same time a neighbor returned a draft horse to the family. The neighbor issued a statement with a remark on Peters' odd behavior as he passed the group of outlaws. Peters told the neighbor that the family had gone to visit relatives in Prescott and wasn't expected home for several days. The neighbor, suspecting foul play, discovered the family shot to death soon after. He rode to the fort to inform the captain. An arrest warrant was issued and a posse formed, but Peters had already left the area. Eventually apprehended near the mining town of Bisbee, his trial was swift. Judged a flight risk, Peters was sent to the fort to await transport to Tucson and then on to Yuma Territorial Prison via rail.

"Your partner in this endeavor will be Harrison Sparks, the bounty hunter who tracked down Peters and took him into custody."

"And he's all right with sharing the job with a partner?" Claire asked. What she really meant to say was a *female* partner but chose to let the implication speak for itself. Bounty hunters were a different breed, independent and territorial. She didn't blame them. She'd heard stories of some being swindled out of their rightful payments when a lawyer or an unsavory lawman decided they deserved the reward instead.

"You're to meet Sparks at Fort Huachuca in two days' time," Van Houten replied, ignoring her question. "The transfer must be done at night. There's talk of a gang of roughs camped nearby although the soldiers have had no luck in locating them. We assume they're waiting to set upon anyone who attempts to move Peters. Leaving under cover of darkness ensures a head start of several hours at least."

Claire narrowed her eyes. "Does Mr. Sparks know he's to have a partner?"

Van Houten cleared his throat. "Not exactly, no."

"Then my welcome is not ensured."

"I will provide a letter of instruction containing the seal of the governor's office. Sparks will have no choice but to accept your presence."

Claire leaned back in her chair. She'd swayed the opinions of men before. But an inauspicious start with someone she would need to rely on and who needed to rely on her throughout such a dangerous journey didn't sit well.

"Is there no plan for more than the two of us? I'm not saying no to the job but why not hire a larger group to fend off Peters' gang?" Unpleasant memories of the attempted train robbery in Colorado by Jack "Sheriff Killer" Abrams rose in her mind. "I'd feel a whole lot better if there were more firepower than just myself and the bounty hunter."

Van Houten agreed. "Your services will only be required to Tucson. At that point a group of deputy marshals drawn from farther afield will accompany Sparks and the prisoner on the rest of the trip. I'm afraid the governor has decided that a lean transport party is more nimble than a larger group for the Tucson leg of the journey. Besides, there are few men I or the governor would trust to remain quiet about our plans to move him at night. As you know, the men we do trust are otherwise engaged."

He had a point. Employing a smaller group did make changing tactics easier. Was she signing her own death warrant? Peters' men were known to be ruthless, cutthroat outlaws, men who didn't care who they killed or why. Claire mentally shrugged off the idea. She'd been up against ruthless men before.

This was her chance to prove herself—and not only to the governor. When she and Sparks successfully delivered Peters to Tucson her reputation and viability would only grow. She'd be able to write her own ticket. Besides, she'd been to Tucson several times and knew the route well.

"Since my good friends the Flys vouch for you," she said, "I accept your offer."

The look of relief on Van Houten's face told Claire he'd likely offered the position to others who refused.

She wondered if they knew something she didn't.

Van Houten gave Claire money for provisions and she stocked up on ammunition for the Peacemaker and the Winchester, and food for both her and her horse, Rose. She wrapped the tomahawk in the blanket Thomas had given her and secured them and the beaded bow and quiver of arrows to her saddle. The next day she left Tombstone, headed to Fort Huachuca.

She wore her hair tucked under her hat in case she met anyone and kept her bandana around her neck, allowing her to raise it if the dust and dirt got too thick, or if someone got too close. She also kept a Green River hunting knife concealed in her boot as a backup.

Claire relished the solitude of riding alone and found herself humming a Gilbert and Sullivan tune from *HMS Pinafore*. The sun on her shoulders, and the familiar scent of leather and horse sweat and Rose's comforting gait made everything right with the world. Leaving Tombstone had been a godsend. She didn't miss the political machinations by the townspeople, preferring her own company to just about anyone except Mollie and Doc. Most of the folks in Tombstone tired her with their unwavering quest for power and money and gossip. The idea of Tombstone—the possibility of striking it rich and anything goes—had been what drew her to the mining town. But those same ideas now repelled her. She'd had enough of shallowness, greed, and the mean-spiritedness that accompanied that greed.

She took her time, enjoying the scenery and keeping a watchful eye out for renegades but the trip was uneventful. As the sun sank low on the horizon creating a brilliant purple and orange sunset, she climbed a slight rise. Below her stretched Fort Huachuca.

Recently re-designated from a camp to a fort, Fort Huachuca was situated at the base of the Huachuca Mountains. Established in 1877 to defend against the Chiricahua Apache and secure the border with Mexico, the fort's strategic location assured its continued existence: the tactical advantage of the Huachuca Mountains at its back, good visibility in the other directions, plentiful trees, and fresh water.

Claire waited until darkness fell before she rode into camp and asked to see the commanding officer. She didn't remove her hat or bandana in an attempt to remain anonymous in a fort filled with soldiers. The captain in charge glanced at her papers and then directed her to the jail where Peters was being held.

"You'll find Sparks there, too," the captain said. "Be warned, the man is about as friendly as a rattlesnake."

"Thank you, Captain," she replied, deepening her voice.

She made her way to the jail—a square rock building with slat iron bars for cell doors. The darkened interiors of each cell obscured her ability to see inside.

In the light of a lantern under a nearby mesquite, a broad-shouldered man lifted a saddle onto one of two horses and cinched it tight. The second horse had already been loaded as had a mule standing next to it. Additional provisions lay at the man's feet.

Not wanting to startle him, Claire cleared her throat to

announce her presence. The man turned to see who was there, squinting in the darkness.

"What do you want?" he asked. He was tall and lean with a beard and dark, longish hair that curled at his shirt collar. Claire figured his age was anywhere from late twenties to late thirties. Hard to tell with folks who lived their lives outside.

"Are you Harrison Sparks?"

He nodded, a wary look clouding his face. The butt of a Colt .45 stuck out from his gun belt and he wore a bandolier slung over his shoulder. A pair of worn leather boots sporting Mexican spurs graced his feet. An oilcloth duster hung from a nearby branch.

Claire pulled out the governor's letter and handed it to him. "I'm to ride with you to Tucson."

Sparks took the letter from her and held it up to the light to read. The lines around his eyes deepened. "Says here I'm supposed to give you all due respect and privilege." He handed back the paper. "With all due respect you need to get your skinny ass back to where you came from and leave me be." Sparks picked up part of his provisions and slid them into a saddlebag.

"With all due respect, Mr. Sparks, I'm coming with you."

His back to her, Sparks' shoulders went rigid. "Not a chance in hell," he growled. He went for his Colt and spun in place. His gaze dropped to the pistol already in her hand.

"I'm sorry." Claire injected as much sarcasm into her tone as possible. "You were saying?"

His expression guarded, Sparks glared at her before re-holstering his gun. "I didn't catch your name."

Claire decocked the Peacemaker. "That's right. You didn't."

"Kinda young for this type of work ain't you?"

"That's rich, coming from someone of your advanced age." She almost laughed out loud at the look on his face. Apparently she'd struck a chord.

Sparks resumed packing. "You sound like you ain't even

passed puberty yet." He let out a frustrated sigh and rounded on Claire. "Dammit, kid. Just because you got friends in high places don't mean you get to endanger my life."

Claire narrowed her eyes and stepped toward him, forcing him back. The tree got in his way and he stood his ground.

"Watch your mouth, Sparks," she said, jabbing her finger into his chest, her anger cresting. She'd about had enough of bull-headed men. "I'm as good or better shot as you are, which means I'll probably save *your* skinny ass, so go to hell." She glared at him, her breath coming fast.

Scowling, Sparks brushed past her. "Let's settle this once and for all."

Claire squared her shoulders and spat back, "Fine with me. The sooner the better."

Sparks breezed past the guards and stormed into the captain's quarters. The captain looked up from his paperwork in surprise. "Mr. Sparks, Mr. Whitcomb." He nodded at them both. "What seems to be the problem?"

"What the hell's the meaning of the governor's request?" Sparks snarled. "You know I work alone."

Seething, Claire retorted, "The governor requires me to accompany Mr. Sparks and the prisoner to Tucson." She nodded at Sparks, who looked like he was struggling mightily to keep his temper in check. "This jackass is trying to prevent me from carrying out my assigned duties."

The captain sighed heavily and leaned back in his chair. He nodded at Claire and held out his hand. "Let me see the letter again."

Claire handed the paper to him and crossed her arms as he read it. She glared at Sparks, but he ignored her, his eyes front and his fists clenched.

"Says here you're to treat C. Whitcomb with all due respect." The captain refolded the document and handed it back to Claire. "Sorry, Harry. Like it or not Whitcomb here is going along." He shrugged. "Hell, man. It's only a couple of days. You could do with the company. It's not like Peters is a good conversationalist."

Sparks snorted. "I don't need help. And I don't want any, either."

The captain gestured at Claire. "Says in the letter that Whitcomb's a crack shot and cool as a cucumber under pressure. I'd venture that those are good qualities to have when you got bandits or renegades on your heels."

Sparks crossed his arms, clearly unconvinced.

Claire rolled her eyes. "We're wasting time. The sooner we get on the road the farther we can travel before daylight."

The captain looked at Sparks. "He's right, Harry."

Harry pulled in a deep breath and exhaled in disgust. "I won't give up any of the reward," he warned. "I captured Peters, fair and square."

"Nobody's saying you have to share the money, Harry." The captain shook his head, the lines around his eyes pronounced in the glow of the lamp. "Did you even read the damn letter? Whitcomb's being paid through the governor's office and only gets the money if you both deliver Peters to the train alive."

At the captain's words Sparks's demeanor transformed and his shoulders inched down. He shifted his weight. "Fine." He turned to Claire. "You'd best keep up. I'm not waitin' on you."

"Don't worry about me, *Harry*." Claire gave him a scathing look. Harry snorted, turned on his heel, and left.

Claire turned to follow him out but stopped when the captain cleared his throat.

"I sure hope you're as good as that letter lets on," the captain warned. "You'll need to be."

Claire touched the brim of her hat in acknowledgement and walked outside.

The ride to Tucson had just gotten a lot longer.

CHAPTER 13

They left without incident, traveling several miles in silence. The night sounds—insects buzzing and chirping, a coyote's lonely howl—were all around them. Claire enjoyed watching the bats swoop through the air hunting for insects, and the occasional coyote slide past on its quest for prey.

For his part, Peters didn't attempt to converse with either Harry or Claire for the first dozen or so miles. His wrists bound tight to the saddle horn, he kept to himself and appeared to doze fitfully. Occasionally Harry pelted him with rocks to keep him awake, to which the prisoner took umbrage, but that was the only sign of life from the outlaw.

To Claire's surprise Sam Peters was small in stature and might have been considered handsome if a person didn't take into account his murderous ways. He wore his blond hair slicked back, and he had a quick, intelligent gaze set beneath a high forehead. At the fort, he'd studied Claire long and hard as Harry secured him to his horse and only spoke to her once when he asked her name. Claire told him to call her Whitcomb.

Riding in the cool of the night had a different quality than that of the daytime—instead of the blazing sun they navigated by the blue light of a half-moon. The deep shadows played tricks on Claire's eyes, revealing places an outlaw or renegade could lie in wait to ambush them. Claire remained alert for anything that might signify movement and kept her fears to herself.

No sense giving either of them reason to taunt her. She could just hear Harry chide her for being nervous after her boldness back at the fort.

Along the way they stopped to water their horses at a small creek and stretch their legs. Peters said he needed to piss, and Harry insisted on guarding him. Claire would be expected to take her turn when the time came, and she was willing, but it looked like Harry decided to assert his influence over the prisoner.

Fine with her.

The issue of her own relief caused Claire a brief moment of consternation. Doing her business in the dark was one thing— her inability to pee standing up wouldn't be noticed and thus no commentary would be forthcoming. But during the daylight hours she'd be stuck. She vowed to go as long as possible without either of them finding out she was female. She had no illusion they'd treat her differently once that little secret was out.

The horizon lightened, signaling the approaching dawn. Dark clouds gathered in the distance near a range of low-lying mountains. A blustery wind whipped up, bringing with it the smell of rain. Harry spurred his bay, taking Peters by surprise when Peters' horse, connected to Harry's by a lead, bolted after him. The mule brayed its objection as it trotted behind Claire.

By the time they reached the foot of the mountains the rain had started. Harry dismounted and Claire did the same. He untied Peters from his horse, then tied the prisoner's wrists together and led both him and the horse up the rocky incline. Claire, Rose, and the mule followed, carefully avoiding the loose shale.

Two-thirds of the way to the top they came to a wide ledge.

At the back stood a deep cave with a good-sized overhang carved into the sandstone. A shallow pool of water graced the entrance, and the three horses bent their heads to drink. Claire removed the bag of feed she'd bought in Tombstone. When Rose finished drinking her fill Claire took her under the overhang, pulled off her saddle, and fed the mare.

Harry bound Peters' ankles and settled him inside the cave out of the weather, then came back out and saw to the other animals. Not a word had been spoken between them.

I could get used to this, Claire thought.

She rummaged through her saddlebag and found some Johnnycakes and a package of jerky, which she offered to Harry.

"Much obliged." Harry nodded, taking the food. He dropped his bags on the ground before sitting nearby.

Claire glanced behind them at Peters. "Shouldn't we offer him some?"

Harry gave her a look. "Murderers get squat, far as I'm concerned."

"You mean to starve him?" Claire didn't see how that would work, since the order to bring him in didn't give the option of dead.

Harry snorted. "If I had my druthers I'd kill the bastard right now." He ripped off a piece of jerky with his teeth and chewed. "But no, I ain't going to starve him." He reached inside one of his saddlebags for a piece of hardtack, which he tossed to Peters. Harry turned to Claire and asked, "Better?"

Claire gave him a dry stare. "Much." She scanned the horizon as she ate, looking for riders who might have followed them. So far there were none. "Think we evaded them?" she asked, keeping her voice low so Peters wouldn't hear.

Harry shrugged. "For now, maybe."

After their meager lunch Claire found the book by Mark Twain she'd purchased in Tombstone and settled in to read. Harry ignored her and Peters and stared morosely at the rain.

"Once the rain stops I could try my hand at hunting," Claire said. "We passed some javalina tracks."

Harry's brows drew together, reminding her of the storm. "I don't plan for us to be here the whole damn day."

"Oh? I figured you wanted to keep traveling by night."

Harry shook his head. "We're only staying until the storm passes. I don't like to waste time."

"Well, then. That puts a different cast on things." She shrugged and opened her book again. "I'll wait until we're on our way. Be more critters closer to nightfall anyway."

Still scowling, Harry gave her a curt nod. He stretched his legs in front of him and crossed his arms, getting comfortable.

"Why don't you rest while I keep watch?" Claire suggested. "At your advanced age you need more sleep than the rest of us." A loud snort came from inside the cave, indicating Peters overheard.

Harry scowled and raised his middle finger. Claire grinned.

About an hour later Claire had put her book away and was combing Rose, thinking about new ways to conceal her pistol, when an ungodly sound jolted her out of her reverie. After a quick search she traced it to Harry, fast asleep near the cave entrance. She walked over and kicked his foot. When he didn't wake she kicked harder. Still, he didn't stir.

"Harry." She shook his shoulder but he remained asleep, snoring like a locomotive. "Harry," she urged, "wake up. Renegades." Perhaps the possibility of Indians, however remote, would snap him awake.

He answered with another loud snort and then whistled through his nose. She stood back, wondering how to rouse him, when Peters called out.

"Holy key-rist. I bet they can hear him all the way to Texas."

He had a point. She knelt next to Sparks and lightly slapped his cheeks. Still no response. She tried a bit more force, but that only managed to interrupt the snoring before it started again. Finally Claire slapped him hard with her open hand.

"Wha—what's that?" Harry bolted upright. Claire leapt out of the way, barely dodging his flailing arms.

He shook his head and looked up at Claire. "What the hell you lookin' at?" he growled.

Claire crossed her arms. "You've got quite a snore there, Harry." She nodded toward the cave. "Peters thought maybe someone was strangling a moose." Snickering could be heard from inside. Claire stifled her own laughter.

Harry was not amused. "Mind your own business, Whitcomb."

"I'm serious, Harry," Claire said, her voice stern. "You could sleep through a stampede. I couldn't hardly wake you." She frowned, adding, "How in God's name have you not lost every fugitive you captured?" A prisoner could easily slip away while Harry was sound asleep. He'd never know.

Harry climbed to his feet and glared at her. "Like I said, mind your own damn business. I done just fine without you riding my ass." He stomped over to the opposite side of the ledge and proceeded to relieve himself.

Vexed, Claire shook her head as she turned to peer into the cave. "You doin' all right in there, Peters? Need some water or anything?" As her eyes grew accustomed to the darkness, the prisoner's silhouette became solid.

"Thanks, but I'm doin' fine. Better'n ol' Harry there."

This time Claire didn't join in his merriment. How was she going to get Harry to stop snoring? She didn't like their odds of evading Peters' gang if he continued.

THEY RESUMED their journey once the storm passed. While Harry remained quiet, Peters got talkative.

"So what's your story?" he asked Claire. "Why'd our esteemed governor choose you to guard me?" He grinned at her. "You his nephew or somethin'?"

"I never met the governor," Claire answered truthfully.

"By the looks of things you're kinda wet behind the ears." Peters narrowed his eyes. "You gonna tell me how you got the job? It ain't like I'm your average outlaw." The proud look on his face told her all she needed to know about him.

Claire shook her head. "Right time, right place I guess." She glanced at Harry who didn't react although she could tell he was listening. "I guess the governor didn't think quite so highly of you as *you* seem to." She turned in her saddle and gave Peters a sympathetic smile. "To be honest you'll need practice to hold a candle to the outlaws I've known."

That elicited a chuckle from Harry. Peters studied her again, a calculating look on his face. To Claire he appeared to be working out who she was. Let him try, she thought.

He'd be wrong.

CHAPTER 14

They made good time and after nightfall set up camp next to some cottonwoods near a swiftly running creek. Claire collected wood and started a small fire to cook the rabbits she'd shot with her bow earlier that afternoon. Harry couldn't hide his surprise when she made the kills, commenting on her ability with the bow and arrow. She shrugged it off, saying she'd gotten lucky.

After dinner Claire checked Rose for burrs and gave her a thorough combing before she retired near the crackling fire. A pack of coyotes howled in the distance. The moon rode low in the sky, telling her it wasn't especially late yet. Harry hobbled the horses and the mule so they could graze, and bound Peters to a nearby tree. He took a seat near the fire, pulled his hat down over his eyes, and settled against a downed cottonwood.

"I'll be expectin' you to keep first watch," he said.

"I figured." Claire didn't mind. Being alone allowed her to relax after a day in the saddle. She stared into the fire and thought about Doc, and Wyatt, and all the people she'd met in Tombstone. Soon, her mind turned to where she wanted to go after this job was finished. She was feeling restless. San Francisco was a possibility—she'd heard good things about the bustling city. Or, since it was getting near springtime, maybe she'd check out Deadwood in the Dakotas. She might even run into Calamity Jane while she was there. She'd like to have a drink with the sharpshooter someday.

Harry started snoring again, interrupting her musings. Claire did what she could to wake him or turn him over, but he wouldn't budge. Eventually his loud snorks and whistles evened out, leaving things not exactly quiet but quiet enough. Relieved, Claire banked the fire so it wouldn't be seen by passersby and went to check on Rose and the other animals. Rose had been acting skittish since dinner. Claire figured a pack of coyotes were nearby and wanted to keep the horses and mule from getting too spooked. On the way she passed Peters, who appeared to be sleeping soundly. She soothed Rose and the others with gentle conversation and some sugar cubes, then moved off behind some trees to answer the call of nature.

Finished, she was buttoning her pants when something moved in the shadows. Startled, she reached for her pistol.

"Hold it right there."

Claire froze at the man's voice. Heart pounding, she squinted into the darkness trying to make out his features. A twig snapped as he stepped toward her, revealing a man with dark, unkempt hair surrounding a long, thin face. A day's growth of beard added to the angular shadows cast by the moon. His eyes glittered as he aimed his pistol at her chest.

"Damnation," he remarked. "You either a half-breed and growed your hair out, or yer a girly." He grinned. "Looks like I hit the jackpot." He moved closer, and she wrinkled her nose at the stench. He hadn't seen the inside of a bathhouse in a long time.

Claire eased her fingers around the grip of the Peacemaker. He hadn't shot her yet, which meant he had something else in mind first.

She calculated the distance between them, keeping her right side turned away. He most likely wasn't alone. She thought of drawing her knife, but he wasn't close enough. A gunshot would be heard by other outlaws in the area. She'd have to hope they'd think it was their man shooting.

"Please, don't hurt me," she pleaded, stalling for time and hoping to lure him closer. "I'll give you whatever you want."

"Don't mind if I do." He lowered his gun and reached for his fly as he took another step toward her.

Claire brought up the pistol and fired.

The sound cracked through the air like thunder. The outlaw's eyes bugged out and he clutched his chest. He collapsed to his knees and fell headfirst into the dirt.

Claire picked up his gun and slid it into her gun belt, then moved quickly through the trees to the camp. The red glow of the banked fire showed three men surrounding Harry, who was now awake. The set of his jaw and fierce look in his eyes spoke to his anger at being ambushed. Another man appeared with an unbound Peters in tow.

"Kill 'im and let's go," the man with Peters said in a low voice.

"What about Johnny?"

"How many shots did you just hear?" Peters asked.

"One."

"Which means he'll be joining us shortly." The obvious annoyance and superior tone of Peters' voice told Claire the rest of the gang answered to him.

"Want me to go see what's takin' him so long?" asked the man nearest to Harry.

Claire sighted on him and squeezed the trigger. The bullet carved a hole in the outlaw's forehead, and he dropped where he stood. She immediately pivoted and shot the next in line. He yelled as the round hit him, and she fired again, but he moved out of range. The remaining gunmen scattered with Peters in the lead.

Claire broke cover, firing both her gun and the dead outlaw's weapon. By this time Harry had gained his feet and was firing at the escaping figures. A gunman cried out in the darkness, signifying another outlaw wounded or down. Claire sprinted after the rest, stopping only when she heard the sound of horses galloping off into the night.

She raced back to camp to saddle Rose. Harry had the same idea—he'd already saddled the bay and had tied a lead on the mule and Peters' horse. He turned to say something to her and froze. His eyes widened and his mouth opened like a fish.

"What?" Claire asked, irritated that he was at a loss for words in such a fraught time. He was the one with the reputation for being the big, bad bounty hunter.

"You're a…woman?"

The astonishment on his face would be something she'd never forget. "So what?" she growled. "Get on your damned horse, Harry. If you hadn't noticed, the prisoner escaped."

Her words broke the spell, and he quickly mounted the bay. "What happened to the one they called Johnny?"

"He's been taken care of." Claire said. She slapped the reins on Rose's flank. She and the mare took off like a shot after Peters and the last of his gang. Harry soon caught up and they continued apace.

The outlaw's tracks weren't difficult to find, but their luck ran out at the edge of a feeder creek.

"We should split up and head in opposite directions," Claire suggested. "When one of us finds them, ambush the gang, recapture Peters, and bring him back to camp."

Harry shook his head. "You think I'm going to let you collect my reward? The contract don't say anything about *who* has to deliver him to the prison. Hell, a jackrabbit could do it and they'd still have to pay."

"I'm not interested in your reward, Harry. I don't need it." Her frustration at his bullheadedness reached a boiling point. "Not everything's about money." Without a backward glance Claire headed south along the creek. *That man is about as pigheaded as they come.*

Harry rode past her and crossed the stream, then paralleled her. "They're headed to Mexico."

Claire bit back a retort. He had a point, though. The border wasn't far and was the most likely destination. At least covering both sides they had a better chance of finding out where Peters and his gang left the creek.

But not if the outlaws had headed north.

The longer they didn't find evidence of the outlaw's tracks the more Claire's anxiety rose. She decided to follow the creek a bit farther before she reversed direction and rode north.

Harry whistled low, directing her attention. She urged Rose to his side of the creek to see what he'd found. Harry pointed to a set of deep prints in the muddy bank, then to a series of broken branches next to a narrow gap in the bushes.

Claire dismounted to get a closer look at the prints. Most of them were obliterated from multiple markings, but a few had the unmistakable shape of a horseshoe imbedded in the damp mud.

"They're shod," she said to Harry as she climbed back into the saddle. Unshod horses would have indicated a possible Indian presence.

Harry nodded. To his credit he didn't lord it over her—they both knew there was a fifty-fifty chance the outlaws rode north to throw them off their trail before heading south to Mexico. They'd gotten lucky.

Heartened, Claire and Harry followed the tracks. When the prints grew faint Claire would dismount and study the terrain like Thomas had taught her—looking for stone rolls, depressions and pocks, and broken or crushed vegetation. One surefire way of noticing changes was sideheading, which involved getting low enough to the ground to get a good sightline of the trail. Depressions were much more pronounced at that level. By this time the moon had traveled higher, shedding its blue light across the landscape and making her job easier.

The outlaws' tracks led them to a deep canyon before disappearing. Claire brought Rose to a halt and dismounted. After several minutes of searching she returned.

"The canyon's blocking the moonlight," she said. "The sheer rock walls are high and the opening's narrow. There's more shale than hard ground as far as I looked. Tracking through the canyon will be difficult unless we use a torch." That lent its own problems. "I suggest we rest up and wait until dawn to continue. If they know their way through these rocks, and I'm betting they do, they'll have the upper hand, especially in the dark."

Harry nodded. "Agreed." They took the animals to higher ground to set up camp in case a storm surprised them during the night, turning the canyon into a river.

Once the animals were seen to, Claire unrolled her bed next to a rock still warm from the day's heat. They wouldn't risk a fire in case the outlaws were camped nearby. Harry laid his gear out a few feet from her.

Claire was almost asleep when Harry cleared his throat, startling her. "What is it, Harry?"

"I, well, I think we need to discuss what happened tonight."

"What happened? You mean how our fugitive escaped?" What on earth could they have to talk about? They had to track his gang and recapture him, pure and simple.

"What happened…earlier this evening."

Claire racked her brain, trying to come up with what he was talking about but couldn't figure it out for the life of her.

"I'm sorry, Harry. You're going to have to be more direct because I have no earthly idea what you're going on about."

He cleared his throat again. "The fact that you're…that you're a woman."

Claire rolled her eyes in the dark. So that's what was bothering him. She chuckled.

"What's so gol-danged funny?" Harry asked, obviously offended. "You deceived me from the get-go. That don't warrant a lot of trust."

She choked back an angry response. "I knew you'd have a problem." She pushed herself to a seated position and pulled her duster close to ward off the chill. "If I recall correctly, you weren't too happy having a man join you—how do you think you would've reacted if you knew I was female?" She peered at him through the darkness but couldn't make out his expression. "I can hunt and shoot and track as well or better than most men and you've seen me do it. Can we just let it go?"

There was a long pause, then he sighed. "I ain't never worked with a woman before." He was quiet a little longer but then climbed to his feet and began to pace. "How in hell am I s'posed to capture Peters with a woman to look after?" he grumbled.

Weary, Claire heaved a deep sigh. "The same way as if I were a man. Look," she said. He stopped pacing. "Can you do something for me?"

"Depends what it is." There was wariness in his tone.

"Can you just go back to pretending I'm a man—"

Harry shoved his hands in his coat pockets and resumed pacing.

"Hear me out. Pretend I'm a man for the foreseeable future, until we find and capture Peters. I'll even wear my hair like I did before, see?" She gathered her hair at the back of her neck and tucked it under her hat. "It'll be easier to pretend that way."

Harry turned to look at her. She couldn't read his face, could only make out the whites of his eyes gleaming in the moonlight.

"And how do you expect me to do that?" He took a step away, then pivoted to face her. "It ain't like I can unsee what I saw."

Claire closed her eyes. Why did it have to be this hard? So many of the men she'd met before—Doc, Wyatt, Mart Duggan, Thomas—had accepted her as a gunslinger. What was Harry's problem?

"Did you ever meet a man by the name of John Henry Holliday?" she asked. "Doc Holliday?"

"I know of him. Can't say as I ever met him though."

"You know his reputation?"

Harry nodded. "What does Doc Holliday have to do with the price of tea in China?" There was that annoyed tone again.

"Doc and I were friends. He took me shooting and gave me pointers."

Harry scoffed. "For all I know you're making up stories." He spread his arms wide. "It ain't like I can ask the man now, can I?"

"No, you can't. But you need to ask yourself why I'd lie about a thing like that when you could check my story as soon as you got back to Tombstone. I invite you to ask anyone in town. Lord knows my reputation suffered because of my associations with both Doc and Wyatt Earp."

That got Harry's attention. "You're friends with the Earps?"

"I am."

"If you're as good as you say and friends with Wyatt to boot, then why ain't you with the posse out looking for his brother's killers?"

"Because Wyatt felt the same way you do." Wyatt's rejection of her offer to join the posse still stung, but she'd be damned if she'd let Harry know that.

"Aha!" Harry pointed at her in triumph. "If Wyatt didn't want you along, then why the hell would I?"

"That's not the point."

"It is exactly the point."

Claire removed the governor's letter and held it up. "Governor Tritle knew I was a woman, as did his representative. *They* didn't have a problem hiring me for the job." She put the letter back in her pocket. "And neither should you."

"Yeah, well, I'll bet they never had to work with a dadblamed woman, either," he muttered.

"Or a dadblamed, pigheaded bounty hunter," Claire muttered

back. She turned away from Harry, lay her head down, and closed her eyes. In the distance, a lone coyote howled. She waited for its pack to join in, but there was only silence. The coyote was all by itself in the desert night.

I know exactly how you feel, she thought.

Claire woke at dawn. Harry was still out cold so she answered the call of nature and then fed the animals. She decided to name the mule Harry, although she felt a little bad—it wasn't near as stubborn as Harry was.

She started a small fire and made coffee, then wolfed down a Johnnycake and a piece of salt pork. She filled a tin cup with coffee and brought it to Harry as a peace offering. The aroma woke him. She held out the cup.

"Thanks," he said, taking the coffee. The steam curled into the early morning air, dissipating with the dawn.

"The dew's up," Claire said, nodding toward the mouth of the canyon. "Should make it easier to track if we get going." Once the sun rose the dew would dry, removing another clue to the outlaws' whereabouts.

"Yup." Ignoring the scalding temperature of the coffee Harry drained the cup and handed it back to Claire.

"I already fed the horses and the mule."

He narrowed one eye and said, "How long you been awake?"

Claire shrugged. "Less than an hour. Thought I'd let you sleep. Because of your age and all."

Harry snorted a laugh. "Just how old do you think I am?"

"Older than me I'd reckon."

"Says you. How old are you? Nineteen? Twenty, maybe?"

Claire widened her eyes in mock offense. "Why sir, you know it's quite rude to inquire as to a lady's chronology."

Harry gave her a look that said he wasn't buying her act.

"I'll be twenty-eight next month," she answered.

Harry looked at her in surprise. "Huh. Sure fooled me. Woulda pegged you younger."

"Well?" Claire demanded. "I told you mine, now you tell me yours."

"Thirty-five."

"Huh. I would have thought…oh, never mind."

"Would've thought what?"

She stifled a smile at his annoyed tone. "That you were a lot older."

Harry snorted. "Madam, did you know it's quite rude to insult your betters?"

"Lordy you're easy to tease."

The corner of Harry's mouth twitched in what might have been a smile. Claire hid her grin by lowering her head as she rolled up Harry's bedroll.

Claire banked the fire and stowed the rest of their supplies while Harry saddled the bay. Twenty minutes later they headed out.

At first, the outlaws' tracks were easy to follow. Once inside the canyon both Claire and Harry had to dismount and lead the animals over the slippery shale. A broken fetlock spelled disaster for a horse, and Claire had no intention of losing Rose.

About an hour later the shale turned to limestone, which gave way to hard-packed sand. They rounded a boulder and came across the remnants of a camp, most likely the outlaws'. Burned wood from the fire scattered in a wide arc and supplies were left strewn about: a canteen here, a bedroll there. Claire slid from her horse and studied the prints. She identified several as the outlaws' horses, but there were also some new prints.

She glanced at Harry. "Looks like the outlaws had company."

"Apache?"

"That would be my guess."

Harry nodded toward a group of creosote bushes. "What's that over there?"

Claire followed his gaze. Something dark lay on the ground next to the shrubs. She walked toward it to get a better look.

She heard the flies before she saw the body.

One of the outlaws lay facedown next to the bush. Blood matted the back of his head where something sharp had cleaved his skull.

"Well?" Harry called.

"Pretty sure it's one of Peters' gang."

Harry got down from his horse and walked over to join her. "The Indians did us a favor by evening the odds. Maybe there's more than one dead."

Turned out it was just the one outlaw. The rest of the gang had either gotten lucky and escaped or been taken by the Indians. Claire and Harry climbed back onto their horses and resumed tracking.

"So you know," Harry said, "there's two kind of Apache— peaceful and otherwise. Geronimo's followers, the Chiricahua, they're what you call renegades. They like to stir up trouble more often than not and would rather kill you as look at you."

"And the other kind?"

Harry shrugged. "Like I said, peaceful. More amenable."

"I would guess the Apache who attacked the outlaws' camp were of the Chiricahua type?"

"Yep. One thing about them, though. If you can get 'em to talk first instead of fight you got a good chance of survivin' the encounter. But they can be touchy."

"Can you blame them?" Claire asked. What happened to the

Apache sounded a lot like what happened to the Utes in Colorado. Broken treaties, broken promises, greedy settlers and miners. Nobody caring what happened to an entire people. Most of what passed for diplomacy tended to be outright land grabs.

Harry shook his head. "Can't say as I do. They surely didn't get a fair shake. But knowing that don't make 'em any easier to deal with."

"You have a lot of experience in that regard?"

"A little." He nodded at her bow and quiver. "Looks like you had some dealings with the tribes too."

"They're gifts from a friend."

"An Indian friend."

Claire nodded. "Thomas." Memories crowded her mind, and she fought back a sudden sense of nostalgia.

"Thomas, eh? Did he ever tell you his Indian name?"

"No. Said he was part of the white man's world now and had to shed his old self. Like a snake sheds its skin."

"Sounds like your Thomas is as sensible as they come. I reckon he'll do fine."

"I reckon."

They rode a while in silence. Claire dismounted at regular intervals to check the tracks, making sure they didn't lose the trail. The canyon opened up to a wider valley with a slow-moving creek. Sheer rock walls stood sentry on each side but were farther apart than before. Claire and Harry stopped to let the horses drink and graze while they ate their midday meal. Birds flitted between tree branches and sang to each other. A pleasant interlude.

They'd started to pack up when Claire felt a prickle at the back of her neck. Without a word she slid the Winchester free and walked around Rose to where Harry stood next to his horse. She gave him a look. Harry's gaze dropped to the Winchester and he raised his chin. He slid his own rifle free of the scabbard and scanned the horizon. Claire turned in a circle, searching the tops of the cliffs.

There.

She caught sight of one, then two, then three men on horse-back silhouetted against the brilliant blue sky. Hoof-beats pounded through the canyon, echoing against the rocks.

The Apache had arrived.

CHAPTER 16

L et me do the talkin'," Harry warned. "Put your rifle away but keep it handy."

Claire nodded and checked to make sure there was a round in the chamber before she slid the Winchester back into its scabbard. Harry eyed the modified rifle before he turned to face the oncoming horsemen.

Claire's breath caught at the fierceness of the five warriors. All wore their dark hair long and flowing. All sported breechclouts and boots and carried spears adorned with feathers; two wore headbands, while one went bareheaded. The remaining two wore brimmed hats. All had single-shot rifles slung over their backs. The bareheaded one had a pair of field glasses around his neck and a revolver in his gun belt. Two of the others wore revolvers in addition to the rifles.

A raiding party.

Harry waited for them to stop before nodding at the one with the field glasses. He said something in a language Claire didn't understand. The warrior lifted his chin in response. He flicked his gaze over Claire, taking in her and Rose, the rifle, and the

Peacemaker, then returned his attention to Harry. He replied in the same language.

"What did he say?" Claire asked, keeping her voice low. She didn't want to set them off—her instincts told her to treat them like she would a stick of dynamite.

Very carefully.

"I told him we're tracking a group of outlaws and asked if he'd seen them. He said that depended on who was asking."

"Well? What are you going to tell him?" Field Glasses studied Claire with interest. Unnerved she forced herself to stare back at him, unwilling to show fear. He cocked his head and then seemingly dismissed her.

Harry cleared his throat and said something to Field Glasses. Field Glasses shook his head and nodded toward the horse Peters had been riding. Harry replied, then reached into his saddlebag for a colorful wool blanket, which he presented to the Apache. Field Glasses smirked and said something to the man on his left. He turned back to Claire and Harry and raised his rifle. Claire tensed and shifted her stance in a bid to brandish the Winchester and start shooting if need be.

Harry set the blanket on the ground and took a step back.

"What's happening, Harry?" Claire whispered.

"Seems they want the horse in exchange for safe passage. Says he can show us where the outlaws went."

"So give him the horse and let's be on our way."

"Ain't that easy." Harry brought up his hands to show he meant the raiding party no harm. "If I fold and give 'em the horse without dealin' they'll think we're easy pickin's and take everything we got."

"We can't let that happen, Harry." Fear of losing Rose spiked through her. Not now. Not after all she and the mare had been through together.

"I need something else I can trade—something I can offer to show our respect and sweeten the pot instead of giving in to his original demands an' makin' him think I'm just another scared white man."

"I have an idea." She moved with care to Rose's opposite side and untied the bow and quiver of arrows from her saddle. She went back and laid them next to Harry's blanket. Field Glasses motioned for her to bring the items to him.

Claire glanced at Harry, who nodded. Heart thudding, she picked up the gifts from Thomas and brought them to him. The Apache's eyes lit up as he studied the fine beadwork on the bow and quiver. He passed the bow to the man closest to him, then removed one of the arrows from the quiver and inspected it from tip to end. After all five of the men had inspected the gift he said something to Harry. Harry replied, then turned to Claire.

"He wants to know how you came across such fine workmanship. I told him they're gifts from a friend."

Field Glasses said something else. This time his voice was sharp. Claire looked at Harry for translation.

"He says how does he know you didn't take this from its original owner by force?"

Claire widened her eyes. "Tell him I would never do such a thing. Never. Tell him Thomas was a great and dear friend—a member of the Ute tribe, with whom we were at peace."

Harry relayed what she said. Field Glasses stared at her long and hard. Claire became increasingly uncomfortable but stood her ground.

"Tell him these gifts mean the world to me," she continued, "but I am prepared to give them as a gift to show my good faith."

Harry did as she asked. After a tense moment, Field Glasses nodded and said something. Harry flexed his hands and said, "He accepts."

"Really?" Giddy with relief, Claire let out the breath she'd been holding. She wouldn't have to give up Rose. The mare, evidently sensing her change in mood, snorted and pawed at the ground.

Harry picked up the blanket and handed it to Field Glasses. Then he walked over to Peters' horse, untied the lead, and brought it to the band of warriors. He and the leader exchanged words, and the five of them rode off the way they'd come. Claire glanced at the ridge above them. The others had disappeared.

"Sorry about your bow and arrows," Harry said as he walked back to join Claire.

"I'm sure Thomas would appreciate their new owner." She turned to mount Rose and realized her knees were weak. She took a deep breath to steady herself before climbing onto Rose's back. "Did he tell you where to find Peters?"

Harry nodded as he climbed back into his saddle. "Over that ridge a piece. Shouldn't take more than a day to catch up with them."

"Did he say how many were left?"

"Says there's four in all."

"That means there were at least eight to begin with since you and I killed three and the Apache got one."

"Yep. Pretty good odds, don't you think?" He grinned at her, transforming his face into something almost pleasing.

Claire returned the smile. "I surely do."

Claire and Harry rode through the day, covering several miles with single-minded purpose. The outlaws kept to the creek, leaving an easy trail to follow. The only thing Claire could figure was that the outlaws believed they'd lost their pursuers so didn't bother covering their tracks.

The sun sank low on the horizon, casting long shadows across the desert terrain and painting the sky deep orange and purple. Claire got down off her horse to study the tracks. They were fresher than before and their gaits had changed, telling Claire the outlaws had slowed their pace.

A large grove of cottonwoods could be seen in the distance, taking advantage of the creek.

She nodded at the trees. "If I was looking for a place to make camp for the evening I'd probably choose near that stand of cottonwoods."

"Have to agree with you there." Harry dismounted and bent to fill his canteen from the creek. He took a long drink and studied the area. "I reckon if we wait til nightfall we'll have the upper hand. What do you think?"

That was a new development. Claire glanced at Harry, surprised. "Did you just ask for my opinion?"

Harry gave her an exasperated look. "Don't make this harder than it needs to be."

"You're right. I'm sorry." She gauged the distance between them and the grove. "I'll go on foot to see what we're dealing with. Shouldn't take long. Once I'm back we can make a plan."

Harry tended to the horses as Claire moved along the creek toward the cottonwoods. The bullfrogs had started to croak, bringing the evening alive and covering up any sound she made. The more she narrowed the gap the slower she went, until she was creeping along the muddy riverbank.

The smell of cooking meat hit her, reminding her how hungry she was. She parted a clump of feather grass and peered through.

Four men sat around a small campfire, eating from metal plates. She caught sight of Peters and her heart raced. One of the men said something to him and he laughed. Their horses were tethered to a rope strung between two trees. All the men wore pistols, and there were three rifles visible. There was a slight rise covered in tall grass to the east of them.

The perfect place to hide.

Claire backed away from the scene and quietly moved to the rise to make sure of its tactical advantage. She was right—the spot revealed a clear view of the camp. She made her way back to where Harry waited and relayed what she saw. Harry again asked her opinion on what she thought they should do.

She thought for a moment before answering. "They're not going to give up Peters without a fight. There's four of them and two of us. I say we wait until they're asleep. I'll sneak into camp and take out the sentry, then release their horses. Next, I'll go for the others. That's where you come in. There's a rise to the east with a clear line to their camp. If you position yourself right you should be able to give me cover in case things go to hell and Peters makes a run for it."

"By the looks of that modified rifle of yours it should be you on the rise, covering me."

"Sure you can be quiet enough? Spook the horses too early and we lose our advantage."

"Don't worry about that. I can be real stealth-like when the need arises."

Claire nodded. "Fine. That works as well as my idea. I'll need your field glasses."

Harry studied her for a moment. "You talk about killing like it's nothing." He raised an eyebrow. "Can't say I ever met a woman like you before."

"You must keep company with the wrong type of woman."

Harry chuckled. "I must."

They shared a cold meal of the remaining Johnnycakes and salt pork, opting not to build a fire and possibly give away their location. Darkness fell with the swiftness peculiar to the desert, and the stars emerged like ice shards on a velvet blanket. Crickets and bullfrogs sang and an owl hooted, keeping company with the yips and howls of a distant pack of coyotes. Neither Claire nor Harry were about to sleep.

"What's your story, Harry? What drew you to bounty hunting?" Claire kept her voice low in case it carried.

Harry sighed and clasped his hands behind his head. "I tried ranchin' after the war but stayin' in one place didn't suit me. I prefer a more variable lifestyle, something with a challenge where the grass don't grow under my feet. I'm good with a gun and have a kind of sense about outlaws—I can usually figure out where they're goin' and why."

"All good qualities for a bounty hunter."

"And the money's good, long as you can fight off the human carrion."

"Sounds like a lonely life," Claire mused.

"There's a difference between lonely and alone. I tend to appreciate the alone parts."

Claire thought about what he said and decided she agreed.

"What made you want to become a lady gunslinger?" he asked. "Did something happen to make you this way?"

"You could say that." Claire wondered if she should tell him about her past. Something had shifted in their relationship—a kind of grudging respect, she supposed. He was still one of the most stubborn, bullheaded men she'd ever met, but he'd proved himself by treating her with the same respect as anyone else.

"You gonna tell me what that was or do I have to guess?"

"It's hard to talk about." She took a deep breath and told him everything, from when the white men murdered Josiah and her children and burned her home, to Blankenship and how he'd wanted their claim and killed to get it. About how she wanted revenge in the worst way and how Mart Duggan and Thomas had funneled her rage into learning how to shoot and ride and strategize.

She was vague about the part where she killed Blankenship in cold blood, but he got the idea. Then she went on to tell him about the train robbery and working as a security guard for the actress, Isabella King. About killing the assassin sent to murder her, about her friendship with Doc and riding shotgun for the stage. She ended with witnessing the gunfight at the O.K. Corral and Wyatt's refusal to let her ride with the posse.

"After that I figured it was time to move on, to find something and somewhere else."

"How's that goin'?"

She shrugged in the dark. "Haven't made up my mind yet. It feels like I have unfinished business back in Leadville, although I don't know what that might be. I tend to sleep better in the mountains."

"I know what you mean. Years back I spent some time in

Western Montana. There's a peace to the mountains I ain't never found anywhere else. Probably cause of the air."

Claire smiled. "Probably."

They fell silent, each with their own thoughts. At moonrise they gathered their weapons and moved stealthily toward the outlaws' camp.

The bullfrogs were still active, covering the sound of their advance, but the crickets grew quiet. Harry split off and headed for the horses on the other side of the camp. The fire still burned, casting an orange glow onto three bedrolls but only two sleeping figures. Claire moved quietly toward the rise and took her position with her rifle, using the field glasses to search for the sentry and the missing outlaw. So far she hadn't seen either.

Patience, Claire. One of them was probably relieving himself. If that was the case, Harry might be able to subdue both the outlaw and the sentry. Thomas's voice echoed through her mind. *Wait until the time is right.*

She took a deep breath and let it go. Then, suddenly, one of the gunmen emerged from the shadows to the left of the campfire. He stirred the fire with a branch and tossed it aside, then walked to the empty bedroll. Claire brought up the rifle, sighted him in, and curled her finger around the trigger. At the same moment she heard a click and felt something hard dig into her spine. She froze.

"I'd be real careful if I was you." The sentry kept his voice low. "Put it down."

Claire set the rifle on the ground.

"Hands in the air."

She raised her hands.

"Who else is with you?"

"It's just me."

"Where's your partner—the bounty hunter?" He prodded her with the barrel.

"Headed to Mexico. Said he figured that's where you all went."

"Why ain't you with him?"

"Because I didn't agree."

"Looks like you were the smart one. Then again, maybe not." He chuckled. "Get up and walk."

Claire climbed to her feet. He picked up her rifle and slung it over his shoulder, then relieved her of the Peacemaker, which he slid into his gun belt.

"You gonna kill me?" she asked in a trembling voice. He might underestimate her if he thought she was afraid.

"Not until we get to Mexico. You're what I like to call insurance in case that bounty hunter catches up."

"He doesn't like me much so I don't see how I'd be any good to you."

"You tryin' to get yourself killed?"

He pushed her forward and she stumbled. She slowed her pace, and he thrust the barrel into her spine. She balked.

"Move," he growled, and shoved her harder.

Claire pretended to fall. When she hit the ground she reached inside her boot and grasped the hilt of her knife, pulling it free. She swiveled to face her captor and sprang to her feet. At the same time she shoved the outlaw's gun barrel away and buried the blade just beneath his ribs. His gun went off, but the bullet went wide.

Ears ringing, Claire yanked the knife free and stabbed him again. His eyes bulged with shock and he fell to his knees. A rifle blast rang out near the camp followed by yelling, sounding the alarm.

Claire retrieved her knife and wiped the blood and tissue on the man's shoulder. She grabbed the Winchester and pistols and turned toward camp. Keeping to the shadows, she ran.

CHAPTER 18

A heavy exchange of rifle fire echoed through the night, the acrid smell of gunpowder mingling with the smoke of the campfire. The bandits shouted to each other as they scrambled for cover. All pretense of stealth gone, Claire slid her knife into her gun belt, sighted the Winchester, and fired.

Taking fire from two directions, the outlaws scattered. Claire hit one of them as he ran for cover and cartwheeled to the ground. Then she sighted on Peters, tracking him to a downed cottonwood near the creek. Careful to keep the trees between herself and the fugitive, Claire got as close as she could without exposing her position.

While Harry and the remaining outlaw exchanged gunfire, Claire shot at the log where Peters was hiding. Wood chips exploded from the stump where she'd seen him last.

"Come on out, Peters," she yelled. "Toss your gun over here. You know Harry won't stop til he brings you in."

There was a pause, then, "Maybe you and me can cut a deal, Whitcomb."

Claire smirked as she reloaded. Might as well play with him, at least until Harry finished off the other gunman. "What'd you have in mind?"

"I got money. Lots of it. I'll give you half if you let me go."

"That so? Well, let me think on that."

"I'm dead serious. There's a load of gold bullion not ten miles from here, buried in the ground near some hot springs."

"And just where'd you get the bullion?" This was getting interesting. There might be a reward for the gold's return.

"I won a map in a card game. The other feller swore on his mother's grave there was more gold than you'd ever care to spend in a lifetime."

"And why would I believe you?"

"Why wouldn't you? You and me, we know each other. I think we'd make a great team. And hell, we'd both be rich. No need for robbin' or killin' anymore."

Sure, Peters. "Where is this treasure map? I mean, if I have to go with you somewhere to get it, well, you can see how that might present some problems."

"No, no. I got it right here."

Claire peered around the trunk. Peters' arm shot up from behind the log, and he waved something in his hand.

"Say you're telling the truth," Claire mused. "What's to stop you from killing me on the way there?"

"Well now, that's a good and fair point. I guess you'll have to take me on my merit."

"How about this? How about you show some good faith by throwin' your gun my way and then come out from behind that log with your hands up?" Harry and the other gunman were still going at it, by the sound of sporadic gunfire. She needed to hurry Peters up so she could help Harry.

"You interested in my proposition?" he asked.

"I give you my word."

"Okay then. I'm coming out."

Claire glanced around the tree as a revolver sailed over the trunk toward her. "Now the other one." She was bluffing, but she doubted he'd give up one gun so easily if he didn't have a backup.

There was a pause, then a second pistol flew over the log and landed near her with a thud.

"Anything else?" she asked.

"That's all I got."

"Come on out, then," she said, picking up both weapons. "But keep your hands in the air where I can see them."

Peters climbed to his feet with his hands held high. "Sounds like your partner's otherwise engaged. We should probably skedaddle." He made a show of looking around. "Where're the horses? We'll need that mule of Harry's to transport all the gold."

Claire sighed and shook her head. "I don't think so, Peters. But thanks anyway." She aimed the Winchester at his chest. "On your knees."

Peters remained as he was. "I shoulda known you weren't bein' truthful."

Claire pulled a length of rope from her coat pocket. "Aren't you a clever boy?" she said, the sarcasm thick. "On your knees. Now." Peters did as she said.

The gunfire had stopped. A moment later Harry called out. "Whitcomb?"

"Over here. I got Peters."

Peters groaned. "Now you gone and done it."

He started to lower his arms, but Claire engaged the modification and aimed at his heart to make her point. "Don't move."

Peters froze.

Harry joined them and took the rope from Claire.

"The other guy?" Claire asked as he corralled Peters' wrists and tied them together.

"In hell where he belongs." He finished tying Peters and hauled the fugitive to his feet. The look on Peters' face was not a happy one. Harry patted him down, looking for weapons. When he got to his boots he paused, then reached in and pulled out a derringer.

"I knew he had another gun," Claire said.

Harry checked the other boot. "Nothing. You got more rope?"

Claire fished another length of rope from her coat pocket and tossed it to him. Harry proceeded to hobble Peters by tying his ankles together.

"How in blue blazes do you expect me to walk?" Peters asked.

Harry stepped back. "Who says you're gonna walk?" He nodded at the log. "Sit down and stay there." He turned to Claire. "I'll get the horses while you keep an eye on him, all right?"

Claire nodded. "I need to talk to you a minute."

Keeping the rifle trained on Peters, Claire and Harry stepped out of hearing range.

"Peters offered me half a shipment of gold bullion if I let him go," Claire said in a low voice. "Says it's ten miles from here near some hot springs."

Harry looked at her with interest. "Think there might be a reward?"

Claire shrugged. "Can't hurt to check, right?"

"You trust him to lead us to it?"

"Not hardly. He's got a map he won in a card game, although it could've been a feint so I'd let him go. I haven't laid eyes on it yet." She shrugged. "Up to you. This is your operation. It'd delay you gettin' him to Yuma by a day or two."

Harry nodded slowly, thinking. "There's some hot springs ten miles west of here but he knows the area so it could be him making up a story to buy time."

"True enough. But why buy time now? It's not like anyone else is coming for him."

"You have a point." He walked back to Peters, stood him up, and started to dig through his pockets.

"What the hell are you doin'?" Peters asked, trying to see what Harry was up to.

Harry reached inside the outlaw's coat pocket and pulled a piece of paper free. "What have we here?" He unfolded the paper and held it up to the moonlight. Squinting, he held it closer, then at arm's length, but gave up and handed it to Claire. "It's too damn dark. I can't make it out."

"Dammit, Whitcomb. You was supposed to keep quiet." Peters glared at her, his expression fierce.

Claire ignored him and handed Harry her rifle. While he covered Peters she studied the paper. She could make out some markings but not much more. She folded the map and handed it back to Harry. "It's definitely a map. We'll have to wait until we get to camp before I can say for sure where it leads to."

Harry nodded and handed her the rifle. "Probably ain't anything. I'll go get the horses."

After Harry left Peters continued his glare-down.

"What'd you think I was going to do?" Claire asked. "Throw in with a murderer?"

Peters drew his brows even closer together and spat, "You just lost out on a whole lotta gold, Whitcomb."

"You don't say? But wait a minute—" She cupped her hand to her ear, acting like she heard something. "Why yes, I do believe it's the call of the 'I have the map' bird." She lowered her hand and smiled as sweetly as she could at him. "Your offer might've worked on someone who was hurting for money or just plain greedy. I know it may be news to you but not everyone is as corrupt as you are."

Peters shook his head and huffed out a disgusted breath. He sat on the log and turned away from Claire.

She smiled at his childish actions as visions of what she might do with the extra reward money danced in her head. If he was telling the truth.

That was a big if.

CHAPTER 19

The next morning Claire and Harry both studied the map while savoring their coffee near the fire. Peters was tied to the base of a tree a few yards away, looking out of sorts.

Harry pointed at a series of upside-down Vs on the paper.

"These markings might represent the foothills to the west of us. And this here," he tapped the wavy lines that indicated a water source, "is where the hot springs are, give or take."

Claire raised an eyebrow. "You mean he might be telling the truth?"

Harry nodded. "But there ain't any indication of where the gold's supposed to be." He shrugged. "You see anything pointing to a location?"

"Nope." She turned to Peters. "Where's the rest?"

"What do you mean?" Peters replied. "It's all right there."

Claire walked over to him and showed him the map. "Then you tell me where the gold's supposed to be?"

Harry added, "If there ain't anything more to this, then I say we deliver Peters to prison first before we head to the springs to dig around."

"Sounds like a plan," Claire said as she folded the map and rejoined Harry.

"Wait a minute."

Claire and Harry turned to look at Peters.

The fugitive grimaced. "There is one last piece that ain't on there."

"And that would be?" Claire asked.

"The guy from the poker game told me where it's buried. It ain't on the map in case someone got hold of the darned thing that weren't supposed to."

"Which means we need you." Harry gave Claire a look that said he wasn't surprised.

"What do you think?" she asked. "Should we give it a try?"

Harry nodded. "I believe we should. Like you said, it'll only delay us a day or two."

Peters said something under his breath. Claire walked back to where he was sitting.

"I'm sorry, Peters, but I couldn't make out what you just said."

The outlaw scowled and looked away. "I said, that gold ain't yours."

"Well, I can pretty much bet it isn't yours either." She crossed her arms and contemplated the outlaw. "It's not like you're going to be able to use it anytime soon."

"Or at all." Harry dropped to his haunches in front of Peters and gave him a drink from his canteen. "You're going to hang, Sam Peters," he said, screwing the cap back on. "Justice for that family of seven you murdered, and all those trains and stages you robbed."

Peters spat at Harry but missed. "Ain't like you're lily white."

Claire gave Harry a sidelong look. "Do tell."

Harry shook his head. "He don't know what he's talkin' about."

"Oh, don't I? What about them women and children at the

Centralia Massacre? I suppose you didn't have nothin' to do with that?"

Harry rounded on him with a raised fist, a red flush spreading from his neck to his ears. "Keep your trap shut 'bout things you don't know."

Peters grinned. "Looks like I hit a sore spot."

Harry took a deep breath, exhaled, and unclenched his fists. "Leave it be, Peters."

"Touchy, touchy."

"He's just trying to goad you into doing something you'll regret, Harry." Claire returned her attention to the map. "If we leave now, we'll have plenty of daylight to look for the gold. Then if he's lying, we can cut our losses, make camp, and leave early in the morning. We'll be in Tucson by tomorrow night."

Harry nodded. "The marshal gave me three days' grace either side to get him to the train. That'll be cutting it short but I believe it'll work."

"Great. Let's move out."

They loaded up their bedrolls and supplies, and Harry tied Peters to the mule, making sure to run a line between his ankles underneath the animal's chest.

A brilliant blue sky stretched before them as they set off. Claire inhaled the fresh morning air, glad for the chance to be on the road again. A few hours later they reached the foothills that Harry thought might be depicted on the map. The horses picked their way through a narrow canyon as they headed for the springs. The temperature had spiked, taking the ride from pleasant to hot, but a slight breeze whispered through the trees, helping to cool them.

They stopped near a burbling stream set into the rocks next to a stand of desert willow. Claire removed the horses' saddles and let them graze while Harry saw to Peters and the mule.

Harry joined her and pulled out the map, flattening it on top of a large rock. "The way he tells it, the cache is buried at the top of a rise near a rock that looks like an animal." He nodded downstream. "As I recall, the springs come out over there by that rock shaped like a cat."

Claire followed his gaze and realized that he was right—the boulder had the look of a reclining feline. She glanced back at the map, her excitement growing. "Shall we?"

"We shall." Harry stopped to remove a shovel from his supplies, then followed Claire over the gray stones lining the stream.

A short distance from camp they came upon a quiet pool. Claire dipped her hand in the water and found it deliciously warm. Thoughts of a long soak filled her mind. Maybe she'd be able to slip off later in the day.

Harry glanced at the map and pointed to the top of a conical-shaped feature to their right. "Looks like we climb."

"How did you get Peters to tell you where to look?" Claire asked.

"Pain. A lot of pain."

The two of them headed toward the top of the rise, stopping every so often to catch their breath. Three-quarters of the way up they came to a flat area surrounded by dark stone. Claire and Harry exchanged looks.

"It's as good a place as any," Harry said. "Time to start diggin'." They had a good view of Peters from where they were and he appeared docile, so they set to work.

Claire began moving the larger stones clear while Harry used the shovel to break through the hard-packed dirt and caliche. Forty minutes later they'd barely made a dent.

Claire sat on a nearby rock and wiped the perspiration from her face with her forearm. "Might I suggest a stick of dynamite?"

Harry snorted and leaned on the shovel. "Could be we're chasin' our tails."

"Maybe." Claire took a sip from her canteen and offered it to

Harry. He took a drink and handed it back. "I'm not ready to give up just yet, though. Are you?"

Harry grinned and shook his head. "Not hardly."

They worked a while longer and made some headway with Claire pushing aside the dirt and rocks Harry shoveled out.

An hour later, Harry hit something hard.

CHAPTER 20

Claire and Harry exchanged looks. Claire's heart raced. Could it be that Peters was telling the truth? The joy of discovery ricocheted through her. She nodded at Harry.

"Well? What are you waiting for?"

Harry leaned on the shovel and fixed her with his gaze. "I just want to make clear—if what we've hit is gold and we can figure out who it belongs to, then we return it to its rightful owner, reward or no."

"Agreed. And if we can't determine ownership? What then?"

Harry shrugged. "Then we split it fifty-fifty."

"All right, then." She nodded at him. "Dig away."

Harry bent to the task, picking at the edges of what turned out to be a large wooden box.

Claire glanced at Harry. "That looks like it's the same size as a Wells Fargo treasure box." She'd seen many of the strongboxes during her time riding shotgun on the stage. The size was right, but she'd have to see more to know for certain.

Harry grunted as he shoved the blade beneath the chest and bore down on the handle. The box shifted, breaking through the hard-packed dirt. Claire grasped the edge and heaved, throwing her weight into dislodging their find. Harry joined her, and they managed to drag it out of the hole they'd created.

Claire studied the case, searching for the familiar Wells Fargo name but the surface bore no markings. They tipped it over and found the same. The leather handles had rotted through, leaving only the wooden pegs used to affix them to the sides. The oak slats that made up the box had shrunk, due to the dry desert conditions, leaving gaps. The box had a metal clasp on the front, which was the only metal evident other than the padlock.

Harry raised the shovel and brought it down on the lock, which broke immediately. Claire removed the padlock and unlatched the clasp before opening the lid.

Inside was a stack of gold bars unlike any Claire had ever seen. "What kind of bullion is this?" she asked Harry. She lifted one of the rectangular bars from the box. The rough surface and lighter weight didn't match the heavier, smoother bars Claire had seen and handled. She turned it over. There was no identifying mark on the bar itself.

Harry picked one up and studied it. "Mining companies always mark their bars. So do banks." He placed it back into the box. "This don't look like any gold bars I ever seen."

"Maybe they're Mexican?"

Harry shook his head. "If they are, they're older than the conquistadores. A long time back I seen a bar of Spanish gold in a traveling curiosity show—accordin' to the hawker they pretty much always stamped their bars."

"What if they had to move quickly?"

"Could be. Either way, it's like findin' a gold nugget lyin' on the ground."

He was right. "So that means…"

Harry nodded. "No marks means there ain't no way to find the owner. Anybody can claim it's theirs. Might as well be us."

That shed a new light on things. "So, are you saying we're rich?"

"Appears to be the case." Harry grinned, his brown eyes sparkling in his sun-darkened face.

Claire's mind raced at the prospect. All they had to do now was transport the gold to Tucson and have it assayed. Claire weighed the bar in her hand. "I'd venture this weighs about the same as two pistols—somewhere around four, maybe five pounds." She moved aside the top layer of bars and counted each one beneath them. "There's forty-eight bars here. Let's say they're four and a half—no, make that four and two-thirds pounds. That makes the total weight a little over two hundred and twenty-three pounds. Peters is round about one-fifty, give or take. The mule could probably carry at least half the bars and I could make room for some of them in my saddlebags. But it could pull the whole darn thing if we made a travois."

Harry glanced at her. "You did that in your head just now?"

Claire almost rolled her eyes but stopped short. "What if I did?"

"Nothin'," he said with a shrug. "I ain't never met a woman who could do sums that fast without a pencil and paper."

"Can't you?" Claire's husband, Josiah, had been good at math, but he always let her take the lead in anything to do with multiplication since she was so quick with the answer.

"Well, of course I can."

Claire studied him for a moment, trying to decide if she should explain to him that a woman's brain was just as good as a man's, but decided to let it go. Let him figure it out on his own.

"Think the box would survive sliding down the hill?" Claire eyed the route they took up the rise, thinking about the wear on the desiccated wood.

He dusted off the box. "The case ain't exactly built to specifications." He pointed out the crudely joined oak slats. "Wells Fargo reinforces the corners and edges with metal. This is just wood. And dried-out wood, at that."

"Then we'll have to carry it down."

"Possible, but I've got a better idea. Wait here."

Harry made his way down the hill back to camp and returned a short time later, carrying his oilskin coat. He stopped for a moment to catch his breath before he laid it out on the ground near the box.

"Help me lift the box onto my coat."

Claire did as he asked, and they heaved the box on top of the rugged material. Harry dusted off his hands and gestured to the bottom of the rise. "I'll hold on to the edge and pull—you push from behind. Plenty of loose shale for it to ride on to the bottom."

It took a bit of pushing to get things started, but his idea worked. Aside from getting dirty and acquiring a small tear where one of the box's corners dug into the fabric, Harry's coat was still presentable. They each took a side, lifting from the bottom, and walked the box back to camp. Peters watched them like a hawk tracking prey.

"Guess the map was right," he said. "Whatever you found is mine, fair and square."

Harry and Claire ignored him as they brought the box next to one of the willows and set it down.

Harry squinted at the sun on its way to the horizon. "We used up most of the day—don't make no sense to leave now. We should turn in early and get a good night's sleep. We can load the bars in the morning and be on the road by sunup."

"Sounds good. What do you say we build a travois so we can transport the whole thing to Tucson?"

"It'll slow us down some."

"Agreed. How far is it? Can we travel it in a day?"

Harry nodded. "Shouldn't be a problem. I'd reckon we could get there before the assay office closes."

"Perfect."

Harry cut several willow branches and Claire helped him lash them together. By the time they'd finished it was late afternoon. Claire gazed downstream, lost in thought.

Harry followed her gaze. "What?"

Claire shook herself from her reverie and smiled. "I was thinking about how nice a soak in those hot springs would feel right now."

Harry arched an eyebrow. "Do tell. You go on ahead and do whatever you need to. I'll see to supper."

"Really?" Claire grinned, happier than she'd been in months. Without thinking, she stood on tiptoe and kissed him on the cheek. He smelled of sweat and grime and warm, sunburned skin. She stepped back and said, "We can take turns, if you want."

He avoided her gaze and nodded toward the springs. "Get along."

She gave him another grin, then reached inside her saddlebag for a face flannel. It would have to do. Of course with the afternoon still warm she'd dry off in no time, even without a towel. She grabbed a clean shirt and made sure to bring her canteen.

Without a backward glance Claire raced downstream, her heart light in anticipation of the relaxing bath ahead.

CHAPTER 21

Claire rinsed out her underthings and laid them on a warm rock to dry, then washed her face and body. The pool depth was perfect—when she sat on the rocky bottom the hot water came up to her chin, completely covering her.

Maybe I can sleep here tonight, she mused, and giggled at the thought.

The pool was big enough that she could stretch out on her back and gaze at the sky as she floated. White, puffy clouds scudded across the wide expanse of brilliant blue, then disappeared behind the walls of the canyon. She closed her eyes, savoring the quiet. Everything else disappeared—she didn't care at all where she might be headed after Tucson.

Oddly enough the thought of delivering Peters to the marshals and saying goodbye to Harry brought a twinge of regret. She'd come to respect Harry despite his gruff pigheadedness and would miss him and his steady ways.

If he asked her to, would she stay?

True, he enjoyed moving around and experiencing new things, but his stubbornness would likely make him hard to convince of anything that he didn't already think was true. She'd had enough of that kind of silliness from her father. She wished he was more like her husband, Josiah, had been. He'd a quick mind and would reconsider his views if there were enough facts to support them.

On the other hand, Harry had a stable job, which was definitely a consideration. It wasn't as though outlaws were going to disappear anytime soon. There'd always be a need for bounty hunters.

Would she be happy with a job like that? Always on the road hunting bandits and the worst of the worst? Now that she thought about it, it did sound kind of fun. Interesting at least. She leaned her head back and took a deep breath, exposing her chest and stomach to the warm desert air.

Rocks skittered behind her and she quickly sat up, swiveling in the water to see what had made the noise.

She caught a glimpse of Harry, partially concealed by a willow about five yards away. He ducked out of sight but not before she got a look at his expression. It was a mixture of guilt at being caught and something else—a look she hadn't experienced since her ill-fated night with Doc Holliday.

Claire stifled a smile and pretended not to see him, partly so she wouldn't cause him further embarrassment but also because she'd decided she was going to do her best to tease him.

Turning her back to him she lifted an arm from the water and ran her hand along its flesh, caressing her shoulder and tilting her head back in a show of pleasure. She thought she heard a sharp intake of breath but couldn't be certain.

The ability to do something daring and not have to confess it —for she would surely not admit to trying to arouse Harry for fear of him thinking her a loose woman—gave her a little thrill. She ran her fingers through her hair and arched her back, then sank below the surface, astonished at her brazenness.

You had better be ready to answer for your actions, Claire Whitcomb, she chided herself. What had come over her? She shook her head at the thought. Living out West had certainly changed her. In polite society her actions would be construed as wanton and base.

And what's so bad about that? The thought spiraled through her mind, unbidden. *Who will even know?* Her reputation was already questionable. What more could she lose?

Why, Claire Whitcomb—you little tart. She smiled to herself.

Time to end the teasing. Keeping her back to Harry, she floated to where her clothes dried in the sun. She slowly rose from the water to give him ample opportunity to take his leave without being seen. It wouldn't do to give the man heart failure.

When she deemed he'd had plenty of time to depart she exited the pool, dried off, and put on her clothes, feeling one hundred percent revived. She took her time walking back to camp, enjoying how relaxed she felt after days in the saddle and living rough. Right before she reached camp she piled her hair up under her hat to continue her pretense of being a man for Peters' benefit.

She stopped to stow her things in her saddlebag and walked over to where Harry sat in the shade of a willow, cleaning his gun.

"Have a good bath?" Harry asked.

She stifled a smile at his studied nonchalance.

"It was wonderful. You really must have a turn." She nodded toward Peters who sat slumped against the tree. "It appears our guest is napping. Now would be a good time for you to go before it gets dark. I'll keep an eye on things here."

Harry finished putting the revolver back together, slipped it into his gun belt, and stood. "As long as you're comfortable watchin' him."

Claire smiled. "Why so solicitous, Harry? You've never had a problem leaving me alone with him before."

"No?" Harry gave her a look that sent a flutter of excitement through her. "Well, then, I'll take my leave." They locked gazes for a brief moment before he touched the brim of his hat and said, "Ma'am." He walked to his bags and pulled out his shaving kit and a flannel, then made his way downstream, whistling.

Claire had never heard him whistle. Come to think of it, she hadn't ever seen him act lighthearted. She watched until she couldn't see him anymore before heading to her saddlebags, intending to repack her things.

"You smitten with him or somethin'?" Peters asked, a look of revulsion on his face.

Claire pulled out some items and redistributed them, making more room. "Why, you want him?"

Peters scoffed at her rejoinder. "Funny, ain'tcha? Nah, I prefer women. The loose, willing kind."

"Well, I can understand that, Peters, bein' as that's the only kind that'd want you."

"Says you."

Ignoring him, Claire continued to pack her things. She unwrapped the tomahawk and took a moment to admire its handiwork, happy that she hadn't had to give up all of her gifts from Thomas.

"Whitcomb." There was an edge to Peters' voice.

Annoyed, Claire turned to see what he wanted. His eyes were as wide as saucers and he appeared unnaturally stiff, kind of like rigor mortis had set in. "What?" she asked. A jolt of concern flickered through her.

Peters rolled his eyes and puffed out his cheeks with short breaths. Beads of sweat rolled down the sides of his face.

The tomahawk still in her hand Claire stood, concern pushing through her dislike of the outlaw. "Are you having some kind of fit?"

Then she saw the snake.

Coiled in an undulating pile not two feet from him, the distinctive brown and white diamond shapes along its scaly body would have been enough to identify the deadly rattlesnake. As if to emphasize its lethality the tip of its striped tail rattled in warning.

The snake moved, shifting into a strike position.

"Do something," Peters hissed.

Claire hurled the tomahawk at the snake. The blade landed with a thud, embedding itself in the ground and severing the snake's head from its body. The tail shivered before falling lifeless on the remaining coils.

Peters let out his breath in a rush. "Damnation." Breathing heavily, he leaned his head back and closed his eyes. "I could've died right then and there."

Claire walked over to the snake and pulled the tomahawk free. "I hear they taste good." She slid the blade under the rattler's body and lifted it off the ground.

Peters stared at her in disbelief. "I almost died and all you can think of is supper?"

She rolled her eyes. "Don't be so melodramatic. Besides," she added, "it's not like you're long for this world. Personally, death by rattlesnake sounds a whole lot better than death by hangin,' don't you think?"

Peters clapped his mouth shut and glared at her.

She smiled sweetly and walked back to the saddlebags with the rattler. "You're welcome, by the way," she called over her shoulder.

Peters didn't give her any more trouble, and she completed her task of rearranging her saddlebags. Then she saw to the horses and Harry the mule. Finished with that, curiosity got the better of her, and she went downstream to see what could possibly be keeping Harry so long. In her experience men didn't take their time in the bath like women did.

Not wanting to scare the daylights out of him, Claire crept up behind the same tree she'd seen Harry use when he was watching her bathe and peered around the trunk. He was floating on his back the same as she'd done, staring up at the slowly darkening sky. She was about to turn around and leave him be when he stood up.

She caught her breath at the sight of him. There was no indication under his shapeless, everyday clothes of the fine male physique presented to her now. Unable to tear her gaze from his lean waist and well-muscled arms, broad shoulders and shapely buttocks, she wasn't prepared when he turned.

Their eyes met. Her heart hammered in her chest, but she didn't turn away. He'd shaved his beard, giving him the appearance of a much younger man. She wet her lips and he smiled.

She clapped her hand over her mouth as the realization hit her. She'd just done the exact same thing as he had earlier. A warm flush of embarrassment wound its way to her cheeks. Mesmerized by the intensity of his gaze she found herself staring right back at him.

You'd best stop now, Claire. If you keep staring at the man he's going to think it's an invitation.

Well, what if it was?

Claire made her decision. Without breaking eye contact she stepped from behind the tree and slowly walked toward him. He remained hip deep in the pool, watching her approach. She unbuttoned her shirt and cast it aside, then stopped and removed her boots, placing them on a flat rock next to the pool. His eyes grew dark and her heartbeat quickened. She unbuttoned her dungarees and slid them and her underthings off. His gaze moved along her body, giving her a delicious thrill.

With a quick movement she waded into the pool and walked toward him with single-minded intent.

CHAPTER 22

"Where in tarnation've you two been?" Peters' plaintive whine greeted Claire and Harry when they returned to camp. "There mighta been another damn snake for all you cared."

Harry gave Claire a puzzled look and she shrugged. "Long story—no need to worry about supper, though."

Peters studied them both. His annoyance turned to suspicion and his eyes widened. "What the—if I didn't know better I'd say you two got to know each other in a carnal sense."

Claire hid her grin but not before Peters saw it.

The fugitive's shocked expression said it all. "That—that ain't—"

"Shut up, Peters." Harry's sharp tone brooked no argument. The outlaw snapped his mouth closed. "Now, what was this about supper?" Harry asked Claire, ignoring the outlaw's obvious astonishment at what he thought were two men having a love affair.

She pointed to the dead rattlesnake hanging on the tree branch where she'd left it. "I've never cooked a snake before but heard they're good eating."

Harry removed it from the branch, inspecting it as he did. "Pretty good size. How'd you kill it?"

"Tomahawk."

Harry nodded as though Claire killing a rattler with a Ute tomahawk was the most natural thing in the world. The thoughts floating up through Claire's mind took her by surprise. She studied Harry as he set to skinning the reptile, wondering again what it would be like to work side by side with the bounty hunter.

Stop it, Claire. You slept with the man once. It isn't like he asked you to marry him.

She shook her head to rid herself of the silly fantasy and got busy searching for wood to build a fire.

After they'd eaten their fill and were relaxing near the fire, Harry went to his saddlebags and returned carrying a bottle of whiskey. He took a swig and offered some to Claire.

"You've been holding out on me." She smiled and had a drink, enjoying the warm sensation in her belly.

"That was some fine rattlesnake." Harry tipped the bottle to Claire in a toast. "May your tomahawk always be at the ready when a snake is nearby."

Peters had evidently gotten over his shock at his captors' apparent love affair and was particularly talkative. "You shoulda seen him, Harry." Unable to use his hands, Peters snapped his head forward to mimic a chopping motion. "Bam! That snake's head came clean off, quick as you please."

Harry gave Claire a sidelong glance. "Not only are you good with a gun and a bow and arrow, but you can throw hell out of a tomahawk." He shook his head and took another drink. "I stand by what I said before; I ain't never met anyone like you, Whitcomb."

Claire smiled and took the bottle. She held it up and said, "Same to you, Harry," then handed it back. "What was Peters talking about earlier? Something about a massacre?"

Harry gazed into the fire. "He's dead wrong."

"No I ain't," Peters protested. "You was one of them bush-whackers under Bloody Bill. I should know. I was there too."

"Shut up, Peters. You don't know what you're talkin' about." He took another swig. "I left for Texas when Bill Anderson ordered the murder of them unarmed Union soldiers."

Peters scoffed. "Then you're a coward."

"What he asked was a bridge too far, Peters. The war was pretty much over by that point anyway."

"Bullshit. You was the only one who lost their nerve, you know that? Remember Jesse? Guess what he's doing now?"

"Robbing banks and stages. Him and Frank are the reason I became a bounty hunter."

"Jesse James?" Claire asked.

Harry nodded. "He was one of the worst in a band of cutthroats. He enjoyed killin'."

"I've heard stories of the war—how brutal it was." Claire placed her hand on his arm. "I'm sorry."

"Aww," Peters growled. "Keep it to yourselves, wouldja?" He tipped his chin up and asked, "Why don't you send a little of that firewater my way?" When neither Claire nor Harry responded he added, "C'mon. Grant a dyin' man his last wish?"

Claire and Harry exchanged looks. Claire climbed to her feet and carried the bottle to Peters and gave him a drink. She turned to rejoin Harry when Peters straightened his legs and captured her ankles with his own. Claire tripped and fell to her knees. Peters was on his feet in an instant.

Before Harry could react the outlaw grabbed Claire's collar and yanked her backward, crushing her windpipe. Fighting for air she grabbed at the front of her collar, trying to rip the fabric as Peters' arm snaked around her neck and pulled her to him. Something sharp nicked her skin as her hat fell off and her hair tumbled free.

"Well, well, what do we got here?" Peters asked. "A woman. Shoulda known, eh, Harry?"

Claire could feel the fight leaving her—she had to get air, now. Black spots danced before her eyes. Harry had climbed to his feet and was advancing toward them. The look on his face would've put the fear of God into anyone—except a man like Peters who was staring at death either way.

"Stop right there or I'll slit your woman's throat."

Harry stilled.

Peters tightened his grip and Claire kicked at the ground, trying to pull in a tiny bit of air. Inside, she screamed for breath, but it was no use.

She tried everything she could think of to loosen Peters' hold, but her strength waned. Peters pressed the sharp object deeper into her neck, drawing blood. She closed her eyes. Perhaps she would see Josiah and her children sooner than she thought.

The knife.

With her last ounce of strength Claire stretched to reach inside her boot and grasp the hilt of the hunting knife. She unsheathed the blade, and in a reverse arc, brought it down behind her head, stabbing him as many times as she could.

The pressure let up and she sucked in a sweet breath of air. Choking and gasping, Claire crawled away, grateful for the reprieve. Her breathing ragged, she collapsed to the ground, fighting the blackness still threatening to envelop her.

"Don't do it. It's cold-blooded murder if you do." Peters' voice shook with fear.

Claire opened her eyes and rolled onto her side. Pistol aimed at the outlaw, Harry loomed over Peters, who held his hands up in an attempt to ward off what was coming. Blood covered Peters' face and shoulder. Claire pushed herself to her knees.

"Kind of like what you did to that innocent family, right?" Harry said through gritted teeth. "Did they beg for their lives too?"

"What about the reward?" Peters pleaded. "You kill me and it's over. They want me alive."

"I don't need the damn reward." Harry growled and cocked the hammer.

"No, Harry—don't," Claire gasped.

The bounty hunter paused. "You tell me one reason why I shouldn't send this piece of shit to hell right now."

"Look." She climbed to her feet. "I'm fine. He didn't hurt me." She put her hand to her neck. Her fingers came away wet, but the blood was minimal. Not nearly as much as what covered Peters.

"He intended to. In my book that's the same thing." Harry stared at the outlaw, the rigid set of his body reminding her of a coiled rattlesnake before the strike.

"Harry. Don't. Let the law take care of him."

Peters stayed silent, his innate common sense likely telling him not to tangle with the man and his gun.

Harry narrowed his eyes as he stared down Peters. Claire didn't know what else to say to keep him from shooting.

A moment later his stance shifted. The tension eased and his shoulders relaxed. "All right." He nodded. "We'll do it your way. For now." He pulled a length of rope from his pocket. "Here." He handed her his gun. "You keep this on him while I tie him up."

Claire aimed the pistol at Peters. "What'd he use to get free in the first place?"

"That piece of shale over there."

The rock lay several feet from the outlaw. "I thought we made sure to remove it all," Claire said. Both she and Harry had swept the area free of anything sharp that could be used to cut the ropes.

"My guess is he beat us to it."

She made sure to kick the sharp stone far away from Peters as Harry corralled his hands behind him and wrapped his wrists several times with the rope. Then she and Harry hauled him back to the tree and wound several lengths of rope around his chest. Claire tied his ankles together for good measure. She wiped off the blood covering his face and shirt to check the knife wounds. None were life-threatening. As long as they delivered him to Tucson before infection set in, he'd live.

Claire decocked Harry's revolver and handed it back to him. He ran his thumb over the cut on her neck. Claire held his gaze. Something in their depths shifted and he stepped back.

"I'll take first watch," he said in a gruff voice.

"All right." Claire frowned at the change in his demeanor but decided to let him work things out on his own. Still shaky from the attack she laid out her bedroll and slipped between the blankets. Sleep was hard to come by.

CHAPTER 23

Claire woke Harry at sunrise with a cup of fresh coffee. She'd taken the early morning watch, eager for him to catch up on his rest. He'd been gruff at the changeover but she'd chalked up his bad mood to the early hour and lack of sleep.

Harry accepted the coffee with a grunt and nothing more. She busied herself breaking camp and saddling Rose. Then she stowed some of the gold bars in each of Harry the mule's saddle-bags, careful to even out the weight so that it could carry Peters as well.

The mule balked at the extra weight. Claire shifted a couple of bars but the animal brayed in protest.

"Shh, Harry," she soothed. "It'll be all right." The mule quieted, but by the look in its eyes she could see she was in for a fight. With a sigh she pulled out the bars and turned to put them back in the box.

Harry stood not two feet from her, an irritated look on his face.

"What?" she asked. She hoped he'd say something, anything to help her understand his mood, but his demeanor suggested a coolness that hadn't been there yesterday.

"Did I hear you call the ass 'Harry'?"

Claire grinned sheepishly. "You have to admit the name kinda fits."

Harry didn't say anything as he attached his bedroll to the back of his saddle.

"Oh, come on, Harry. I meant it as a joke." She looked from Harry the mule to Harry the man. "Mule-headed? Get it?" But Harry remained silent, his expression stern.

Claire stepped in front of him and crossed her arms. "Why aren't you talking to me?" she demanded. "Did I do something wrong?"

Harry sidestepped her and slid his rifle into the scabbard.

Frustrated, she moved in front of him again. "What do I have to do to get you to say something?"

Harry stopped what he was doing and without looking at her replied, "We need to get Peters to Tucson. After that we split the gold and go our separate ways."

Claire's breath caught. "What? I thought—I thought we were..." What had she thought? He'd never said anything to make her believe he wanted anything more than what they'd shared in the hot springs.

Harry answered her, his voice low. "You thought wrong."

Hurt and anger scrambled for dominance in Claire and she clenched her fists, digging her nails so deep she came close to drawing blood. How dare he treat her like that? Her cheeks warmed with anger and shame. The thought of getting her Peacemaker crossed her mind, but she decided against it. He was a man, and no man was worth the noose.

"Oh, I see," she said, putting an edge to her voice—cold and hard like his heart. "You got what you wanted and now you think you can cast me aside. Well, I'm here to tell you, Harry Sparks, I wouldn't give you the time of day if you were the last man on God's green earth." Afraid of the depth of her anger she stalked away before she could lose control.

Peters watched the exchange with a grin. "I'd be more than happy to take his place, Claire, darlin'. Looks like you're in need of a real man."

Claire rounded on him, her rage at a boil. "Shut the hell up, Peters," she snarled, and punched him in the face.

Peters yelped and struggled to grab his nose with his bound hands. Blood poured down his face. "You broke by dose," he screamed.

"If you don't shut up I'll break more than that," she growled, shaking her hand from the pain.

Harry ignored them both and brought the mule to the travois they'd built the day before. The mule balked as Harry attempted to back it up to the carrier.

With some satisfaction Claire watched him try to harness the stubborn animal with little success. Finally she relented and picked up the opposite pole. Without a word they moved the travois into position and attached it to the mule's tack. Then, still not speaking, they hoisted the box filled with gold and settled it on the frame. Harry secured the crate to the frame and covered it with a blanket, which he bound to the box with more rope.

Claire finished loading Rose and handed Peters a rag to stem the bleeding. He gave her a murderous look, but she was past caring. As soon as Harry tied Peters to the mule, they headed for Tucson.

As far as Claire was concerned they couldn't get there soon enough.

It was early evening before the trio reached Tucson. Thankfully one of the assay offices was still open, and they dropped off the gold to be tested. Peters hadn't shut his mouth for the first several miles. Claire had grown tired of his blathering on about how he was going to bring charges against Claire, and that he deserved a share of the gold for giving them the map. Evidently Harry had enough of him too and gagged the outlaw. The bounty hunter had kept to himself, and Claire obliged him, her hurt and anger at his coldness filling her with a burning desire to take her leave as soon as practicality allowed.

They made their way along the dusty streets of Tucson past squat adobe buildings and the new gaslights that had recently been installed. Even though it was one of the biggest cities in the Arizona Territory, the town still had the same feel as a Mexican village she'd visited with Doc the autumn before.

Harry secured Peters at the Pima County jail for the night. Harry was to meet with the marshals in the lobby of Porter's Hotel the next day before boarding the train for the trip to Yuma Territorial Prison. Citing business to attend to elsewhere in Tucson, Harry left Claire to her own devices. Relieved she didn't have to endure his sullen demeanor, Claire took a room, had an early supper, and retired for the evening.

What had she done to change his attitude so abruptly? Claire lay on her bed and went over what had happened the day prior. He'd been fine after they'd been together. She had assumed they'd talk things through before he left for Yuma. Now, all she wanted to do was leave and never set eyes on the pigheaded jackass again.

The same went for the mule.

Claire spent a restless night tossing and turning but finally fell into a dreamless sleep.

Loud voices in the hall woke her. Sun streamed in through her window, telling her it was later than she'd like. She bounded from her bed and threw on her clothes before rushing out the door.

The morning was a warm one with clear blue skies, promising a hot day ahead. Claire shaded her eyes as she and Rose approached the assay office. There weren't any horses tied to the hitching post in front. Perhaps she beat Harry. She couldn't remember when he said the train was due to leave—she thought it might have been midmorning, which was still an hour or so away.

She entered the low-ceilinged adobe building and walked over to the man behind the counter. He looked up from his task, his round eyes magnified behind a pair of wire-rimmed glasses. A boy of about seven hid behind a table and peeked out at her, his brown eyes wide as saucers.

"May I help you?" he asked. The nameplate on the counter read *W. Jacobs, Esq.*

"Mr. Jacobs?"

"Yes."

"I'm C. Whitcomb. My partner, Harrison Sparks, dropped off fifty bars of unmarked gold yesterday evening. I was wondering if you'd had a chance to determine its worth?"

Jacobs' eyebrows shot up. "Indeed I have." He paused, evidently considering how he should address her.

"Mrs. Whitcomb," Claire prompted.

He nodded. "Mrs. Whitcomb." Emboldened, the young boy crept closer to Claire but ran back behind the table when she smiled at him. Jacobs waved at the child. "Elizondo, *vamos!*" With a giggle Elizondo disappeared into the back room. Jacobs put down his tools and gave her a serious look. "The gold Mr. Sparks brought in is some of the purest I've ever assayed. How did you come across it, if I may be so bold?"

"I'm afraid I'll have to leave that story for Mr. Sparks to tell. I'm on my way out of town and need to pick up the certificate for my portion."

"But Mr. Sparks has already been by."

Claire tensed and narrowed her eyes. "When was that?"

"Earlier this morning." Jacobs pulled a thick envelope from under the counter, which he handed to her. "He left you this."

Claire took the bulky envelope that was addressed to her. Inside was a bundle of bank notes and nothing more. She rifled through them, mentally calculating the amount. A small fortune. She glanced at Jacobs who watched her with interest. "Is this all he left?"

Jacobs nodded.

"Did he ask you to give me a message?"

"No, I'm sorry."

Claire nodded. That was it, then. Harry obviously didn't want to chance meeting her that morning. He and Peters were probably already on the train headed for Yuma.

"The bars are reminiscent of a cache of gold an explorer found near Lima, Peru several years ago," Jacobs offered. "I was fortunate to have witnessed the assay."

"Were you able to determine its provenance?"

Jacobs shrugged. "Without corroboration no one knows where it came from. Given the history of the area it was most likely gold taken from the native tribes by the Spanish and melted down for transport."

"I wish I could help you with the story," Claire said, "but it appears you know more than I do."

She thanked Jacobs and left. At least Harry had been fair. He could have taken all the money.

Well, Claire, she thought, *you learned another valuable lesson. Just because you feel something for someone doesn't mean they'll return the same.* It wasn't like she'd had a lot of experience with men. She'd married Josiah at seventeen and become a mother within the year. Doc was the only other man she'd been with, and that hadn't turned out very well. At least they'd parted as friends.

Claire stowed the bank notes in her saddlebag and climbed into the saddle. She glanced at the sky and contemplated where to go next. The thought of the Rocky Mountains tugged at her with a long-buried yearning. Had she gained enough distance from the terror of the "Whitcomb Massacre" so that she could return? She'd like to see Thomas and Mart again, as well as Augusta Tabor and Esther. Perhaps she was ready to go back. If she got there and the memories were too fraught with ghosts, she could always leave and try someplace else.

"You ready to go home, girl?" she asked Rose and leaned over to pat the chestnut mare's neck. As if she understood, Rose nodded her head and whinnied softly.

CHAPTER 24

Leadville, Colorado – Spring 1882

Claire finished dressing and gave herself the once-over in the floor-length mirror. Although the corset still took some getting used to, the unfamiliarity of wearing a dress had worn off like an old habit. She still wore men's clothes when she and Rose went riding but had taken to dressing like the townswomen in order to fit in and go about her business without garnering curious stares. Besides, Leadville had changed since she'd been gone, becoming more civilized and settling down to the day-to-day business of commerce. Certainly the odd shootout happened, usually late at night, but the city was nowhere near the lawless mining town she'd left two years before.

She'd seen Thomas a few times, but not Mart Duggan. Unfortunately, Mart's livery business had failed, and he'd taken a job as a deputy south of Denver in Douglas County.

Claire patted the pistol secreted in the pocket of her skirt, then did the same to her hair, tucking an errant strand back into place. She picked up her reticule and was about to leave when there was a knock at the door.

Thinking it might be Esther or Thomas stopping by to ask her to lunch, she smiled and swung the door wide.

Before her stood Harry Sparks. Her breath caught at the sight of the bounty hunter, and the smile froze on her face.

He cleared his throat and fiddled with the hat in his hand. With a look of surprise his gaze wandered from her face to her dress, then back to her face. He'd recently shaved and wore his hair slicked back with pomade in an attempt to corral the unruly curls at the nape of his neck. Claire had to stop herself from staring at his full lips and took a deep breath before letting it go in a rush.

"Harry—"

"Claire—"

They both stopped, waiting awkwardly for the other to speak. When he didn't say anything, Claire said, "What a surprise." She smiled, ignoring the feelings that rushed back—a mixture of anger, shame, sadness, and affection, all mixed up with a large dose of confusion. "What are you doing in Leadville?"

Harry worried the brim of his hat and looked at the floor. His face had grown even darker from the sun, giving him an exotic look that brought out the whites in his deep brown eyes. She caught a whiff of cologne, something she'd never in a million years imagine him using.

"I heard someone say you had taken a room here and wanted to pay my respects."

"Oh? And who might that someone be?" Perhaps he'd looked up the Tabors in an attempt to locate her. *Stop it, Claire. Don't read anything into this. He wouldn't go that far to find you. This is just a coincidence.*

"I read that article they wrote about you in the *Daily Star*. The *Tombstone Epitaph* ran the story, too."

A reporter from the local newspaper in Tucson had tracked her down in Leadville and interviewed her about her adventures transporting the notorious outlaw Sam Peters and how she and Harry had killed his gang and fought a renegade band of Apache. The last had been due to the reporter's incorrect assumption and fertile imagination, but he hadn't asked her to correct his story so there wasn't much she could do. He'd titled the article, "Arizona Legend Claire Whitcomb: Lady Gunslinger and Intrepid Indian Fighter."

Claire had made certain that the reporter included Harry in the story, citing his sterling record as a bounty hunter and giving him credit for killing more than half the outlaws.

"And?"

"Folks have taken to calling me Dead Shot." The tips of his ears grew red. He cleared his throat again. "That's not—oh, never mind. Can I come in?" He gestured to her room. "I feel the fool standing out here in the hallway."

"Oh. Of course." Claire moved aside so he could enter, then double-checked the hallway for nosy neighbors. Thankfully no one was there. She closed the door and crossed her arms as she turned to face him.

Harry looked around the room, his gaze settling on her gun belt and bandolier slung over the chair near the window.

"You came to see me?" she prompted.

"Look, I don't blame you for being mad. I've been mad at myself if you want to know the truth."

"Oh? Whatever for?" She couldn't keep the sarcasm from creeping into her voice.

Harry took a deep breath and let it go. "For the way I treated you in Tucson."

"Hmm." She wanted to add, "and not for the way you treated me at the springs?" but thought better of it.

"I should have at least left you a note explaining my reasoning."

"And that would be—?"

"When Peters got the drop on you all I wanted to do was kill him." He shook his head. "For the first time in my life I lost control. If you hadn't brought me back to my senses the undertaker'd be measuring him for a box and we'd be out the reward. It scared the hell out of me."

"I understand that well enough." She sighed. "But that doesn't explain why you left Tucson without a word."

He gave her a sheepish look. "I couldn't face you. I figured taking Peters to Yuma would be the end of things—that I'd forget you and move on."

"How did that work out?"

He caught and held her gaze. "I couldn't forget you, Claire."

A flare of happiness ignited inside her as she searched his eyes. Was he telling the truth? *He came all the way to Leadville, Claire. What do you think?*

She tamped down the happiness and asked, "Is that why you're here? Or are you searching for a fugitive and just decided to look me up?"

The hurt and surprise in his eyes told her what she needed to know.

"No, ma'am. After seeing that article I figured you'd be here, so I came to find you."

"What if I hadn't been here?"

"Well, then I would've kept lookin'. I'm pretty good at that." His lips curved into a half smile.

She couldn't help herself—she smiled back. The relief on his face was instantaneous. Claire wanted to laugh out loud—from the easing of the tension that had permeated the room to her joy at the realization he cared for her like she did him. She moved into his embrace and laid her head on his shoulder.

"What now?" she asked, pulling away. She searched his eyes for an answer.

"I've got an idea I think you might like." He pulled out a newspaper advertisement and handed it to her.

She read it and looked up. "You want to go to Alaska?"

Harry nodded. "But not to look for gold. I received a letter from an acquaintance who's in San Francisco where he's laying in supplies. He invited me to join him when he heads back north. Says word is starting to get around about the gold strikes and believes there'll be a rush like there was to California in forty-nine. I thought to use some of my money from the gold bars to purchase supplies and resell them to the miners."

"You mean open a general store of some type?"

Harry nodded. "All it takes is a tent and some poles. What do you think? Hell, at the very least it'll be a grand adventure. If things don't work out like we want we'll figure something else."

His idea sounded good, but Claire wasn't completely won over. "You say it'll be a grand adventure and I'll give you that. But what kind of assurances do I have that you won't up and leave me once we get there? Or even on the way?" She wanted to believe him, but she was no fool. A woman alone in the wilderness of Alaska was a vastly different experience than what she had done up to now.

"I thought you might say that." He reached inside his coat pocket and brought out a ring, which he held up for her to see. He dropped to one knee and said, "Claire Whitcomb, would you do me the honor of accepting my hand in marriage?"

Claire studied him for a moment, thoughts swirling through her head. "May I think about your kind offer?"

Harry's face fell at her words, and he lowered the ring. "Of course." He cleared his throat as he climbed to his feet.

She placed her hand on his arm. "Please don't feel badly, Harry. It isn't that I don't want to be with you. It's just that...I hadn't ever thought about getting married again. After Josiah died I think I figured that was all for me. One marriage, one great love." Harry's expression looked even sadder, if that were possible. She rushed to continue. "I'm honored that you asked me to be your wife, truly I am. I'm sorry. I need to go for a walk." Claire opened the door and hesitated. "Will you wait for me in the restaurant? I shouldn't need more than an hour at most."

"It's not like I have anything else pressing."

Claire walked out the front doors of her hotel and onto the teeming, bustling street. She went through as many scenarios as she could think of, trying to figure the absolute worst thing that could happen with each. Once she'd worked those out to her satisfaction she wrestled with the biggest worry of them all: did she love Harry enough to throw in her lot with him? Would she be happy as his partner if not his wife? Did she really want to go to Alaska?

As she thought through the answers to those questions she got the feeling someone was watching her. She looked up and searched the crowd, wondering if perhaps Thomas or Esther might be nearby. Not seeing anyone familiar Claire continued along the wooden boardwalk. The crowd parted to accommodate a lone figure standing in the middle of the thoroughfare. There was something familiar in the man's posture, although she couldn't quite put her finger on what it was.

As she drew near the man turned. Claire gasped in recognition.

"Doc?"

He smiled, his china blue eyes still clear and sharp. But he'd changed in the months since she'd seen him. The emaciated man who stood before her now was a shadow of his former self. *How could he have lost so much weight in such a short amount of time?*

"Why Miss Claire," he drawled. A rattle shook his frail body, and he quickly covered his mouth with a handkerchief. When the coughing fit passed he folded the blood-spattered material and slipped it back inside his pocket. "How nice to see you."

The urge to give him support was overwhelming. Instead, she took his arm in hers and clasped it tight to her side. "It's wonderful to see you, Doc." They walked a few paces in comfortable silence, allowing the rest of the town to rush past. The swinging doors to the Silver City Saloon emerged to their right. "Shall we have a drink and catch up?" she asked as she steered him inside.

They had a seat at a table and ordered whiskeys. Doc seemed to lack energy and was content to sit and watch the patrons drink and play cards. Their drinks came and Claire sipped hers as Doc threw his back.

"What brings you to Leadville?" She eyed him nervously—he really didn't look good. His skin was paler than she remembered, and it hadn't been that long since she'd seen him last. His clothes hung on his thin frame, giving him the appearance of someone who bought their clothing a size too large.

Doc signaled to the bartender for another round even though Claire hadn't finished her drink. Then he turned to her. "I was on my way to Glenwood Springs to take the waters when I crossed paths with an itinerant card sharp who mentioned there was money to be made here in Leadville."

Claire nodded. "Well, then I'm glad we ran into each other."

Doc studied her for what seemed an overly long time. Soon she became restless under his gaze and asked, "May I ask how long you think you'll be in town?"

He shook his head. "Not long, I'm afraid. The altitude isn't good for my lungs. I plan to make my way to the springs in short order."

Claire raised her drink as the bartender delivered Doc's second. He raised his and they touched glasses. "To old friends."

"To old friends." Doc threw the second drink back and delicately wiped the corners of his mouth. "I should like you to accompany me there."

Claire choked on the whiskey and set down her glass. "I'm sorry—I thought you just asked me to come with you to Glenwood Springs."

"I did." Doc watched her closely. "Is that unimaginable?" He spread his hands wide. "I'm still the same man you knew in Tombstone—albeit a tad thinner." His chuckle turned into a full-blown coughing fit.

Alarmed, Claire rummaged in her reticule for a handkerchief but he waved her away and produced his own.

When he'd finished coughing and could breathe again he wiped the perspiration from his forehead and put the kerchief away. "I've been assured that once I'm at a lower altitude and take the waters that my infirmities will dissipate of their own accord. I will then see what fortunes I may wrest from the good people of Glenwood Springs and the surrounding environs. I'd like you to be there with me."

Claire gave him a look. "What about Kate? I think she'd be quite unhappy if I were to do what you ask."

Doc's expression became dour. "Kate and I have parted ways, never the twain shall meet or some such nonsense."

"I'm sorry to hear that, Doc. I know she loved you."

He shrugged. "She surely had a strange way of showing it, didn't she?"

"That she did." Claire finished her whiskey. "What happened with the posse? Is Wyatt still on the warpath?"

Doc smiled ruefully. "We hunted down three of the curs responsible. When we got back to Tombstone there was a warrant for our arrest."

"On what charges?"

"Murder."

That explained why Doc was in Colorado instead of Arizona Territory. "Where's Wyatt?"

"He and Josephine left town about the same time as I did. No sense sticking around and pressing our luck with another trial. This one wouldn't go as well as the last, I fear. Besides, the mines are flooding. Tombstone is dying. I believe Wyatt and that actress are in Gunnison, dealing faro." He shrugged. "They appear happy." He stared morosely at his empty drink. Claire waved at the bartender for another.

She studied Doc, remembering the times he'd taught her the finer points of shooting, of their days riding in the desert, of gambling at the Alhambra and the Occidental. Unbidden, an image of Harry crowded out those memories, catching her off guard. She placed her hand in Doc's.

He gazed into her eyes, searching. "I believe I feel a rejection coming on."

"You know I care for you, Doc. I always will. But I've met someone and I'd like to see where things go." Her admission was as much a surprise to her as it appeared to be for Doc.

"He is a very lucky man." The bartender set his third whiskey on the table and left. Doc threw it back and set the empty glass on the table. "Give him my regards—and my utmost admiration." He patted her hand. Then, using his silver-topped cane, he climbed to his feet. Claire rose at the same time. He took her hand and raised her fingers to his lips, reminding her of their time together. "Take care of yourself, Claire Whitcomb. And make sure this lucky man does right by you. Tell him if he doesn't, he'll have to answer to Doc Holliday."

As she watched him leave, sadness and a bittersweet longing for bygone days filled her. Brushing the tears from her eyes, she made her way back to the hotel.

And Harry.

CHAPTER 25

Juneau, Alaska – 1888

Claire closed the door to the woodstove and turned to clean the table of flour. The sourdough starter given to her by one of the miner's wives created some of the best bread she'd ever eaten. She'd even taken to making pancakes with it, topping the fluffy stacks with her homemade huckleberry syrup.

As she cleared the table and put away the mixing bowl, her hand brushed the pocket holding a letter the postmaster had dropped off earlier. She'd almost forgotten about it in her rush to finish the baking.

Now she slid it from her pocket and studied the handwriting. It was obviously female, with large loops and swirls. Claire wondered who might be trying to contact her. The postmark was a few months old from a town in Colorado she'd never heard of. She wiped her hands on her apron and tore open the envelope.

Dearest Claire,

Greetings from an old friend. I hope this letter finds you well, if at all. I'm writing to you at a last known address from the postmaster in Leadville. I'm certain you'll want to know that which I am about to impart, since we both know and love the subject of this letter.

I write this to you with deep sadness to tell you of Doc's passing. I was with him at the end, at the Glenwood Springs sanitarium. He mentioned you before he died and asked that I write to you when the time came. He cared deeply for you and fervently wished for your happiness and contentment.

I am well, although in mourning for the man who brought such adventure to my life as I'm sure he did to yours.

I do hope that you remember me with fondness, as I do you.

With much regard,
Kate Elder Holliday

A wistfulness overcame Claire as memories of her days in Tombstone filtered through her mind. The time she'd spent there was brief, like a flash wildfire in the forest of life. She was sad at Doc's passing yet relieved he was no longer in pain. A smile curved her lips—if there was a heaven Doc would certainly be dealing faro and drinking only the finest whiskey along with his good friend Morgan Earp.

A scream interrupted her thoughts and she ran to the window, her heart pounding like a dozen horses' hooves. Outside, Harry stood with his back to the cabin. Callie, their five-year-old daughter, faced him down like a true gunslinger, wearing a gun belt cut to size, her favorite dungarees, a long-sleeved shirt, and a wooden pistol carved by her father.

Callie pretended to shoot and Harry fell to his knees, acting out his death throes for all he was worth. Claire smiled as she watched, proud of her daughter and her husband, thankful for her life and the unmatched beauty and wildness of their surroundings. The untamed nature of the Alaskan wilderness allowed their daughter to grow up free and unfettered by the constraints of "civilized" society. Claire had taken to teaching Callie how to track animals by making up games to hold the attention of a child. As Callie grew older both Harry and Claire were committed to training her in everything she'd need to make her way in the world, giving her the ability to survive and thrive on whatever path she chose to follow.

Harry and Claire still tracked down fugitives, allowing them both to inject an element of duty and danger into their lives—although Alaska provided ample opportunity to keep them both engaged. Even so, Harry was already talking about their next grand adventure, fueling Claire's and Callie's imaginations with tales of lost cities and exotic people in the jungles of Mexico and on the dark continent of Africa.

She set the letter on the table and headed for the door, past the modified Winchester leaning against the wall for emergencies and the beautiful, beaded tomahawk that hung above the fireplace. Rose's familiar whinny reached her from outside and she smiled as she walked through the door to join her family.

Legends are made and, if lucky, burn brightly and hot, leaving the world better for the light shown upon them. Claire had been fortunate in her life to have known many who could be considered such—but none shone as brightly as the two people who turned and smiled at her now.

ACKNOWLEDGMENTS

Writing a book that includes historical characters is somewhat of a tricky business—I tried to hew as closely to historical timelines and descriptions as humanly possible, taking only a few liberties here and there. The description of the shootout at the O.K. Corral is drawn largely from the extensively researched and informative book *The Last Gunfight: The Real Story of the Shootout at the O.K. Corral - And How It Changed the American West*, written by Jeff Guinn. If you have any interest in events leading up to the infamous thirty-second gunfight and beyond, that's the one to read. Bud Philpot's death during the botched stage robbery was one of the seminal events leading up to the shooting, as was the misinformation and gossip that followed. Questions still remain as to whether Doc Holliday took part in the attempted robbery, as he had no alibi at the time. Even so, research suggests he had no role and most likely tried and failed to stop his friend Billy Leonard from taking part.

Kate Elder's betrayal of Doc to Johnny Behan along with her leaving town during the trial is true. In later years, Kate wrote a memoir in which she stated that she and a woman friend had witnessed the infamous shoot-out through a window at Fly's

Boarding House. It didn't take much to imagine Claire as that friend. Kate was also reported to have been with Doc in his final hours at the sanitarium in Glenwood Springs.

Harry Sparks and Sam Peters are fictional, although bounty hunters often transported prisoners to Yuma Territorial Prison. The gold Harry and Claire found is based on tales of Spanish plunder discovered in the desert on both sides of the border.

A huge thank you to the usual suspects: my wonderful partner Mark for his unfailing support and wicked sense of humor; early readers Ali, Jenni, and Michelle; Jim Van Houghten for double-checking the accuracy of the weapons I had the characters use; Charles Ray for reading and commenting on an early draft; Cathy Speight for the same; and of course the fantastic ARTeam—I couldn't do this without you guys.

Writing is never a solitary endeavor.

ABOUT THE AUTHOR

DV Berkom is the USA Today bestselling author of action-packed, riveting action-adventure and crime thrillers. Known for creating resilient, kick-ass female characters and page-turning plots, her love of the genre stems from a lifelong addiction to reading spy novels, thrillers, and action/adventure stories.

A restless soul and adventurer at heart, she spent years moving around the US and traveling to exotic locations before she wrote her first novel and was hooked. More than a dozen books later, she now makes her home in the Pacific Northwest with her husband, Mark, and several imaginary characters who like to tell her what to do. Her most recent books include Claire Whitcomb Westerns *Legend, Gunslinger,* and *Retribution,* and Leine Basso thrillers *Shadow of the Jaguar, Dakota Burn, Absolution,* and *Dark Return.* DV's currently hard at work on her next novel.

For more information, visit her website at www.dvberkom.com. To be the first to hear about new releases and subscriber-only offers, go to: bit.ly/DVB_RL

ALSO BY D.V. BERKOM

LEINE BASSO CRIME THRILLERS:

A Killing Truth

Serial Date

Bad Traffick

The Body Market

Cargo

The Last Deception

Dark Return

Absolution

Dakota Burn

Shadow of the Jaguar

KATE JONES ADVENTURE THRILLERS:

Kate Jones Thriller Series Vol. 1

Cruising for Death

Yucatán Dead

A One Way Ticket to Dead

Vigilante Dead